SPRINKLES, SECRETS & Other Stories

SPRINKLES, SECRETS & Other Stories

INCLUDES
IT'S RAINING CUPCAKES,
SPRINKLES AND SECRETS,
AND FROSTING AND FRIENDSHIP

LISA SCHROEDER

Aladdin

NEW YORK LONDON TORONTO SYDNEY NEW DELHI

ALADDIN

An imprint of Simon & Schuster Children's Publishing Division

1230 Avenue of the Americas, New York, New York 10020

This Aladdin paperback edition May 2022

It's Raining Cupcakes copyright © 2010 by Lisa Schroeder

Sprinkles and Secrets copyright © 2011 by Lisa Schroeder

Frosting and Friendship text copyright © 2013 by Lisa Schroeder

Frosting and Friendship interior spot art illustrations

copyright © 2013 by Nathalie Dion

Cover illustration copyright © 2022 by Bambi Ramsey

All rights reserved, including the right of reproduction

in whole or in part in any form.

ALADDIN and related logo are registered trademarks

of Simon & Schuster, Inc.

For information about special discounts for bulk purchases,

please contact Simon & Schuster Special Sales at 1-866-506-1949

or business@simonandschuster.com.

The Simon & Schuster Speakers Bureau can bring authors to your

live event. For more information or to book an event contact the

Simon & Schuster Speakers Bureau at 1-866-248-3049

or visit our website at www.simonspeakers.com.

Book designed by Karin Paprocki

The text of this book was set in Mrs Eaves.

Manufactured in the United States of America 0422 OFF

2 4 6 8 10 9 7 5 3 1

Library of Congress Control Number 2022933924

ISBN 9781665907354 (pbk)

ISBN 9781439157220 (*It's Raining Cupcakes* ebook)

ISBN 9781442422650 (*Sprinkles and Secrets* ebook)

ISBN 9781442473980 (*Frosting and Friendship* ebook)

These titles were previously published individually.

Contents

It's Raining Cupcakes

For my sweet brother, Jim

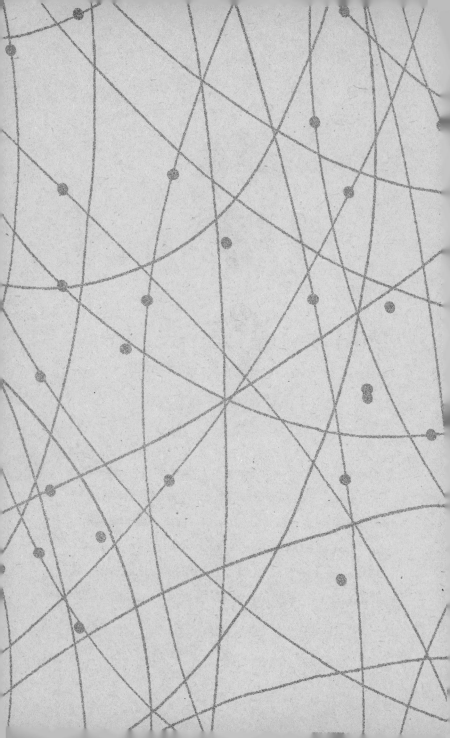

Chapter 1

red velvet cupcakes

A CLASSIC THAT NEVER LETS YOU DOWN

The whole cupcake thing started a couple of years ago, on my tenth birthday. My mom tried a recipe for red velvet cupcakes with buttercream frosting. She said, "Isabel, this recipe comes from a very famous cupcake shop in New York City called St. Valentine's Cupcakes. We're going to make these cupcakes for your party!"

Now, my mother isn't big on birthday parties. Since I was six, I've pretty much planned my own party, from the handmade invitations we deliver right down to the candy we put in the goodie bags.

But baking is what Mom loves. And it's the one thing we've liked doing together. She told me once there's something really satisfying about throwing stuff into a bowl and watching a mess turn into something wonderful. And she's right. There is.

That year for my birthday party, only four girls were coming for a sleepover: my best friend Sophie, plus two other girls from school. With such a small group, Mom thought cupcakes made more sense than a big cake.

Those cupcakes turned out delicious. Better than delicious. Amazingly fabulous. And from that day on, all Mom could talk about were cupcakes. Dad and I listened, because we were just glad she was talking about something. When she started talking about opening a cupcake shop, we listened and nodded our heads like it was the best idea ever. I don't think either of us *really* thought it was the best idea ever. But after years of trying odd jobs here and there, and complaining about how they were too easy or too hard, too weird or too boring, too right or too wrong, it was nice to hear good stuff for a change.

The talking turned into more than talking last year, when she convinced Dad to buy an old Laundromat with an apartment upstairs. It's called a walk-up apartment, and they're more common in big cities, like New York City or Chicago, than the town I live in: Willow, Oregon, population 39,257.

Mom didn't see a Laundromat. She saw a cute cupcake shop where she could make cupcakes every day and finally be happy. I think that's what she saw. I'll admit, I didn't see that at first.

We moved into the apartment right away, even though the cupcake shop wouldn't be ready for a while. Mom and Dad took out a loan and hired a contractor to do the work downstairs.

As a bunch of big, burly guys hauled the washing machines out of the building and into a large truck, I asked Mom, "Where will they go to wash their clothes now?"

"Who?" she asked.

"The people who brought their baskets of dirty

laundry here every week. Where will they go?"

She looked at me like I had a washing machine for a head. "Well, I don't know, Isabel. But it really doesn't matter, does it? I'm sure there are other Laundromats in town."

"Seems like running a Laundromat, where people wash their own clothes, would be a lot easier than running a cupcake shop, where *you* have to bake all the cupcakes."

Mom sighed. "I don't want a Laundromat. Who would want a Laundromat? I want to bake cupcakes. I want people to walk into my warm, wonderful shop and tell me how much they love my cupcakes. Besides, it won't just be me doing all the baking. Grandma's going to help. And you can even help sometimes."

Maybe it was the fact that this new adventure had forced me to move away from my best friend, Sophie, who'd lived right next door. Maybe it was the fact that my mother expected me to help without even asking if I wanted to. Or maybe, deep down inside, I didn't think Mom would be able to pull off this cupcake thing. All I know is I still wasn't sold.

"But I don't get it, Mom. Do you really think people

are going to want to eat cupcakes in a place where they used to wash their dirty, stinky socks?"

This time she looked at me like she wanted to shove a dirty, stinky sock into my mouth. "Isabel, Dad assures me we can turn it into an adorable cupcake shop. Let's not look back at what's been, but look ahead to what might be. Okay?"

Was that my mother talking? I must have given her a funny look, because she shrugged and said, "I heard it on TV. I thought it sounded good."

While Mom and Dad were busy getting the shop ready and organizing the apartment, I'd ride my bike up to the public library for something to do. I'd sit at a table right next to the travel section and read books about the places I wanted to visit someday.

See, my aunt Christy is a flight attendant. She sends me cool postcards from all over the world. When she came to visit last time, I asked her if she liked her job, and she said she doesn't just like it, she *loves* it. She gets to meet interesting people and see fascinating places. I asked her if she thought I could be a flight attendant someday, and she smiled real big and said, "You would make a fantastic flight attendant, my dear Isabel."

As I read those books, I'd dream of taking a cable car ride through San Francisco, or watching a Broadway play in New York City, or eating pastries outside a cute little café in Paris. Compared to those places, our town of Willow seemed about as interesting as dry toast.

I'd never been anywhere outside the state of Oregon. Grandma calls me a native Oregonian, like it's something to be proud of. What's there to be proud of? The fact that I own three different hooded coats, because it's the best way to be ready when the sky decides to open up and pour?

A couple of days after we moved in, Dad and I went to the dollar store because he needed to buy some clipboards and pads of paper for him and Mom. He said there was a lot to do in the coming days, and he wanted to help Mom stay organized. Dad is good at making lists. Not just good. He's the King of Lists. He usually scribbles them on whatever he can find—the back of an envelope, a corner of the newspaper, a piece of toilet paper. I thought it was sweet how he wanted to help Mom out and buy real paper for a change.

While he scoured the store for list-making supplies, I wandered down the aisles with a single dollar bill, looking for something interesting to buy. In a bin next to dollhouse-size bottles of shampoo and conditioner were a bunch of white plastic wallets with tiny pictures of suitcases on them. I picked one up and opened it. A piece of paper was stuck inside that said, "Passport Holder."

I imagined a girl like me eating a bowl of soup at a restaurant in Athens, Greece. Suddenly she bumps the bowl, and soup spills all over the table. She gasps when she notices her passport is sitting there on the table. But then she breathes a sigh of relief, because she remembers she bought a passport holder at the dollar store to keep her passport safe. She opens it and finds the passport perfectly soup free.

Of course I had to buy it. Even if I didn't have a passport to put inside the passport holder.

When I got home, I put little pieces of paper inside it to make a mini-notebook. I carried it around with me everywhere, and whenever I had a thought about traveling, I wrote it down. This is what I wrote the first day:

I want to go
on many journeys.
I want to meet interesting people
and experience new things.

—Isabel Browning

As I wrote that in my passport-holder-turned-note-book, I realized something important. If I ever wanted to get past the Oregon-Idaho border, I needed to make a plan. A fantastic, incredible, big moneymaking plan.

And I thought turning a Laundromat into a cupcake shop was hard.

Chapter 2

strawberry lemonade cupcakes

THE PERFECT PICK-ME-UP

It says 'The Bleachorama,'" Sophie said, when she finally came over for a visit the day after the Fourth of July. We were standing in front of our building, piles of sheetrock and boards on the sidewalk, and guys carrying tools at every turn.

They hadn't taken the tacky neon sign down yet. If I was in charge, it would have been the first to go.

"Mom's getting a new one made. Guess what she's calling the shop?"

"Caroline's Cupcakes?" Sophie asked.

I shook my head. A worker carrying a can of cream soda walked by. I waved at him. He waved back.

"Cupcakes R Us?"

I shook my head again. "You'll never guess. So I'll just tell you. It's Raining Cupcakes."

"It's Raining Cupcakes?" she asked. "That's the name?"

"Yep. You know, 'cause it's almost always raining in Willow. Now it'll be raining cupcakes."

"Riiiight. Okay, show me your room. Can we take the fire escape?"

"Sophie, are you kidding? Dad would kill me. We have to go the normal way."

"Have you met Stan?" she asked, pointing to the sign STAN'S BARBER SHOP on the building next door to ours.

"Yeah. He's round and bald and has a big, bushy mustache. And he's really nice."

Stan and his wife live upstairs, in an apartment down the hall from us. The first time I met him, I knew I'd like him. He smells like shaving cream, and he loves to tell knock-knock jokes. When I told him my name, he told me this one:

"Knock-knock."

"Who's there?"

"Isabel."

"Isabel who?"

"Isabel out of order? I had to knock!"

I led Sophie between the two storefronts to a door. Behind the door is a little room that doesn't hold much of anything except mailboxes along one wall and the stairs that take us up to the apartments. Dad told me they constructed buildings like ours to make the most out of the space, and to allow people other than the owners of the shops to rent the apartments above them.

"Then why did we move?" I'd asked him. "We could have stayed where we were and rented the apartment out to someone else."

He just smiled and said, "Your mom liked the idea of walking to work."

Living at work is more like it, I thought.

As Sophie and I walked up the old, creaky stairs,

she whispered, "Chickarita, this place is majorly cool."

We got to the top and turned to the right. As we approached the door, we heard Mom humming a tune, happy as a sparrow on a spring day.

"Wow, guess cupcakes really do make her happy," Sophie said.

"For now." I didn't have to say any more. Sophie knew. My mom has more moods than there are sparrows in Oregon, and that's a lot.

When Sophie and I walked into the tiny family room, I noticed it still didn't feel like home. It felt like someone else's place with our worn-out furniture and some of the equipment Mom had bought for the bakery.

The fan hummed in the corner, adding more noise to the room than cool air. Dad swore we'd get an air conditioner for the window as soon as we could afford it. Until then, during the hot months of July and August, we'd have to dream of cold December days and drink lots of ice-cold drinks.

Mom sat in the old, tan La-Z-Boy, with a cookbook in her lap and a whole pile of them stacked beside her on the end table. "Girls, do you think pineapple cupcakes would be good?" she asked.

"My mom and I make pineapple upside-down cake all the time," Sophie said. "My little brother thinks it's disgusting. But it's my dad's favorite."

"Oh, you're right," Mom said. "I don't think Isabel and I have ever baked pineapple upside-down cake. Have we, Is?" I shook my head. "Hmmm, I wonder why. Anyway, they wouldn't be quite the same, but I bet they'd still be good. I'm adding it to the list."

"How many flavors are you up to?" I asked, walking toward the kitchen. "Hey Soph, you want a root beer?"

She gave me a nod and followed.

"Seven," Mom said. "I figure I need at least eight to start with. Of course, we'll have to come up with new ones as we go along. Fun, exciting flavors will keep people coming back. Isabel, you can help me come up with catchy little sayings to go with them. You're good at that kind of thing."

"Sure," I said. "I can do that." I reached into the fridge, grabbed two cans of root beer (my favorite), and handed one to Sophie.

"How about if you have a flavor of the month?" Sophie said, popping the top. "You know, like the ice cream shops have?"

Mom gave a little squeal. "Sophie, that's brilliant! Flavor of the month. Why didn't I think of that? So, what should our first month's flavor be?"

"When are you opening?" asked Sophie as she sat down on the plaid couch.

"Should be August fifteenth," Mom said. "They're working fast and furious down there to make it happen."

"Hottest month of the year," I said. "Maybe something with 'cool' in the title. Cool as a Cucumber?"

"Ewwww," they said at the same time.

I laughed. "Okay, maybe not." I took a drink of my root beer. "What about root beer cupcakes? Or iced tea?"

"I know!" Sophie said. "Strawberry lemonade! Nothing says summer like strawberry lemonade."

Mom clapped her hands together, "Yes! I can cut up some strawberries and add a splash of lemon. Perfect! Sophie, you're a genius."

Sophie hadn't even been there five minutes and my

mom had already called her brilliant and a genius. But that's Sophie for you.

Mom set the cookbook down and jumped up. "I think I'll go buy the ingredients right now and make some. And I need some new cupcake pans, since the ones I ordered for the bakery are too large and don't fit in the oven up here. If you two are still around, you want to help me? It'll be fun. We haven't baked together in a while, with the move and everything."

I had to admit, strawberry lemonade cupcakes sounded pretty good to me. "Sure, Mom. We'll probably be here."

"Okay. If you need anything, your dad is down-stairs, going over some things with the contractor. I won't be gone long."

After she left, Sophie said, "Wow, she really *is* happy."

I nodded. "She's never been this excited about anything. I just hope it lasts."

"Okay," Sophie said, pulling on my arm, "show me your room!"

"Close your eyes," I said.

"What?"

"Come on, just do it. I'll lead you. Trust me."

She put her hands over her eyes while I gently pulled her behind me down the hallway and into my room.

"Okay, you can open them."

Now it was her turn to squeal. "Isabel, it's totally purplicious! How come you didn't tell me?"

"'Cause I wanted to surprise you," I said. "Isn't it just so cool?"

We stood there, admiring the pretty walls, partially covered with posters of the places I dreamed of visiting: the Space Needle in Seattle, Niagara Falls in New York, the Dover Castle in England, the Swiss Alps in Switzerland, and lots more.

The person who lived in the apartment before us had painted the bathroom and the two bedrooms really bright colors. Mom and Dad's room was turquoise. The bathroom was orange. And my room was purplicious, as Sophie and I liked to say. Our favorite color.

I walked across the room and turned on the fan. Sophie chugged the rest of her root beer, then did a belly flop on my freshly made bed. "Lucky girl. You get to have a cupcake shop where you can eat all the cupcakes you want *and* the most fabulous room I've ever seen."

I set my can on the nightstand and sat down beside her. "I guess. I miss the old neighborhood, though." I reached over and grabbed her hand and squeezed it. "I miss you, Sophie Bird."

She laughed and rolled over. "You haven't called me that in a long time. Oh my gosh, remember that day?"

How could I forget? We'd climbed a huge oak tree at the park down the street from our duplex. I stopped at about the fifth branch up because it was high enough for me. But not Sophie. She wanted to go higher. She went so high, I yelled up at her, "What do you think you are, a bird?"

It took her forever to get down. At one point I thought I was going to have to get help. But she did it. She's amazing that way. She accomplishes whatever she sets her mind to.

In fourth grade she'd wanted a puppy. Her mom was allergic, so she'd always said no when Sophie asked. But Sophie decided she couldn't live without a dog any longer, and researched and researched until she found a great breed that doesn't shed and is hypoallergenic. Within six months, she had her very own Havanese puppy named Daisy.

In fifth grade she decided she wanted to be the school's spelling bee champion. She studied words from the dictionary every day for months. It didn't surprise me at all when she won and went on to the state championship.

In sixth grade she ran for class president. She wrote speeches, made posters, and went on campaign walks down the hallway, shaking people's hands. They said she won by a landslide.

As I sat there with her, I wondered what she would accomplish in seventh grade. And I thought maybe, just maybe, I could get her to help *me* accomplish something.

I envy birds who can fly.
I want to fly too.
On an airplane.
—IB

Chapter 3

peanut butter and jelly cupcakes

KIDS GO WILD OVER THESE

I need to find a way to make some money," I told Sophie as she picked up a *National Geographic* from my nightstand. Mr. Nelson, my sixth-grade social studies teacher, had given it to me.

"Won't your mom pay you for working in the cupcake shop?"

"I don't think so. They have to pay back the loan

they've taken out, and there won't be a lot of money left over. Besides, I'm not old enough to work, so it's not *really* working, you know? And I bet it won't be very often. I mean, I have school. I have a life!"

"And turtles!" Sophie said, as she picked up one of my many stuffed turtles that lay at the end of my bed. "You can't bake cupcakes, Chickarita. The turtles need you!"

I snatched the turtle from her hands. "Yeah, to save them from the turtle haters of the world like you!"

My grandma got me a stuffed turtle for my fifth birthday. I sort of became obsessed with them. She still gets me one every year, so now I have, like, a whole army of turtles.

Sophie sat up and tossed the magazine back where she found it. "Okay. So what do you need the money for?"

I bit my lip. I wasn't sure if I should tell her. What if she didn't understand?

"Don't laugh, okay? I want to go on a trip. It's so pathetic that I've never been anywhere outside of Oregon!"

She sat up straighter. "Ooh, a trip! How fun! Maybe you can go to Disneyland. I had so much fun when we went a few years ago. Okay, so Hayden screamed like his arm was being cut off at the sight of Mickey or Goofy, or any of the other characters, but still. It was a blast."

I decided not to tell her that a trip to an amusement park wasn't really what I had in mind. She kept talking. "Well, I know Mrs. Canova across the street from us is looking for a mother's helper to watch her three-year-old twins. She's doing cooking shows and selling kitchen tools in people's homes a couple of nights a week. She wants someone to come a few hours a day and watch the boys while she works in her office, making calls and doing computer work. She asked me to do it, but I'm leaving for camp in a few days."

I felt my stomach tighten up. I'd forgotten she was going to camp. "How long are you going to be gone?"

"Three weeks. Well, camp is for two weeks, but after Mom and Dad pick me up, we're going to the Grand Canyon for vacation."

My stomach got even tighter. "You get to see the Grand Canyon?"

She stood up and stretched, her arms clasped above her head. She reached to the right just slightly, reminding me of a tall, lean ballerina.

"Yeah. If I survive the car ride. Hayden's latest obsession is the solar system. The whole way there, I'll have to listen to him spout off facts about Saturn and Mars and every other planet in the galaxy. I don't get it. Who cares about planets that are millions of miles away?"

"Girls," Mom called from the other room, "I'm back. Want to come help make the cupcakes?"

I looked at Sophie and shrugged. "You want to?"

She started walking toward the door. "Sure. But wait. Are you gonna go see Mrs. Canova?"

"Yeah, I probably will, if Mom and Dad say it's okay. Little kids aren't my most favorite thing in the world, but how hard can it be?"

She laughed and threw her arm around me as we walked down the hall. "Oh, sure. A piece of cake. Or should I say, cupcake?"

I got the job and started a couple of days later. I think scrubbing floors with a toothbrush would have been easier than babysitting two toddler boys.

"No, Lucas, don't—" But I was too late. The bowl of water he'd been using to dip his paintbrush in was now all over the kitchen floor. Frustrated that his blue blob looked nothing like a stegosaurus, he had grabbed the bowl and dumped its contents.

Logan sat in his chair, paintbrush out like a sword drawn for battle, little chuckles coming from his mouth as he said, "Dat's funny."

The chuckles turned into a full-blown laugh as they watched me on my hands and knees, trying to sop up the water with a big wad of paper towels.

"It's not funny," I told them. "We have to be careful when we're painting. Very, very careful. You understand, Lucas?"

Lucas nodded his head, then grabbed his paint-brush and painted across the kitchen table. "Keep paint on paper."

Knowing that paint on a table is much worse than water on a floor, I tried to jump up and clean it before it dried. Normally that would have been fine, except the floor was slippery, so my flip-flops couldn't get a firm grip, and I ended up back on the floor. Total face plant.

Lucas and Logan threw their paintbrushes in the air like confetti to celebrate the occasion, and laughed until they cried.

Me? I just cried.

When I got home, a pretty pink sign with elegant black lettering greeted me.

It's Raining Cupcakes

I ran up the stairs, excited to tell Mom how great the sign looked. After I turned the corner when I reached the top of the stairs, I ran right into Stan, carrying suitcases in both hands.

"Isabel," he said, laughing. "You in a hurry?"

"Oh, sorry. Hey, are you going somewhere?"

"Just getting them out of storage. We don't leave for another week. Judy and I are going to jolly old England."

My heart leaped at the thought. "You're going to England? What part?"

"The northeastern part to start with. County Durham, North Yorkshire, and Northumberland."

"You'll get to see Durham Castle! And the Durham Cathedral!"

He chuckled. "Have you been there, Isabel?"

I shook my head. "I just read a lot."

He nodded like he understood. "Well, you probably know more about the place than I do. I'm not much into traveling. More of a homebody myself."

"Then why are you going?"

He smiled. "Because I have a wife who has wanted to go to England for years. I surprised her and bought tickets for an anniversary gift. Our thirtieth is coming up in a couple of weeks. Anyway, I'll send you a postcard, how's that?"

"I'd love that. Wait, are you closing your barber shop while you're gone?"

He nodded. "I figure with all the construction going on, it's for the best anyway."

The way he said it made me feel funny. Was he

angry that we had moved in and things were changing in the neighborhood? Maybe he had liked having a Laundromat next door. And maybe he didn't *like* cupcakes.

He must have read my mind. "No worries, though. You're sprucing up the neighborhood. I bet my business increases tenfold thanks to you."

That reminded me of something I'd been wondering about. "Hey, who lives in the third apartment up here? I haven't seen anyone else around."

"That'd be Lana. She's away on a trip herself. To visit family, I believe. Can't remember when she's due back. But anyway, you'll like her. She's a real nice gal."

I smiled. "See ya later, Stan. Have fun packing."

"Knock-knock," he said.

"Who's there?"

"Stan."

"Stan who?"

"Stan back! I think I'm going to sneeze!"

Ha, more like, Stan gets to go to England and Isabel doesn't. No fair!

I pulled my passport book out of my back pocket, along with the tiny pencil I carried, and wrote:

Queens live in castles.
I'd love to visit a castle
and feel like a queen
for a day.
—IB

When I walked into our apartment, a gray, smoky haze greeted me. And the smell! It was like when cheese from the pizza drips onto the bottom of the oven and burns, only worse.

"Mom? Dad?"

"In here!" Dad yelled.

He was in the kitchen, using a towel to wave smoke away from a cupcake pan.

"What happened? Where's Mom?"

"She's in her room. Go open all the windows and then see if she's all right."

I went around the apartment and opened every window. It was sunny and warm outside—not much of a breeze—so it didn't help a whole lot.

When I got to her bedroom, I found Mom sitting on her bed, staring out the window. I sat down next to her.

My stomach felt funny. Nervous. Mom let things get to her so easily. Little things that most people can just laugh off. But not my mother. I'd learned over the years that talking to her when she was upset about something was like that game where you walk across the yard with an egg on your spoon, the whole time trying not to drop the egg. As I sat next to her, my mind whispered, *Careful, be careful, step slooowly*.

I thought of the time she had planted a garden a few years ago at our duplex. She was excited about growing her own carrots, radishes, and tomatoes. Things seemed to be going along pretty well. The plants started growing, and we could see the first signs of some yummy vegetables. But then one morning she woke up and discovered a bunch of gopher holes. Dad said they could try traps, but she wasn't interested. She just gave up. Said she wasn't meant to be a farmer, and that's why we have grocery stores anyway. So while the moles had a party in our backyard, Mom spent the rest of the day in her room.

Grandma told me one time that Mom is missing the gumption gene. Of course I had no idea what gumption was. It sounded to me like some kind of terrible soup. When I told Grandma that, she laughed and explained that it means spirit or spunk. When things don't go quite right, Mom's solution is to just give up.

"Mom?" I asked.

She didn't answer.

"Are you all right? Did you burn yourself or anything?"

She shook her head and sighed. "I'm fine. Just not cut out to make cupcakes."

I turned and faced her. "Mom, everyone burns things. We put something in the oven and we forget. Remember that one time I burnt a batch of snickerdoodles? I felt so bad, and you told me not to worry, because it was just one batch and we still had plenty of dough to make lots of cookies for the bake sale. Now I'm telling you, don't worry! You're the best baker I know. Come on. Cheer up! The sign is *so* beautiful. It made me excited when I saw it. Didn't it make you excited?"

She turned to face me. Her mousy brown hair was kind of messed up and her green eyes looked sad.

But for a moment, there was a little sparkle in them. "It is beautiful, isn't it?"

"Yes! So be happy, okay? Now I'm going to make dinner for us tonight. You rest if you want to, but I'm coming to get you in thirty minutes."

"Thanks, Is."

I gave her a quick hug before I re-entered the smoke zone.

"Is she okay?" Dad asked. He was sitting on the couch, checking things off the list on his clipboard.

"Yeah. I think she's just worried. I mean, it's a scary thing, opening a new business, right?"

Dad looked at me. He tried to smile, but the wrinkles in his forehead told me he was worried too. "You're right. It's scary for anyone. She'll be fine. We just need to stay positive even when she worries."

"I'm going to make dinner. Tacos all right?"

He turned the TV on and started flipping through the channels. "Sounds good," he said. "Thanks, honey." When he came to a baseball game, he stopped. I could tell from the uniforms that the Red Sox were playing the Yankees. Dad's a huge Red Sox fan.

"Did you know Stan is going to England?" I asked

him as I leaned up against the back of the sofa behind where he sat. He turned and looked up at me for a second, and I noticed how tired he looked.

He'd been working long hours downstairs, helping to get the cupcake shop ready. During the school year, he taught high school math, but every summer he spent his time differently. One year he taught summer school. Another year he painted the inside and outside of our old duplex. This year he was helping to get the cupcake shop ready. As I thought about it, I realized the guy never stopped. Never took the time to rest. I know some people like to keep busy, and maybe it was his way of dealing with Mom and her stuff, but still, it just didn't seem right to me.

"Yeah," Dad said. "Stan told me. Sounds like a great trip."

"Dad, how come we never go anywhere? Isn't it just completely sad that I've never even been on an airplane?"

He reached over and patted my hand resting on the top of the sofa. "Sad? No. Disappointing? Maybe. When you get older, you can travel all you want, how's that?"

"Well, that's why I want to be a flight attendant. But really, do I have to wait that long?"

He gave a little grunt as one of the batters struck out. Then he looked back at me. "Didn't your aunt Christy say she'd take you on a trip when you turn sixteen?"

"That's four years, Dad. Four long years. How come we can't take a vacation? A real vacation? You need one! We could go to Florida or Mexico, or what about Australia?"

He laughed. "Australia? You've never even been out of Oregon and suddenly you want to see Australia?"

"I want to see everything! And anything! I'm so tired of Willow. Aren't you?"

He turned back to watch the game. "No," he said quietly. "This is our home, Isabel. We belong here."

We belong here? Or we're stuck here? I wanted to tell him there was a difference. But instead I went into the kitchen and made tacos. Just like I belonged there.

Chapter 4

chocolate coconut cupcakes

TASTE LIKE A MILLION BUCKS

I was a complete idiot and took the babysitting job without asking how much I'd get paid. When Mrs. Canova paid me on Friday for the two days I'd worked that week, she gave me thirty dollars. That was only fifteen dollars a day. Okay, I didn't actually work the whole day, just a half day. But still, I guess I'd expected a little more. It was hard work trying to keep up with those boys!

I was complaining to Sophie about it the day before she had to leave for camp, after I'd spent the afternoon repairing the damage caused by the dual cyclone known as Lucas and Logan. While I'd been doing the dishes after snack time, they'd decided to take the books off the bookshelf in their room and wipe the pages clean with the flushable wipes they found in the bathroom.

"Wipes are for your bottoms, not your books," I told them when I walked in and saw what they were doing.

They just laughed, like always.

"Well, think of it this way," Sophie said, trying to shove another sweatshirt into her already full suitcase. "By the end of the summer, you should have a few hundred bucks, right? That might be enough money to buy an airplane ticket."

"Yeah, right. If I want to go to Pocatello, Idaho."

I lay on her bed, looking at her bookshelf and the soccer and softball trophies she'd won over the years. Her parents had always encouraged her to try new things. She'd played sports, taken piano lessons, and participated in the summer children's theater program until now, when she was finally too old.

I'd never done any of those things. My mom thought sports were dangerous. We didn't have a piano. Or any instrument, for that matter. When I asked for a guitar one time, Mom said noise gave her bad headaches, as if she didn't think I could actually make the thing sound good.

As for the theater, I could never picture myself up on a stage. Sophie's good at that kind of thing. But not me. While she was gone, I'd stay home and read books, or watch soap operas, waiting for our antique clock to chime four o'clock. That was when Sophie would come home, and we'd play outside before dinner.

Now Sophie smacked her forehead with the palm of her hand in a very dramatic way, snapping me back to reality about my moneymaking dilemma. "Oh my gosh, Is, I have the perfect solution. I can't believe I almost forgot to tell you. Does your mom still get *Baker's Best* magazine?"

"I don't think so," I said. "At least, I haven't seen one lying around lately. Why?"

She reached over and opened the top drawer of her desk. I sat up as she handed me a magazine, open to a page that read BAKING CONTEST FOR KIDS AGES 9—14.

"A baking contest?" I asked her, my heart starting to pound inside my chest. "Are you going to enter?"

She nodded, and her eyes got really big. "Grand prize is a thousand dollars. But you have to come up with a recipe on your own. No one can help you. Not your mom, not your grandma, no one."

My eyes skimmed the rules. They were looking for a completely original dessert recipe. Each entry would be graded on easiness to prepare, uniqueness, presentation, and taste. All entries had to be postmarked by August 1, which wasn't that far away.

When I got to the bottom of the paragraph, I jumped off the bed. "Finalists will be flown to New York City along with one parent or guardian for a bake-off!" I yelled. "Sophie, we could go to New York! The Statue of Liberty. Metropolitan Museum of Art. Radio City Music Hall!"

"Does it say how many finalists there'll be?" she asked.

"No. But wouldn't it be fun if we both made it?"

She sat down on her suitcase, reached down, and flipped the latches closed. "It would be a blast." Then

• 40 •

she pointed her finger at me. "As long as you know I'm in it to win."

I smiled. "What do you want the money so bad for, anyway?"

She stood up and took the suitcase off her bed, and then, with a loud grunt, dropped it on the floor. "The future. As for the present, I think I packed too much. I have to pack in case it's ninety degrees or forty. How come Oregon's weather is so unpredictable, anyway?"

"Wait a minute. What do you mean the future? Like college?"

She took the magazine from my hand and threw it on the bed. "Maybe. Come on. Time for you to go home so I can get my toiletries packed. Isn't that a stupid word? Toiletries? It makes it sound like the stuff comes from the toilet."

She walked me to the door, and I gave her a quick hug. "See you when you get back," I told her. "I'll be practicing recipes while you're gone."

"I should have waited and told you after camp," she said. "Now you have the unfair advantage. Especially since I'll only have a few days to make the deadline when I get home. I'll have to work fast."

"Hey, maybe while you're at camp, you'll come up with a new and improved s'more recipe."

"How can you improve the s'more? It's, like, chocolaty marshmallow perfection."

"Bye, Sophie Bird. See you in three."

"Bye, Chickarita. Be good."

I made a quick note in my passport book:

I've heard walking down a busy sidewalk in New York
is like swimming in a sea of people.
I love to swim and I love people,
so of course I would love
New York!
—IB

I hopped on my bicycle, my thoughts turning faster than the spokes underneath me. A trip to New York and a thousand dollars!

I knew I just had to win that baking contest. Even if it meant, for once, that something didn't go Sophie's way.

Chapter 5

carrot cake cupcakes

PETER RABBIT'S FAVORITE

When I got home, Grandma was there, helping Mom in the kitchen. The apartment smelled spicy, like cinnamon.

"Izzy!" Grandma said when I walked in. She was the only one who ever called me that. "Just in time to try our latest creation. After I get a hug, of course."

I wrapped my arms around her tiny waist and let

her squeeze me real tight, being careful not to bump her pink pillbox hat.

Grandma always wears a hat. Her closet has two long shelves with stacks of hatboxes piled high. Inside are hats with veils, hats with beads, hats with feathers, hats with sequins—just about any kind of hat you can imagine. My grandpa was in the hatmaking business for a long time, until hats went out of style. He moved on to other things, but he always had a soft spot for hats, and it made him happy when Grandma wore them. Even after he died a few years ago, she kept wearing them. Some of the hats she has are probably sixty years old, and she usually has a crazy story about each one. I never know if she's serious or just making it up.

"Nice outfit," I told her when I pulled away. Underneath her apron, I could see she had on a tailored white and pink pantsuit. Since she always wore a hat, she felt like she had to dress up to match.

"Thanks, cupcake," she said. "You're looking quite ducky yourself."

"Ducky" is Grandma's favorite word. Says it all the time. Drives Mom crazy.

"This hat," she continued, "is just like one the First Lady Jackie Kennedy wore that sad, sad day her husband died. I met Jackie Kennedy once, many years ago, at a fundraising dinner, did you know that? Lovely lady. We exchanged the usual pleasantries, then she leaned in to whisper in my ear. Why, my heart started racing, because I thought she was going to tell me some big secret. But you know what she said?" She paused to give a little giggle. "She told me that I had a smudge of lipstick on my teeth. Wasn't that kind of her? It really felt like we had been friends forever."

I nodded like I always did when she started talking about people like that. Then my eyes traveled around the kitchen. A stack of dirty bowls sat next to the sink. About eight trays of cupcakes, most with one missing, were scattered across the gray Formica countertops. "Doing a little baking, huh?"

"Oh yes. We've been perfecting one of our eight flavors. Carrot cake with cream-cheese frosting. Want to try the latest batch? We just frosted them."

I shrugged. I didn't really *like* carrot cake. "No, thanks. Are you sure you want carrot cake as one of the eight? I mean, is anyone really going to pick carrots over chocolate?"

The whole time Grandma and I had been having this exchange, Mom stood there, not saying anything. But as soon as I said that, she snapped out of her trance, throwing her towel on the counter. "She's right. She's absolutely right! What are we doing? We keep trying and trying to get this recipe right, when it shouldn't even be one of the eight flavors. It's boring. Vegetables are boring! We can't do carrot cake. We can't, Mom. We need to find something better."

Grandma wrapped her arm around Mom's shoulders and started leading her out of the kitchen. "Why don't you go take a rest? We've been on our feet all afternoon. Izzy and I will clean up in here. We can try again tomorrow."

"Wait!" I said. "Mom, before you go, I have the best news. Sophie told me about a contest in *Baker's Best* magazine. It's a baking contest for kids, ages nine to fourteen. We're both going to enter. The grand prize is a thousand dollars!"

They both turned around and looked at me,

Mom's eyes much brighter. "A baking contest? Will the finalists be on TV?"

"Um, I'm not sure. Anyway, I have to come up with a recipe and enter by the first of August. And the finalists are flown to New York City. Can you believe that? New York!"

"Oh, Isabel, you should come up with a cupcake recipe. If you make it into the finals, it could be great advertising for our little cupcake shop. We could even feature your cupcake—Isabel's cupcake—as one of the flavors of the month."

I looked over at Grandma. She just smiled, not saying anything. It felt like my heart had jumped up into my throat.

I tried to choose my words carefully, so I wouldn't upset her. "But Mom, cupcakes are your thing. Why can't I do my own thing? Besides, if I make cupcakes, they'll think you helped me with the recipe."

The corners of her lips turned down just slightly. "If you tell them you came up with it yourself, they'll believe you. Please, Isabel? This could be a chance for us to show the country our great little shop here. What does it matter what kind of recipe you enter, anyway? As long as you're in the finals, right?" She smiled again. "Oh, this is going to be great. I can't wait to see what kind of cupcake recipe you come up with. All those times we've baked together will come in handy now, won't they?"

And with that, they turned and walked toward Mom's bedroom.

I went to the sink, put the stopper in the drain, and turned the water on full blast. I threw beaters, scrapers, and silverware into the water, creating splash after angry splash.

How dare she tell me what to bake for the contest! Why was everything about *her*? Couldn't she think of *me* just once? What a stupid idea. They'd call me a cheater for sure. I didn't care what she said. I wasn't doing it.

Grandma came back in and stood beside me at the sink. She reached over and turned the water off. I hadn't noticed that the water in the sink was about to overflow. "You didn't add soap," she said softly.

I reached under the sink, grabbed the bottle of dishwashing soap, and squirted a bunch into the sink. "There. Now we have soap."

She rolled up her sleeve, stuck her hand in the water, and stirred the water hard. Bubbles rose to the surface. Then she turned and looked at me, her eyes soft and warm, like a blanket you reach for when you want to curl up and read a book.

"I know it must be hard, honey. You had to move. Your mother is stressed about getting this business off the ground. Your dad is busy working downstairs. All I can say is, follow your heart. Think about it, and do what your heart tells you to do. You have a good heart, I know that as sure as I know your grandpa loved hats."

Well, my heart sure didn't *feel* very good. "Grandma, I thought this was all going to make her happy. I mean, it's been me and Dad walking on eggshells around her for so long, and then, with this cupcake idea, she was finally thinking about something besides her problems for once. I thought things were going to be different. Better, you know?"

I blinked real fast, trying to keep my eyes from getting teary.

She gave me a squeeze, her wet hand cool on my shoulder. "You are an amazing girl, Izzy. I'm sorry it's so hard for you sometimes, but your mother loves you very much. Thank goodness she has you, honey. And you know, I think deep down she is happy. We just can't see it right now because of all the other stuff she's feeling too. It's stressful right now, but it'll get better. So try not to worry, okay?"

Easy for her to say. She didn't have to live with Mom.

While Grandma went to work washing the dishes in the sink, I walked over to a pan of cupcakes, ready to change the subject. I might like parties, but pity parties aren't my idea of a good time.

"What are we supposed to do with all these cupcakes?" I asked.

She shrugged her shoulders and smiled. "Those are the rejects. They weren't quite moist enough. They may not have had enough oil in them. Or she may have overmixed them. I'm not really sure. In any event, you can throw them away. The good batch is over there."

I followed her pointed finger to a plate of cute little cupcakes set aside, all nicely frosted, with two sliced almonds crisscrossed in the center of each.

"I'm going to go see if Stan and his wife are

around. Maybe they'll take some of these. We can't eat them all."

"That's a ducky idea, Izzy. I'm sure they'll appreciate that."

I walked down the hall to Stan's apartment and knocked, but nobody answered. Wondering if they'd already left for their trip, I went down the stairs and out the door, to see if the barber shop was open.

I hadn't been inside his shop before. There were two stations with big, black swivel chairs in front of mirrors along the right side of the shop. Along the back wall was a sink with a chair in front of it, and a shelf of shampoos and other products sitting above the sink. Up front, by the large picture window, sat a row of chairs with a coffee table in front of them, piled high with magazines. Two old guys sat there, reading the newspaper.

Stan was cutting a kid's hair, while the kid's dad stood beside him, watching.

"Well, Isabel, how nice to see you," Stan said, holding his scissors up in the air. "Need a trim?"

Without thinking, I reached up and touched my straight, short brown hair. Did it look like I needed a trim? Wasn't a barber just for men? "No, thanks. I'm good. I actually brought you some of my mom's cupcakes. We're doing a lot of baking and sampling, and one family can only eat so many, you know?"

"Pass them out," he said, waving the scissors around. "Except for Phillip here. He needs to wait until he's done. Otherwise he'll be picking hairs out of his food right and left. And it won't be the chef's fault."

By now the two men had set their newspapers down. They each took a cupcake and thanked me.

The dad standing next to his son took two. "I'll hold Phillip's until he's done."

"Well, land sakes," I heard from behind me. "This is one doggone good cupcake. You make these, miss?"

I turned around. One of the men was wiping frosting from his top lip, using his finger. I realized I should have brought napkins. Cupcakes can be messy.

"No. My mom. She's opening up a cupcake shop next door. The grand opening is August fifteenth. You should stop by. It's going to be really great."

"Delicious," the other man said. "Give your mother our compliments."

I felt my heart flutter in my chest. They liked

them! They liked the cupcakes. I couldn't wait to tell her. That'd give her a good boost of confidence.

Stan unsnapped the cape around the kid's neck, and the kid jumped out of the chair. "Can I have mine now?"

I started to warn him that it was carrot. He might be disappointed. But I didn't say anything, just bit my bottom lip and waited. Maybe the kid liked carrot cake. Maybe it was his absolute favorite. Yeah, right, and every kid begs to eat their brussels spouts.

He bit into it, looked up at his dad, and said, with a mouthful of cupcake, "Mmmmmm. That's good."

"I know," agreed his dad. He looked at me. "They really are delicious. Thanks for sharing."

I smiled. "You're welcome."

Stan walked over and took two from the plate I was holding. "I'll take these home with me when I'm done here. The perfect dessert after supper tonight. Judy'll be thrilled."

"Good. Hey, when do you leave for your trip?"

"Tomorrow," he said. "We'll be back in a couple of weeks."

"Take lots of pictures. And don't forget to send me a postcard!"

"Okay, I will. See you when we get back."

I waved to everyone as I started to walk out.

Behind me, I heard Stan say, "Knock-knock."

The kid answered. "Who's there?"

"Phillip."

"Phillip who?"

"Phillip the gas tank, I'm running low."

I heard the boy laughing as the door closed behind me.

Back upstairs, Grandma had the kitchen just about cleaned up. Dad was standing there, talking to her. I handed him the plate, only half full now. "I took them down to the barber shop and passed them out. They loved them. I want to tell Mom."

Dad took hold of my arm as I started to leave, a nervous smile on his face. "Isabel, I just went in to see her. Please, don't say anything to upset her. This is a really hectic time for her."

Like he needed to tell me that. While I walked down the hall toward her room, I could feel my heart pounding in my chest. What would she say when I told her they liked the cupcakes? Would she even believe me? What if she brought up the contest again? Would I have to lie and tell her I would make cupcakes when I wasn't sure what I was going to make?

I took a quick right, went into my room, and shut the door. I'd tell her later. Or maybe it wasn't that big of a deal after all. Maybe I didn't even need to mention it.

I thought of Stan getting ready to go to England, and how I would have loved to be getting ready to go on a trip right about now.

*Getting a postcard means
someone is thinking about you.
It's also like getting a little piece
of the place the person is visiting.
I love getting postcards.
When I travel someday,
I will send lots and lots
of postcards.
—IB*

Chapter 6

banana cream pie cupcakes

WHEN IT'S HARD TO DECIDE WHICH

DESSERT SOUNDS BEST

For the next couple of weeks, I spent most of my time either babysitting the twins or reading travel books in the library. And I thought about the baking contest. A lot. I couldn't figure out what to do. I didn't *want* to make cupcakes. But nothing else seemed quite right either. A pie sounded too difficult. Cookies were too ordinary. A cake was hardly different from cupcakes. I didn't know what to do.

It was fun to get a postcard from Stan in the mail. He sent me one with Durham Castle on the front. On the back he wrote:

> Dear Isabel,
> We're having a jolly good time here. The weather's been truly grand. I miss everyone back home, however. Hope the cupcake shop is coming along splendidly. It's sure to be a smashing success.
>
> > Cheerio, Stan

I took it along with me to show the twins. They weren't impressed. "We want to swim!" Lucas said.

"We want to swim, we want to swim, we want to swim!" they chanted, marching around the family room.

We went outside to the backyard, only to find the kiddie pool completely empty.

"If I fill it up, the water's going to be *really cold*."

Lucas nodded his head hard, his blond curly hair flopping in his eyes. Those curls were my ticket to telling them apart. Logan didn't have nearly as many.

While Lucas nodded, Logan clapped his hands, like he'd never heard anything so exciting. *Really* cold water? Yay!

I dragged the hose over, stuck it in the swimming pool, and turned the faucet on. "Let's go inside and read books until it's full."

They didn't move.

"Come on, boys. It's going to take awhile."

They still didn't move.

"Please? If we're going to be sitting out here all afternoon, I want a book to look at." I had spotted a beautiful book about Colorado on their bookshelf the other day that I was dying to read.

The boys stood there, hypnotized by the water running from the hose into the pool. For once they weren't climbing something, spilling something, or tearing something apart.

"Okay, you stay here," I told them. "I'll be back in a second. But listen to me. Do not get into that pool. Do you understand me? If you get in, I'm throwing it away. You'll never, ever be able to swim again. You got that? DO NOT GET INTO THAT POOL."

"Okay," Logan said. Lucas nodded in agreement.

I ducked inside, kicked my flip-flops off, and ran to the front of the house where the living room was, all the while wondering how mothers of young children ever got anything accomplished. It seemed amazing that they weren't all walking around completely filthy from not having showered for months. Unless they were waking up at four a.m. every day and showering then. Maybe that was their trick.

I snatched up the book about Colorado, but as I did, my eyes couldn't help but scan for others. There were a lot. I took one called *50 Amazing Things to Do in Chicago*, and another one about Ireland, then hurried to the backyard.

When I got there, Mrs. Canova, or Sue as she insisted I call her, was standing there, arms crossed in that "I'm so appalled with you" way, as two completely dressed boys walked around inside the pool, kicking and splashing water at each other.

"Isabel?" Her eyes pierced mine.

I gulped. "Yes?"

"Did you leave them out here by themselves with a pool of water?"

"Well, it was filling up and—"

Her eyes narrowed even more as she stepped closer to me. "Did you, or did you not, leave them unattended with a pool of water?"

I looked down at my toes, the red nail polish I'd put on a month ago starting to chip away. Obviously, she already knew the answer to that question. She had found them outside, and I wasn't anywhere around.

"Yes," I whispered. "I'm sorry."

The boys' laughter filled the air. I listened to it, trying to make myself breathe. But I couldn't. It was like someone was standing on my chest, pressing harder and harder.

She reached over and took the books from my hands, then walked toward the sliding glass door. "I'm sure you understand, I can't have someone watching my children who displays such a lack of judgment. Do you know an accident can happen just like that?" She snapped her fingers. "I'm going to get my checkbook and pay you for the past five days. Please, stay here and watch them for another minute. And then your services will no longer be needed here."

After she left, I went over to the pool. I wanted

to cry, but I didn't want them to see me like that. I didn't want *her* to see me like that.

"Bye, boys. I have to go now."

"You throw it away now?" Lucas asked.

It made me smile. He asked like it was no big deal. Like it wouldn't matter to them one bit. Maybe they didn't even know what it meant.

"No. I'm the one being thrown away. I'll see you guys later. Be good for your mommy, okay?"

Sue came back and handed me my check. I apologized again, but she didn't say anything. She didn't have to. Her eyes said it all.

I knew I had to tell my parents. Not just tell them I wasn't working for Mrs. Canova anymore, but tell them *why*. If I made something up, like I quit or something, word would get back to them that I'd lied. Mom knew a lot of people in Willow, and she'd eventually find out, whether I told her or not.

Still, I didn't go home right away. I rode my bike to the library, the hot air stinging my eyes, making them water.

Okay, so maybe it wasn't the hot air.

For the first time in a long time, I didn't go to the travel section when I got to the library. I went to the cookbook section instead. It was time to come up with an idea. No more excuses.

"Isabel?" said a familiar voice as I was sitting at a table, looking at a lemon torte recipe.

I looked up.

"Mr. Nelson," I said, louder than I should have. "What are you doing here?"

Okay, stupid question. He was holding a stack of books. "Oh, you know, summer vacation is for reading, right?"

"Right." I smiled.

It was weird seeing my social studies teacher in shorts and a T-shirt. He looked different. Not like a teacher at all. More like an ordinary guy.

"Cookbooks?" he asked. "Taking up a new hobby?"

I shut the book. "I guess. I'm entering a baking contest. The finalists get to travel to New York City for a bake-off. Figured it might be my only chance to fly on an airplane and go somewhere interesting."

He sat down across from me. "Sounds like fun. My wife and I had a layover there on our way to Germany last summer. Stayed a couple of days so we could take in a Broadway play. It's an amazing city. All the people there? I don't think there's any place like it." His eyes smiled at me. "You'd probably love it there, Isabel. Seems to me you're quite the people person."

I wasn't sure what to say to that. "What part of Germany did you go to?" I asked as I picked at an annoying hangnail on my thumb.

"Frankfurt, Berlin, Hamburg, Heidelberg. We went all over. It's a beautiful country. Didn't care for the food much. But everything else was fantastic."

"Where are you going this summer?" I asked.

He leaned back in his chair, tipping it off the floor a little. It was funny to see an adult do that. I always got in trouble for it at home. "We're going to Washington, D.C., in a couple of weeks."

I sighed. "I'd love to go there. I'd see the Capitol Building, the Washington Monument, and the National Museum of Natural History for sure."

He laughed. "Yep. We'll see all of those."

"You're so lucky. Sometimes I feel like I'll be stuck in Willow forever."

Mr. Nelson tilted his head a little and looked at

me kind of funny. "Is everything all right at home, Isabel? Your parents doing okay?"

"Yeah. Just busy. We're getting ready to open a cupcake shop. You know where the Bleachorama used to be? The building is now the future home of It's Raining Cupcakes."

"Wow, that's exciting!" He stood up. "I'll have to stop by. I love cupcakes."

"That'd be great! We open on August fifteenth."

"Okay, Isabel, I need to get going. But I'll try to come by for the grand opening. And good luck with that contest. Are you going to make cupcakes?"

I shrugged. "I don't know yet."

"See ya later," he said.

"Say hi to the president for me!"

I pulled out my passport book and wrote in it:

Mr. Nelson made me love
reading about other places.
But reading about places
and going places
is just not the same.

—IB

* * *

I told Mom and Dad about the pool incident over a dinner of fried chicken and mashed potatoes. Mom didn't say a whole lot, just shook her head and pushed the food around on her plate.

"I feel bad, you know," I told them, wanting them to believe me. "I'd never want anything to happen to those little boys."

Dad took a drink of milk. "Drowning accidents can happen so fast. It probably just scared Sue something fierce. She's mad now. But she'll get over it. You apologized, right?"

"Yeah. But I don't think she believed me."

"It's okay," he said. "Look at it this way. We're getting close to opening day. Your mom could probably use some help with grocery shopping and testing some more recipes. Right, Caroline?"

"I suppose," she said, staring off into space.

"Mom, aren't you excited?" I asked. "You open in just a few more weeks! I've been telling everyone I see."

She stood up and took her plate to the counter. "Don't remind me. I'm not ready. I don't know why

I thought we could be ready by the fifteenth. It's too soon." She turned around. "David, I think we should wait. I think we should postpone the opening."

Dad stood up. "Honey, we're not going to wait. All the guys have been working so hard to have it ready. You just have cold feet. That's all. But Isabel getting fired is a blessing in disguise. She can help you with whatever you need—running errands, trying new recipes, advertising. Put her to work."

I sighed. There went the rest of my summer vacation.

While they continued their discussion, I snuck off to my room. I took a seat at my desk, feeling defeated about the entire day and thinking maybe I should just crawl into bed, when I saw two pieces of mail that had come for me.

The first was a postcard from my aunt, with a picture of the St. Louis Gateway Arch on the front.

Dear Isabel, I've been to St. Louis many times and never took the time to go up to the arch. It was fun!

The view from the top was incredible, and there's a cool museum inside about Lewis and Clark and their trip. Hope all is well with you. Is the cupcake shop coming along nicely? Love, Aunt Christy

The second was an envelope with Sophie's handwriting. I ripped it open and read.

Dear Is,

　　Camp sucks. I think I'm getting too old or something. Every activity seems lame, lamer, and lamest. I mean, canoeing on the lake isn't fun. It's work! Just ask my biceps. And archery? I used to be happy just getting the thing somewhere on the target. But now? No way. I want to hit the bull's-eye, baby! And of course, it's impossible. So I get frustrated and throw the thing on the ground. And then they yell at me. And then I cry. And then . . . well, you get the idea.

I want to come home. Next year, when my mom tells me I have to go, I'll just stay at your place and eat cupcakes for breakfast, lunch, and dinner for two weeks. Your parents won't mind, right?

What's going on in Willow? Working on your recipe? How are Thing 1 and Thing 2, otherwise known as Lucas and Logan? I don't know why I'm asking you questions. By the time you get this letter, I'll be on my way to the Grand Canyon, so you can't write me back. Can't wait to catch up when I get home.

Time for campfire. At least there won't be any singing tonight. Rachel's guitar somehow tragically lost all its strings. I wonder how that happened?

Campily yours,
Sophie

Thanks to Sophie, my stinky, stinkier, and stinkiest day ended on a happy note. I folded up the letter, tucked the envelope into a desk drawer, and crawled into bed underneath a blanket of turtles, figuring I'd better quit while I was ahead.

Chapter 7

coconut mango cupcakes

A TASTE OF THE TROPICS WITHOUT

GETTING ON A PLANE

The next day, Mom and I were going through all the boxes that had been delivered, trying to figure out if we still needed to buy anything. Mom didn't say a word. She just emptied the boxes, took notes on her clipboard, and mumbled to herself every once in a while.

I wanted to tell her it'd be okay. I wanted her to know I thought it was great that she was trying to make a dream come true. I wanted to say *something* to make her feel better about everything. But I didn't know what to say. How many times had I wished I'd been born with the knowing-just-the-right-words-at-the-right-time gene, like Sophie had? More times than there are red-eyed tree frogs in the forests of Costa Rica, that's how many.

I decided maybe the best thing to do was to talk about something completely different. "Mom, where did you and Dad go on your honeymoon?"

She looked up from her clipboard with her left eyebrow raised. "What? Why?"

I shrugged. "You've never told me. And I'm curious."

"Well, we went to the Oregon coast. Stayed in a cottage for a week. It was very nice."

I peeled the packing tape off the top of the box in front of me. "You didn't go to Hawaii? Or Mexico? Or the Caribbean? Don't most people go to places like that?"

"Sometimes. And your father wanted to, I think.

I just couldn't do it. I couldn't envision myself getting on a plane."

My hands stopped moving, and my eyes looked up at her. "What do you mean?"

She stood up, a pair of wooden spoons in her hand. "I'm afraid, Isabel. I'm afraid to fly."

"You never told me that. How come you never told me?"

She shrugged. "I guess it never came up."

I could feel my heart racing. It didn't come up? All those times I'd rambled on about how I'd love to be like Aunt Christy, flying here and there and everywhere? All those times when I'd asked, "How come we never *go* anywhere?" Her response had always been brief and generic. "It's just not in the budget," or "Maybe someday we'll be able to."

Once again, it was all about *her*. The anger inside of me grew, like a cupcake expanding in the oven. I gritted my teeth and tried to sound as sweet as a chocolate chip cupcake. "Is that why we've never gone anywhere outside of Oregon?"

She made a checkmark on her clipboard. "Oh I don't know, Isabel. There are a lot of reasons.

Anyway, I know you want to travel. And you can blame me if you want to. But just think, you have the whole world to look forward to when you're older."

I started to respond to that with something I probably would have been sorry about later, but I didn't get the chance. There was a knock at the door.

I ran to open it before Mom had even taken a step. As the door flew open, Stan's big smile greeted me.

"You're home!"

"We just got in," he said. "And I wanted to bring you these." He held up a white box. "I thought you might enjoy one of my favorite treats from England. I bought these on the way to the airport and carried them with me the whole way. Judy thought I'd lost my mind. But jam tarts are delicious. And you were so kind to share your cupcakes with us."

I took the box from his hand. By now Mom was standing behind me. "Please, Stan, come in. But you'll have to excuse the mess. We're just going through the equipment for the shop. Not long until we open, you know."

He nodded as he stepped inside. "Yes, I know. August fifteenth, right? Those carrot cake cupcakes were wonderful, Caroline. Very moist and tasty. If your shop had been open, I'm sure Judy would have run downstairs and bought a half dozen more. I predict you are going to have more business than you can handle." He rubbed his belly. "And I predict my already large waistline will be getting even larger."

I looked at Mom, and she was all smiles.

"I got your postcard," I told him. "Thanks for sending it. Did you like the castle?"

"We sure did," he said. "That was actually one of many we saw. We had a great time. I'll have to show you the pictures one of these days."

"I'd love that," I said.

He looked around at the clutter on the floor. "Well, I don't want to keep you. Let me know how you like those tarts, Isabel."

He opened the door and stepped back into the hall.

"Knock-knock."

"Who's there?"

"Jam."

"Jam who?"

"Jamind? I'm trying to get outta here!"

"Bye, Stan," I said.

I skipped to the kitchen, carrying the box of tarts.

"Mom, come try a jam tart," I called, the anger I'd felt earlier now set aside on the cooling rack.

"No, thanks," she said. "I'm not really hungry." She paused, then called out, "Hey, I just remembered, how is that cupcake recipe coming along for the contest?"

I pulled a slightly squished but sweet-smelling jam tart from the box and took a bite. It was the most delicious thing I'd ever tasted.

"I'm, uh, still working on it."

"Do you need some help?"

That was pretty much the last thing I needed. "You can't help, Mom. That's one of the rules, remember?"

Besides, I thought, as I took another bite of the scrumptious tart, *I don't think you'll want to help me once you find out I'm submitting a jam tart recipe instead of a cupcake recipe.*

I pulled out my notebook.

Cupcakes are popular.
So is Disneyland.
Popular is good,
but it doesn't always mean
the best.
—IB

Chapter 8

root beer float cupcakes

A GOOD CHOICE EVERY TIME

At the library, I found hundreds of recipes for jam tarts. The basic recipe was pretty simple. But that didn't mean anything. I needed to make something different. Something all my own.

The tricky part was going to be baking jam tarts without Mom knowing what I was up to. If she found out, I knew her feelings would be hurt.

One afternoon I finally had the apartment to myself while Mom was running some errands and Dad was working downstairs. I'd just finished baking a batch of tarts that I'd made with some fresh lemon juice squeezed into the pastry crust. They were good, but still not something really different or totally fantastic.

I was racking my brain as I drank my second can of root beer, trying to figure out how I could make the world's greatest jam tarts, when I heard voices outside the apartment. As keys jingled, I heard Dad. And then Mom!

I grabbed the pan of tarts and ran to the family room, and without really thinking, I threw open the door that leads to the fire escape. And just like that, I was standing on the platform, looking down at the street below, with a pan of tarts in my hand.

I swear, sometimes I am not the sharpest knife in the drawer, as Mom likes to say. Why didn't I just go to my room and throw the pan under my bed? Now I was stuck out there until they left, unless I wanted to suddenly appear and have them ground me forever.

They'd told me probably a hundred times the fire escape was off-limits.

The door has glass in it, so I had to go to the very edge of the platform and stand against the railing to keep them from seeing me.

People scurried along the sidewalk below, completely unaware that I was standing above them. I put my hand over my mouth to keep myself from giggling at the thought of jam tarts suddenly raining from the sky. But the pastry in that batch was on the heavy side, and the last thing I wanted to do was to give someone a concussion. I could just picture someone going to the emergency room claiming they'd been hit on the head by a jam tart falling from the sky.

I stood there for a long time, listening to my parents chatting away inside, although I couldn't hear specifically what they were talking about. I took a bite of a tart and wondered if they might be worrying about me. I always left a note letting them know where I was going.

There were stairs that dropped below the platform I was standing on, and those stairs were one way out of the tight spot I'd gotten myself into. The problem was that the stairs didn't go all the way to the sidewalk. If I took the stairs, I'd have to jump from the last rung to the sidewalk. I couldn't tell how far it was, but from where I stood, it looked like a long way.

So I waited. And I waited. Then I had to go to the bathroom. Bad. I made a mental note to skip the two cans of root beer the next time I decided to hang out on the fire escape for an hour.

Finally I decided I had two choices. Die at the hands of my father, or die at the hands of the sidewalk below. It was a hard decision. But I decided my father might end up being a bit more forgiving than the concrete sidewalk.

I walked into the family room, and neither of them were around. I smiled and did a little skip across the floor. Maybe I could actually get to my room and throw the pan under my bed like I should have done in the first place, and everything would be fine.

I thought I just might make it when I heard my mom from her room.

"Isabel?" She peeked her head out of the bedroom. "Where have you been? You didn't leave a note."

Then she looked at the pan in my hand. "What's

that?" Now she came all the way out. "What's going on, Isabel?"

"I, um—"

Dad came out of the bathroom across from my room. "Hi, honey. We were getting a little worried. Where'd you run off to?"

"That's what I was just asking her," Mom said.

As we stood there in that cramped hallway, about a hundred lies fluttered through my brain like butterflies in a meadow. But I knew each one would result in more questions and more lies, and I'm a horrible liar.

My shoulders slumped in defeat. "These are tarts. I was trying to come up with a recipe for the baking contest. I was afraid you'd be mad that I wasn't making cupcakes, so when I heard you coming in, I ran onto the fire escape."

They both looked at me as if I had just told them I'd robbed a bank. Which right about then, sounded like a better way to make some cash than trying to make jam tarts in a cupcake house.

"I'm sorry, okay? I shouldn't have gone out there. It was stupid, I know."

"I'm disappointed in you, Isabel," said Dad. "The fire escape is off-limits. You know that."

I hung my head and nodded.

Mom took the tarts from my hand. She looked so sad, I thought she might start to cry. "You really aren't going to submit a cupcake recipe for the contest?"

I shrugged and tried to look her in the eyes, but it was too hard. I looked down at the floor again. "I, uh, I don't know. I was just playing around. You know, experimenting. I don't know what I'm going to submit yet."

Dad put his arm around Mom and took the pan of tarts with the other hand. "They look good, don't you think, Caroline? Want to try one?"

She shook her head. "No, thanks. I'm going to go lie down and read. I'm tired."

"You do that." Dad nodded. "Isabel and I are going to have a little chat about the fire escape and how it's only to be used when, you know, there's an actual *fire*."

The way he said it, I couldn't help but smile. My "thanks for trying to lighten the mood" smile.

He took her to their room while I went into the

kitchen to clean up. He came out a minute later and set the jam tarts on the counter, then walked over to me and gave me a hug.

"What am I going to do, Dad?" I said, my head resting on his chest. "Jam tarts or cupcakes?"

He pulled away and brushed my bangs out of my eyes. "I'm afraid I can't answer that for you, sweetie. It's your decision."

I sighed. He didn't have to say it with words. His eyes were begging me to make it easy on her. Easy on him. Easy on all of us.

He looked at his watch. "I gotta run. I have an appointment with a vendor downstairs. We're getting bids for the glass cases."

"Okay. See you later."

He started to walk away, then turned around. "Oh, and Is?"

"I know, Dad, I know. Stay off the fire escape. Unless there's—"

"—a fire," we both said at the same time.

"Good girl," he said as he waved and scurried out the door.

I went to my room and plopped down in my

desk chair. The thing was, jam tarts were different. Special. When I was thinking about them, and baking them, it really seemed possible that I might actually get out of Willow some day.

I took out my passport book and made a note:

A fire escape is really not
an escape at all.
Traveling to New York,
now that would be an escape.

—IB

Chapter 9

fudge brownie cupcakes

THE BEST OF BOTH WORLDS

The next couple of days were not ducky at all. I walked around like a dazed and confused cartoon character with question marks floating above my head.

Mom seemed to have her heart set on me entering a cupcake recipe. I wasn't sure it mattered, and I wondered if it would really be as great for our cupcake shop as she thought it would be.

Finally, after thinking about it so much my head actually hurt, I decided I needed to get over it and just do a cupcake recipe.

I threw myself into creating the best cupcake recipe ever. I became determined to come up with something no one had ever heard of. Nothing in the kitchen was off-limits. Boy, did I make some strange cupcakes that week.

Peppermint bubblegum cupcakes. Fruit salad cupcakes. Peanut butter, banana, and marshmallow cupcakes. The list went on and on.

I played around with recipes all week, in addition to helping Mom move all the equipment downstairs and testing a gazillion recipes for her. About then, I think I would have been over the moon with happiness if someone had told me I'd never have to eat another cupcake as long as I lived.

The shop downstairs looked better each day as we got closer and closer to the grand opening. They still needed to paint the walls inside and get the glass display cases moved in, along with a few other things. But the kitchen space in the back of the shop was ready to go. Now Mom spent most of her time down there, getting familiar with everything. After Stan raved about her cupcakes, her nerves settled down, which I felt thankful for.

Dad had taken on the role of marketing director. He was placing ads in the newspaper and on the radio, trying to get the word out about the grand opening. The telephone poles throughout town were plastered with pink and green flyers.

Things seemed to be going along pretty well, I guess. So I probably should have known something terrible would happen. I mean, isn't that how it works? Just when you think you have it made, *bam*, something bad happens.

I was on my way home from the library, the day before Sophie was due to come home, when a disaster of the worst kind happened. A disaster no one could ever have predicted. Not a natural kind of disaster. No, this disaster was of the man-made kind. A disaster called Beatrice's Brownies.

Beatrice's Brownies was the latest chain to take the nation's sweet tooth by storm. There had been stories on the news lately of cars lined up for blocks and blocks when one opened in a new location.

Part of it was the fact that the brownies had unique flavors. Bavarian cream brownies, banana split brownies, mint chocolate chip brownies, and lots more. But the other part was the experience the customer had once inside a Beatrice's Brownies store. Each customer was greeted with a brownie sample and a Dixie cup of cold milk. Then they could walk upstairs and get a firsthand view of the kitchen down below, where huge vats of brownie mix were stirred and then poured into extra-large pans. My parents and I had watched an entire TV special on the Beatrice's Brownies craze a few months back.

I about fell off my bike when I saw the sign being hoisted onto the old Burrito Shack building. They had been working on remodeling the building for a while, but not a word had been said about who or what was moving into the building. It had all been very hush-hush. But not anymore.

Cars slowed to a crawl, everyone's eyes fixed on the sign. I watched as people pointed and put their hands over their mouths. This was the biggest thing to happen to the town of Willow since the big flood of 1997, when the whole west side of town basically went under water.

I stood there, feeling sick to my stomach, like I'd eaten two dozen carrot cake cupcakes. How could we compete with Beatrice's Brownies? As the question ran through my brain over and over, only one answer kept popping up: We couldn't.

And then an even bigger question popped up. How could I tell Mom the news?

I told myself I just had to come out and tell her when I got home. But she was so happy with the strawberry lemonade cupcakes she'd made that afternoon, I couldn't do it. Then I told myself I had to tell her over dinner. Except Dad wouldn't stop talking. He told us he had passed out those strawberry lemonade cupcakes to all the workers downstairs, and they had praised her name up and down and sideways. I didn't want to be the wet blanket! Or in our case, the burnt cupcake.

Luckily, they didn't turn on the TV at all that night, so they didn't see the local news. After dinner, Mom went back down to the shop and Dad left to play cards with some teacher friends. I decided I could wait until Sophie came home to tell Mom. Sophie could help me figure out how to break the news. How to break her heart was more like it.

With the place to myself, I went into the kitchen to work on my recipe some more. The deadline was only five days away. As I pulled a bowl out of the cupboard, I thought of Mom's final list of cupcake flavors for the first month. Her list of eight looked like this:

Old-Fashioned Vanilla   Peanut Butter and Jelly
Cherry Devil's Food   Chocolate Coconut
Carrot Cake   Banana Cream Pie
Pineapple Right-Side-Up Strawberry Lemonade

If it had been up to me, I'd have had at least one more chocolate recipe on the list. People love chocolate. Beatrice's Brownies proved that.

And that's when it hit me like a chocolate coconut cupcake upside my head. Chocolate jam tarts. Flaky, chocolaty pastry with fresh strawberry jam in the middle.

It was perfect.

Brilliant!

And absolutely, positively *not* a cupcake recipe.

Still, I wanted to try it and see how the tarts turned out. I couldn't help it. I had to know, would they taste as good as I thought they would?

I made a batch of tarts, writing the ingredients down on a recipe card as I went along.

They tasted *so* good! In a word, amazing.

I paced the kitchen floor as I finished the tart, my thoughts and feelings chasing each other round and round, like a puppy chasing his tail.

After a good thirty minutes, I figured out, it really came down to one question: Make myself happy or make my mother happy?

I had to choose. Simple as that.

Except there wasn't anything even close to simple about it.

Chapter 10

s'mores cupcakes

CAN'T GO WRONG WITH CHOCOLATY

MARSHMALLOW PERFECTION

I thought about calling Grandma and asking her for advice. But I'd already asked her that day when I first told her and Mom about the contest. She'd told me to follow my heart. She'd said I had a good heart. A good heart?

A girl with a good heart would set her own feelings aside, I thought. That was the good thing to do. The right thing to do. Even if it was the sad thing to do. Sad to me, anyway. Submitting a cupcake recipe would make Mom happy. I needed to do it for her.

With that, I made up my mind. For good this time. I dumped the rest of the tarts into the garbage can, hoping I hadn't just dumped my chances to go to New York City right along with them.

Then I got back to work, wishing and hoping I could come up with a fantastically amazing cupcake recipe. I still had chocolate on the brain, and I was thinking about Sophie coming home the next day and wondering what recipe she would make, when I remembered talking about s'mores. Chocolaty marshmallow perfection, Sophie had called them. Well, what if I put that chocolaty marshmallow perfection into a cupcake?

I stayed up into the wee hours of the morning mixing and baking, perfecting the recipe. When Mom came in late herself, I had her taste the latest batch. She smiled and said it was delicious. Then she said good night and headed to her room. I'll admit I had hoped for a bit more encouragement. More excitement. More something. But she was tired, and

I told myself it didn't matter, I had a recipe to enter (even if it wasn't the best chocolate jam tart recipe ever to be invented).

When I went to my room, I wrote the cupcake recipe on a card in my best handwriting, put it in an envelope, and stuck it in my desk drawer until I could get the mailing address from Sophie. Then I wrote in my passport book:

> Maybe someday
> I can live somewhere in England
> and open a jam tart shop.
> I wonder, would I long
> to visit Willow then?
> —IB

I fell into bed that night exhausted and slept late, which wasn't like me. Usually the morning traffic on the road in front of our building woke me, but I slept through it.

When I finally did wake up, my first thought was that Sophie would be home soon. The happiness in that thought was quickly replaced with a sickening sadness when I had my second thought. I needed to tell Mom about Beatrice's Brownies.

After I threw on my robe, I went to my window, slid it open, and put my cheek against the screen. The blue sky and warm air told me it was going to be hot. Down below, two ladies stood at the corner, one of them pointing at the cupcake sign. They walked up to the building and peeked inside the window.

I knew Mom, without the gumption gene, wouldn't take the news about Beatrice's well. But I also believed, as I watched those ladies, our cupcake shop could be something special. I just needed to figure out how to convince my mother of that.

I found Dad sitting at the kitchen table, his hands hugging a cup of coffee and the Sunday paper laid out in front of him. On the front page it read WILLOW WELCOMES BEATRICE'S BROWNIES and below it was a big picture of the sign I'd seen yesterday.

"Dad?" I asked.

He jumped a little, startled to hear my voice.

"Hey, good morning, punkin."

I pointed at the paper. "Did Mom see that?"

He shook his head. "She's in the bathroom. We

need to tell her when she comes out. It's important that she hear it from us."

I sat down. "I saw them putting the sign up yesterday, on my way home from the library. I should have told her last night. But I just couldn't."

He nodded. "I know. It's hard." He took a drink of coffee. "At least it doesn't open until Labor Day weekend. That buys us some time. I mean, hopefully she'll see it's not the end of the world. We're just going to have to work a little harder, that's all."

I gave him a funny look. Was he talking about my mother?

We sat there, waiting. "You hungry?" he asked me.

I shook my head. Then the phone rang.

I jumped up and grabbed the phone in the kitchen.

"Hello?"

"Isabel, it's Grandma. Did you hear the news?"

I sighed. "Yeah. Dad and I are here, waiting to tell Mom."

"Tell me what?" I heard Mom's voice from behind me.

"I'll be right over," Grandma said.

"Okay. Bye, Grandma."

I hung up and walked back over to the table.

I looked at Dad. He looked at me. I think about then we were both wishing for a miracle. Like suddenly the president of the United States would declare brownies unfit to eat and brownie shops everywhere would be forced to close. Or a big rock band would swing through town, see our shop, and write a song about it. It'd shoot to number one and our shop would be famous. They'd put me in their music video. And insist I come on tour with them. And . . .

"Tell me what, Isabel?" Mom said again.

Dad walked over and put his arm around Mom. "Honey, I don't know how to say this, so I'm just going to come right out with it. Beatrice's Brownies is opening a store near here. It made the front page of the newspaper today."

I watched as her cherry-pink cheeks turned the color of buttercream.

"Mom, it's really not that big of a deal. I mean, okay, yeah, it's Beatrice's Brownies. But the excitement will wear off, and people will realize that a cute cupcake shop is way better than a stupid chain brownie store."

Her shoulders slumped, and one hand reached up to her heart, as if her hand pressed there could keep it from beating too fast. "Beatrice's Brownies? Here in Willow?"

Both Dad and I nodded. He handed her the newspaper. "It's going to be all right, though, Caroline. I was telling Isabel, we just have to work a little harder."

She stared at the picture in the paper. "Work a little harder? Are you kidding? We could work day and night for months and never come close to getting the kind of business they're going to get. And once you have a box of scrumptious brownies, you think you're going to stop and get a box of cupcakes, too? Of course you're not. Which means we're doomed. Doomed before we even had a chance." She threw the paper on the table and stomped down the hall to her room.

After her door shut, I asked Dad, "What do we do now?"

He got up and grabbed his clipboard off the

kitchen counter. "I don't know. I'll be back later. I need some air."

As he walked toward the door, I wanted to tell him to go in there and be a cheerleader. He was giving up too easily. He needed to give her his best rah-rah-rah! But my dad's not like that. He's never been like that. Give him a fraction to reduce or a project to work on, and he's all over it. But words of encouragement? Not his thing. I thought about making him a list.

1. Use a soft, calm voice.
2. Smile, but not too much, or it looks fake.
3. General phrases like "Try not to worry" or "It'll be okay" are good.
4. And specific words that will make her smile and feel good about herself and her cupcakes are even better. What those specific words might be, I don't know, since I'm not good at that kind of thing.

I started to get up and go in there myself, and try to find the right words. But something told me she wouldn't listen to me. Because I'd had my doubts. I had told her a Laundromat would be better than a cupcake shop. Easier than a cupcake shop. And knowing her, she'd probably remind me of that.

I sat there, staring at the picture on the front page, wishing it would disappear, so maybe, just once, Mom could be happy. And maybe, just once, all of us could be happy.

Right then, it seemed about as impossible as me flying across the world and seeing the Great Wall of China.

Chapter 11

hawaiian sky cupcakes

THE BLUE COCONUT BUTTERCREAM WILL MAKE YOU GO "WOW"

Grandma came over, all dressed up in an emerald green dress along with little white gloves and a white hat with a feather. She marched down the hall and told Mom she had five minutes to get ready because they were going out.

"I think the best thing to do today is get her out of here and get her mind off cupcakes for a while. Let her stew for too long, and she'll be ready to give up for sure. Wouldn't you agree, Izzy?"

I nodded. Grandma always seemed to have the right answer.

"Do you want to go with us, honey?"

"Sophie's coming home today. She's been gone three whole weeks. I can't wait to see her. Is that all right?"

"Of course. I know this is hard for you, too. You should go see your friend and have a ducky good time. Tomorrow we'll regroup. Make a plan. And we must never, never, never give in. That's what Winston Churchill said, Isabel. He was a wise man. We would do well to follow his advice. Your grandpa met one of his relatives, you know. I can't quite remember her name. But, oh, your grandfather was tickled pink about meeting one of Churchill's relatives, that's for sure."

"Never give in," I said. "Okay. I'll try."

She shook her finger at me and smiled. "Never, never, *never* give in. That's three nevers. Got it?"

"Got it."

She hugged me. "It'll be okay, my darlin' Izzy. You'll see."

The phone rang, so I ran to get it, hoping it was Sophie.

"Chickarita!" she shouted in my ear. "I'm home!"

I squealed. "Yay! Can I come over?"

"Yeah. Just be prepared. Suitcases and dirty clothes are everywhere! They might put you to work doing laundry or something. On second thought, I'll wait for you out front. Hurry, before they suck me into the bottomless pit of chores to be done."

I laughed. "Okay. I'll be right there. I have so much to tell you!"

"Oh, good. Hey, wanna go to the Blue Moon? I'm craving some fries big-time. Plus, that way, Hayden can't barge in and interrupt us with stories of how aliens are here on earth, living among us, ready to snatch us at any given moment and take us back to their planet for research."

"I'm on my way. Bye."

After I hung up, Grandma said, "I presume she's home?"

"Yep. I'm going over there and we're going out to lunch. Tell Mom where I'm at?"

She nodded. "I'll be sure to tell her. And I'll leave your dad a note. Have fun!"

I flew out the door and down the stairs, then grabbed my bike from the storage closet underneath the stairs.

Just then, a pretty woman in shorts and a T-shirt with long black hair walked up to the door, carrying a suitcase and wheeling one case behind her.

I quickly put the kickstand down and went and opened the door for her.

"Thanks," she said, walking in and dropping everything in front of her. "You must be one of the new neighbors." She stuck her hand out. "I'm Lana. I live in the third apartment upstairs."

I took her hand and shook it. Gently but firmly, like my grandpa had taught me when I was three years old. "Oh, hi. I'm Isabel. I wondered when you'd be back. Stan said you were on a trip?"

She nodded. "I'm just getting back from staying with my family in Hawaii. That's where I'm originally from."

"Oh, cool," I said. "Which island?"

"The Big Island."

"Wow. I'd love to go there someday." I pointed to her suitcases. "Want some help carrying these upstairs?"

"Oh, that'd be great. Thanks. Times like this it'd be nice to have an elevator, you know?"

I grabbed one of the suitcases and started up the stairs. "Is Hawaii as beautiful as it looks in pictures?"

I could hear her flip-flops clicking behind me. "Well, even more so, I think. No other place like it, really."

When we reached the top of the stairs, I stopped and let her go ahead of me. She pulled her keys out of her purse.

"Is it your family who is opening the cupcake shop?" she asked.

"Hopefully. I mean, we're supposed to open August fifteenth."

She turned back and looked at me, a puzzled look on her face. "You don't sound too sure. Things not going well?"

"Oh, they're going fine, I guess. We're just nervous

because Beatrice's Brownies is going to be opening a few blocks over."

She fiddled with her keys, trying to find the right one. "Well, I like cupcakes a lot better than brownies, so you'll have at least one customer. I'll have to mark my calendar."

The door swung open, and she hung back so I could go in ahead of her. Past the little entryway was the family room, just like our apartment. But that was where the similarities ended.

"Whoa," I said as I set the suitcase down. Every wall was painted with a beautiful Hawaiian scene. Palm trees, a blue and green ocean, surfers, and even a girl doing the hula in a grass skirt.

"This is incredible. Who did it?" I asked, looking at Lana.

She smiled. "I did. I'm so glad you like it."

"You're an artist? Really? Do you do paintings, too, or just, um, walls?"

She laughed. "Murals are my specialty, but yes, I also paint on canvas."

Just then, I realized that Sophie would probably

be wondering about me. "Oh, man, I have to go. Sorry, Lana. My friend is waiting for me."

"No problem. It was great meeting you, Isabel. I'll go over and introduce myself to your parents. I'm sure I'll see you around."

"Bye!"

I ran down the stairs and hopped on my bike, my feet pumping faster than the thoughts whirling around in my brain. Now I had one more cool thing to tell Sophie. So much had happened in the past few weeks, I didn't even know where to start.

A few minutes later I reached the street with the yellow duplex that I'd called home for five fun-filled years. When Sophie saw me pedaling toward her, she jumped out of the grass where she'd been sitting and came running down the sidewalk, waving her arms in the air like a crazy person.

Laughing, I glided to a stop and put my foot down. I stood beneath a tall maple tree in front of a big white Colonial-style house Mom had always admired. It was hot out, and I'd worked up a sweat on the short ride over. It felt nice to stand in the cool shade for a couple of seconds, the smell of cut grass drifting through the air.

Once Sophie reached me, she grabbed my hand, jumping up and down, flapping my arm as she screamed, "I'm home, I'm home, I'm home!"

I laughed. "I know, I know, I know!"

"Did you miss me?" she asked.

"Are you kidding? I have so much to tell you. Get your bike and let's get something to eat!"

While I waited for her, I pulled out my passport book for a quick note, since Lana's and Sophie's trips were both on my mind.

> There are so many places I want to visit.
> When I'm a flight attendant,
> I can visit the Grand Canyon one day
> and be in Hawaii the next.
> I can't imagine
> a more perfect job.
> —IB

We couldn't really talk while we rode, because we had to ride single file in the bike lane. When we finally got to the Blue Moon, we both started talking as we walked up to the door.

"Okay, just hold on," Sophie said with a giggle. "We have to be orderly about this. You know, like show-and-tell in first grade. First I'll share something and you listen. Then you share something and I'll listen."

"Hey," I said, crossing my arms and sticking my bottom lip out. "No fair. You get to go first."

She laughed and pulled me inside the diner, a wave of cool air greeting us. A waitress walked by, carrying two plates with burgers and fries. The smell made my stomach rumble. "Go ahead and sit anywhere, girls," the waitress said. "I'll get you some water right away."

The Blue Moon is this funky little retro place where a lot of the middle school and high school kids like to hang out. Black-and-white pictures of our town back in the fifties and sixties hang on the walls. There's a jukebox in the corner, and the booths are the old style with red vinyl seats.

As the Beatles song "Yellow Submarine" blared from the jukebox, we slid into a booth, the waitress right behind us with two glasses of water and menus. "Hot out there?" she asked.

We both nodded as we picked up the glasses and started chugging.

"I'll be back to take your order," she said.

My lips tingled from the cold water. I set my glass down. "Okay. Start."

She stuck her finger in the air as she finished draining her glass.

"Sophie, how dare you quench your thirst at a time like this. Talk. Now!"

She started laughing, which meant water spewed out of her mouth and all over the table.

Then *I* was laughing. I grabbed some napkins from the silver napkin dispenser and wiped up the mess.

"Ah," she said, once she got her laughter under control, "I missed you, Chickarita."

"I missed you, too, Sophie Bird. Now start."

"Okay, first, remember I wrote in my letter to you that camp was not fun? You got my letter, right?" I nodded. "Good. Well, the day after I mailed that, guess what?"

"What?" I asked.

"It got fun. I mean, really fun." She leaned in like she had to tell me the world's best secret. "Fun you spell like this: K-Y-L-E."

Chapter 12

pink champagne cupcakes

SWEET YET SOPHISTICATED,

JUST LIKE GRANDMA

My mouth flew open. "You met a boy?"

She nodded. "He's so cute. And funny. Hilariously funny. You would like him. He's just like us."

"How old is he? Where does he live? Are you, like, boyfriend and girlfriend now?"

"Whoa, wait a sec. Okay, let's see. He's going into

eighth grade, so one year older than me. He lives in a small town in Washington. It's close enough so we *could* visit each other. Maybe. And my boyfriend? How am I supposed to know? We held hands three times and we hugged twice. Oh, and we wrote each other lots of notes. So what do you think? Boyfriend and girlfriend?"

"Sounds like you are to me!"

She clapped her hands together and squealed. "Oh, good, I think so too." But then the corners of her mouth turned down, and the sparkle from her eyes disappeared. "Still, I can't stand it that I don't even know when I'll see him again."

I nodded, like I'd had ten boyfriends and I understood, even though I hadn't had one and I really didn't.

The waitress came back, and we ordered two shakes along with an order of fries to share.

"Okay, your turn," she said.

"Mine comes in three parts. First part. I got fired from my babysitting job at Mrs. Canova's."

Her mouth dropped open. "No way. Are you serious?"

"I left them alone in the backyard for about a

millisecond, and she freaked out. Okay, so there was a pool of water involved and she had every right to be furious, but still. Firing me was kind of extreme, wasn't it?"

She nodded. "Very."

"Second part. My recipe's all ready to go for the contest. I just need the address."

"Holy guacamole, I have to get cooking," she said. "Literally."

"Yeah, Soph, you better. August first is just a few days away."

She leaned back in her seat, tucking her hair behind her ears. "No problem. I'll whip something up tonight or tomorrow, and get it in the mail. Remind me to give you the address when I get home. Okay, what's the third part?"

"The third part is the worst." She leaned in when I said that, her eyes big and round. "Beatrice's Brownies is going to open just a few blocks away from us. Mom is devastated. Like so devastated, I think she wants to give up."

"No!" Sophie said. "She can't give up. You guys have worked so hard."

The waitress brought our fries and milk shakes. We started sipping on our shakes, both of us quiet for a minute.

"We have to figure out a way to help her," Sophie said. "I know we can make the cupcake shop work. I just know it."

"You'd better come over a lot in the next couple of weeks," I told her as I took the ketchup bottle and squirted some on the french fry plate. "You need to rub some of that determination onto my mother."

The next morning I got out the contest address Sophie had given me the day before and wrote it down on the envelope that held my recipe. I found a stamp in the desk in the family room, walked down to the corner and, with my fingers crossed, dropped the envelope into the big blue mailbox.

The magazine didn't say when finalists would be contacted, but I guessed it would be awhile. I wanted to be selected more than anything I'd ever wanted, but it was out of my hands now. I had other things to worry about, anyway.

The construction workers were back in full

force. A truck sat out front, and guys were carrying enormous boxes from the truck into the shop. I figured the glass cases had finally arrived. The cases where the cupcakes would be beautifully displayed, causing little kids to lean onto the glass, oohing and aahing, their grimy fingerprints a gift they'd leave behind for me to wipe away with a bottle of Windex and a good rag.

"Good morning," Grandma's voice said from behind me.

I turned around. Today she wore a navy blue skirt with a pale yellow jacket and a big floppy navy blue hat.

"Grandma," I said, "you're here early."

"We need to have a family meeting. You know, get our cupcakes in a row. Your mother and I didn't discuss business at all yesterday. She loosened up a couple of hours into our shopping trip, and I think she had a good time. But now it's back to work."

I nodded. "Grandma, we're so lucky to have you. What would we do without you?"

She looped her arm through mine, and we went inside. "Well, Izzy, I'm glad I have you, too."

Upstairs, Mom made pancakes while Dad read the newspaper.

"Grandma's here," I called out as we walked in.

We sat at the table, and Mom brought a plate of steaming pancakes over along with a small pitcher of warm syrup. "Would you like a plate, Mom?" she asked.

"No, thank you. I've already eaten. I'll take some coffee, though, if you have it."

Dad and I started piling pancakes on our plates, while Mom poured Grandma her cup of coffee.

"This week," Grandma said, looking very businesslike, "we all need to focus on advertising. Every minute of every day needs to be getting the word out about the cupcake shop. I ordered some postcards with coupons we can send out. We definitely need to get around town and pass out samples. Oh, and I've contacted a newspaper reporter who would like to interview us."

"A newspaper reporter?" Dad asked as he wiped his mouth with a napkin. "That's great, Dolores. How'd you manage that?"

"Easy," she said, as Mom slipped a mug of steaming

coffee in front of Grandma, then sat down beside me. "I called the paper up and told them they were missing out on the truly interesting stories surrounding the opening of Beatrice's Brownies. How is a big, corporate, national chain going to affect family businesses? Is it the kiss of death? Will one small business be finished before it ever even started?"

"Mother!" Mom gasped. "We have to talk about ourselves in comparison to Beatrice's? I don't want to do that. Why can't we just talk about It's Raining Cupcakes? You know, what we have to offer and why we're special?"

"Because," said Dad, "your mother is a genius. A story like this will garner sympathy. It will get people in our corner. It's exactly what we need. Nice job, Dolores."

My mom sighed. "Are you sure this is a good idea?"

Grandma nodded. "Completely ducky. Beatrice's Brownies will be the villain. We'll come out smelling like roses. Or cupcakes, in this instance."

I smiled as I finished the last bite of pancake. I was right. We were *really* lucky to have Grandma.

"So when's the interview?" Dad asked.

Grandma tapped her watch. "Today. One o'clock."

"Today?" cried Mom. "No, no, no. I can't do it today. That's too soon."

Grandma reached over, put her hand on Mom's arm, and spoke in her calm but firm voice. "It's not too soon, Caroline. It's just in time. We need to get the word out about the shop now. And honestly, I don't want to give you a whole lot of time to fret over it. We'll do it today, and it'll be over with."

Mom stood up and paced the floor. "I just don't know. I don't know if I can do it. David, can he interview you? I'm not good at this kind of thing."

"How about if he interviews all of us?" I suggested. "He can ask a question and whoever wants to answer it does."

"Sure," Grandma said. "I think that's a fine way to handle it. After all, every one of us is invested in this thing one way or another. Not just Caroline."

I looked at the clock in the kitchen. It said 10:10. "We have three hours to clean the place up and get ready. What should I wear, Grandma?"

She smiled. "It's all taken care of. Your mother and I bought you some new clothes yesterday on our shopping expedition. Wait until you see what I picked out for you!"

I stood in my bedroom, looking in the full-length mirror hung on the back of my door. How do you spell style? G-R-A-N-D-M-A! Boy, did she know how to pick it out.

She'd bought me a cute pink sundress with a black, short-sleeved jacket trimmed in pink that went over it. I hardly ever wore dresses, but this one made me want to wear them more often. She'd also bought me a pair of black sandals with short heels (which I now wore), two pairs of pants, and some fun summer tops to go with them.

I heard the doorbell ring and looked at my watch. It wasn't quite one o'clock, so I assumed it was Sophie. She'd called while I was dusting earlier, and when I told her we were getting ready to meet with a newspaper reporter, she'd asked if she could come and watch.

I heard Grandma's heels *tap*, *tap*, *tap* across the

hardwood floor. I decided to let her greet Sophie and send her back to my room so I could surprise her with my newfound style.

When she opened my door, she gasped and cried, "Whoa, Chickarita!"

I spun around. "You like?"

"But you're not done yet," she said, as if she was talking about a tray of cupcakes baking in the oven. "We need to do something about your hair. Come. Sit down."

She nudged me over to the chair in front of my desk and grabbed my hairbrush off the dresser. "Do you have any barrettes or ribbons or anything?"

This coming from the girl with the best hair in town. Natural blond, wavy—but not in an obnoxious frizzy way—and totally cooperative with whatever she wants to do with it on any given day.

"Sophie, my hair is short. I don't need barrettes, and I never put anything in my hair. You know that."

"You don't have *anything*?" she asked.

I shook my head.

"Hold on. Let me go see if you have something I can work with."

She walked out and left me sitting there, wondering what was so wrong with my hair. It was brown, it was short, and I never had to do anything to it. Just wash it and go. Then I realized, maybe *that's* what was wrong with it. Maybe it looked like all I did was wash it and go.

She came back with a bottle of gel Mom had gotten ages ago at the salon. I think she used it one time and never touched it again.

"Sophie? What are you going to do exactly?"

She squirted some of the gel into her hands and rubbed them together. "I don't know. I just want to try something."

I sat there as she rubbed the stuff through my hair, trying to sculpt it this way, then that way. She worked a lot on my bangs, trying to force them over to one side. She was taking forever. Then the doorbell rang.

"He's here!" I yelled, jumping up and whacking her in the chin in the process.

"Ow!" she cried.

"Sorry. Come on. We have to go."

I turned and faced her.

"Oh no," she said.

"What? What's wrong?"

I dashed over to the mirror. And shrieked. "Sophie! I look like Elvis. Only uglier!"

She tried to laugh. "I guess a little of that gel goes a long way. But come on, it doesn't look *too* bad."

"Doesn't look too bad? Are you kidding me?"

I grabbed the brush, bent over so my hair hung upside down, and brushed my hair as hard as I could. I thought maybe I could brush some of the gel out and fluff my hair a little bit. But when I flipped my head back and stood up, my hair stuck straight up everywhere.

Sophie burst out laughing.

"Girls, come on, the reporter's here," I heard Grandma say.

I peeked out of my bedroom. Grandma was looking right at me, and she clapped her hand to her mouth.

"I need another minute, Grandma." She nodded, her eyes wide with both shock and amusement.

I shut the door again and started brushing, my best friend laughing so hard she was absolutely no help. Not that I wanted her help, of course. I decided I never wanted her help again.

At least when it came to my hair.

Chapter 13

cherry devil's food cupcakes

WHEN YOU NEED SOMETHING DEVILISH

TO MATCH YOUR MOOD

When Sophie finally stopped rolling around on my bed and wiping tears from her eyes, the first words out of her mouth were, "Put on a hat!"

"A hat?" I cried. "Okay, if it were the middle of February, maybe a stocking hat and some gloves would work. But it's summer, ya loonhead."

She started to laugh again. "Not a stocking hat. You know, a fancy hat, like your grandma wears. Don't you have any old hats she's given you?"

It seemed like the only solution. I ran to my closet and started digging through the piles of old clothes I'd set aside to be taken to Goodwill. Underneath the pile, I found a funny-looking black hat with a little piece of netting that hung in front. Right. Perfect if we were going to a funeral.

"Isabel!" my dad called. "Hurry up. We're waiting for you!"

I tossed aside a blue one with a big white flower on the side. Ug-lee! And then, from way in the back of my closet, I pulled out a little pink hat with a bow along the side.

I dusted it off and fluffed it up, then stuck it on and ran to the mirror. It wasn't bad. "What do you think?" I asked.

"Just ducky. Now go out there and sell cupcakes!"

I walked out like I'd been planning to wear the hat all along. Grandma gave me the biggest grin when she saw me.

"Like grandmother, like granddaughter," Dad said to Mom.

"Hi, Isabel," the reporter said, sticking his hand out. "I'm Patrick."

"Very pleased to meet you," I said, trying to sound as sophisticated as Grandma when she says it.

The four of us sat on the couch, while Patrick sat across from us in the La-Z-Boy. Since there weren't any more seats, Sophie stood next to the end of the couch.

Patrick started off by asking Mom and Dad questions about the original concept of a cupcake shop, who came up with it, why did they think it would be successful, that kind of thing. Then he got into asking us how we felt about Beatrice's Brownies.

"Well," Grandma said, "I'm sure you can understand our lack of enthusiasm over the opening of the store. They are a huge corporation and have mostly targeted large cities. Until now. Why come here, to our cozy town of Willow? What is there for them to gain? Not a thing, except crushing the hopes and dreams of families just like ours, who are trying to make a decent living in the neighborhoods where we grew up."

"What do you think, Isabel?" Patrick asked me. "Have you ever had a brownie from Beatrice's? Think the kids will prefer them over your cupcakes?"

I put my hand on my stomach, the butterflies flapping their wings hard in there. He'd asked me a question directly. I had to answer him.

I smoothed my dress across my lap and started talking. "No, I've never had one of their brownies. But we watched a special about them on TV. Their brownies look pretty good, I guess. And people seem to like them. Will kids want brownies or cupcakes? Well, I hope they'll want cupcakes, but we'll just have to wait and see."

I sat back and breathed a sigh of relief that it was over. I'd been as honest as I could be. I glanced over at Sophie, expecting to see a thumbs-up. Instead her eyes were bugging out of her head; she was waving her hands back and forth and mouthing the words, *No, no, NO!*

Dad noticed and spoke up. "Sophie, is there something you'd like to say? We've known you for so long, you're like part of the family now. Come over here and take a seat."

He got up and made room for Sophie to sit next to Mom. Patrick asked Sophie for her full name and wrote it down in the little notebook he'd brought with him.

"What about you, Sophie? Think the folks in Willow will prefer brownies over cupcakes?"

"Are you kidding me?" said Sophie. "No way. Those brownies are terrible. They aren't chock-full of chocolaty goodness like the commercials say. More like chock-full of artificial flavors and preservatives. We can guarantee you that It's Raining Cupcakes will give you a fresh, homemade cupcake just like Grandma used to make every single time you come to visit."

And with that, she pointed to Grandma and smiled, like the reporter had a TV camera in his hand instead of a notebook.

I sat there fuming, my hands balled up into tight fists. The nerve! How could she make my answer sound completely wrong? It wasn't wrong. It was honest. Besides, how did she even know the brownies were terrible? Had she ever tried one? What if the company sued her for saying something mean like that?

I started to speak, to add something more newsworthy to my answer, when Sophie piped in with some more words of wonderful wisdom.

"I'm so sure people like cupcakes better than brownies, or any other dessert for that matter, I entered a cupcake recipe in a special baking contest for kids. Just you wait. I bet my cupcake recipe will win!"

I couldn't believe it. Out of all the desserts she could have entered, she'd picked a cupcake recipe? I glared at her and almost said something, but just then the doorbell rang.

Patrick jumped up from his chair. "That'll be the photographer. I want to get a picture of all of you downstairs, in front of the shop. Then I'll have a few more questions for David and Caroline, if that's okay."

They nodded, and we all stood up. When Sophie finally looked at me, she gave me the thumbs-up sign. By then I was sure she was out to make me look as stupid as possible. First the hair and then making me look bad during the interview. What was next? Pushing me out of the photo at the last second?

Dad greeted the photographer, and then we all walked downstairs. Sophie walked beside my grandma, chatting it up with her like they were best friends.

I reached up and fixed my silly hat, knowing I needed to stand next to Grandma for the photo, so people would think we dressed up like that on purpose. As I walked down the stairs, I saw Lana getting her mail.

"Hey, Lana," I yelled, waving at her.

"Hi, Isabel," she called back.

Sophie looked back at me, a question mark in her eyes. I had forgotten to tell her about Lana and her beautiful murals. Well, good. Let her wonder who the strange, pretty lady was who knew my name.

Outside, the photographer arranged us the way he wanted. The three adults stood in back, and Sophie and I stood in front of them. "I need to switch with her," I told him.

"How come?" Sophie asked.

"So the only two ladies wearing hats in the photo are standing next to each other."

"It doesn't matter," said Sophie.

"Well it matters—," I didn't get to finish.

"Fine," the photographer said. "Doesn't make

any difference to me. Please switch and let's get this going while the sun is behind a cloud. Makes for a much better picture that way."

We made the switch, and then he said, "Say 'cupcakes.'" I didn't say "cupcakes" and I didn't smile, since I couldn't find one single thing to smile about.

Patrick pulled Mom and Dad aside to talk to them a little more. Sophie and I stood there on the sidewalk with Grandma.

"I think it went just ducky, don't you, girls?"

I didn't answer. I was too mad. But Sophie spouted off a bunch of stuff, including how she was positive no one would eat at Beatrice's once they read the article and learned that Beatrice's brownies were filled with artificial flavors and preservatives.

It was then that I found my voice. My loud voice. "Sophie, do you even know if that's *true*? I don't think you should have said that. There are better ways to earn customers, don't you think?"

Her mouth dropped open, like she couldn't believe what she'd just heard. I wanted to pop a cupcake into her big mouth. A whole carrot cake cupcake. Unfrosted.

"Well it was better than what you said, Miss Wishy-Washy. 'I hope they'll want cupcakes, but we'll just have to wait and see.' I thought the whole reason for the article was to MAKE PEOPLE WANT TO EAT YOUR CUPCAKES!"

"Okay, girls," Grandma said, "that's enough. Come on. You both had the best of intentions. And you did a lovely job. Now patch things up between you, what do you say?"

Neither of us said anything for what seemed like forever.

"Sorry, Isabel," Sophie finally said. "I was just trying to help. But I'm going home now. You're obviously mad at me. Call me later if you want."

Before I could say anything, she took off down the sidewalk and around the corner.

Grandma pulled me to her and gave me a hug. "For goodness' sake, Isabel, what is wrong? One minute everything's ducky, and the next it's like World War Three."

I looked down and kicked a little pebble across the sidewalk. "I can't stand it, Grandma. She does everything better than me. And what she wants, she gets. It's not fair. She has a dog, and a boyfriend, and she even got to see the Grand Canyon."

Grandma laughed. "I didn't even know you wanted a dog. Or a boyfriend."

I leaned up against the front window of the cupcake shop, the glass cool on my back. "I don't. But I guess she did. And she got what she wanted. That's my point. I want to go on a trip. Do I get to go? No. I want Mom to be happy. Is she? Mostly no! I want to look good for a picture in the paper, and something as simple as that doesn't even work out. See what I mean? I don't even know why I entered that stupid baking contest. Of course she's going to win."

"But you entered?" Grandma asked.

"Yes. I mailed it yesterday."

She reached out and grabbed my hand, then gently rubbed it with hers. It felt small against mine. Fragile. "Things don't always go our way, Izzy. But I'm proud of you for sticking your neck out and trying. If you don't try, nothing happens. But if you try, well, you just never know. That's what you want your mom to understand, right?"

I nodded and sighed. "I miss the old days, Grandma. I miss the days when Mom and I would bake together because it was fun. Will it ever be fun again?"

"I do believe it will be," she said, pulling on my hand, leading me back to the door to go inside. "Think positively. Stay focused on the possibilities. What do you say?"

I couldn't answer. Because I was starting to believe less and less in possibilities and more and more in plain, rotten luck.

Chapter 14

old-fashioned vanilla cupcakes

FOR THOSE WHO LOVE THE FAMILIAR

I didn't call Sophie. And she didn't call me. Instead I threw myself into the cupcake business. Grandma and I made about a gazillion cupcakes over the next week and went around the whole town, passing them out to anyone and everyone. We stood in front of the library, the swimming pool, and Mother Goose Park. Along with the cupcakes, we gave people a postcard Grandma had made with a coupon for two dollars off the purchase of a dozen cupcakes. Again and again, people told us how delicious the cupcakes were and that they'd be sure to stop in when the shop opened.

Of course, Mom didn't hear any of it because she stayed home. She mostly sat in her room, or on the couch watching TV. We tried everything to get her to come with us, but she seemed determined to give up.

I went to the library and checked out a bunch of books to see if something might help her. Some of them had pretty interesting titles.

Don't Be a Fraidy Cat: How to Live Like You Have Nine Lives
How to Find Your Happy Place in a Sad World
From Worrywart to Hopeful Hero in Ten Easy Steps

I left a couple on the coffee table in the family room and a few others on the nightstand in her room, so all she had to do was pick one up and start reading.

"We only have another week until we open," I

said to Dad one night while he and I sat watching TV. "What if she can't do it? Are *you* going to bake cupcakes?"

He turned and gave me a slight smile. "I'm a fine cupcake baker, thank you very much."

"Fine cupcake eater is more like it," I said.

"That too," he said, standing up. "And now I'm going to bed. Don't stay up too late."

"Good night, Dad."

"Good night, sweetheart."

"Hey, Dad?" I said, before he reached the hallway.

He stopped and turned to me. "Yes?"

"Do you think everything's going to be okay?"

He put his hand up and rubbed his scruffy cheek. "Yes, I do. We just have to carry Mom through this right now. She doesn't believe, so we'll believe for her until she's ready. That's what families do, you know?"

"Yeah."

He turned around. "See you in the morning."

Suddenly I felt tired. Exhausted. I thought about what Dad said as I turned off the TV and went to my room. In my passport book, I wrote:

When I travel, I will pay someone
to carry my luggage everywhere I go.
It will just be so much easier that way.

—IB

The next morning Dad woke me up, shaking me and saying my name.

I sat up, afraid the place was on fire or something. "What is it? What?"

"Look!" he said. "They put us on the front page!"

He shoved the paper in my face. I had to blink a few times to focus.

The headline read, LOCAL FAMILY KEEN ON CUPCAKES, NOT BROWNIES.

When I saw the picture, I wanted to throw up. I looked completely ridiculous in the hat. On Grandma a hat looked normal. Stylish. But on a twelve-year-old girl? Just. Plain. Stupid.

I fell back and pulled the covers over my head.

"What?" Dad said. "What's wrong?"

"Nothing," I mumbled. "I need to wake up. I'll be out in a little while. I'll read the article then."

He got up and left me alone to consider my options.

A. Use my babysitting money to buy up every newspaper I could get my hands on and then burn them.

B. Hitch a ride to Idaho and take up residency there.

C. Color my hair purple so no one would recognize me as the girl in the stupid hat.

D. Just accept the fact that I was the stupid girl in the hat, and it would blow over eventually.

I got up and put my robe on. At least Dad seemed happy about the article. Then I remembered what Sophie had said during the interview, and I wanted to see if they'd put it in the article.

I walked out and grabbed the paper off the table.

"Has Mom seen it yet?" I asked.

"No. She's still asleep. I hope it cheers her up."

I scanned the article, looking for quotes. My name

was mentioned only once, in the beginning, when we were introduced as the family who owned the shop. Nothing I actually said was included. Sophie, on the other hand—"a close family friend," according to the article—was quoted as saying, "It's Raining Cupcakes will give you a fresh, homemade cupcake just like Grandma used to make."

Even though Sophie sounded like she was being paid to plug our cupcakes, it was a good article. The reporter wrote about the different flavors, the flavor-of-the-month idea, and the hominess of the shop. I could see people reading it and wanting to come and try our cupcakes.

"Well?" Dad asked.

"It's good. Really good. Except for the picture, where I look totally ridiculous. But it should make Mom feel better."

He stood there, sipping his coffee. "I think it's good too. Maybe her fear will lessen a bit after she reads it."

"What are we doing today?" I asked. "Passing out more cupcakes?"

Dad shook his head. "We're taking the day off. You

deserve it. Why don't you and Soph go to the pool? Or see a movie? Get out and have some fun."

"I don't know. I'm pretty tired. Maybe I'll just stick around here. Read a book or something."

"Whatever you want," he said, heading toward the bathroom. "I'm going to get ready for the day."

I sat down at the table and flipped the paper over, so I wouldn't have to look at the embarrassing photo. I imagined Sophie looking at it and dropping to the floor in hysterics. She'd probably cut it out and send it to her *boyfriend*. They'd write back and forth about the idiotic girl wearing the old-lady hat. Sophie would brag about how she was totally going to beat the idiotic girl in the baking contest she'd entered. He'd tell her that of course she would beat the idiotic girl. She was good at everything. Not just good. Fantastic.

Mom came out of her room, snapping me out of my depressing thoughts. She walked over to the coffeepot and poured herself a cup without a word. It was like I wasn't even there.

"Mom? The article ran today. You know, the article on the cupcake shop? It's really good." I got up and tried to hand her the newspaper.

She swatted at it and turned her head away. "I don't want to read it. It doesn't matter. I've decided we're selling it. I can't make it work. I just can't."

I grabbed her arm. "Mom! Come on. Don't give up yet. We haven't even opened."

She shook my hand loose. "Please, Isabel. Just stop. My mind is made up."

"I know you're scared, but you'll feel better once we open. I know you will. It's just the unknown right now that's making it hard."

She stood at the sink, staring past me. "Nothing has ever gone my way. Why should this be any different?"

And when she said that, I felt an electrifying current run through my body. I thought of Sophie and how I'd gotten so mad at her. How I'd complained to Grandma about nothing going my way. How I'd pushed Sophie away because I felt like that.

I looked at my mother, standing there, so sad and afraid. And I knew one thing as sure as I knew I'd love New York City. I didn't want to be like my mother.

Chapter 15

cherries jubilee cupcakes

JUST LIKE LOVE, IT'S OH-SO-SWEET

Dad asked me to leave so he could have a private talk with Mom, so I showered and left.

I wasn't sure exactly where I was going, but I had an idea. I just needed to find a little courage first. I ran into Lana downstairs as she walked through the door, carrying a grocery bag. Her hair was tied back in a ponytail and she wore overalls splattered in paint.

"Hey, Isabel, how's it going?"

I sighed and leaned up against the wall. "I don't know. Wait. That's not true. I do know. Terrible."

"Oh, no. Sorry to hear that." She paused, like she was trying to decide if she should say the next thing she was thinking. "Well, do you have a few minutes? I'll show you what I do when I need a pick-me-up."

I shrugged. "Sure."

I followed her upstairs and into her apartment. She put the bag of groceries on the counter. Then she waved at me to follow her toward the back of the apartment.

The second bedroom in her apartment wasn't a bedroom at all. She had turned it into a painting studio, with canvas and easels set up around the room and a big drawing table next to the window.

The paintings were incredible. One of them was a picture of a hillside, with rolling green hills and little flowers blooming in the sun. Another was a picture of the beach with a little girl walking in the sand. It looked so real, it was like I was looking out the window, watching the blond-haired girl walk along the water, admiring the big blue ocean.

Lana went to the closet and grabbed a long white jacket and handed it to me. "I have a friend who is a scientist. Lab coats make great smocks."

I put it on and buttoned it closed in the front while she tore off two big pieces of paper from a roll that sat in the corner.

She laid them in the middle of the floor, and then she went to a bookshelf and picked up some pie tins. Lana took bottles of paint off another shelf and squirted some paint into the tins.

"Okay, Isabel, when was the last time you painted with your fingers?"

I smiled. "Um, never?"

Her mouth opened wide. "What? You've never finger-painted?"

I shook my head.

She smiled back at me. "Well, this will be fun!"

She dropped to her knees, stuck her fingers into the blue, and then swirled it around at the top of her piece of white paper. Then she put her hands in some white and went back and mixed it in with the blue swirls she had just made. The blobs started to look like clouds.

"Cool!" I said.

I kneeled next to her and stuck my fingers in some red. It felt cold, wet and kind of sticky. On the paper, I swirled my fingers around and around, making big and little circles.

I did the same with the blue, and when the blue and red mixed, I had red and blue on the paper, but I also had purple.

"Purplicious," I whispered.

"It's fun to mix colors, isn't it?" Lana said.

I looked at her paper where she had painted clouds and the sun and was working on a flower growing out of the ground. She'd done that all with her fingers!

Mine looked like something a two-year-old would do. Just color and squiggles. And suddenly I wanted more color. More squiggles.

I put all my fingers in the paint this time, then moved them hard across the page, in big, sweeping motions, going this way and that way. Soon there weren't any distinct lines, but instead, waves of color across the page.

Finally I dipped my index finger in the red, and right in the middle of the wavy mess, I painted a heart.

I leaned back and looked at it. Lana stopped what she was doing and looked with me.

"It's beautiful," she said. "What does it make you think of?"

"My insides," I said. "Waves of love, of anger, of sadness, of everything, all mixed together."

She nodded. "But that heart you drew? That shows me that love is the thing that matters most to you. That even when everything is messy, your love is there, shining through."

"Do you think that might be a wave of courage?" I asked, pointing to a brownish-grayish wave of paint next to the heart.

She smiled. "You know, that looks *exactly* like a wave of courage. Wow. How did you draw that so clearly?"

I stood up and grabbed the picture. "Thanks, Lana. That was fun. I think I'm going to take this and give it to someone."

"You might want to let it dry first," she said. "It's pretty wet."

"That's okay. If I walk over, it'll dry on the way."

We went out to the kitchen and washed our hands. I took the smock off and handed it to her.

"Thanks again, Lana," I told her as I walked to the front door. "I hope she likes it."

She wiped her damp hands on the front of her overalls. "Actually, Isabel, I'm pretty sure she'll love it."

I went home to tell Dad I was going to Sophie's, and then I started on the long walk to the yellow duplex. I held the picture flat in my hands, so it could dry in the warm rays of the sun, Lana's words echoing in my ears.

When everything is messy, your love is there, shining through.

I hoped with all my heart Sophie would see that too.

Chapter 16

peach cobbler
cupcakes

PERFECT FOR FAMILY GATHERINGS

I'm pretty sure the walk to Sophie's that warm
August day was one of the longest ones of my entire
life.

When I got there, Hayden answered the door,
talking to me through the screen door, Daisy barking
like crazy behind him. "What's the secret password?"

"Huh?" I asked.

"What's the password?"

"Um, open sesame?"

"Bo-ring."

"Okay. How about, Mars is red?"

He raised his eyebrows and smiled. "I like it. You may enter."

I walked through the door, and Daisy jumped on me as if to say, *Notice me, love me, pet me!*

"Alien invasion, alien invasion!" Hayden yelled.

"Hey, who are you calling an alien?" I asked as I bent down to pet the dog. She rolled over, giving me her little white belly to scratch.

If only my life could be as easy as a dog's, I thought.

"Alien or not, Daisy sure is happy to see you." I looked up. Sophie stood there, looking cute as always, wearing black shorts and a frilly yellow blouse.

I stood up, my heart beating quickly in my chest. I swallowed hard. "I hope she's not the only one," I said softly.

"Chickarita," she said. "To my room."

I followed her there. Her room smelled good, like baby powder. She sat on her bed, bouncing up and down slightly. I could tell she was nervous too.

"I'm sorry," I said. "I was a jerk. Jealous of you, I guess." I went over and kneeled in front of her. "I brought you a peace offering. Please, forgive me?"

She laughed and pulled me to my feet. "Stop it. Of course I forgive you. And I'm sorry for criticizing your answer during the interview. I was just trying to help. The last thing I wanted to do was upset you."

I nodded. "I know."

She took the picture from my hands. "Wow, this is cool. Did you make it?"

I wiggled my fingers in front of her face. "With my very own hands."

She laid it on her nightstand. "I love it. Thanks, Is. So, did you see the picture of us? In the paper?"

I rolled my eyes. "Unfortunately."

"It's fine. And the article is good. I predict big sales."

I sat on her bed. "Well, I predict no sales. Mom wants to sell the place. I shouldn't be surprised. I mean, the woman is afraid to get on an airplane. Actually, I'm pretty sure she's afraid to do *anything*."

"You're so not like her," she said.

I looked at her. "What? You don't think so? Sometimes I worry I'm too much like her."

She shook her head. "No way. If I handed you a ticket to Peru right now, you'd go. Even though it's a billion miles away and who knows what kind of food you'd eat there or if they have humongous spiders that kill people. You wouldn't hesitate. You would just go. And that day the reporter came over? Most people would have stayed in their room, using the worst hair day in the history of the universe as their excuse. But not you. You went out there and did what you needed to do."

Daisy nudged the door open with her nose, ran in, and jumped onto the bed in between us. Both of us reached over to pet her.

"But I really didn't do what I needed to do. I didn't help my mom at all. My answer to that reporter's question was so lame. And I knew it. *You* did what needed to be done. *You* knew the right thing to say. Not me. And that's why I got mad. Because I wish I could be more like you."

"What do you mean?"

"You're so determined, Sophie. And you know what you want."

She stood up and faced me. "So tell me. What do *you* want?"

I sighed and put my head in my hands. "I just want to get out of Willow." I looked at her. "Get away from this place that seems to makes my mother crazy. I can't stand it."

She crossed her arms over her chest. "Can't stand what? Willow? Or your mother?"

It felt like she'd stuck a knife in my chest. It hurt. It hurt so much, tears came from deep inside that tender, hurting place in my heart.

As soon as she said it, I knew she was right. It wasn't Willow I wanted to get away from. It was my own mother. Because I had no idea how to relate to her. To talk to her. To help her. All those years I'd tried, I could never understand why she couldn't be happy. Why wasn't being my mom enough? Why was she always looking so hard for something else to make her happy?

Sophie sat down and wrapped her arms around me. She let me cry for a long time.

"I'm sorry," I told her when I pulled away, because my nose was running a lot and I didn't want to get snot on her pretty yellow blouse.

"Me too," she said. "I shouldn't have let you wear that stupid hat. See? I'm not so perfect either."

When I got back to the apartment, I didn't go home. I went into the cupcake shop. It was Sunday, and the workers weren't around. The door was locked, but our apartment key also opened the shop door, so I was able to get in.

The glass cases were all assembled and in place. They looked amazing. I could just picture tray after tray of little cupcakes in various colors and flavors. Next to the cases was a light pink counter. I went and stood behind the newly purchased cash register sitting on the counter.

"Oh, good morning, Mrs. Johnson. What can I get for you? One dozen banana cream pie and one dozen carrot cake? Are you sure on the carrot cake? Oh, of course, yes, they're your husband's favorite. Yes, I know, men can be odd about their food choices, can't they?"

"And what will it be for you, Stan? Oh, why yes, of course, the chocolate coconut are jolly good indeed. Three dozen, you say? Oh, I hope we have enough. It's been busy today."

I could picture it all so clearly, it was as if I'd done it a thousand times. The cupcakes, the people, the fun conversation.

I turned around and ran my finger along the clean counter where just yesterday, Grandma and I had worked, making cupcake after delicious cupcake.

I pulled the passport book out and wrote this:

Food brings people together.
All over the world,
people gather together and eat.
In America, churches have potlucks
and neighborhoods have barbecues.
I like that about America.
—IB

My family needed the cupcake shop. Because we needed to be brought together.

Chapter 17

chocolate caramel cupcakes

THERE'S A HIDDEN TREASURE

INSIDE EACH ONE

Visiting the cupcake shop gave me an idea. A great idea. An incredible idea. An idea that I could only hope Mom would like.

I did what I needed to do to set the idea in motion, and then I went to find Mom. She was sitting next to Dad on the couch, reading a magazine while he watched a baseball game.

I sat down next to her and took a deep breath. "Mom, I want to tell you something."

"Isabel, I don't think—," my dad began.

"Dad, please. Maybe you don't think this is a good idea, but I need to do this. I need Mom to hear me say that I want to bake cupcakes with her. Remember, Mom? We used to bake all the time, and we loved it. That's all this is—another baking session, just a little bigger this time. We're throwing stuff in the bowl, and yeah, it's a big mess for a while. But we'll keep stirring, and we'll cross our fingers, and we'll hope that when we pull the batch out of the oven, it will be something wonderful. A wonderful cupcake shop, just like you wanted."

She didn't say anything. I stood up and took the books that I'd gotten from the library off the coffee table and set them in her lap.

"Mom, we can do this. You believed once, right? Just believe again. If you'll try, meet me in the cupcake shop tomorrow morning at nine. I have a surprise for you."

I walked out and down the hall toward the front door. "Dad, is it all right if I go see Stan and Judy for a few minutes?"

He nodded, so I left.

Stan was home, since it was his day off. And Judy was there too. I'd only talked to her once or twice, but she made me feel like I'd been to their home a hundred times.

"Come in and sit down, Isabel," she said. "I'll get you some lemonade. And we have cookies. You like cookies, right?"

"Yes, thanks."

Their apartment was a lot like ours, although much cooler, since they had an air conditioner. It had old furniture that had seen better days. Bookcases filled with books once read, now just taking up space. And lots of pictures hung on the wall. Stan sat in a big, stuffed green chair. I sat across from him, on the floral couch.

"Nice article in the paper today," he said. "Good

photo, too. I bet you have a ton of business on opening day."

"I hope so," I replied. "Hey, is that your son?" I pointed to one of the pictures on the wall.

"Yes," he said, smiling proudly. "Yes, it is. He lives in Texas now. He should be coming for a visit around Thanksgiving."

"Were you close?" I asked. "When he was growing up?"

Judy brought me a glass of lemonade and a plate with two cookies. "Are you kidding? They fought all the time. They're very different from each other."

I took a bite of the peanut butter cookie. It tasted good. I hadn't had a cookie in so long, it made me want to go home and bake some. "What do you mean?" I asked.

Stan leaned back and put his feet on the stool in front of him. "He loved to be busy doing things. Going places. Seeing things. Me? I like sitting around, talking to people. That's why I like cutting people's hair. All day long I get to hear interesting stories from people."

I nodded and kept eating my cookie.

"Like yesterday, this guy Rupert was telling me how he went to a rummage sale at his church, and he's walking down the aisle, looking at all the junk. And then he spots this long, skinny black case. And he's thinking, what could be in that case? Of course he looked, and it was a sword with this old-looking handle and some papers inside written in what seemed to be Japanese. It looked interesting, so he bought it. Well, he did some checking, and do you know that sword is from the 1800s and is worth thousands of dollars?"

"Really?" I asked. "How much did he pay for it?"

"You won't believe it."

I set the empty plate down on the coffee table. "How much? Like a hundred dollars?"

"Two dollars and fifty cents!" Stan slapped his knee and laughed. "Can you believe that craziness?"

"Is he going to keep it or sell it?" I asked.

"Ahhh, see, you're like me. You want to know more. And to me? That's the most important part of the story. Sure, finding a treasure is exciting, but what are you going to *do* with the treasure?"

"Well?" I asked. "What did he do?"

Stan started laughing again. I liked his laugh. When he laughed, it was like his whole body laughed, not just his mouth. Like he felt the happiness in every bone of his body.

He pulled out a handkerchief and wiped his forehead with it. "Well, he said he's going to keep it. Because just looking at it and thinking about it, like where it's been and how it's survived this long, is an amazing thing. He said he can always sell it if he needs the money someday. But for now, the treasure makes him happy."

I nodded as I thought about that. Owning the sword made him feel good. And that was enough.

"Stan!" I said, jumping up. "That's it! We need to get my mom to understand that it's not about the money or success or any of that. It's about the *treasure*. It's about having a cupcake shop and sharing with the people who visit every day. Who cares if Beatrice's Brownies sells more than we do? It doesn't really matter, does it?"

He smiled. "I think you're right, Isabel. I may not be living in a mansion, and I'm sure there are plenty more successful barber shops than mine. But who cares? Mine is perfect for me."

"Can I borrow your phone? That's why I came here, actually. I need to call my grandma, to tell her to meet me downstairs in the morning. I didn't want my parents to hear, because it's a surprise."

He pointed toward the kitchen. "Help yourself. Have another cookie if you'd like too."

As I walked toward the kitchen, he said, "Knock-knock."

"Who's there?"

"Sherwood."

"Sherwood who?"

"Sherwood like to have a cupcake shop downstairs!"

"Me too," I told Stan. "Me too."

I talked to Grandma, and she agreed to come over at nine o'clock, bringing something with her that I needed. I asked Stan to be there too and to bring a little something as well.

When I left and went back home, I knew I had done everything I could.

Now it was up to Mom.

I bet it's scary sometimes,
traveling in a new place.
But you take along maps
and a cell phone,
and you know help is there
if you need it.
—IB

Chapter 18

grandma's applesauce cupcakes

TASTE JUST LIKE HOME

The next morning I woke up early. Like six a.m. early. I got dressed, then grabbed my keys and the envelope of babysitting money I'd been saving. I reached inside the envelope and pulled out the small pile of bills, fanning it the way I'd seen thieves do it on TV. Except I wasn't a thief. I'd worked hard for that money, hoping to see something besides the sidewalks of Willow, Oregon. I felt a little twinge of pain about giving it up, but a little voice inside me told me I would travel someday. Just not today.

Besides, I'd been thinking it was just like Stan said. Maybe it wasn't really going places and seeing things that mattered. Maybe it was just doing your best to enjoy the people around you. Like that day with Lucas and Logan. While the pool filled with water, I should have taken my shoes off and gotten in the pool with them. I should have splashed and laughed and stopped thinking about those books and what I *didn't* have, and instead just been glad for what I *did* have.

I tiptoed out the front door and down the stairs and went around to the front door of the cupcake shop.

What I saw when I walked inside the shop made me smile so big, my cheeks felt like they were going to crack to pieces.

All night long Lana had stayed up, painting a mural on one of the walls to look like a rolling countryside with green hills, a big tree in the corner, and a bright blue sky. No matter how rainy it might be outside, people would feel like they were sitting next to a sunny countryside inside our little shop. It was perfect.

"Lana," I squealed. "It's so beautiful."

She wiped her hands on her overalls and carefully walked down the ladder. "The tree isn't finished yet." She looked at her watch. "I should have it done by nine, though."

I couldn't stop looking at it. "Beatrice's Brownies might have Dixie cups full of milk, but they have *nothing* like this." I turned and looked at her. "You must be so tired. Thank you. Thank you very much."

"You're welcome, Isabel. I hope your mom likes it. I hope it makes her excited to be in the cupcake business."

I handed Lana the envelope of money. "I know you probably get paid a lot more than this. But it's all I have."

"No worries," she said, taking the envelope. "I'm happy to help you guys out. And you can pay me the rest in cupcakes, how's that?"

I reached out my hand. "Deal."

I sat and watched Lana paint for a while. But I

didn't want to make her nervous, so I went back upstairs and put on the coffee. While it dripped into the pot, I wrote in my passport book:

People travel to see beautiful things.
But really, beauty is everywhere,
isn't it?
—IB

Dad came out, and I'm pretty sure I was still smiling like a chimpanzee, because he asked me, "What are you up to, young lady?"

"You'll see," I said. "Do you think she's going to show up?"

He went in the kitchen and pulled a mug out of the cupboard. "I don't know, honey. I hope so."

I went downstairs to wait. Lana was cleaning up, so I helped her carry the paint back upstairs to her apartment. It was good to have something to keep me busy.

At 8:50 Grandma showed up with the pink ribbon and the thumbtacks like I had asked her to. She was dressed in pink from head to toe for the occasion.

Literally. Pink suit, pink hat, and pink shoes.

When she walked in and saw the mural, her hand flew to her mouth as she let out a big gasp. "Oh, Izzy, it's incredible."

"I know," I said, stepping back to admire it again with her. "Lana, our neighbor, did it for us. Do you think Mom will like it?"

She came and gave me a hug. "She's going to love it. That was so sweet of you."

We strung the pretty ribbon from one end of the store to the other, straight across, about waist high.

I looked at my watch. Nine o'clock.

"You want me to go check on her?" Grandma asked.

I shook my head. "She has to do it on her own." 9:05. 9:10.

Grandma paced the floor, her heels clicking on the parquet floor as she walked.

I heard the door open and quickly turned around.

"Hey, sorry we're late," Stan said, with Judy next to him. "Is she here yet?"

I shook my head. "Not yet." My shoulders slumped. "Maybe she's not coming. Why should today be different from any other day? I'm so stupid. Just because I go in there, hand her some books, and tell her I have a surprise for her, I think that's going to make a difference?"

Grandma came over and put her arm around me. "Why should today be any different? Because, my dear Izzy, you just never know. Maybe reaching out to her yesterday, in the special way that only you can, is just what she needed. Why, I remember one time, I was feeling down about the state of the economy and worried about your grandfather's business in the worst way. And about that time, I got the nicest letter from Patricia Nixon. You know, President Nixon's wife? I had written her a letter because I wanted her to know I was thinking about her while her husband was going through a terrible time. Well, she wrote me back, and that letter did wonders for my spirits. It was a simple gesture. But it meant so much."

I heard a noise and looked up. The door opened slowly, Mom's face visible through the glass at the top of the door. I held my breath, waiting for her to see the wall behind me.

Dad came in right after her. When she walked in, she looked at me, and then I watched as she noticed the rolling hills and the blue sky. I moved to the side so she could take it all in. Just like Grandma, her hand flew to her mouth in shock. Then her eyes got crinkly and tears started to form.

I ran to her and gently grabbed her elbow. "Mom, don't cry. Don't you like it?"

"Oh, Isabel, I think it's just about the most beautiful thing I've ever seen. You did this for me?"

I looked around the room. "Well, I think I did it for all of us."

She nodded and turned to give me a hug. "I'm so sorry," she whispered. "I'm working on an attitude adjustment, I promise."

When she pulled away, she looked around the room. "Thanks for being here, everyone."

Stan walked toward Mom with a pair of scissors in his hand. "Caroline, these have been very lucky for me over the years. Not once have I cut off an ear or scratched a cheek." We laughed. "Will you please do the honors and cut your ribbon? This shop is your little treasure. Cherish it. Share it. Love it. And I promise, when you do that, others will love it too."

"Thanks, Stan," she said as she took the scissors from his hand. She looked over at me. "And thank you, Isabel. Thanks for continuing to stir to make something wonderful when I couldn't do it. You're the best."

She looked around the room one last time. And then, without any hesitation, she cut the ribbon.

And we all clapped for a really, really long time.

Chapter 19

lucky lemon-lime cupcakes

BETTER THAN A FOUR-LEAF CLOVER

To say we were busy the first couple of weeks doesn't even begin to describe it. We were slammed. But of course, it was all good, and Mom's confidence grew, thank goodness.

A storm blew through, and it rained the first few days we were open, which meant that all the moms who would normally take their kids to play in the fountain in the park brought them to our place to have cupcakes instead. Mom said it was entirely appropriate that it rained on the day It's Raining Cupcakes opened.

Everyone we knew, plus many more we didn't, showed up the first day. I couldn't believe how many teachers from the middle school came. I think Mr. Nelson must have sent them all a note or something. He stopped by too and brought some cool pictures of Washington, D.C., with him.

Sue Canova brought her twin boys by for a cupcake, and when she saw me, she gave me a hug and told me there were no hard feelings. At least I think that's what she said. The boys were jumping up and down and yelling, "Cupcakes, cupcakes, CUPCAKES!" so it was a little hard to hear.

But the best surprise was having Aunt Christy drop by. She came right from the airport, still dressed in her flight attendant uniform. She gave me a bag of goodies from different places she'd visited in the past couple of months. My favorite souvenir was a miniature Statue of Liberty. I'd been checking the mail every day, expecting to hear about the baking contest, one way or the other. But so far I hadn't heard a thing.

Christy couldn't stay long, as she had another flight that evening, to Chicago. We sent her on her way with a belly full of cupcakes, which she said was icing on the cupcake after visiting with us for a while.

As she left, she told us she would tell all the people traveling to Oregon to make sure they stopped in at It's Raining Cupcakes. I know Mom appreciated that a lot.

The first day, we opened at noon and ran out of cupcakes by three. People were really nice, though, and sat at the little pink tables drinking coffee or tea and talking about how they'd just have to come back the next day and get some cupcakes.

The next morning Grandma, Mom, and I tripled the number of cupcakes we made. This time, we had enough to get us through our regular closing time, five o'clock.

Mom had decided that for all our sakes, the shop would be open five days a week, Tuesday through Saturday, and only in the afternoons. "We don't want to work ourselves to death," she'd said.

Beatrice's Brownies had a great opening weekend, of course. We got in line with everyone else to check it out. The brownies were good, but their chocolaty goodness didn't make any of us cry in despair or anything. By then Mom knew her cupcake shop was special in and of itself.

The day after Labor Day, Dad and I had to go back to school. Grandma and Mom said they'd be fine without us and not to worry. Still, I did—just a little.

Sophie and I ended up with three classes together, which made us extremely happy. She came home with me after school, so we could talk about our first day.

"I miss Kyle so much," she said, as we sat at the kitchen table, drinking some iced tea before we went downstairs to see how Mom and Grandma were doing.

"Has he written you back yet?" I asked.

She shook her head. "I can't believe it. I thought we had something special, you know? But that reminds me. Guess what I did get in the mail?"

"What?"

"A letter telling me I didn't place in the baking contest. I'm so bummed. Did you get one?"

I shook my head. "Maybe I should run down and check the mail right now." I started to get up and find the mail key when the phone rang. I thought it might be Mom calling from downstairs to ask why we hadn't come to see her yet.

"Hello?" I said.

"May I speak to Isabel Browning?" a woman on the other end said.

"This is she."

"Isabel, this is Julia from *Baker's Best* magazine. I'm so glad you answered the phone. I'm calling to let you know that you are one of our finalists for the baking contest you entered last month. Congratulations!"

I backed up against the counter and grabbed onto it to keep myself steady. "Are you serious?"

She chuckled. "I'm very serious. We loved your recipe. It was so different from anything else submitted. Very original."

Sophie came over with a puzzled look on her face. *Who is it?* she mouthed.

I covered the mouthpiece with my hand and whispered, "The baking contest."

"Isabel, is everything all right?" Julia asked.

"Yes, sorry. I just can't believe I'm really a finalist!"

By now Sophie was clapping her hands together really fast, although quietly, and jumping up and down.

"Isabel, we look forward to seeing you in New York in November. You'll get a packet in the mail in the next week with all the information. Please give it to your parent or guardian who will be accompanying you on the trip, so it can be completed and mailed back to us right away."

"Okay, I will. Thank you very much."

"Congratulations again, Isabel. Bye."

When I hung up, Sophie grabbed my hands and pulled me around in circles. "You get to go to New York, you get to go to New York!"

I laughed as we spun around and around. When we stopped, we stood there, holding hands. I squeezed hers and said, "I'm so sorry, Soph. You didn't place."

She reached out and hugged me. "It's okay! You get to go on a trip, just like you wanted. That's more than enough to make me happy."

"Thanks, Soph."

"Come on. We have to tell your mom and your grandma. They are going to die when they hear!"

I gulped. "That's what I'm afraid of." But she pulled me along, smiling like there wasn't a thing to worry about.

As we walked downstairs, I said, "Sophie, what did you want the thousand dollars for, anyway? You never really told me."

She stopped before we went through the door and closed one eye, like she was thinking. "I'm not sure I want to tell you."

I put my hands on my hips. "What? What do you mean? Come on. You have to tell me."

"Okay, fine. But you can't tell anyone. Promise?"

"Promise."

"I want to take acting lessons. And singing lessons too." She smiled. "You know how much I loved those theater camps. My mom found some more for next year that I can do with other teens. But when she talked to the camp director, he said a lot of the kids take professional lessons throughout the year. And if I want to get better, so I can be a professional actress someday—"

"Oh, Sophie Bird," I said, "you will make a *maahvelous* actress someday. I can just see you on the big screen. When you move to Hollywood, can I come and visit?"

She laughed. "Absolutely, Chickarita. Just be prepared. I don't think it's anything like Willow."

We kept giggling and talking as we made our way to the cupcake shop. Lana was sitting at a table with a cup of tea, reading a book. I waved at her, and she waved back. The other tables were filled with people I didn't recognize. That was a good sign. It meant people were coming because they'd heard the cupcakes were good, not because they knew us.

We walked back into the kitchen. It smelled yummy, like always. A mix of cinnamon, vanilla, and chocolate all rolled into one. Grandma greeted me with a hug. Mom had bought each of them official cupcake "uniforms" to force Grandma to stop wearing fancy dresses to work. I almost hadn't recognized her the first day she showed up in khaki pants and a pink T-shirt with the words IT'S RAINING CUPCAKES printed on the front.

She'd said, "Now I'll have to style my hair every day. That's the real reason I wear hats, you know. Nothing like a hat to fix a bad hair day." It made me laugh, because I knew about that trick!

When I saw Mom, my insides felt like someone had taken a mixer to them. She walked over and put her hand on my forehead. "You don't look very good, Isabel. Is everything all right?"

"Mom," I said, my voice shaking just a little, "remember that baking contest?"

"Of course I remember."

"Well, they called to say that I'm one of the finalists."

She squealed and clapped her hands together. "Isabel, that's wonderful!"

I gulped. "You know the bake-off is in New York, right? An adult has to go with me. Do you think Dad can get some time off work in November to take me?"

Mom walked over to the counter and opened a drawer. She pulled out a book and held it up. It was

Don't Be a Fraidy Cat: How to Live Like You Have Nine Lives.

"I liked it so much, I bought my own copy," she said. "I've been doing visualization exercises. If I keep at it, I bet I'll be ready to go in November." Mom turned to my grandma. "You can keep things running for a few days, can't you, Mom?"

"Of course," she said. "I'll be happy to."

I couldn't believe it. I let out a big sigh of relief. She was really going to try. Try to get over her fears. For me.

Mom looked at me. "Oh, I can't wait to visit St. Valentine's Cupcakes! And take you to a Broadway play. And—"

Sophie grabbed our hands and started jumping up and down. "You're going to New York, you're going to New York!"

As I giggled at silly Sophie, I noticed something out of the corner of my eye. I turned and looked, which made everyone look. A young guy with a mustache and major bedhead hair stood there, holding a laundry basket full of clothes.

"Can I help you?" Mom asked.

"I think I'm lost," he said. "I'm looking for the Bleachorama."

Mom turned around and looked at me, and I could tell she was trying not to laugh. We were both thinking of that day I had asked her where the people would go who needed to wash their clothes.

She walked around to the front and took his basket from him. "Mother, will you get him a cupcake and some milk, please? I'm going to take these upstairs and wash them for him."

"Wow," he said. "That's some service. A place that does laundry and gives you cupcakes. I'll have to tell all my friends."

"NO!" we all shouted. Then we burst out laughing.

But as Mom walked out the door, she turned around with a twinkle in her eye. "You know, now that I think about it, you could be onto something there. I mean, Beatrice's Brownies certainly doesn't—"

"You have an adorable cupcake shop, just like you wanted," I said, interrupting her, as I walked over and put my arm around her. "Let's leave it at that, okay, Mom?"

She looked around and smiled a relaxed, happy smile. "I do, don't I?"

• 182 •

Later that night, I wrote in my passport booklet as
I daydreamed about our trip to New York City.

I journeyed to a place
where it's always raining cupcakes.
I didn't need a passport,
but I met a lot of interesting people
and experienced new things.
Even though the trip was a little bumpy,
I got there just fine.
—IB

Chapter 20

the dr. seuss cupcake

THIS ONE WILL SURPRISE YOU!

When we arrived at our hotel, I called Dad and then Grandma to let them know the flight went just fine. Mom brought along a special compact disc Aunt Christy had sent her for people afraid of flying. She played it during both the takeoff and the landing to help her relax. It seemed to work. The rest of the time, she browsed cooking magazines, looking for inspiration for new cupcake flavors.

As for me, I felt nervous and excited and a hundred other things, so I didn't know what to do with myself. Mostly I just looked out the window and tried to enjoy every minute of the flight. I loved it when we took off—it didn't scare me at all. As we flew higher and higher, I watched the buildings and roads get smaller and smaller. Eventually, it looked like a town for dolls—everything was so tiny. But my favorite part was approaching New York and seeing the Statue of Liberty from the plane. I got all teary-eyed, and when I looked at Mom, she was right there with me. Incredible.

The cab ride to our hotel was a different story. I swear I almost peed my pants! There were cars everywhere, and lots of honking going on. Our driver didn't speak English very well, so we couldn't understand much of anything he said, even though he talked to us almost the entire time. I wanted to tell him to be quiet and just drive. I kept grabbing Mom's leg when he'd slam on his brakes or squeeze in between two cars in another lane. I should have asked Mom for her relaxation CD.

Finally we made it to our hotel in one piece. Mom and I were superexcited, because the magazine had put us in a hotel right in the middle of Times Square.

"Do you think we'll see anyone famous?" I asked her.

"That would be fun, wouldn't it? But just think, Isabel, after you win that baking contest, *you'll* be the one who's famous!"

Every time she mentioned the contest, my stomach felt like I was on another cab ride. I told myself I didn't care if I won or not. It didn't really matter, because I'd gotten to take a great trip, and that was the best prize of all. Still, part of me did want to win, because it'd be something I'd remember forever. And also because I knew Mom hoped to get some free publicity out of the deal.

We had Friday afternoon and evening to do whatever we wanted, and then early Saturday morning a car would pick us up and drive us to the bake-off. Saturday night we would attend a fancy banquet, where the grand prize would be awarded to the winner. Then Sunday we'd be on our own again, to do more sightseeing before we flew back home Monday morning.

After we got settled into our hotel room, which was small but nice, we headed right out to our first stop—St. Valentine's Cupcakes. Out of all the things we planned on seeing and doing, I think the cupcake shop made Mom the most excited.

We got directions from a man at the front desk, then we went outside and started walking. Just like I imagined, the street felt like one big beehive, buzzing with people. Almost everyone walked fast, so Mom and I found ourselves hurrying too, even though we had no reason to. I could just imagine Sophie there, making fun of the way everyone walked, and then going slow on purpose just to be different and annoy people.

The cupcake shop looked like something from a TV show. I knew it would be beautiful—but *wow*. First of all, the place was huge, like five times the size of our little shop. Round tables were surrounded by lovely chairs with deep red seat cushions and high chair backs made of brass with a heart shape at the top of each one. The walls were painted a shiny gold color, and different heart-shaped paintings hung on them. The glass cases that displayed the cupcakes went from one end of the room to the other end and wrapped around in a big L shape. I couldn't believe how many cupcakes there were to choose from!

The line went all the way out the door, and shortly after we arrived, it made its way down the sidewalk.

"See," I told Mom, "people get just as excited about cupcakes as they do about brownies."

She smiled as she looked at a menu she had picked up from a stand by the door. "What kind are you going to get?"

I shrugged. "I don't know. How do you even choose?"

"I'm going to get the Lucky Lemon-Lime. Figure we can use all the luck we can get for tomorrow."

The lady behind us leaned in and smiled. She was about Mom's age, with warm brown eyes. She wore a red knitted hat with a cute little bow just above the brim. "I'm getting a dozen of those for a party tonight, along with a dozen of the Dr. Seuss. They're all wonderful, but those two flavors are my favorite."

"There's a cupcake called the Dr. Seuss?" I asked. "What's it made out of? Green eggs and ham?"

That made her laugh. "I don't really know. They keep it a secret. But trust me, it's fabulous!"

When we reached the counter, I decided to try the Dr. Seuss. We also ordered some tea, which came in the most adorable little teapot I'd ever seen, in the shape of a white rabbit.

We took a seat, and Mom bit into her cupcake. "Mmmm, Isabel, it's magnificent. Try yours."

I started to peel the paper off. "Maybe we should have come here after the bake-off. My s'mores cupcakes are going to seem so ordinary now."

Mom stopped chewing, and her eyes got big and round. "Isabel. Don't you know? Didn't she tell you on the phone?"

"Know what? What do you mean?"

"Honey, you aren't baking cupcakes tomorrow. You're baking chocolate tarts."

I blinked my eyes. I blinked them again. Did I hear her right? No, I couldn't have.

"What?" I asked. "What are you talking about?"

She smiled. "I saw that tart recipe sitting on the counter. And the jam tarts in the garbage can. They looked incredible. So I made a batch myself, in the shop's kitchen one day. Isabel, they were truly out of this world. I ran out and got a copy of the magazine, found the address, and mailed the tart recipe for you, just in time to meet the deadline."

"But, but—" It was hard to find the words as my brain tried to understand what she was saying. "You mean I submitted two recipes? Is that even legal?"

"The entry form said you could enter up to three."

"But how do we know the tart recipe won?" I asked.

She reached into her purse and pulled out the papers I had given her to complete. "It says right here, in the letter they sent with the paperwork."

I followed her finger and read the very last line of the letter. "We are looking forward to meeting you as well as Isabel, and tasting her delicious chocolate jam tarts!"

"I'm sorry, sweetie," she said. "I was wrong to make you feel like you had to enter a cupcake recipe. I get so wrapped up in my own stuff sometimes, I forget what's really important."

I didn't have time to say anything. The lady with the red hat came by our table, carrying her boxes of cupcakes. "What do you think?" She looked at my cupcake with no bites taken out of it. "What? You haven't tried it yet? Well, go on, try it!"

I reached down and took a bite. First I tasted chocolate. Then I tasted something sweet and crunchy. Jelly beans! But there was something else I couldn't quite figure out.

I sat there chewing and thinking. "I know. Bananas! Chocolate, jelly beans, and bananas. It's so good! It's like they threw a bunch of stuff into a bowl, not sure how it would turn out, and surprise, it turned out fantastic!"

My mom looked at me, and then up at the lady, and said, "I need to remember that cupcake when I'm worrying about whether or not things are going to turn out okay."

She laughed and said, "You and me both. Where are you ladies from, anyway?"

"Willow, Oregon," Mom said as she reached into her purse and grabbed a business card. "I own a cupcake shop there, as a matter of fact."

The lady took her card. "Wow, you've come a long way, haven't you? Well, enjoy your trip!" She waved and disappeared into the hive of buzzing New Yorkers with her boxes of scrumptious cupcakes.

"You know, Isabel," Mom said as I took another bite of my cupcake, "I brought along one of my It's Raining Cupcakes T-shirts. I was going to wear it tomorrow, but maybe it'd get more attention if you wore it. What do you think?"

I smiled. "Sure. I can do that."

When we got back to the hotel, I bought postcards in the gift shop.

Dear Dad,

Here's a list of things New York has taught me:

1. Have a tissue ready when you see the Statue of Liberty for the first time.

2. Go to the bathroom before you get into a cab in New York City.

3. Cupcakes can be like people. Sometimes a little different, but still good.

Love, Isabel

S'mores Cupcakes

Cupcakes

1 cup all-purpose flour

¾ cup granulated sugar

½ teaspoon baking soda

½ cup butter or margarine

⅓ cup water

3 tablespoons unsweetened cocoa

1 egg, lightly whisked

¼ cup buttermilk

Frosting

¼ cup unsalted butter, softened

1 ½ cups powdered sugar

½ teaspoon vanilla

1 7-oz. jar marshmallow cream

4 graham cracker squares

15 Hershey Kisses

Preheat oven to 350°. Line muffin tins with cupcake
papers.

In a large mixing bowl, mix flour, sugar, and baking soda together with a whisk. In a saucepan, melt the butter/margarine with the water and cocoa on low heat. When completely melted, remove from heat. Whisk egg in a separate bowl and add to flour mixture, along with the melted butter/margarine mixture, buttermilk and vanilla. Beat with electric mixer on low until smooth.

Fill cupcake liners half full. Bake 18–20 minutes, until toothpick inserted into center comes out clean. Let cupcakes cool completely before frosting.

For frosting, beat softened butter, powdered sugar, and vanilla until smooth. Add marshmallow cream and mix. Spread on cooled cupcakes with knife.

Use a food chopper to finely chop graham crackers, or break into pieces and put in a plastic bag and roll over them with a rolling pin. Set aside.

Unwrap candy kisses and place one on top of each cupcake, then sprinkle graham cracker crumbs across the top.

Makes about 15 cupcakes.

Grandma's Applesauce Cupcakes

Cupcakes

3 medium or 2 large Granny Smith apples

½ cup water

cinnamon and sugar mixture

1 ⅓ cups all-purpose flour

1 teaspoon baking soda

1 teaspoon baking powder

1 teaspoon ground cinnamon

½ teaspoon nutmeg

¼ teaspoon ground cloves

½ teaspoon salt

½ cup granulated sugar

½ cup firmly packed brown sugar

½ cup canola oil

2 eggs

Frosting

1 8-oz. package cream cheese, softened

½ cup unsalted butter, softened

2 teaspoons vanilla

2 cups powdered sugar

Preheat oven to 350°. Line muffin tins with cupcake papers.

Peel, core, and cut apples into small, bite-size pieces. Place in a large, microwave-safe bowl. Add water and generously sprinkle with cinnamon and sugar. Microwave on high 3 minutes, check and stir, and repeat 3 to 4 times, or until apples have softened to a chunky applesauce texture.

In a small mixing bowl, stir together flour, soda, powder, spices, and salt and set aside. In the mixing bowl with the applesauce, add sugars and oil and whisk together. Whisk eggs in separate bowl. Add to apple mixture and whisk together. Add the flour mixture to the apple mixture slowly, stirring with a wooden spoon until just combined.

Fill the muffin tins about three-quarters full. Bake 20—22 minutes, until toothpick inserted into the center comes out clean. Let cupcakes cool completely before frosting.

For frosting, beat cream cheese and softened butter together with a mixer until smooth. Mix in vanilla. Add powdered sugar and mix until creamy. If you have a pastry bag, you can pipe frosting onto the cupcakes.

Makes about 18 cupcakes. These are best eaten the day they are made.

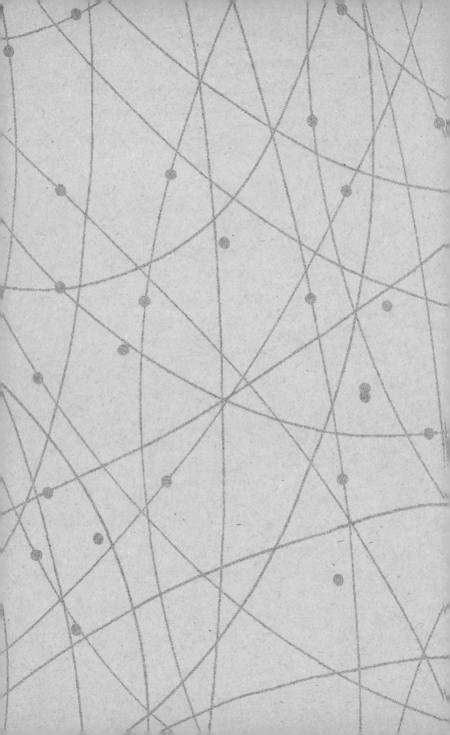

acknowledgments

A heartfelt thanks to Sara Crowe for loving this book from the start. To Alyson Heller and the team at Aladdin, thank you for your hard work to help make this book what I hope will be a delectable treat for those who read it. Lisa Madigan and Lindsey Leavitt, I owe you a lifetime of cupcakes for giving me your love, support, and writerly wisdom at just the right times. To Scott, Sam, and Grant, thanks as always for everything. Now we have a good excuse to eat lots of cupcakes. Be glad I didn't write a book about cucumbers.

Sprinkles and Secrets

For my dear friend, Lisa—
I had so much fun remembering our magical afternoon
together watching WICKED *as I wrote this book.*
Love you, LK!

Chapter 1

chocolate ice cream

THE ULTIMATE COMFORT FOOD

I think there are two kinds of happiness.

There's the real kind of happiness when you *have* to smile because you feel so good inside. It's like you've just eaten the most delicious cupcake or cuddled with the most adorable kitten. When you look around, everything looks like it's trimmed in gold. Beautiful. Joyful. Happy.

Then there's the fake kind of happiness. Something is supposed to make you happy. Your brain keeps saying *you should be* happy *about this* and you want to be, but no matter how hard you try to feel the real happiness, for some reason you can't. So you smile anyway and put on the best happy show you can because you don't want to look like a bad person. Sometimes, though, if you're lucky, the fake happiness eventually and magically turns into real happiness.

Today I'm supposed to feel happy and excited. Instead I feel sad and jealous. No one knows that, though. I made sure of it. All day at school I was the picture of happiness. I should get an Emmy for my performance today. Or an Oscar. Or, at the very least, a new tube of lip gloss, because my lips are really dry from all that smiling.

As I ride my yellow mountain bike home, my legs pumping hard and fast and my face all scrunched up and ugly because I don't have to pretend to be happy anymore, I think of that horrible old woman, Miss Gulch, from *The Wizard of Oz*. The one who took Toto from Dorothy? I probably look like her. What a scary thought.

I take a deep breath, slow down my sad and jealous legs, and tell myself to relax. And then I turn my thoughts to the list of things I go to when I'm in serious need of cheering up. Well, not an actual list. That might be weird to have a piece of paper with *Sophie's List of Pick-Me-Ups* written at the top and then a list of items that fill the page.

Usually I'm a pretty happy person. But there are some days, like today, when the world feels like a big, rotten tomato. (For the record, I hate tomatoes.)

I go over my mental pick-me-up list and realize that with the long, boring weekend stretching out ahead of me, I'm going to need almost every single thing on the list to help me through it.

First on the list is my dog. Daisy is a Havanese, which means she's an adorable, white bundle of fluffiness. And before you think I'm really shallow and only love my dog because of how she looks, when I say she's cute, I mean even her personality is cute! When she wags her tail, which is a lot of the time, her whole body wiggles. She has a small collection of stuffed animals (ones I used to play with) that she's claimed as hers, and she loves it when I grab one and throw it so she can chase it and bring it back to me to play tug-of-war. And when I've worn her out from tossing a bear or a tiger down the hallway a hundred times, she'll set the stuffed animal down, crawl into my lap, and paw at my hand as if to say, *Pet me, pet me!* See? So cute!

Next on the list is my best friend, Isabel. What can I say about Isabel? She's the best friend a girl could have. She used to live in the duplex next to ours, but they moved last summer so her mom could open a cupcake shop. The shop is called It's Raining Cupcakes, and Isabel and her parents live in an apartment above it. I think it's pretty great, and I'm happy her mom is living out her dream, but I miss having Isabel right next door. We still see each other a lot, but won't this weekend, which brings me to the actual reason the world feels like a big, rotten tomato.

Isabel is out of town, in New York City, so she can't be a part of my cheer-myself-up plan. In fact, her being in New York City is the reason I'm not happy. She entered a baking contest through a magazine and her recipe was good enough to earn her a spot in the bake-off. The finalists all flew to New York this morning, where they'll compete in the bake-off tomorrow.

I'm the one who told Isabel about the contest. I'm glad she got to go, but I wanted to go too! I wanted to compete for the grand prize of one thousand dollars. That's a lot of money, and it would have paid for some singing and acting lessons, something I really want to do so I can be an actress someday.

When I woke up this morning, it hit me pretty hard that Isabel was in New York City while I was stuck here, in the small town of Willow, and my happiness quickly disappeared. It'll be back one of these days—hopefully by the time Isabel gets home and tells me whether or not she won the contest.

In the meantime, back to my list. Musicals. I love, love, LOVE musicals. Movies like *The Sound of Music*, *The Wizard of Oz*, *Annie*, *Hairspray*, *Mamma Mia!*, and *High School Musical*. I have a whole collection of musical movies I've gotten as gifts since I was six years old. When I'm feeling down, I pop one in and snuggle up with my favorite blanket and a good snack. Soon everything fades away. In fact, it fades away so much that halfway through the movie, I'm usually up and singing along. I can't help it! It's like I want to be in the movie singing those songs so bad, I just have to get up and do the closest thing to it—singing and dancing around in my bedroom (usually in my purple pajamas).

Fourth on the list is shopping. I don't even have to buy anything, it's just fun to look at all of the cool clothes, sparkly jewelry, and beautiful shoes. Sometimes I'll try on shoes I know my mom would never approve of in a million years and pretend I'm a movie star with a red-carpet event I have to attend. You know, like it's absolutely crucial that I have the right pair of shoes. Now that's a type of pretending I don't mind at all.

Finally, chocolate. There's a little plaque that hangs in our kitchen. It's been there for as long as I can remember. It says HAND OVER THE CHOCOLATE AND NO ONE GETS HURT. I can just imagine a bank robber going into a bank, strolling up to the counter, and saying those words. At first, the bank teller is terrified. But when the robber demands chocolate instead of money, the teller says, "Oh, honey, I sure do understand. It's been one of those days, huh?"

I love chocolate. It's definitely my snack of choice, when given an option. I know, I know. I should be eating apples, bananas, and carrots, and I do eat those things, I swear! But like my mom always says— everything in moderation.

Last summer, as I thought about a cupcake recipe for the *Baker's Best* baking contest, I knew I wanted my recipe to include chocolate. I mean, if you have two flavors of cupcakes sitting side by side, one with chocolate and one without, I bet people choose the chocolate one most of the time. The recipe I finally ended up submitting for my entry was one for watermelon chocolate cupcakes—chocolate cake with a watermelon-flavored frosting. (See? I like fruit, too!) My whole family thought they were amazing. But I guess the judges didn't agree. Stupid judges.

Stupid sadness and jealousy.

When I get home, I put my bike in the garage and go in the house. Daisy greets me at the door with her usual jumping, spinning, and *pet me, pet me* routine.

"Hello, adorable dog of mine and number one on my list," I whisper, petting her as she rolls over, giving me her belly to scratch.

After a sufficient amount of scratching time, I stand up. "Come on, Daisy. You want a treat?"

She follows me into the kitchen, her tail wagging so hard it's practically picking her up off the ground. I toss her a Milk-Bone, get a spoon from the silverware drawer, and then grab the chocolate ice cream from the freezer.

I don't even get a bowl. I sit on a stool at the counter and dig in.

"Sophie, is that you?" Mom calls from the other room.

"No, it's a stranger raiding your freezer."

Mom appears, smiling. I have to say, my mom is so cute. No, not Daisy-cute, but girlie-cute, I guess. She wears her blond hair short but stylish, and she has a round face with big blue eyes. And she always wears the cutest clothes, not like she's trying to be sixteen again, just fresh and fun. Today she's wearing jeans and a pink T-shirt that says WAG MORE, BARK LESS.

"Hi, honey. How was school today?"

I shrug my shoulders, partly because I don't want to tell her about my rotten tomato day and partly because my mouth is full of chocolatey, creamy goodness.

"I've been thinking about you," she says. "Thinking about how you're probably a little sad to be here and not in New York City like Isabel."

The way she looks at me and the way her caring comes through in her voice, I feel tears rising up. I blink hard a few times, then I shrug again, scared that if I try to talk about it, I'll have a full-blown tearfest going on. And I don't want that. The whole point of the chocolate ice cream is to cheer myself up!

"I have a surprise for you," she says, her face now literally beaming.

I swallow my mouthful of ice cream. Thoughts of a tearfest disappear at the mention of the word "surprise." I totally forgot that's another one on my list of pick-me-ups! Except, it's sort of hard to make a surprise happen by myself.

I wait, my spoon frozen in midair.

She brings her hand around from behind her back, and she's holding three tickets. I lean in, my eyes squinting, trying to read the small words.

My spoon makes a loud clanking noise as I drop it on to the counter and grab the tickets from her hand.

I can't believe it.

Wicked, the musical.

We're going to see *Wicked*!

Chapter 2

chocolate-covered peanuts

THEY SING AND DANCE IN YOUR MOUTH

I squeal, jump off my stool, and grab my mom so hard that I'm afraid for a second I might have broken her rib or something.

I let go. "Sorry, are you okay?"

She laughs. "Yes. Are you?"

"Mom, how did you get these? When—?"

"One of my customers has a sister with some

connections to Broadway Across America. Good ones, obviously. When I heard *Wicked* was coming to Portland, I asked if she could help me get some tickets. And so she did."

I can't believe it. Other kids at school have seen the show when they've traveled to places like New York City, San Francisco, and Miami, and they always come back raving about it. The story, the songs, the performances—all of it is supposed to be spectacular to watch. I've read it's the story of how the Wicked Witch of the West in *The Wizard of Oz* came to be wicked.

"When is it?" I ask.

"Tomorrow night."

"There are three tickets here," I say, grabbing the rapidly melting ice cream and sticking it back in the freezer. "Who else is going with us?"

"I thought you might want to ask a friend to come along. If not, Hayden might like to see it."

Ugh. Hayden. Okay, my eight-year-old brother is definitely not on my list of pick-me-ups. In fact, he just might have the ability to totally ruin what could turn out to be one of the best nights of my entire life.

My brain goes through my list of friends from

the theater camps I've attended the last few years. Choosing one of them makes sense because I know they would love a live musical production as much as I would.

"Lily!" I decide. "I'll ask Lily. She's perfect. I hope she can go."

"Better call her right away," Mom says. "If she's free, tell her we'll pick her up at four tomorrow. We'll stop and get a bite to eat on the way. The play starts at seven. We'll be home really late, so maybe ask if she can spend the night with us."

"Okay." I give my mom another hug, a much gentler one this time. "Thanks, Mom. You are now officially on my pick-me-up list."

She smiles. "That's a good thing, right?"

"You're on there with chocolate! Yes, it's a good thing."

As I'm heading to the phone, Hayden comes in carrying what looks to be a spaceship made out of toilet-paper tubes. He's obsessed with all things outer space.

"Hayden," Mom asks with a funny look on her face. "Where did you get those?"

"Mom, don't worry," he says. "I got them out without unrolling all the paper. Well, except for one. And I folded the paper up really neatly. Anyway, with most of them, you can hardly tell the tubes are gone!"

I grab the phone and take it to my room, and leave Mom alone to handle that situation.

Lily is really excited. Her parents give her permission to come with us and spend the night so I give her all the details. After I hang up, I lie on my bed, thinking of all the fun times we had together at theater camps and missing them.

Last summer, the only camp I went to was the two-week overnight camp my parents have sent me to the last few years. It wasn't nearly as fun as theater camp, although two good things did happen. One, I met this cute guy named Kyle who was really nice. Well, I thought he was nice. He never wrote to me or called me like he promised. Okay, scratch that. One good thing happened. One of the camp counselors, Marcella, recorded everyone's talent show performances. She said she was so impressed by my performance, she planned on showing it to her mom. I thought that was a strange thing to do until she explained that her mom is an agent, and she's always looking for talented young people to star in commercials and TV shows. Of course, here it is November, a long way from July, and Marcella hasn't gotten in touch with me.

That does it. Overnight camp was a complete bomb. Which is why I'm going to do everything possible so I don't have to go next year and can go back to theater camp here in Willow instead. I just need to figure out a way to make some money for lessons. Otherwise, I'm afraid they'll give me the role of a tree or something else equally humiliating. I'm so much more than a tree, I know I am!

When I leave my room to tell Mom that Lily is going with us to the play, I hear Hayden talking in the bathroom. "But, Mom, why is the tube so important? The toilet paper will still get the job done, right?"

On Saturday, Mom and I spend almost the whole day getting ready for our big evening. Mom gives us both manicures after we eat lunch, and then we go through all of our clothes before we settle on what dresses we're going to wear. I decide to wear a pale-green dress I wore to a wedding last year that still fits. Mom chooses a simple black dress she said she's had forever, because it's the kind of dress that never goes out of style.

After that, I curl my shoulder-length blond hair and put in two small, sparkly barrettes to dress it up a little. When we finally head out to the family room to say good-bye to Dad and Hayden, Dad whistles at us.

"Who are you and what have you done with my wife and daughter?"

We laugh and then Hayden says, "Eh, Sophie, you look better in your purple pajamas."

I give him a swat with the small handbag Mom lent me.

"Drive safely," Dad says as he kisses Mom on the cheek. "And enjoy the show." Then he leans in and kisses me on the forehead. His breath smells like peanuts.

"It's going to be so awesome," I say.

"Oh, wait a second!" Dad hustles into the kitchen and pulls out a bag of chocolate-covered peanuts. "Here, take these along. They'll have snacks during the intermission, but they'll cost almost as much as the tickets to the show."

Mom sticks them in her purse and then we say good-bye.

As I put my seat belt on, I turn and look at my beautiful mom. "I'm not dreaming, am I? We're really doing this?"

"I promise, you are wide-awake." And then she starts singing, "We're off to see the wizard . . ."

And I burst out laughing.

Chapter 3

chocolate-chip
pancakes

TRY THEM FOR A SWEET SUNDAY

MORNING BREAKFAST

The play is incredible.

Brilliant.

Dazzling!

I laugh. I cry. I cheer! We all do. When it's over and the actors take the stage for their bows, I applaud as hard as I can, wishing there was another performance so we could experience the magic all over again.

"I'm pretty sure that was the most amazing thing I've ever seen," Lily says as we stand in line waiting to buy a CD. We want to listen to it on the way home. I look at her and realize she's glowing, and it's not because of the sparkly coral dress she's wearing.

"Me too!" I say.

We get our CD and head outside. The night is cold and clear. I look up, but the tall buildings of downtown Portland prevent me from seeing the moon or very many stars. We rush to the parking garage, shivering the whole way. When we get in the car, Mom turns it on and cranks up the heat.

I lean in toward the front seat. "Just so you know, I'm now more determined than ever to find a way to pay for some singing and acting lessons."

"You need to help me come up with the hottest look in doggy fashion," she says as she puts the car in reverse. "We could make millions. Then you'd be set."

I turn and look at Lily, who has a puzzled look on her face. "My mom designs and sews clothes for dogs. Her company is called The Pampered Pooch."

"That's, um, different," she says, trying to be nice. Both Mom and I laugh.

"Do you have a dog, Lily?" Mom asks her.

"No. Just a big yellow cat."

"So you probably don't get the whole doggy-fashion thing."

"Not really," she says. "I mean, don't they already have fur coats?"

I reach over and tap Mom's shoulder. "See? Isn't that exactly what I said when you told me you were going to start the business?"

"Well, if you ever have a good idea for a new doggy look, Lily, be sure and let me know. Sophie's acting career may depend on it."

I pop open our new CD and hand it to Mom to put into the car's player. And just like that, we're back in the magical world of Galinda, Elphaba, and Fiyero once again.

The next morning, Lily and I make chocolate-chip pancakes. Hayden comes in, jumps up and down, and tells us that last night he finally convinced Dad to let him watch *Star Wars*. They have a movie date next Friday night, and lucky me, I'm invited too.

"I've waited my whole life to see *Star Wars*," he tells us. "I didn't think I could go on a minute longer. Out of all my friends, I'm the only one who hasn't seen any of the movies. But now it's finally going to happen."

For once, I can actually relate to my annoying little brother. "That's how I felt about *Wicked*. I'm happy for you, Little Brother Man. So why does Dad think you're suddenly ready?"

"I told him it wasn't fair that you got to see *Wicked* on stage. So I told him to give me one good reason why I couldn't finally see *Star Wars*."

"What'd he say?"

Hayden takes a big piece of pancake, dips it in the syrup, and shoves it in his mouth. "He couldn't think of anything, Soph. Not one reason! So he looked at me and said, 'Okay, Hayden. Next weekend. *Star Wars*, here we come.'"

He's done eating in about two minutes flat, thank goodness. "Catch you girls later. I've got a top-secret project I have to finish."

"Don't touch the toilet paper!" I yell.

"Funny kid," Lily says. "He reminds me of that one boy Henry, at theater camp. Do you remember him?"

"Oh, the supersmart kid who memorized every single president of the United States, including their dates of birth? Yeah, I remember."

We're quiet for a second, both of us lost in the memories.

"Lily, the last time we talked, you said you were thinking about taking voice lessons. Did you sign up?"

"Yeah, I did."

"Do you like them? I mean, are they fun?"

She shrugs and takes another bite of pancake. "I don't know if fun is the right word. My teacher really pushes me. But yeah, I like them."

Envy tugs at my heart. "You have such a beautiful voice," I tell her. "I bet you'll be on a stage someday, singing and acting."

She blushes, and tucks her straight brown hair behind her ear. "I don't know. I hope so. It's what I want more than anything."

"Yeah. Me too," I say as we put our dishes in the dishwasher. "So what do you want to do now?"

"I've been dying to see your friend's cupcake shop. Could we walk over there?" She checks the clock on the microwave. "My mom won't be here for another couple of hours."

Lily lives on the other side of Willow and is in eighth grade at the other middle school in town. I'm surprised she hasn't made a trip to the cupcake shop yet. When she mentions it, I think of Isabel and the baking contest. Maybe Isabel's grandma, who's running the shop while Isabel and her mom are out of town, will know who won the contest. I'd love to find out!

"Sure. Just let me tell my mom where we're going."

When we get outside, it feels cool and crisp. No rain, luckily. The walk goes quickly as we talk about school, the play, and theater camp.

"I'm so glad you called me," she says as we turn the corner, It's Raining Cupcakes now in sight. "I mean, not just because of the play. It's been fun, hanging out with you."

I smile. "Yeah, it's been really fun."

When we get up to the shop, a closed sign hangs from the door. We both mutter "oh no" at the sight.

Lily peeks in the window. "It's adorable! Wow, look at that gorgeous mural on the wall."

"Yeah, it's very cute," I say. "Sorry they're not open. Guess we'll have to come back another time."

"It's a date," she says.

Just as we turn to head back home, Stan, Isabel's neighbor, comes through the door that leads to the apartments above the shops. He owns the barbershop that sits next door to It's Raining Cupcakes. He's supernice.

"Sophie!" Stan says. "So wonderful to see you." He gives me a strange look. "You know Isabel doesn't get back until tomorrow, right? Or did you come by to get a haircut from your favorite barber?"

I laugh. "No. See, my friend Lily here wanted to see the shop and have a cupcake. I forgot they're not open on Sundays. Have you heard anything about Isabel?"

"Haven't heard a thing," he says. "And I'm dying to know too! You could go up and knock on their door. I bet her dad is home and he probably has the answer."

I wave my hand. "No, that's okay. I'll wait and hear

it from Isabel. I'm sure she wants to be the one to tell me anyway."

He looks at Lily. "Well, I hope you do come back. From what I hear, they could really use the business."

I get a funny feeling in my stomach when he says that. "What? What do you mean? Are things not going well?"

His round cheeks turn a rosy-pink. "Oh for Pete's sake, look at me, spouting off things that are none of my business. I do apologize."

"No, it's fine. I mean, I won't say anything to Isabel about it. Are things really bad? What have you heard?"

He looks down at the ground for a second, then back at me. "Let's just say, in the words of Isabel's grandma, things are far from ducky in the cupcake world."

"That's awful," I say softly. "Isabel hasn't said anything to me about it. I wonder if she knows?"

"I sure know how to ruin the mood, don't I?" Stan says. "I better turn it around quickly! Knock, knock."

Lily gives me a funny look.

I shrug. "He loves 'em."

"Who's there?" she asks.

"Icy," Stan says.

"Icy who?"

"Icy you again someday soon, okay?"

We wave and start walking home. My feet feel heavy, like my shoes are bricks. I don't want to go home. I want to do something to help Isabel's family. But what? There's not one thing I'd be able to do.

"You okay?" Lily asks.

"I just feel bad for Isabel and her family. They've worked so hard. I don't want their business to fail, you know?"

"I bet Beatrice's Brownies has made it hard on them," Lily says. "Their location is better. And their brownies are so good. We've probably been there ten times since it's opened."

My heart sinks even more. I bet Lily's family is like a lot of families. Beatrice's Brownies is a big chain, with stores all across the country. They put a lot of money into advertising, something a small business like It's Raining Cupcakes can't do.

Lily must sense it's time to change the subject.

"So what's going on with Isabel? I didn't quite get what you guys were talking about."

"She's in New York," I explain. "She competed in this big baking contest yesterday. If she wins, she brings home a check for a thousand dollars."

She smiles. "That'd be awesome. Do you think her parents will let her keep it all? And what would she do with money like that?"

"Isabel wants to travel. We dream of being onstage while Isabel dreams of seeing beautiful places."

"Wish I'd known about that contest," Lily says.

"No, because then you'd probably be in New York City too, and you would have missed going to see *Wicked* with me."

"You're totally right. That performance was worth way more than a thousand dollars anyway."

Yeah. I like how this girl thinks.

Chapter 4

chocolate milk

IT COMES FROM SWEET COWS

Before Isabel left, we agreed to meet at the Blue Moon Diner right after she got home so she could tell me if she'd been crowned Queen of the Baking Contest.

At school on Monday, it seems like National Ask-About-Isabel Day. Everywhere I go, someone asks me if I've heard from her yet. I try to keep my face happy and my answer short—"Nope, not yet, but I'm seeing her after school." By the end of the day, I'm exhausted. I head home, and even there, I'm not safe from interrogation.

I walk through the door and give Daisy a good belly rub. Hayden comes up to me and asks, "Sophie, when does Isabel get back?"

"She should be back by now. We're meeting up in an hour."

"I've heard aliens love New York City. What if she didn't make it home? What if they abducted her and instead of making it back home to Oregon, she's somewhere in outer space, trying to send us a message so we can save her?"

I shake my head. I've given up trying to tell my brother there is no such thing as aliens. "Hayden, that's a good point. I think you better try to construct a device to receive the message they're trying to send."

His eyes got as big as flying saucers. "Really? What do you think the device should be made out of?"

I think on this for a few seconds. "Tape. Lots and lots of really sticky tape. And paper, of course. The expensive kind Dad keeps in his top desk drawer. Good luck, Little Brother Man."

Before he turns to go, he gives me a big grin and a full-on salute. Finally, a little respect. I'll have to give orders involving aliens more often.

I sit down at the kitchen table, pull a textbook out of my backpack, and try to read. But my brain just can't focus. So then I go to the bathroom to freshen up, which means putting on some bubblegum lip gloss and running a brush through my hair. Thirty seconds later, I check my watch. Fifty more excruciating minutes. I'm about to go to my bed and lie down because death by waiting seems inevitable at this point, when the phone rings.

I hear Mom answer it as I come out of the bathroom. Then she calls, "Sophie, where are you? It's for you."

It has to be Isabel. Maybe her plane's delayed. Or maybe she's extremely excited, and she can't wait to tell me. Or, maybe she's feeling too high-and-mighty to meet up with a low-life peasant like me, and wants to cancel our plans.

"Who is it?" I whisper.

"A girl named Marcella?"

My counselor from summer camp. How weird that I was just thinking about her the other day.

"Hello?"

"Sophie! It's Mar! How are you?"

"I'm fine. How are you?"

"Fantastic! Listen, I have great news. I finally got around to showing my mom your talent show performance this past weekend when I was home from college. She thinks you are just the cutest thing."

"She does?"

"Yes! Of course she does. I told you, that performance was totally impressive. Anyway, my mom is hoping you and your mom might be willing to call and talk to her about signing with her talent agency in Los Angeles. She thinks she could get you into some commercials really easily. Maybe even a spot on a TV show. You have the looks, you have the voice—actually, you've got it all, according to her."

I look at my mom, then back at the phone. Is this for real? Commercials? TV shows?

"Sophie?" Marcella asks.

"Sorry. I—I think I'm in shock. Are you serious?"

She laughs. "Would I joke about something like this? Get a piece of paper so I can give you her phone number. She's really excited to talk with you."

Somehow I manage to make it over to the counter where I find a pen and notepad. After she gives me the number, I thank her and we hang up.

"What was that about?" Mom asks.

I speak slowly, as if I need to hear it coming out of my mouth to believe it. "One of my camp counselors says her mom wants me to sign with her agency."

"Agency? What kind of agency?"

I look at the phone. I look at my mom. It *really* happened. I grab Mom's hands and start jumping up and down. I can't even talk for a few seconds. Finally I yell, "Mom, a talent agency! Like, for actors. She saw a recording of my talent show performance, and she thinks I've got it all! Those were her exact words!"

Mom pulls me to her and wraps her arms around me. "Oh, Sophie, that's wonderful. Should we call her now?"

The clock on the microwave tells me if I don't leave soon, I might be late for my diner date with Is. But a talent agent wants to talk to me!

I go to the fridge and chug some chocolate milk right out of the container. When I'm done, I wipe the milk mustache away and I smile. "Yeah. Let's call her!"

Chapter 5

french fries dipped in a chocolate shake

A GREAT SWEET-AND-SALTY SNACK

When I finally get to the Blue Moon, Isabel is in a booth, waiting for me. Her face, along with the empty water glass sitting in front of her, tells me she's been here for a while.

"Chickarita," I say as I slide into the seat across from her. "Sorry I didn't get here sooner. Something of epic proportions came up and I couldn't get away."

"I was beginning to wonder if you'd forgotten about me," she says as she picks at a hangnail.

The waitress walks up to our table, and we order our usual: chocolate shakes and French fries.

After she leaves, I lean in and wait until Isabel's brown eyes meet mine. "I'm sorry. I'm here now, right? So tell me! Tell me everything! Did you win?"

A smile spreads across her face like the sun breaking through the clouds, and in that moment, I know. I know she came here, flying on her bike, ready to tell me she won and then she waited and waited some more. Her enthusiasm must have deflated like a balloon with a leak in it.

"I won," she says. Then, like she almost can't believe it, she says it again, louder. "Sophie, I really won!"

I clap my hands together and squeal. A few people look over at me, which makes us both laugh. "Oh. My. Gosh. Isabel! This is the coolest thing EVER! Tell me. Tell me what happened!"

"The day of the bake-off, I was so nervous. I mean, it's one thing baking in your own kitchen, but it's another thing to bake in this big convention center where they have a bunch of little kitchens set up, one for each contestant. And the whole time I was in my little kitchen, I kept thinking, judges *are going to be eating what I make*. It was pretty scary."

"Wow," I say. "So you got there and they had all the ingredients for your cupcakes, and you just started baking?"

She smiles. "Yes. Except I didn't make cupcakes. I made chocolate jam tarts. Mom sent in the recipe I'd wanted to do all along. She felt bad, I guess, about wanting me to submit a cupcake recipe. Anyway, the chocolate jam tart recipe is the recipe they wanted me to make. And luckily, the day of the bake-off, everything went really well, and the tarts turned out perfectly. Some of the other contestants had a terrible time with their recipes, burning things or forgetting to add important ingredients. I'm pretty sure, on a different day, mine wouldn't have won. I feel so lucky!"

"You are talented, Is, not lucky. And can I just say that chocolate jam tarts sound so delicious. And different! Will you make them for me sometime?"

"I think Mom is going to feature them at the cupcake shop next month. You can come every day in December and have one if you want."

The waitress brings our order and we dig in as Is tells me about New York City and all the things they did while they were there. They visited a fancy cupcake shop, climbed to the top of the Empire State Building, and saw a Broadway musical.

"Which one?" I ask.

"*Wicked!*"

"No way! Are you serious? I saw *Wicked* this weekend too, in Portland. My mom got tickets and surprised me. Wasn't it good?"

"I loved it," she says. "I kept thinking, someday Sophie will be in a play like this."

I smile. Isabel pauses to take a sip of her shake, then she says, "I wish you could have been there, Sophie Bird. We would have had so much fun."

"It's all right, Chickarita. I'm over it. Sort of." I take a napkin and dab at my eyes. It makes her laugh.

"So, what are you going to do with the prize money?" I ask. And when I do, I realize any jealousy I felt is gone. I'm truly happy for her. She totally deserves it.

Her face lights up. "Oh! It's going to be so fun. My parents and I are going to spend a few days up in Seattle. See, at the bake-off, there was a boy in the kitchen next to me named Jack. When I asked him what he was baking, he said, 'I can't tell you, because I'm on a secret baking mission. If I told you, I'd have to kill you.' And I said, 'Wow, you mean they really let spies into this thing?' And then he leaned over and whispered, 'No, actually, they don't. And you better not breathe a word of our conversation to anyone, understand?' Anyway, Jack lives in Seattle and his mom owns Penny's Pie Place. Doesn't it sound cute? My mom wants to see it! And since I've never been to Seattle—"

"Isabel, wait a second." I raise my eyebrows. "Do you *like* Jack?"

She gives me this shrug that says, *I'm not going to admit it, but I'm pretty sure I do.* "I don't know. All I know is that he's nice and really funny."

I smile. "I think I know how you feel."

She starts to say something, but I wave my hand and say, "No! We aren't going to talk about the rotten-boy-from-camp-whose-name-must-never-be-spoken-again. So just forget about it. It's over and that's that. When are you going to Seattle?"

"During winter break, in December. We'll get to see the city all decorated in lights! And, Sophie, here's the best part: Mom and Dad said I could invite you to go with us!"

"Really? Me and you in Seattle?"

"I know, right? So you have to ask your parents when you get home, okay?"

"Okay, I will."

"Can I get you girls anything else?" the waitress asks. We tell her no thanks and go to work finishing off the fries.

"Oh, before I forget, I brought you something," Isabel says.

She reaches into the pocket of her jacket and pulls out a little notebook. It has a picture of the New York skyline across the front with the words I ♥ NEW YORK.

I smile. "Thanks, Is. It's cute! Not sure what I'll write in it, but I'll think of something."

"Yeah, you'll think of something," she says. "Hey, hold on. What thing of epic proportions happened before you got here? You haven't said."

The butterflies I felt earlier as I talked on the phone with Mrs. Parks come rushing back. I still can't believe how my whole life has changed in the course of an hour.

"Well, it turns out one of my camp counselors, Marcella, has a mom who is a talent agent. And she's interested in signing me. She thinks she can get me into some commercials, and maybe even a spot on a TV show."

Isabel's brown eyes get big and round, like two chocolate cupcakes. "Sophie! Why didn't you say anything sooner? That's ten times more exciting than me winning a baking contest. You're going to be famous!"

I laugh. "Well, it's kind of early to be saying that. She's sending me a contract and we have to mail her some photos, then she'll let me know if there are any auditions that might be a good fit. I'm trying not to get my hopes up, you know?"

Ah, who am I kidding? My hopes are already higher than Seattle's Space Needle!

Chapter 6

chocolate gum

IT WILL SATISFY THAT CHOCOLATE

CRAVING IN A PINCH

Tuesday morning, I roll out of bed, take a shower, and get ready. When I get to the kitchen for breakfast, Dad hands me the *Willow Gazette*. I squeal when I see my best friend's picture with the heading "Isabel Browning Takes First Place in National Baking Contest." I read the entire article and when I'm finished, I'm so excited. Today will be a really fun day for Isabel.

"It's exciting!" Dad says. "She won a thousand bucks? Somehow you left out that small detail when you were telling us about it last night. Guess you were too busy thinking about the talent agent who wants to sign you, huh?"

I smile. "Yeah. That could be it. Oh, and Isabel wants to spend the money on a trip to Seattle with her family. She asked me to come too. Can I go? It'll be over winter break."

"I don't see why not. Sounds fun. Check with Mom, though. Make sure she isn't secretly planning a family trip to Tahiti or something."

"Wow, that'd be some surprise. Even better than tickets to see *Wicked*."

I scarf down a piece of toast and some juice, and then I'm out the door and on my way to school. What a difference a few days make. There will be no fake happiness today. Only the real kind, thank goodness.

When I get to school, a crowd has gathered around Isabel. I try to squeeze my way in, but I don't have much luck. I can hear some kids laughing, and then Isabel says something so quietly, I can't make it out.

When the first warning bell rings, everyone takes off, and I'm able to get to our locker, where Isabel is standing.

"Congratulations!" I say, reaching in to get my science textbook. "You made the front page of the paper! And they mentioned the cupcake shop. I bet that will help business."

She looks at me funny. "Why would you say that?"

Uh-oh. "I mean, it's a good thing, that's all. Good for you, good for your parents. It was a great article!"

I slam our locker and look at her. "You okay? You don't seem as happy as I thought you'd be."

"You know how the paper mentioned the prize money?" she whispers.

I nod. "Yeah. So?"

"A couple of the kids were joking about it just now. One said I'd probably be going on a shopping spree and would come back with a new Coach purse or something. Then the other one said after that I'd be too good to eat in the cafeteria with them, and I'd have to eat with the teachers instead."

I feel my happiness disappearing faster than a

plate of jam tarts at a coffee shop. "Isabel, don't let them bug you. They're just jealous, that's all."

She bites her lip, quiet for a second. Then she says, "I told them I was taking my family on a trip. Someone said they'd watch for me on the *Spoiled Rich Kids* TV show."

Anger boils up inside of me. "Isabel, listen. You have nothing to feel bad about! You came up with an incredible recipe, and you worked hard to bake that recipe in a bake-off with real judges! Don't let their stupid jealousy bring you down." The words taste yucky in my mouth, because I know, just a few days ago, I was one of those stupid, jealous people. Shame on me. Shame on them.

We start walking to class. "They're acting like I won a million dollars or something," she says.

"Now *that* would be something, huh? You could buy every girl in the whole school a Coach purse."

As I'm turning into my science class, Dennis Holt, a tall, skinny kid I've known since kindergarten, is there and says, "You're buying every girl in the whole school a purse, Isabel? Wow, you *are* rich. What about the boys? What do we get? Maybe a new video game? There's this new one I really want—"

I interrupt him. "She's not buying anyone anything. Especially you." I wave to Isabel. "See you next period."

The bell rings just as I'm taking my seat. Mr. Leonard tells us we'll be doing an experiment with chewing gum. He loves coming up with these crazy experiments to help us learn what all the terms in the scientific method mean. This time, we'll be chewing different kinds of bubblegum to see which type of gum blows the biggest bubble.

I like Mr. Leonard except for the fact that he doesn't let us choose our partners. He seems to get a thrill out of matching me with kids who get on my nerves. For the bubblegum experiment, of course, he assigns Dennis Holt as my partner, who is definitely on my nerves today.

"Hey, Sophie, want to see a dead bird's foot?" Dennis asks when he comes to my desk to work.

Ewww! "What? Why would I want to see that? And why do you have a dead bird's foot? That's disgusting."

He's rummaging around in his binder, like he's looking for it. If he shows it to me, things are going to get ugly. "My cat likes to kill things and bring them to the porch for us to see. The bird's foot was lying there, so I picked it up."

I hold up my hands. "Please, do not show me that thing. And what do you mean, foot? Birds don't have feet, do they?"

"Yes, they do."

I scowl. "No. I'm pretty sure they don't."

"What are they called, then?" he asks.

"Talons. At least on big birds of prey that's what they're called. My brother went through a birds of prey obsession."

"Man, I bet he'd like to see the bird's foot," Dennis mumbles.

I shake my head. Why do boys have to be so weird most of the time? "Can we just get started with the project? Please?"

"Sure." He points to the pieces of gum in front of us. "Pick a flavor, any flavor."

I don't say one word to him the whole time, even though he tries his hardest to get me to talk to him. I simply shake my head yes or no if I have to answer an important question. Halfway through class, I can tell he's getting tired of my silent act.

Mr. Leonard comes over to see how we're doing. He gives us his approval, then says, "You both need to work on the write-up. Don't forget, it's due on Friday. Sophie, I do not want you doing all of the work, understand?"

I look at Dennis, expecting him to make a smart remark, but he just sits there, twirling a gum wrapper between his fingers.

"Okay," I say.

After he leaves, Dennis says, "He hates me."

"He does not hate you. He might think you're lazy, but he doesn't hate you."

"Do you think I'm lazy?" he asks.

I unwrap another piece of gum and pop it in my mouth. Oh my gosh, it tastes like chocolate. Chocolate gum!?

"That depends," I tell him. "How much of the write-up are you going to do? And you have to taste this chocolate gum. It's the weirdest thing."

"Do you want me to do all of it? I can do the entire

write-up if you want me to. I'll prove to both of you I'm not lazy."

I don't trust him with the whole thing. "How about half? You want to do the first half or the second half?"

"I have a better idea," he says. "Let's meet up one day after school and do the whole thing together. How about Thursday? I have other stuff going on after school tomorrow."

I'm silent.

"I promise it'll be fun. And my mom makes really good snacks."

"There's one more thing you have to promise," I tell him. "That after class, you'll go and tell Isabel congratulations on the contest. Tell her you're really happy for her, and mean it. Plus, I want you to apologize for joking about the money."

He sighs. "Fine. But I really don't think what I said was that big of a deal."

"Imagine twenty other kids saying something like it," I tell him. "It *is* a big deal."

His expression changes. I can tell he gets it.

"All right. Sorry."

"Don't tell me. Tell her."

He nods. "Where do you want to meet Thursday?"

I consider the question for a second. "My brother says Mars is pretty cool."

"Ha ha, very funny. How about my house?"

So much for a day filled with real happiness.

Chapter 7

chocolate-covered banana

DIP IT IN PEANUT BUTTER

FOR AN EXTRA KICK

By the time the bell rings, I get the feeling Isabel would love nothing more than to return to New York City and stay there forever.

"Want to come over?" I ask her as we leave school. The sun is shining, but it's cold. I zip my black down jacket all the way up. "We can listen to the *Wicked* CD. Bake some cookies or something?"

She slips her arms through her backpack straps as we walk toward the bike rack. "Thanks, Soph, but I better get home. I have lots of homework. I missed two days of school, remember?"

A strange noise comes from above. We look up and see a flock of geese flying across the bright blue sky. A couple of them are honking loudly.

"Flying south for the winter," I say.

"Wish I could go with them," Isabel says.

"Oh, Isabel. The stupid, jealous people need to get over it and just be happy for you." Yes, once again I think of myself when I say this, and secretly cringe. "Try to forget about them, okay?"

She bends down to unlock her bike. "I'm trying, but it's hard. I heard someone whispering to a friend that I think I'm better than everyone else now. Where did she get that?"

She stands up and looks at me, her eyes starting to fill with tears. "You've done nothing wrong," I tell her. "Nothing! So forget about them and just hang in there. It'll be old news in a couple of days anyway. Hey, you want me to do something shocking and get caught, so the attention is on me? Toilet paper the principal's house or something?"

She finally smiles. "Thanks for the thought, but no, please don't."

"Okay, well, if there's anything I can do, let me know."

"Sophie Bird, you are the best."

She gives me a quick hug before she gets on her bike and rides away. I look up and think of those geese, flying together in the V formation. They'll stick together and help each other through until they get to their final destination.

Why can't the kids at school be more like those geese?

I pull out the notebook she gave me and decide then and there it'll be a place where I can dream things, big or little, and maybe, just maybe, they'll come true.

Dream #1—
I dream of a school where
no one is mean to one another.
(In other words, everyone
is as sweet as cupcakes,
like my best friend.)

✳ ✳ ✳

When I get home, I find Mom at her sewing machine, working away on something for her Pampered Pooch business. Last year the business really took off and she got so busy, she had to hire a couple of women to help her. Now they also sew doggy clothes in their homes.

It's weird to me how many people believe dogs need clothes. When my mom first started Pampered Pooch a few years ago, Dad and I thought she'd be out of business in six months. Boy were we wrong. Not only do people want their dogs to have clothes, but they want them to have a variety. I mean, do they really think the neighbors are going to say bad things if the dog goes outside wearing the same outfit two days in a row? I guess they do. And thanks to my mom, there are some dogs out there who dress better than I do.

"What are you making?" I ask as I grab a banana from the fruit basket. Daisy begs me with her eyes, telling me she wants a little snack, too. So I take a treat from the special treat container and toss it to her.

"I'm working on bows today," she says.

I pick up a finished one. It's made out of plaid

fabric in pastel colors. In the center of the bow is a button shaped like a bone.

"You want one?" she asks. "I bet it'd look cute on you."

I smile. "Uh, no thanks. I'm good. Hey, what about that leather jacket idea I had? I bet it'd be a big seller."

She takes her scissors and cuts the thread. "I'm still thinking on that. Leather is expensive, so I think it's going to have to be a faux leather of some kind. And besides, dogs like to chew on leather. Can you imagine paying fifty dollars for a jacket and having your dog decide it makes a great chew toy?"

I open a jar of peanut butter and scoop some up with my banana. "I can't imagine paying fifty dollars for anything relating to my dog. I love her, but Mom, that's so ridiculous. Don't people realize there are starving children in Africa? I just think there are a lot more important things to spend money on."

She stands up. "Careful, honey. You're starting to make me feel bad. Although, if they weren't buying the stuff from me, they'd probably buy it somewhere else."

"Mom, I'm hungry," Hayden says as he walks into the kitchen.

I break off part of my banana and hand it to him. "Don't say I never gave you anything."

He takes a bite. "How come I taste peanut butter?"

"Because bananas and peanut butter are awesome together." I give him the peanut butter jar. "Here, try it."

"I'd rather dip it in chocolate. Do we have any of that?"

"Mom, is that okay?" I ask.

"Sure, go ahead."

I take the chocolate-flavored syrup out of the fridge and pour some in a bowl. I cut up Hayden's banana, put it on a plate, and set it all at the kitchen table.

"There you go. Dude, that's some snack you got there. You could even dip the banana slice in peanut butter *and* chocolate. Then you'd have it all."

He pulls a banana slice out of the bowl of chocolate with his fingers, and I watch as chocolate drips down his arm and all over his pants.

Mom glares at me as she grabs a towel and starts

cleaning up his gooey mess. "How about giving the kid a fork, Sophie? And maybe not quite so much chocolate next time?"

As I head to the silverware drawer, I notice Mom has gathered photos of me and piled them next to the phone. "Mom, you're not going to send all of these to Mrs. Parks, are you?"

"No, honey. I pulled them out so you could go through them and choose the ones you like the best."

"So does this mean you and Dad have discussed it?"

"Yes, we have. If this is something you really want to do, we'll support you. I've done some research and talked to some other clients, and Candace Parks is one of the top agents in the business."

"Are you going to be famous, Sophie?" Hayden asks before he licks the chocolate between his fingers on the hand Mom hasn't washed yet.

"Ha, that's what Isabel said. It's fun to imagine big things happening, I guess."

Mom goes to the sink to rinse out the chocolatey dish rag. "How is Isabel, anyway?" she asks. "Was everyone happy for her today at school?"

"Not really. Jealous is more like it. Everyone was focused on the prize money and acting like she's rich now or something. Wouldn't that be nice? Then their business wouldn't be in trouble."

Mom frowns. "Oh no. Sorry to hear that. And what's this about their business being in trouble? Did Isabel tell you that?"

"No, their neighbor, Stan. He let it slip when Lily and I walked over there the other day. Isabel hasn't said a word, and I don't know what to say."

"I'm thinking if she wants to talk about it with you, she'll bring it up. Maybe just wait and see."

I grab the jar of peanut butter and a sleeve of crackers and head for my room. "Okay. Thanks, Mom."

Once I'm in my room, I pull out the notebook Isabel gave me and write down two more dreams.

Dream #2—
I dream that someday
there are no hungry
children in Africa,
or anywhere else.

Dream #3—
I dream that tomorrow
Isabel is back to her
happy self again.

• 262 •

Chapter 8

candy cane dipped in hot cocoa

A CHOCO-MINTY TREAT

There doesn't seem to be as much drama at school today. This is good. Still, Isabel seems quieter than usual, so I ask her to come over after school, using our upcoming social studies test on ancient Rome as a good reason. Studying together is much more fun than studying alone, I tell her. Mostly I just want to try and cheer her up! She agrees, so we ride our bikes to my house, then she calls her mom to let her know.

My mom made pumpkin bread, which we slice up and take to my room, along with two mugs of steaming hot cocoa.

"This bread is so good," I say. I hand her the plate. "Try some!"

Isabel takes a piece. "I love this time of year. Can you believe Thanksgiving is already next week?"

"I know—so many fun things to look forward to. And everyone bakes the yummiest things. I can't wait until Mom and I have our annual Christmas cookie baking day. Is your mom doing anything special with the cupcake shop for the holidays? Besides featuring your fabulous chocolate jam tarts?"

"So far, gingerbread cupcakes and peppermint cupcakes are on the menu, to get everyone in the holiday mood. She's really hoping we'll do a lot of business next month." She pauses. "I haven't said anything to you, but things aren't going very well. She's not even making enough money to pay the loan bill every month."

"Oh, Is, I'm sorry. But hopefully things will pick

up next month. So many people have holiday parties, you know?"

While she takes a sip of cocoa, her eyes light up. "Hey, I totally forgot to ask you about Seattle. Can you go?"

"Yes. Just let me know the dates, and I'll get it on our calendar."

"Okay, I have to check with Mom and Dad and see what they've decided."

We hear the phone ring, and a minute later, Mom pokes her head in. "Sophie, it's for you. It's Mrs. Parks. Do you want to call her back?"

Isabel looks at me. "Who's Mrs. Parks?"

"My agent," I say, smiling. "It's so weird saying that."

"Take it!" Isabel says, pointing toward the door. "Go on, you can't keep your agent waiting. Don't worry about me. I have Julius Caesar to keep me company."

"Okay, I'll be right back."

I step into the hallway and Mom hands me the phone. I shut Hayden's door as I walk by, so I won't be interrupted by Mr. Alien Hunter.

"Hi, Mrs. Parks," I say as I walk into the kitchen. I sit at the kitchen table, and Mom sits across from me.

"Please, Isabel, call me Candace. Mrs. Parks makes me feel old."

"Okay. Candace."

"Tell your parents thanks for overnighting the contract along with the photos. I'm going to ask your mom to take you to a professional photographer for some headshots, but for now, these will do. And I have good news."

I look at Mom and mouth the words "Good news!"

Candace continues. "An ad agency in Portland has put out a call for commercial auditions. It's a big client, and I think it'd be an excellent opportunity for you. The audition is the Monday after the Thanksgiving holiday. Are you interested?"

"Absolutely," I say.

"Wonderful. I'm going to drop all of the details about the audition in the mail to you. Please confirm with me once you receive it, all right?"

"Great, thanks, Mrs.—I mean Candace. Oh, wait, do you know what the commercial is for? I mean, what product I'd be selling?"

Mom gives me a thumbs-up. I think it means this is a good question to ask. "Of course," Candace says. "Sorry, I didn't mention that, did I? It's a wonderful company. I believe there's even a store there in your little town of Willow. Beatrice's Brownies?"

Oh no. I swallow hard. It couldn't be, could it? "Uh, what did you say?"

"Beatrice's Brownies. You've been there before, haven't you? Or are you the one person in a million who doesn't like brownies?"

"Yeah, I've been there," I say quietly.

"Wonderful! All right, Sophie, I have to run, but we'll talk again soon."

"Okay, bye."

"Sophie," Mom asks. "What is it? You look disappointed or something. Who's the commercial for?"

I want to cry. Why, out of the thousands of companies in America, does it have to be *that* one? Isabel's mom almost didn't open her cupcake shop because of Beatrice's Brownies. And now it may be one of the reasons It's Raining Cupcakes isn't doing very well.

Before I can say anything to Mom, Isabel appears. "Hey, Sophie, what'd your *agent* have to say? Don't you just love saying that? Your *agent*? Wait, let me guess. They want to give you your own TV show, right? A series?"

I force a laugh. "Yeah, right. She's working on a big deal for me. Huge! I can't even tell you guys, that's how big it is. She wants me to keep it to myself for now. Besides, I might jinx myself, you know?" I get up and pull on Isabel's arm. "Come on. Let's go study."

"But that's so silly," Isabel jokes. "You're going to be famous! You don't really need an education, do you?"

Oh, I need an education, all right. I need an education on how to choose between the opportunity of a lifetime and ruining my best friend's life.

Chapter 9

chocolate
mole sauce

TRY A HINT OF CHOCOLATE ON

YOUR NEXT ENCHILADA

Mom makes my favorite meal for dinner
to celebrate the audition. The *Wicked* music plays
softly in the background, "for ambiance," Mom
says. She's trying to make it really special. All the
music seems to be doing though is reminding me

how much I want to be an actress, when I really want to forget that right now.

I haven't told her yet which company the audition is with. I said I'd wait and tell everyone at dinner. So now as we sit at the table in chicken enchilada heaven, I decide to break the horrible news. I can only hope my parents will forbid me from doing something that terrible to my best friend. Then all I have to do is call Candace back, cancel the audition, and sit back and wait for something else to come along. Please, oh please, let something else come along.

"Delicious, as always," my dad says, pausing after intense shoveling from plate to mouth to take a drink of water.

"Yeah, Mom," I say. "It's really good."

"Soph, tell Dad and Hayden your good news."

My dad turns and gives me the pirate look. I know, that sounds strange, but it's, like, this grin with one eye practically shut and he just looks like a pirate to me. Or he did when I was five, and the idea stuck. He's got the wavy brown hair, the beard, and the tanned, rugged face. My dad is an electrician, so he's nothing like some of my friends' dads who wear a suit to work everyday. Maybe if he was, I wouldn't be able to spot the hidden pirate in him.

I swallow the bite in my mouth, then take a sip of milk. "Well, I got a call today for a commercial audition."

Hayden does a fist pump. "You *are* going to be famous. I knew it!"

"Sophie, that's amazing," Dad says. He takes his napkin and wipes all around his beard and mustache. "So, what's the commercial for? An interesting product, I hope."

"Yeah, not bran cereal or something yucky like that," Hayden says.

"Oh, it's interesting all right," I say. I take a deep breath. "It's Beatrice's Brownies."

For a second, everyone's quiet. Then Mom blinks a couple of times and says, "Sophie, that's wonderful. That's right up your alley—you love desserts."

I set my fork down. "Mom, it's not wonderful. It's terrible."

"Why?" Dad asks. "I think it sounds fantastic."

Who are these people and what have they done with my family?

"Won't that make Isabel mad?" Hayden asks.

"Yes," I say, nodding. "Yes, Hayden, thank you. It's going to make Isabel very mad. Which is exactly why I can't do it."

Dad scoots his chair away from the table and leans back. "Sophie, this is about you and your dreams, not Isabel. She's a good friend. I think she'll understand."

I look back and forth between Mom and Dad. Mom. Then Dad. "No! You guys need to tell me I can't do it!"

Mom laughs. "Sophie, why would we do that? Don't you want to do it?"

"That's not the point. The point is that I—"

And then I stop. Because suddenly, I'm not sure what the point of arguing with them is exactly.

"Look, honey," Dad says, "if you want to do the commercial, do the commercial. It's not like you're doing it to spite your best friend. You're doing it because it's a good opportunity. And no one would want to deny their best friend a good opportunity. If it was the other way around, I'm sure you'd encourage her to go for it. Right?"

I stand up. "I don't know. I guess I thought you guys would see it the way I see it."

Mom stands up and gives me a quick hug. "Sweetheart, I see where you're coming from. But this is the kind of thing that could lead to bigger things—things that could help make your dream come true. At the very least, go to the audition and see what it's like."

"I agree," Dad says. "If nothing else, it's good practice for the next time."

"Sophie," Hayden says, "maybe they'd let you hold a cupcake in one hand and a brownie in the other."

If only it were that easy.

"Do you want any dessert?" Mom asks.

"I do!" Hayden says.

"No, thanks," I tell her. "Dessert is the last thing I want right now."

I go to my room.

Dream #4—
I dream of the ability
to do the right thing,
even when it's hard.

❄ ❄ ❄

The next day, I do my best to avoid Isabel. I hang out in the library before school and go straight to science first period without going to the locker first.

Dennis catches me in the hallway outside of the classroom. "They're called feet," he tells me. "Not talons. At least on regular birds. You were wrong."

"Whatever," I mumble.

"Hey, I apologized to Isabel like I promised. I really am sorry. I didn't mean to upset her. Or you. So, we're good now, right?"

I look over at him. He seems to mean it.

"Anyway," he continues, pushing his glasses up with his finger, "I thought you might want to know birds do have feet. Not that I wanted to prove you wrong or anything. I was just, you know, curious."

"It's fine. I'm probably wrong about a lot of things."

And as soon as the words are out, I stop in my tracks.

"What?" he asks. "What is it?"

I shake my head. "Nothing." I look at Dennis.

"Okay, have you ever thought you were absolutely, positively right about something? But then everyone else tells you maybe you aren't right after all, and you start to second-guess yourself, even though you *know* you're right?"

He gives me a blank stare. "No. Not really. Hey, do you think birds have ears?"

I laugh. I can't help it. It's so ridiculous, and I can't believe I'm spilling my guts, in a roundabout sort of way, to Dennis Holt.

"I have no idea," I tell him.

"Maybe we can research it," he says. "We're still doing homework at my house later, right?"

Oh no. With all of the stuff going on about the audition, I totally forgot. Well, at least if I see Isabel after school, I have a reason to rush off. "Yeah. I rode my bike. You don't live very far from here, right?"

"You remember! My birthday party in first grade was pretty awesome, huh?"

I shake my head. "You had a Power Rangers cake, Dennis. That was not awesome. At least, not to all the girls you invited."

He laughs. "Power Rangers, activate!"

The warning bell rings, so we start walking toward our classroom.

"I'll meet you at the bike rack after school," he says.

"Okay. And hey, Dennis?"

"Yeah?"

"You're not going to try and show me the dead bird's foot at your house, are you?"

"Don't worry. I know it's not everyone's thing. But, Sophie, I'm curious. What is your thing?"

And before I have time to think twice, the word comes out. "Acting." I let out a big sigh, because the truth really does sort of hurt. "My thing, right now, is acting."

"Cool," he says. "I bet you're good at it."

And all I can think is, *We'll see, Dennis. We'll see.*

Chapter 10

milk and chocolate-chip cookies

THEY MAKE HOMEWORK BEARABLE

When we walk into Dennis's house, it smells delicious, like we've just walked into a bakery.

"Hello!" a woman's voice calls out. "Dennis, I'm in the kitchen."

"Yeah, Mom, I can tell. Whatever you're making, it smells really good!"

We're standing in the living room, where there are more knickknacks than I've ever seen in one place. She has hutches, bookshelves, and end tables full of music boxes, tea cups, ceramic and glass figurines, and all kinds of other stuff. It's totally different from our house. My mom can't stand having knickknacks or useless stuff just sitting around.

Dennis must sense my amazement. "Something else, huh? My mom calls them her treasures." He drops his voice to a whisper. "That's not what I would call them."

"Where does she get it all?" I ask.

"The thrift store. Man, she loves that place. There's nothing here that cost more than three ninety-nine. Except maybe the sofa. I think she got that for nineteen ninety-nine."

I look at the old sofa with pink-and-green stripes. She paid $19.99 for that? I think she got robbed. "So, I guess you could call her a treasure hunter?"

He smiles. "Something like that." He picks up a glass penguin as we walk by one of the end tables.

"Help!" he says in a high, squeaky voice. "Get me back to the South Pole. I'm dying here."

"Watch your feet, penguin," I say. "They're not safe around Dennis."

"Wait a second," he says. "Do penguin have feet?"

I give him a shove. "Stop it."

I follow him into the kitchen where his mom is standing at the counter with a spatula, taking cookies off a baking sheet and putting them on a cooling rack. She's a short woman, and has her brown hair up in a bun. She's wearing a bright red-and-yellow apron and a big smile.

"I hope you like chocolate, Sophie."

"I love it," I say.

"Good. This chocolate-chip cookie recipe is our favorite. It's very unique in that the oatmeal is blended before you add it in. Dennis, you want to pour some milk for you two?"

She puts the spatula down and comes over to me, carrying a plate of cookies. "Don't know if you remember me. I'm Margie."

"I remember. We were just talking about his first-grade birthday party."

"Let's see, was that Power Rangers or Spiderman?"

"Power Rangers," Dennis and I say at the same time. Then he says, "I think I still have some action figures around here somewhere, Sophie. You want to play with them when we're done? You could be the pink one."

I raise my eyebrows at him. "I hope you're joking."

Margie hands me the plate of cookies, then turns to Dennis. "You two can use the kitchen table for your homework. I have laundry to put away. Just holler if you need anything, okay?"

"Thanks, Mom."

"Thanks," I echo.

She leaves and we go to the kitchen table. We set the cookies and milk down and drop our backpacks onto the floor. "Let's eat first," Dennis says. "I'm starving."

I take a bite of a cookie. "These are really good."

"Whenever I have someone come over, which isn't very often, Mom makes them. I think it's because they were Michael's favorite."

"Michael O'Reilly?" I ask.

"Yeah. You know we used to be best friends in elementary school, right?"

"You're not friends anymore?" I ask as I reach for my glass of milk.

"Nah. I don't know if you can tell, but I'm not really the athletic type. I tried. I played soccer and baseball through fifth grade. But I just wasn't good enough. It stops being fun when you feel horrible about how you play all the time."

"What does that have to do with being Michael's friend, though?"

He shrugs. "Sports are his life. Things changed. I don't know. Now he hangs out with his friends he sees all the time at games and practices."

He sounds kind of sad. I don't know what to say. He keeps talking. "You and Isabel, you've been friends for a long time, right?"

"Yeah."

He reaches for another cookie. "That's cool. Does she want to be an actress too?"

"No. Flight attendant. Travel the world and all that stuff."

"It's weird," he says. "I always thought girls were the ones who had problems with friends. And here I am, the one with the problems."

I think of the audition and Isabel. I swallow hard. I don't want to go there. "Well, Dennis, maybe if you wouldn't do odd things, like ask people if they want to see a dead bird's foot, you'd have more friends."

His face turns red. "Can I tell you something?"

"Sure."

"I never really had a dead bird's foot."

"You didn't? Then why'd you say you did? Just to freak me out?"

He shrugs. "I don't know. Sometimes I don't know what to say. There was a dead bird on my porch that morning. It just popped into my brain and before I knew it, I was talking crazy-bird-feet talk."

"Well, I guess sometimes I don't know what to say either." I think of the conversation I need to have with Isabel someday about the audition. It makes my stomach hurt just thinking about it. I'm not sure I'll ever figure out what to say for that conversation.

Dennis stands up and takes the empty plate and glasses to the counter. "We should come up with a saying we automatically go to when we're having a hard time. So we don't say something stupid. Like my dad, he always talks about the weather. And he's always so excited about it. Doesn't matter what it is; it can be forty-five degrees and raining, like it is almost every single day in Oregon, and he'll still want to talk about the weather."

"My dad loves the weather too. The Weather Channel is his favorite channel. What is up with that? Look outside, Dad. There's the weather."

Dennis laughs. "I know, it's the truth."

It's quiet for a minute. "We should get to work," I say.

"What's your all-time favorite movie?" he asks.

"I think I'd have to go with *The Wizard of Oz*. Why?"

"No, see, that should be our question. When we don't know what to say. Movies are a safe topic."

"What's wrong with the standard 'How's it going?'"

"Because all you get is an 'Okay' or 'Fine,' and then what? You're right back where you started. It's a useless question. Like anyone is going to tell you how it's really going. 'Hey, thanks for asking. Man, things are terrible. My grandma's sick, my dog just died, and I didn't have any clean underwear this morning.'"

I'm trying hard not to laugh. He's right. It's true. "Come on. Let's get our write-up done. Tell me what you've got for the hypothesis."

He points his pencil at me. "Aren't you going to ask me what my favorite movie is?"

I look at him and smile. "Power Rangers, right?"

He laughs and shakes his head. "You are never going to let me live that down, are you?"

"Nope. Never."

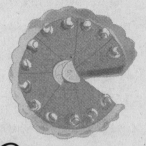

Chapter 11

chocolate pudding

IT CAN SOOTHE EVEN

THE MOST FRAZZLED NERVES

It's Friday, and the audition is still over a week away. As I peek around the corner, waiting for Isabel to leave her locker, I realize I'm being ridiculous. There is no way I can hide from her for an entire week. I'm going to have to tell her. I decide I'll do it at lunch. When she asks me about it, I'll just tell her. Straight out, fast as I can, and it'll be over with. Like ripping off a Band-Aid. She'll be mad. Furious, probably. But I'm going to have to live with it.

I take a deep breath and walk over to our locker.

"There you are," Isabel says. "How's it going?"

I think of Dennis. How he hates that question. And here I am, proof that the question really is useless. Because I can't tell her I'm a mess over this audition thing. Not right now. So I say what I usually say. "Okay. How about you?"

"Dreading that social studies test today. Did you study some more last night?"

"A little bit. I was busy with a science project, though."

She grabs the locker door as I'm about to close it, then takes her lip gloss out of her pocket. She looks in the little mirror we have stuck on the door and moves the wand over her lips.

She turns and smiles. "That's better. Yeah, so I saw you with Dennis Holt yesterday after school. You guys working on something together?"

"Yeah. We have a write-up due today. We got it done yesterday. It actually turned out really good."

"He's kind of different, isn't he?"

"I don't know. I think he's all right. Once you get to know him."

The warning bell rings. "Let's have lunch together, okay?" she says. "I missed you yesterday."

I try to smile. "Yeah, sure. See ya later."

In science, Mr. Leonard gives us a few minutes at the beginning of class to check over our write-ups. We split up into pairs again, and I meet Dennis at his desk this time.

"You want to look it over again?" he asks.

"Not really. But I will."

I take it from him and start reading. "So, big plans for the weekend?" he asks.

"I think I'm watching *Star Wars* with my brother tonight. His first time."

"That is awesome. I still remember the first time I saw the movie. Most amazing thing that's ever happened to me."

I give him a funny look. "You need to get a life, Dennis."

He nods. "I know! You want to help me?"

I look around, wondering if anyone heard him say that to me. "I don't think I can. I have my own problems. Now be quiet so I can read this thing."

He scribbles in his notebook as I finish looking it over. I find one spelling error and make the correction.

"I think it's ready," I tell him. "We did a good job."

"I need a new hobby," he says, still scribbling. "Something fun. I haven't tried anything new since I gave up sports."

"Music?" I ask him.

He shakes his head.

"Martial arts?"

He shakes his head again. "I was thinking something like photography."

"That'd be good."

"I just need a camera."

I sit back in my chair. "Yeah, I'd say that's pretty important if you want to take up photography. Maybe for Christmas?"

He nods. "Yeah. I'll put it on my list."

"Along with your Power Rangers pajamas?"

He gives me an evil grin. "I'm gonna get you one of these days, Sophie. Just you wait."

❋ ❋ ❋

At lunch, Isabel and I find a spot at a table in the corner of the cafeteria. I haven't even sat down and I'm already sweating. My stomach hurts so bad, I didn't take anything from the hot food line. I just grabbed a carton of milk and a bowl of chocolate pudding.

As I sit down, I notice Dennis at a table off to the side, by himself. Does he always sit by himself? I've never noticed before.

"Sophie, what are you doing?" Isabel asks. "You need more than that to eat. You're not on some crazy diet for your audition, are you?"

"No. Just not hungry."

She opens her milk carton, and then pours some dressing on her salad. "Okay, so tell me. Tell me all about the audition. I'm not letting you keep it to yourself one minute longer. I don't care if your agent said you aren't supposed to tell anyone, I am your best friend, and I have to know."

I look over at Dennis. He's reading a book. A book. At lunch! Who does that? The boys down the table from him laugh at someone's joke. Somebody throws a carrot stick across the table. He should be sitting there, having fun. Not alone. What would I do if I didn't have anyone to sit with? If all of a sudden Isabel didn't want to be my friend anymore? Would I be brave enough to go up to a table of girls I don't know very well and ask if I could sit with them? What would I do?

"Sophie?" Isabel says, shaking my arm. "Are you okay? You don't look so good."

I'm breathing fast. I can feel my heart racing. "Um, I don't know."

All I know is I don't want to eat alone. I can't lose Isabel. I just can't.

"The audition is for this new bran cereal," I blurt out. "They want to try to sell it to kids, so they're looking for kids to cast in the commercials. Isn't that the craziest thing you've ever heard? I have to try to get kids to want to eat bran cereal."

She laughs. "Seriously? Bran cereal? Yuck. But if anyone can do it, you can!"

My breathing slows down. I take a bite of my pudding. It tastes good. I take another bite. My stomach feels better. I keep eating.

"So when's the audition?" she asks.

"Monday after Thanksgiving weekend."

"Oh! That's a teacher workday so you won't have to miss school. Too bad, huh?"

I smile and keep eating. I want to dive into this pudding and live there. It reminds me of being little, when a bowl of chocolate pudding made everything better.

Isabel changes the subject then, and starts telling me a funny story about her neighbor, Lana, who's an artist. I'm only half-listening, though, as I watch Dennis get up from the table and leave the cafeteria. Alone.

Chapter 12

candy bars

SO MANY KINDS,

AND EVERYONE HAS A FAVORITE

Dad went all-out on snacks for the big movie night. There's popcorn, lemonade, and various candy bars all laid out on the kitchen counter. Hayden barely eats any of his dinner, he's so excited.

"Couple more bites, Hayden," Mom says. "Or no candy for you."

"Are the spaceships real, Dad?" Hayden asks, before he takes a bite of his hamburger.

"Dude, what do you mean?" I ask. "It's a movie. *Nothing* is real."

"But—"

"Hayden, don't talk with your mouth full," Mom says.

He finishes chewing and swallows. "I mean, did they make spaceships and let the guys fly in them?"

"Let's wait and see what you think, okay?" Dad says. "I don't want to ruin anything for you."

Hayden takes another bite and then jumps up, walks his plate over to the counter, and starts ordering us. "Hurry up, hurry up, hurry up!"

I help Mom clear the table while Dad takes Hayden into the other room.

"I think you should have given him the movies for Christmas, Mom. How are you ever going to top this?"

She takes a sponge to the kitchen table. "Honey, have you been in the toy aisle recently? Something tells me many *Star Wars* products are in our future.

I'm pretty sure this is only the beginning."

"Geez, don't sound so depressed. It could be worse."
I start to throw out a joke about Power Rangers, but
she probably wouldn't get it.

The phone rings, and I answer it.

"Hey, Sophie, it's Lily."

"Hey. How are you?"

"Really good. I wanted to see if we could get
together tomorrow. Maybe go for cupcakes when the
shop is actually open?"

"Uh, sure, we could do that," I say. "You want to
come over here and we can walk again? We can hang
out here for a while too, if you want."

"Yeah, that sounds good. What time should I have
my mom drop me off?"

"How about after lunch, like one o'clock?"

"Sounds good. See you then, Soph."

"Bye."

"Was that Isabel?" Mom asks.

"No, actually, it was Lily. She's coming over
tomorrow."

"Mom! Sophie!" Hayden yells from the other
room. "Come on, it's starting!"

"I'm glad she called," Mom says. "It'll be fun to see her again."

"Come on," I say. "The galaxy far, far away is waiting for us."

"Yes, it is."

Hayden hardly says a word the first half of the movie. Not only that, he hardly moves. He takes a bite of a candy bar when Dad hands him one, and then puts it in his lap, totally forgotten. Normally the kid would have had that thing eaten in ten seconds flat. It's like he's hypnotized. Or maybe he's under the control of the Force.

During one of the battles, my mind drifts to Isabel and how I totally failed as a friend. Her = good. Me = evil. I should wear a Darth Vader costume to school next week for punishment. I'm sure Dennis would love that.

Or maybe I should cancel the audition.

I should.

I really should.

"Mom, will you help me get the popcorn and drinks?" I ask.

I go to the fridge and grab the lemonade. Mom

plugs the air popper in and pours in the kernels. It's noisy. I wait until it's done, and then I tell her about my decision.

"I've decided I don't want to go to the audition," I tell her.

She turns from the stove, where she's melting butter, and looks at me. "What? Why?"

"I can't tell Isabel, Mom. I just can't. I tried today, and I failed. It was horrible."

"Oh, honey. I'm sorry this is stressing you out." She drizzles the melted butter over the big bowl of popcorn. "Why don't you think on it over the weekend. Maybe talk to Lily about it tomorrow, see what she thinks."

"I don't know—"

"We can't call Candace until Monday anyway," she says. "So wait. Sleep on it some more. I really think it's an incredible opportunity, and I'd hate to see you regret it someday."

She hands me the popcorn. "Did you salt it?" I ask.

"Nope. That's your job. I always do too much or too little."

I walk over to the table, grab the salt shaker, and give it four good shakes. Mom reaches in, takes a handful, and pops some into her mouth.

"Perfect."

Well, at least I can do one thing right.

Chapter 13

rocky road
cupcakes

THEY PROVE A LESS-THAN-SMOOTH
ROAD ISN'T ALWAYS A BAD THING

*T*he next morning, it is all *Star Wars* all the time, because Hayden won't stop talking about it and can't wait to watch the next one. Mom finally gives in, so I spend most of the morning in my room, watching musicals. I doodle in my dream notebook while I do.

Dream #5—
I dream of wearing beautiful
shoes in a movie one day.
I wonder if Judy Garland
felt like the luckiest girl in the world
wearing those ruby slippers.

At noon, I make a peanut butter and jelly sandwich and slice up an apple before I jump in the shower. Lily arrives right on time.

"Lily, which Jedi is your favorite?" Hayden asks.

"Hayden. Please stop," I tell him. "Not everyone wants to talk space stuff, okay?"

"I like the short green guy," Lily says. She pretends to be thinking. "What is his name?"

"Yoda!" Hayden yells.

"You ready to go?" I ask her. I look out the front window. "Is it very cold?"

"Yeah, it is."

"Okay, let me get my heavy coat."

"Hey, Lily, did you know Sophie's going to be an actress someday?" I hear Hayden saying. "Maybe someone will see her on TV and put her in a movie. Maybe it'll be a movie with spaceships!"

I walk back out and Lily looks very confused. Yes, my annoying brother will do that to a person. "I'll explain on the way."

Mom comes and says hi to Lily. "We're going to get a cupcake," I tell her.

"Okay, have fun, girls. Call if you decide you want a ride home."

We step outside and it really feels like winter, with the chilly air and the trees almost bare. I zip up my coat.

"Sophie, what did he mean, 'see you on TV'?"

We walk down the front pathway to the sidewalk. I take a deep breath and tell her all about my new agent and the audition.

"That is so exciting!" she says.

"I guess."

She laughs. "You guess? Come on. This could change your whole life!"

"If I tell you the audition is with Beatrice's Brownies, does that change how you feel about it?"

She stops walking, grabs my arm. "No way."

"Yes. Way."

Her face looks almost as pained as my insides have felt these past few days. We continue walking. "What are you going to do?"

"I think I'm going to call my agent on Monday and cancel. I tried to tell Isabel about it last week, but I couldn't do it."

We turn the corner and a blast of cold air comes at us. We walk faster. "What do your parents think?"

"It's crazy. They both think I should do it. It's a great opportunity, Isabel would understand, blah, blah, blah. But what if my commercial was the one to bring their cupcake business down? I would have to live with that for the rest of my life. And maybe without Isabel, which would be even worse."

She looks at me as she holds her coat collar up around her face, trying to keep the cold air away. "But it wouldn't be *your* commercial. You'd be *in* the commercial, but it's Beatrice's commercial. And besides, you might not even get the part. If I were you, I'd go, and think of it as practice for the next audition. I mean, no offense, but I bet not many people get the job from the first audition anyway. It's really competitive!"

"So you'd go to the audition and not tell Isabel who it's with? Just keep it to yourself?"

She shrugs. "Yeah. I mean, a practice audition is not a bad thing. It's not going to hurt anyone."

Hearing her say this fills me with relief. "The only thing is that Isabel knows about the audition. She was at my house when I got the call. I made up excuses as long as I could, but finally on Friday, she said I had to tell her about it. So I lied. I told her it was an audition for bran cereal." I hit my head with my hand. "I can't believe I said that. I wish I could have just told her."

Lily doesn't say anything else. We just walk, our hands tucked into our coat pockets, and our faces buried in our coats as much as possible.

When we reach the cupcake shop, Lily turns to me before opening the door. "Do the audition and then tell her. My mom always says, one thing at a time. That's what you need to do. Right now, focus on the audition and get that over with. When it's all over, you can come clean to Isabel. I mean, what are the chances that the first audition you get called for is their cupcake shop's biggest competitor? It's so crazy it's almost funny. I bet you guys will laugh about it."

She's made me feel so much better. I'm not an evil person. I'm not! No Darth Vader costume for me after all. "Thanks, Lily." I open the door, and the little bell above it rings. "Come on, let's go eat."

We step in, and the first thing I notice is how empty the place is. We're the only ones here.

Isabel's mom, Caroline, walks up to the counter. "Sophie! What a wonderful surprise!"

"Hi! How are you?"

She waves her hand around. "I'd be better if I had a few more customers. But we're fine. Happy about Isabel's win, of course."

I nod and catch Lily out of the corner of my eye, scanning the case of cupcakes. "Oh, this is my friend Lily. We went to theater camp together."

Caroline smiles at Lily. "Nice to meet you. Is this your first time at our shop?"

"Yes. And they all look so good. It's going to be hard to decide."

She lists the flavors, pointing to each one in the case as she does, but I don't hear anything past the first one: Rocky Road. I know instantly, as soon as she says it, that's the one I want.

While Lily tries to decide which flavor she wants, Caroline looks back at me. "Would you like me to call Isabel? See if she wants to come down and sit with you girls?"

For some reason, the thought of seeing Isabel in this empty cupcake shop makes me squirm a little bit. "Um, I think we're actually going to get the cupcakes to go. Right, Lily?"

She gives me a strange look, because that wasn't really the plan. "Oh yeah, right."

"We have stuff to do at home," I explain. "But tell her I said hi, okay?"

She smiles. "Sure will." She turns to Lily. "Okay, what'd you decide?"

"I'm going to try the Raspberry Dazzle. It sounds delicious."

Caroline grabs a pair of black tongs and a little box and reaches into the case to get one of the raspberry cupcakes. I wonder what they do with the ones they don't sell. Do they throw all of them away? It makes my chest ache just thinking about all of those beautiful cupcakes going to waste.

"We'll need a bigger box," I tell Caroline as I reach into my coat to get my wallet. "I want to take home one of each kind."

There goes all of my allowance, which I was going to use for Christmas shopping the day after Thanksgiving. Hopefully I can convince my mom to pay me back. I mean, I couldn't go home with only two cupcakes, could I? That'd be totally rude. And how am I supposed to know what flavor they might like?

One of each is the only solution.

And I sure am good at talking myself into things.

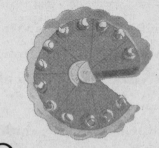

Chapter 14

old-fashioned chocolate cream pie

NOTHING BEATS IT

The week of Thanksgiving all the kids are ready for a break from school, while the teachers make it their mission to cram five days of learning into three. By Wednesday, I'm ready to eat turkey and mashed potatoes until I can't move, lie around, and do nothing all weekend.

First period, I'm counting the hours until the final bell rings.

"Okay, class," Mr. Leonard says as the bell rings, "I'm going to pass your gum experiment papers back to you now. Please pair up with your partner, so you can see my comments and discuss what you might do differently next time. I'd also like everyone to write a paragraph or two about what you liked and didn't like about this particular experiment. It's due at the end of class, please."

Dennis comes over and sits down.

"Think we got an A?" he asks.

"I hope so. Otherwise, you're in trouble."

He laughs. "Me? Why is it my fault? Wait, if we get an A, is that my fault too?"

"Absolutely not."

"You are funny, Sophie Wright. I wish you were a boy."

I start to ask why, but then I think of him eating alone.

"Do you always eat by yourself at lunch?" I ask.

He looks down. Oh no. I've embarrassed him. I

instantly feel bad and wish I could take it back.

"Yeah. Most of the time."

"Ever since you've been in middle school?"

He looks back at me. "No. See, last year me and Hikaru were friends. Did you know him? He was cool. But over the summer, his family moved."

Now I get it. First he lost Michael. Then he lost Hikaru. He's lost two good friends the past two years. That's tough.

Mr. Leonard steps up to our desk. "Nice work, Sophie and Dennis. You did do your share, correct, Mr. Holt?"

I jump in before Dennis has a chance to talk. "We both did the work. He did as much as I did. Maybe even more."

"I'm glad to hear it."

He puts the paper on our desk. We got an A minus.

"I should be partners with you more often," Dennis says. "I've never gotten anything higher than a B in this class."

I grab the paper and start flipping through it, reading Mr. Leonard's comments.

"Oh, before I forget," Dennis says, "I brought you something."

I look up. He reaches into his binder and pulls out a movie. "I thought you might want to watch this. It's really good. You can watch it for research, you know? Since you want to be an actress."

I take the movie and read the title on the case: *Bridge to Terabithia*.

"Isn't there a book with that title?" I ask.

"Yeah. I'm reading it right now. My mom bought the movie the other day, because it was on the five-dollar rack. She asked me if I wanted to watch it with her, so I did, and while we were watching it I thought, *I bet Sophie would like this movie*."

I smile. "Well, it's better than a bird's foot, that's for sure. Thanks, Dennis. I'm curious to see if I'll like it as much as you think I'll like it."

"You will," he says confidently. "You'll like Jess and Leslie, I know you will."

"Okay, kids," Mr. Leonard says. "Get to work on those paragraphs. Or I'm calling your parents and telling them no pumpkin pie or chocolate cream for you. Only mincemeat!"

The whole crowd groans. Dennis leans in and whispers, "I like mincemeat."

I shake my head. Oh, Dennis.

I sneak my dream notebook out of my binder and quickly write down another dream.

Dream #6—
I dream that Dennis will make
new friends. Besides me.
Yes, this is me actually admitting
I'm Dennis Holt's friend.

I think of Dennis as I stare at the table of pies at my aunt Georgina's house. There's the traditional pumpkin and mincemeat, both of which my grandma loves. I stare at the mincemeat and wonder if Dennis was joking about liking it. It looks pretty disgusting. Do I dare try it? No. Maybe next year. Or maybe never. Mom brought an apple pie, because that's Dad's favorite. And then for the kids, there's chocolate cream and banana cream.

Some of the adults are going back for seconds on the turkey and side dishes. But not the kids. We're ready for dessert. There are seven of us, five boys and two girls. All of the boys are in front of me, getting their pieces of pie so they can finish eating and get the annual football game started in the backyard. My uncle Pete, who's athletic and played football in college, is standing in front of me, trying to keep the boys from rushing the pies and tackling them to the ground.

"Uncle Pete, how long do we have to let our food digest before we can start the game?" Hayden asks him.

"Probably an hour." He turns to me. "You want to join us this year, Sophie?"

Before I can answer, Hayden jumps in. "She's too much of a girl. A girl who's gonna be in a commercial and wants to make sure she doesn't mess up her hair." He puts one hand on his hip and the other hand next to his head where he pretends to fluff up his buzz cut. I give him a nice, girlie shove.

"A commercial?" Pete asks. "Really?"

"Uh, well, no." I glare at Hayden. "I just have an audition on Monday. I'm sure there will be a ton of people there and I won't get it."

"Oh, come on!" he says. "Think positively. You've got to believe it to achieve it!"

Yeah, that's Uncle Pete for you. He's the training manager at a car dealership in town and he's always telling the salesmen that the key to selling cars is to visualize the sales and all this other hocus-pocus stuff.

"Well, I did that for the baking contest and it didn't exactly work out too well for me," I say. "Besides, I'm not sure I want to do commercials anyway. I mean, maybe I should wait. Hold out for a spot on a television show, you know?"

"Don't ever pass up an opportunity, Sophie," he says as he helps Hayden dish up a big piece of chocolate cream pie and put it on his plate. "You never know when another one will come along again. Because many times, they never do. Trust me. If you have a good opportunity, you have to go for it. Or, I promise, you'll regret it later."

Geez, has he been hiding in our closets, listening to my mom?

Oh yeah, that's right. They're brother and sister. Same gene pool and all of that. No wonder.

Chapter 15

monster cookies
THEY'RE NOT SCARY, ONLY DELICIOUS

In the car on the way home, Hayden is talking and talking and *talking* about how much fun the football game was. Dad, Uncle Pete, and Uncle Ben played too, and Hayden ended up on Dad's team. Dad let him play quarterback for part of the game. Hayden has never been offered that position before this year. And one of his passes led to a touchdown, which Hayden cannot shut up about.

I turn and look out the window. We're at a stoplight next to the library, which is completely dark, since it's a holiday. I think of Isabel and all the time she spends at the library, looking at books and dreaming of the places she wants to travel.

Isabel understands dreams. I know that. So why am I having such a hard time telling her? Why can't I tell her about this fantastic opportunity that's been handed to me like a pretty platter of cupcakes—even though it may be for her main competitor?

All my life, I've gone after what I've wanted. That's what I do. When I wanted a dog, I looked and looked until I found one that wouldn't make my mom itch and sneeze. If I hadn't done that, where would we be now? Daisy is what inspired Mom to start her business. The Pampered Pooch wouldn't exist, and our lives would be totally different now. All because I wanted something and did my best to make it happen.

But this time, something is holding me back.

Hayden taps my arm. I turn and look at him. He's holding a wishbone. "Make a wish."

"Where'd you get that?" I ask him.

"The chocolate cream pie," he says, his voice full

of sarcasm. "Where do you think I got it? I stole it from the turkey. So go on. Make a wish."

I close my eyes. I start to wish for myself, but it's all so messy, I don't even know where to start. So I wish for the boy who's been on my mind since yesterday. His life is a little less complicated than mine at the moment. *I wish Dennis would make a new friend.*

"When I say three," Hayden says, "start pulling. One, two, three."

When we start pulling, the bone breaks in my favor.

"No fair," Hayden says. "I want a do-over."

"Don't be a sore loser. Besides, you don't need anything anyway, Little Brother Man. You got *Star Wars*, you got a touchdown, what else do you need?"

"What I need is my very own spaceship."

"Well, you know what Uncle Pete says: You've got to believe it to achieve it."

"What's that mean, Sophie?"

I think for a minute. "I'm pretty sure it means no one can really give you what you want except yourself."

❋ ❋ ❋

I can't sleep. We came home and played Monopoly together. Dad has no mercy when we play that game. He won again, just like the last twenty-six times we've played. After that, I went to bed and read for a while. When I closed the book, I felt tired. And I wanted to get a good night's sleep, because Mom and I are going shopping tomorrow. I love shopping on the day after Thanksgiving—it's one of my favorite days of the year.

But every time I close my eyes, thoughts of cupcakes and brownies swirl around in my brain. I want to stop thinking about it! How come my brain doesn't have an on/off switch?

At midnight, I get up to see if a glass of milk will do the trick. And a cookie. We didn't eat anything after Thanksgiving dinner because everyone was so stuffed, but now, I'm kind of hungry.

I reach into the cookie jar and pull out one of Mom's homemade monster cookies, Hayden's favorite. They're made with peanut butter, oatmeal, chocolate chips, and M&M's. Mmmm, so good. As I'm pouring myself a glass of milk, I hear someone behind me.

"Can't sleep?" Dad asks.

I turn and look at him. "No, I'm sleepwalking. I'm dreaming about eating a cookie with milk. And about some guy who looks like a pirate standing in the kitchen talking to me, wearing an old green robe that looks like it's been around since 1970."

"Ah, okay," he says. "I thought you might be worried about Monday."

I take a bite of my cookie. "I don't know what you're talking about. What's to worry about?"

He takes a seat on the stool next to the counter. "Have you told her yet?"

"No."

"When are you going to do that?"

I grab my glass of milk and take a seat next to him. "I don't know. Probably next week sometime. Hopefully."

He picks up the glass of milk and takes a drink. "It'll be okay. You'll see."

My eyes drift from his face to the green robe he's wearing. There are stains on the shoulders. "What are those?" I ask him, pointing.

He follows my finger. "Those are the places where you and your brother spit up on me."

"Gross! Dad, get yourself a new robe, would ya?"

He pulls me in and kisses my forehead. "No way. It's one of the few reminders I have of when you were cute and cuddly. You'd cry and your mom would nudge me to say that it was my turn. So I'd get up, go to your crib, bring you down here, and give you a bottle. Then I'd rock you, burp you, you'd spit up on me, and then you'd fall asleep."

I give him a funny look. "They do make these things called burp rags, you know."

"I know, but sometimes, I'd forget to have one with me or you'd miss or—"

"Okay, okay! I can't believe we're sitting here talking about spit-up."

He rubs my hair and stands up. "I think you're the one who started it."

I look at him, my pirate of a dad in an old, ugly robe, and I can't help it. I love the guy so much. I stand and give him a big hug. We stand there for a long time, rocking back and forth the tiniest little bit.

I yawn and pull away. "Okay. I think I can sleep now. Thanks, Dad."

"Anytime, sweetheart. You want me to burp you too?"

I laugh. "Nah, I'm good, thanks."

Before I go, I look at him for a second. For some reason, I don't tell him very often, but right now, it feels like I should. "I love you, Dad. You know that, right?"

He nods. "It's always nice to hear it, though. I love you too. Sleep tight, Sophie."

When I get back to my room, I pull out my notebook.

Dream #7—
I dream of good sleep, sweet dreams,
and a good deal on a bathrobe
tomorrow morning.

Chapter 16

hazelnut chocolate-chip scones

A TREAT WORTH STOPPING FOR

Mom and I are at the mall by seven a.m. It's about thirty minutes from Willow, in the next city over called Delaney. The parking lot is already full, and we have to park a long ways away. And so goes Black Friday madness. Socks at half-price and five-dollar toasters obviously get people out of bed.

Even though I'm tired from being up so late, my blood is pumping and I'm excited. Mom paid me back for the cupcakes and gave me another twenty, so I have money to get some of my Christmas shopping done. She said we could also look for a new outfit for me to wear to the audition on Monday. After we had our little talk while making the popcorn Friday night, I never brought it up again. And she didn't either. I'm pretty sure that means I'm going.

"I know what I want to get Dad," I tell her as we walk through the big, glass doors. "Can we split up so I can do some shopping for both of you, and meet up later?"

She checks her watch. "Two hours enough time? Or do you need more?"

I shrug. "That should be enough. So meet back here at nine?"

"Yes." She hands me Dad's phone.

I wave it in her face. "You know, if you got me one of these for Christmas—"

"Yeah, yeah, I know," she interrupts me. "Now, let me show you, my number is programmed in, right here." She shows me how to dial her, and after that, we say good-bye and I'm on my own.

I walk toward Macy's, thinking about what I should get my mom. She's really hard to shop for. She's so practical, it's not even funny. Like one year, Dad bought her a gorgeous pair of diamond earrings, and she made him take them back.

"Let's use that money to buy coats for the kids," she'd said. "They need coats a lot more than I need a pair of earrings."

Yeah, diamonds are definitely out. Or cubic zirconia in my case, since that's all I could afford with the pitiful amount of cash I have.

When I get to the store, I go to the men's department first and find a sales rack with bathrobes. I grab a gray one that looks good and isn't too expensive, and take it to the counter. A teenage guy is behind the register. He's got brown hair with long bangs that practically cover his eyes. He brushes them back when I walk up and put the robe in front of him.

"This isn't for you, is it?" he asks. "This is the men's department, you know."

Oh. My. Gosh. He thinks I'm a total idiot. "No.

Really?" I look around. "Wow, I wouldn't have known, what with all of the men's pajamas, boxer shorts, and black socks. Huh." I give him the evil eye. "It's a gift for my dad."

He smiles. "Oh, okay. Great."

Great.

After I pay the guy, I look around, trying to figure out where to go next for a gift for my mom. I could get her a robe too, except I don't think I have enough money left.

I wander aimlessly around the store, passing the perfume section (definitely not practical), the department that sells, um, underwear (practical, yes, but I'm not picking out something like *that* for my mother), and the purses (no way—totally different tastes in that department).

I wander a long time, but nothing is hitting me as right for Mom. I'm about to give in and buy her a pair of gloves, because you can't get more practical than that, when a woman walks by carrying a cup of coffee from a coffee shop. That's when it hits me: Mom loves tea. Adores it, in fact. Except we don't have a tea shop in Willow, so she buys the bags at the grocery store and every once in a while, she'll comment on how she'd give anything to have a good cup of tea.

I head back out to the mall and find a map of stores, crossing my fingers there's a tea shop in the mall, or maybe a place that sells good tea. Nothing. So I run to the coffee shop and ask the cashier if she knows of something close by. She tells me there's a shop at the far end of the mall called Flynn's Irish Shop, and they carry some really good tea.

I'm on my way there when I pass a camera shop, and it makes me stop. I don't know why, but I go inside. There are so many cameras, all shapes and sizes. *What kind would Dennis want?* I wonder. Something small that would fit in his pocket, or a big one that allows you to use different types of lenses? They all are pretty expensive. I bet his mom will shop at the thrift store and try to find him one for $3.99. A picture of a beat-up old camera with a broken lens pops into my brain. She wouldn't do that to him, would she?

If I had enough money, I'd buy him one. But I don't. There's nothing that costs less than a hundred dollars in here.

"Can I help you?" the man from behind the counter asks me.

"No," I say. "Just looking." I start to turn to leave, but then I change my mind. "Actually, I have a friend who wants a camera for Christmas. What's a good kind for someone my age? Something not too, you know, expensive?"

"Yes. Let me show you."

He comes around and takes me down an aisle, and we stop in front of a red camera that's out on display. He walks me through some of the features, and then I ask him to write the name and model number on a piece of paper. When he hands it to me, I slip it into my purse, thank him, and tell myself I can't forget about it.

After that, I go to Flynn's and buy tea from Mom. I don't have enough money left to get Hayden anything. I'll have to wait and buy his gift with my December allowance. I head back to the meeting place and wait for Mom.

She walks up a few minutes later carrying four big bags. "Wow," I say. "You've been busy. Want to show me what you got?"

She winks. "You know I can't do that. Come on. I'm hungry. Let's get a snack, and then we'll shop for the perfect audition outfit."

We go back to the coffee shop where we order some tea and hazelnut chocolate-chip scones. While we eat, Mom pulls out Hayden's list and looks it over.

"Is there anything that doesn't involve space on there?" I ask her.

"Yes," she says. "Number one on his list is a tarantula."

"No," I say. "No, no, no. You can't do it, Mom." She laughs. "Don't worry!"

Just as we're about to get up and leave, someone taps me on the shoulder.

I turn around.

"Hey!" Isabel says. Her grandma Dolores is standing behind her, smiling.

"Hi, Suzanne, hello, Sophie," Dolores says. My mom gets up to greet her.

I stand up and give Isabel a hug. Then I point to her bag. "Let me guess. You just couldn't stay away from the year's biggest sock sale, right?"

She laughs. "Um, not exactly. Takes a lot more than cheap socks to get me out of bed early when there's no school. I bought some Christmas presents for Mom and Dad."

I point to my bags. "Yeah, me too."

"What about your audition on Monday? Are you going to get a new outfit to wear? Something that says, 'I love bran cereal and so will you'?"

I gulp and look at my mom. She and Dolores have stopped talking, and are looking at us.

Oh no.

This is bad. Really bad.

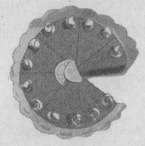

Chapter 17

dark chocolate

RESEARCH SAYS IT'S GOOD
FOR YOUR HEALTH IN SMALL DOSES

I hurry up and answer Isabel before my mom has a chance to say anything. "Yeah, we're on our way right now." I pick up my bags and beg my mom with my eyes not to say a word. "Ready to go, Mom?"

"Ready as I'll ever be, I guess."

"Happy shopping, you two," Dolores says. "Be

careful out there. Those discount-hungry people can get a bit rough."

"Bye!" I call as I rush out into the mall.

I walk fast. Superfast. Like lightning-speed fast.

"Sophie," Mom calls. "Wait up, please."

I slow down, but not very much.

When she reaches me, I don't look at her. "Stop. Sophie, please stop walking."

"Mom, come on, a lot of the door-buster sales end at eleven."

She grabs my arm. "I don't care. Stop, please."

And so I do. When I look at her, I see disappointment all over her face. "You lied to her?"

"I told you, Mom, I couldn't tell her."

"It's one thing to be waiting for the right time to say something. It's another thing to lie!" Her voice is firm. And loud.

I look at the people passing us. They throw pity my way, like candy at a parade.

"Mom, can we not do this right now?" I whisper. "Please? It's embarrassing."

She sighs. "Fine. Let's go home. I think we've done enough shopping for today."

"But what about a new outfit?"

She shakes her head. "I'm not going to reward that behavior, Sophie Wright. We're going home. Give me your dad's cell phone, please, before I forget."

I reach into my pocket, but it's not there. I reach into the other one. It's not there, either. Then I frantically check my purse.

"Sophie?" Mom asks.

I check my pockets a second time. But it's gone. How can it be gone? Wouldn't I have heard it hit the ground if I dropped it?

"Where is the phone?" she asks through gritted teeth.

"I don't know," I whisper.

Mom lets out a disgusted groan. In one minute's time, I've gone from big trouble to seriously BIG trouble.

Mom grabs her bags, walks over to a bench, and plops down. She takes her phone out of her purse and pushes some buttons. She looks at me as she puts the phone to her ear. "You better hope a very kind soul is the one who found it."

She doesn't have any idea.

I stand there and wait, my fate in the hand of some stranger.

"Hello?" Mom says. "Yes, we lost the phone you're holding right now. Are you in the mall?" She listens. "Perfect. We'll be right there. Thank you so much."

She gets up and doesn't say a word. I follow her. We walk through the crowds of people, back toward the end of the mall where the Irish shop is. If I lost it there, she'll want to know what I was doing in that shop. I guess I'd have to tell her, because even a little white lie for the sake of Christmas secrets doesn't seem like a good idea right now.

But instead of the Irish shop, she turns into the camera store.

A short kid wearing a shirt that says PARTLY CLOUDY WITH A CHANCE OF NINJAS is standing at the counter with a petite woman. They're talking to the man who answered my camera questions earlier. I look at the kid hard. He looks familiar.

The salesman smiles and holds out the phone. "So you're the one who dropped it."

"Thank you," I say. "That was almost an epic disaster."

"No problem," he says. Mom steps up and takes the phone from him, and says something I can't hear.

Then the boy says, "Sophie?"

"Yeah."

"I'm Austen. We go to the same school. I have science with your friend, Isabel."

"Hey, I thought you looked familiar. Are you shopping for a camera?"

"Giving my mom some Christmas ideas."

I look at him again, trying to remember something about him. Like who he hangs out with or something like that.

"Wait, are you new at our school?" I ask.

"Yeah. We just moved to Willow last month."

When he says that, the wheels in my head start turning. "Do you know Dennis Holt?" I ask him.

He shakes his head. "The name sounds familiar. He might be in one of my classes, I'm not sure."

"I want to introduce you next week." I look at his shirt. "I think you guys might get along. He likes photography too."

He shrugs. "Okay."

We tell the salesman thanks one more time and then we head home. Mom doesn't say a word to me the whole way.

When I get home, I go to my room and shove Mom and Dad's presents into my closet. Then I grab my dream notebook.

Dream #8—
I dream of a mother
who is not mad at me.

I walk back out to the kitchen and get a square of Mom's favorite dark chocolate, wrap it up in a paper towel, and grab a note card from the little desk in the kitchen. Inside the card I write:

Dear Mom,

I'm sorry about lying to Isabel. I promise I'm going to tell her the truth. I want to get the audition over with so I only have one thing to worry about. Then I'm going to tell her everything. I really hope she isn't mad at me, although now I guess I deserve it if she is.

I know what I did was wrong. I was just so worried about making her mad, especially because their cupcake shop isn't doing very well. I'm really sorry. Please forgive me. You always say, chocolate makes everything better.
Right now, I really hope it does.

Love, Sophie

Mom's in the other room, curled up on the couch, watching a decorating show on television. I drop the card and the chocolate in her lap, and then I go back to my room, where I stay for the rest of the afternoon.

Chapter 18

peanut butter chocolate-chip granola bars

A DELICIOUS, PORTABLE SNACK

I am so glad when Monday finally arrives, I almost kiss the calendar. It'll feel good to get the audition over with so I can get on with my life. Since last night, I've had what my dad calls "haunted-house stomach." It's that feeling you get when you're about to do something both exciting and terrifying. Who knew stepping in front of a television camera would feel just like walking into a haunted house?

I shower, blow dry and curl my hair, and then put on outfit number twenty-one. That is, last night I tried on about twenty-one outfits before I finally decided on this one. It's a black skirt with a light-blue sweater along with my favorite necklace. Grandma gave it to me last year for my birthday. It's a long silver chain with a big, puffy heart hanging from the end of it.

After I'm dressed and have looked in the mirror enough times to make myself sick of me, I go out to the kitchen where oatmeal with blueberries is waiting for me at the kitchen table.

"You look beautiful, Sophie," Mom says. "Are you nervous?"

"Yeah, a little bit."

"Well, try not to worry. You're going to do great."

I eat my oatmeal while she cleans out the dishwasher. When she's finished, she comes and sits down across from me.

"I know this whole thing with Isabel has been

upsetting to you, and I probably didn't help," she says. "But don't think about any of that today. Just do the best you can, and soak up the experience, okay?"

Mom and I already had a long talk about me lying to Isabel. I've promised to tell her this week, and to apologize.

I nod, agreeing to do my best, and I finish my glass of milk. "I'm ready. Can we go?"

She raises her eyebrows before she says, "After you brush your teeth and wipe the milk off the corners of your mouth."

On the way to the bathroom, I run into a sleepy Hayden.

"Break a leg, Sophie," he says. "Why do they say that, anyway? It makes no sense."

"I don't know, Little Brother Man. But thanks. I think."

Soon, we're in the car and on our way to Portland. Mom puts the *Wicked* CD into the CD player and squeezes my leg. "For some inspiration, huh?"

I nod, sit back, close my eyes, and let myself go back to that magical night.

❋ ❋ ❋

It takes about two hours to get to Portland. Mom pulls off the freeway, drives into downtown, and I look up at the big, tall buildings. It's so different from our cozy town of Willow. Mom finds a spot in a parking garage across the street from the building where the audition is being held.

When we get inside the building, a woman at a reception desk greets us. She asks us to sign in on a piece of paper, and then sends us to the fifth floor. Once there, a woman directs us to a long line of kids and their parents. It's noisy. I check out my competition. There are all kinds of kids here—girls and boys, short and tall, average and beautiful. Most of them look to be about my age. A couple look older, but I'm guessing most of them are in middle school, like me.

We wait. And wait. And wait.

When we finally get to the table, Mom pulls the paperwork out of her purse and hands it to the lady sitting on the other side.

She looks at the paperwork, then looks up at me and smiles. "Hi, Sophie. Welcome to the audition. Here is a page of lines. You'll want to work on memorizing a couple of them so you can say them when it's your turn, okay?"

I take the paper from her and nod. She marks some things on one of the pages Mom gave her, then hands me a large piece of card stock with the number 99 written on it. Does that mean ninety-eight people are auditioning before me? I turn around and look at the line that's formed behind me. There's got to be another thirty people there.

It really hits me how competitive this industry is. If there's this many people here for a simple commercial, what's it like when it's an audition for a TV show or a movie? It must be harder to get an audition at that point. I bet the headshots become a lot more important. I wonder if you have to be exactly what they're looking for, or you don't get called in.

The lady sends us to a large room where everyone is standing or sitting around, waiting to have their number called. Mom finds us two seats in the far corner of the room.

I read through the lines. Some of them sound a little cheesy.

Do you ever wake up in the middle of the night, craving a delicious snack? Head to Beatrice's Brownies now and stock up before the snack attack hits!

There's only one thing that beats the homework blues. Come to Beatrice's Brownies for all of your snacktime needs.

We wait through the sixties and the seventies.

I study the lines.

We wait through the eighties and the nineties.

I keep studying.

The boy sitting next to me has been playing cards for the last hour. Guess he feels like he's got the lines down. I think I do too. Wish I had brought a book to read or something. Who knew this would be worse than waiting at a doctor's office? Except here, we're waiting for a different kind of shot—a shot at making our dreams come true.

"You doing okay?" Mom asks as she reaches over and puts her hand on my bouncing leg. "Not too nervous?"

"I might have been, like an hour ago," I whisper back. "I can't remember. All I know is that I'm starving and I want to get this over with and go eat lunch. What time is it, anyway?"

She pulls back the sleeve of her jacket and holds her watch out so I can see the time. It's almost one o'clock. No wonder I'm so hungry. Luckily, I have the smartest mom in the world. She reaches into her purse and pulls out a granola bar. I look around and see other kids snacking too.

Mom leans in while I'm chewing. "Just remember, honey, they probably have something specific they're looking for. Either you have it or you don't. If you don't, it's nothing personal. You just aren't *the one* this time around. You know what I mean?"

Not really, but I nod anyway. How do they know what they want until they see it? That's why so many kids are here today. I think it's my job to make them think I'm the one. Except maybe I don't want to be the one, which makes the situation ten times more confusing.

I finish the granola bar in no time, and am about to go in search of a drinking fountain, when the woman with the clipboard who keeps coming in and calling numbers yells out, "Number ninety-nine?"

Mom squeezes my hand as I get up. "Good luck," she says.

I mumble a quick "thanks" and then make my way through all the people to the door, and follow the woman down the hall and around the corner.

She leads me into a room with a light-blue cloth hanging at the front of the room. I'm directed to stand in front of the cloth and hold my number up in front of me. There's a cameraman not far away with a real-life television camera. I tell myself to breathe. Just smile and breathe.

The lady with the clipboard says, "After you say your name and the agency you're with, you can put your number down. Then look at the camera and say one of the lines. If you need help, we've put a couple of them on the easels here and here." She points to two big easels on either side of the camera that have large pieces of paper taped to them with lines written in big black marker.

"Okay, action," she says.

"I'm Sophie Wright," I say. "CPE Agency." I put my hand holding the number down by my side, and then I smile really big and say one of the lines I could actually see myself saying in a real commercial.

"Tired of store-bought cookies in your sack

lunch? Stop by Beatrice's Brownies and get the dessert everyone will be *begging* you to trade!"

"One more, please," the woman tells me.

"Come and try a Beatrice's brownie today. After all, Delicious is our middle name!"

"Great," the woman says. "That's all we need."

That's it? What was that, about thirty seconds? She walks over, takes my number, and says someone will be in touch with my agent very soon if I'm one of the kids selected.

"Thank you," I tell her. "I hope I did all right."

She smiles. "You did great."

I leave the room feeling like I can leap the tall buildings in downtown Portland in a single bound.

It's over. I did it!

When I make it back to the waiting room, I stand at the doorway and wave to Mom. She rushes over.

"How'd it go?" she asks as we walk toward the elevator.

I shrug. "I don't know. But she had me read two lines, and I didn't mess up or anything." I look at her. "She said I did great. So I guess it went pretty well."

She puts her arm around my shoulders and gives me a squeeze. "I'm so proud of you, Sophie. Good job. Now let's go find some lunch."

In my best fake-actress voice I say, "And we should stop by Beatrice's Brownies and stock up before the snack attack hits!"

We giggle all the way down to the first floor.

Chapter 19

chocolate
jam tarts

A DESSERT LIKE NOTHING
YOU'VE EVER TASTED

*H*ow'd it go yesterday?" are the first words out of my best friend's mouth.

"It's hard to know," I tell her as I grab my science textbook along with my binder.

"I can't wait to hear about it at lunch," she says.

I pull my lip gloss out of my pocket. "I need to do

something else at lunch today. Can we get together after school? Maybe have a chocolate jam tart, since today's December first?"

"Oh, yeah!" she says. "Sounds fun. Meet you at the bike rack, okay?"

"Okay. Oh, and Is, can you do me a favor? You have science class with a new kid. Austen? Can you tell him to meet me here, at our locker, at the beginning of lunch?"

She gives me a little eyebrow raise, which tells me she's thinking I've got a crush on the guy. "No, it's nothing like that. Long story. Will you tell him?"

She shrugs. "Okay. See ya later." She scurries off to class and I touch up my lip gloss before I close the door and go to science. When I get to class, I go to Dennis's desk. He looks half-asleep. I know the feeling.

I drop a card in an envelope on his desk in front of him. He jumps a little, sits up straight, and reaches for it. Inside the sealed envelope is a note I wrote to his mom telling her that Dennis told me he wants a camera for Christmas. I gave her all of the important information for the red camera, since that's the one the salesman recommended. I'm hoping it will improve his chances of getting a new one versus getting one from the thrift store.

"Can you give that to your mom, please?"

He turns the envelope over and reads "Margie" in my best cursive handwriting.

"Should I be worried?" he asks.

I start to joke with him and tell him of course he should be, but I don't want him to rip it open and read it. "No, I promise, nothing to worry about. Just wanted to say thanks for letting us study at your house and for the delicious cookies." He sticks the card into his binder. "Oh, and I need you to meet me at my locker at lunch, okay? First thing after the bell rings."

He gives me a funny look. "Uh, okay. Sure."

I start to walk to my desk when he asks, "Hey, Sophie, did you watch the movie yet?"

"I forgot it in my locker over the weekend. I'm taking it home tonight, though."

"You better watch it," he says.

"I will, I will! I've just been, um, kind of busy."

If only he knew.

At lunch, Dennis gets to my locker first. "Am I in trouble?" he asks. "Was an A minus just not good enough for you?"

"I think I found a friend for you. So remember— talk about normal stuff, none of that bird-foot stuff, okay?"

He's about to say something when Austen walks up.

"Austen!" I say. "This is my friend Dennis. He likes photography too. Or, at least, he wants a camera for Christmas, like you, so he can get into photography. I thought maybe we could have lunch together?"

Austen turns to Dennis and says, "On Sunday, my dad took me steelhead fishing. I took pictures with his camera when he was gutting one of the fish. Wanna see?"

Dennis looks like he's just been offered a hundred dollar bill. "Yeah!"

Austen pulls some pictures out of the back pocket of his jeans. "Have you ever been steelhead fishing?"

"Nah, just bass fishing. Is it fun?"

They start walking toward the cafeteria, lost in a sea of fishing and photography.

I am so proud of myself.

It's a match made in middle school.

After school, Isabel and I ride our bikes to It's Raining Cupcakes. The sweet smell of baked goods greets us when we walk in the door. Today there's a mom with three little kids sitting in the shop. This makes me very happy.

Isabel's grandma is behind the counter. "Hello, Sophie," she says, wiping her hands on a pink-and-white towel. "I'm glad to see you survived Black Friday."

"Barely," I say. If only she knew I'm not really joking.

"Grandma," Isabel says, "I brought Sophie in to try one of the jam tarts. Can we have two, please? With milk?"

"That's just ducky," she says. "Coming right up."

We stand aside and watch as the mom with the three kids tries desperately to keep the frosting situation from getting out of control. That is, out of their hair, off their clothes, and into their mouths.

"Here you go," Dolores says, handing me my jam

tart and glass of milk. Isabel takes hers, and then we take a seat in the corner.

"Isabel, it looks fantastic," I tell her.

She smiles. "I hope you like it."

"You know I will."

And I do. It's *really* good. The flavor of the strawberry jam with the chocolate tart is like nothing I've ever tasted before. I can see why it won the contest.

Just then the little bell over the door jingles, and Stan walks into the shop. He looks over at us and waves.

"Hello, Isabel!" he says. "Long time, no see. My wife sent me to get some of your jam tarts to try. Seems like we've been waiting forever to get our hands on them." He chuckles. "Or our mouths, as the case may be."

"Thanks, Stan. Did I ever tell you it was those tarts you brought from England that inspired my recipe?"

"No, I don't believe you ever told me that. Isn't that wonderful? I'll have to make sure to tell Judy. She gave me such a hard time about bringing those tarts all the way from England. See, I knew there was a reason why I felt so strongly you should have some."

He orders half a dozen and Isabel's grandma boxes them up for him.

"How's business?" he asks her.

Dolores folds her arms across her chest and sighs. "The last month or two has been very slow. We're hoping things pick up now, with the holidays around the corner. The shop will be open seven days a week in anticipation of all of the holiday parties going on in town. We're featuring some wonderful, special flavors for the season. After you've finished those tarts, you'll have to come back and try some gingerbread cupcakes."

"We'll definitely do that," he says. "Thanks, Dolores. Say, did anyone ever call you Dee growing up?"

"Oh yes," she says. "My little sister couldn't say Dolores for the longest time, so she called me Dee. Even today, I'm Dee to her."

"Knock, knock," Stan says.

"Who's there?"

"Dee."

"Dee who?"

"Dee-licious jam tarts for sale!" he says, holding the box in the air.

She laughs, and he waves good-bye and disappears out the door.

"I love that guy," Isabel says.

"Me too," I say, before I finish off the last of my tart. "Is your mom doing okay, Chickarita? I mean, she isn't too worried about business, is she?"

She stacks our plates and pushes them aside. "I don't know. It's hard to tell with my mom. She's trying really hard to focus on the good stuff—the people who love our shop come here again and again. The hard thing is figuring out unique, inexpensive ways to drum up new business. To get people to come and try a cupcake when they haven't been here before. If only we had an advertising budget as big as Beatrice's. Must be nice to be a big, ugly chain, huh?"

I gulp and take a swig of milk. This is when I should tell her.

Right now.

Right. Now.

And then the door of the shop opens again. I watch as a girl with dark, straight hair comes through the door followed by a pretty woman. The girl turns and looks at us.

I jump up. "Lily!"

She waves and walks over to our table.

"Isabel, this is my friend Lily," I say. "I brought her here last week to try the cupcakes. And look, she's back!"

Lily turns to Isabel. "My mom has book club tonight. I told her she had to buy cupcakes for snacks this time. They're *so* good, I just don't understand how business can be slow for you guys."

"How do you know that?" Isabel asks.

Lily's cheeks start to turn pink, almost matching the fuchsia coat she's wearing. "Uh, I—"

Isabel looks at me, her eyes sad. "Did you tell her? Are you telling people my family's business is having a hard time? That's really personal, Sophie."

I grab her arm. "I know it is. But—"

She shakes her head and pulls away from me. "Look," she whispers, nodding at the people in the shop, "I don't want to talk about this right now. I'm

gonna go upstairs. Call me later if you want to."
She turns to Lily. "I hope your mom's friends like
the cupcakes."

After she leaves, Lily says, "I'm sorry." I can tell
she feels really bad.

I sigh. "Don't worry about it."

I'll worry enough for the both of us.

Chapter 20

chocolate-covered strawberries

CELEBRATE!

When I get home, I find Mom working away at her sewing machine, which is the way it will be for most of December. Apparently clothing for dogs is a popular gift item during the holidays. Who knew?

"What are you working on?" I ask as I go to the fridge and grab a bottle of water. A tray of chocolate-covered strawberries catches my eye. That's weird.

Those are something you have for a special occasion. Well, maybe they have a party to go to.

"I'm trying to get twenty of these made," she says. I look over and she's holding up a tiny pink shirt that says FRIENDS FUR-EVER.

I laugh. "Oh, Mom, that is classic. Dogs everywhere are going to hate you, you know that, right? Because a true friend would never put a dog in a shirt!"

She takes a pair of scissors and cuts a thread. "Maybe dogs enjoy wearing clothes, Sophie. Have you ever asked Daisy if she might like it? I mean, how do you know her true feelings on the subject?"

I've told my mom that Daisy will never be caught in anything other than the coat she was born with. Once in a while, Mom uses Daisy for a model, but that's it. The clothes go on, she takes a picture, the clothes come off.

"Mom, seriously, you've seen her face when you put something on her. She looks humiliated. Like you would look if someone told you to run across a football field in your underwear in front of millions of people."

"I actually did that once," she says. I practically

choke on my water. "Just kidding. But your dad, he may have really done it. You should ask him."

My family is so weird.

"Well, I'm going to go watch a movie a kid at school loaned me."

"What movie?"

"*Bridge to Terabithia.*"

"I've read the book," Mom says, "but I haven't seen the movie. You'll have to let me know what you think after you watch it. The story centers around friendship. I bet you'll like it. Speaking of friendship, did you tell Isabel today?"

I bring my hands to my face and shake my head.

"Sophie."

I put my hands up, like I'm surrendering. "I know, Mom. I know! I need to tell her. Tomorrow. I'm going to do it tomorrow no matter what. First thing, at our locker." I make an X over my heart. "Cross my heart and all of that. Now can I go watch my movie?"

"Yes."

Dream #9—
Wouldn't it be great if

courage grew on trees,
so if you needed some,
you could just go out
and pick a basketful?

The movie is good. It's kind of slow at first, but after a while, I'm into it. I'm about halfway through when Hayden pokes his head in.

"Mom needs you in the kitchen," he tells me.

Probably wants me to set the table. Why doesn't she have Hayden do it? I hit the pause button with a big sigh.

When I walk into the kitchen, Mom, Dad, and Hayden are standing there holding fancy champagne glasses. A bottle of sparkling cider is on the counter, next to the platter of chocolate-covered strawberries.

"What's going on?" I ask.

"Congratulations!" Mom and Dad call out. Hayden puts the glass to his mouth and chugs it.

Dad hands me my own glass. "I don't get it," I say. "What are you congratulating me for?"

"Your agent called today," Mom says. "I wanted

to wait until your dad got home to tell you. You got the part!"

I feel my knees buckling. I grab the counter, setting the glass of cider down in front of me. "What? Are you serious? That can't be right."

"Would I kid you about something like this? Running through a football field in my underwear is one thing, but your acting career is quite another."

Dad looks at Mom like she's gone insane.

"What did Candace say exactly?"

"She said you are just what they're looking for. On-screen, you look fantastic, like the girl next door, friendly and approachable. They love you, Sophie! They want to film the actual commercial very soon."

Now I look at Mom like she's gone insane. They *love* me? Did she really say that?

"What did you tell her? Did you say I'd do it?"

"Yes, honey, of course I did! You have the chance to be on television, which could lead to other, bigger roles. Who knows how far this could take you? And they'll pay you! You could take that money and buy some lessons, like you've been talking about."

Bigger roles?

Money for acting lessons?

This is so amazing!

And then I think of Isabel. And it's not so amazing anymore. Part of me wants to dance down the street while the other part of me wants to find a hole and crawl in it.

I try to push the thought of bigger roles and money for acting lessons out of my mind. It's like pushing a huge boulder down the street—I have to push really, really hard. Finally, with what feels like a boulder in my throat, I say, "Mom, I don't think I can do it. You should call her back and tell her I can't."

Dad steps forward and puts his arm around me. "Honey, wait a second. Not so fast. Is this about Isabel?"

"Yes," I say. "I won't make her choose between me and her family. I won't. So I have to be the one to make the hard choice."

Dad gently pulls me over to the table and pulls out a chair. I sit down, then he sits down across from me, and Mom does the same.

"Can I go to my room?" Hayden asks, his hands full of chocolate-covered strawberries.

Dad's soft, warm eyes don't move from my face. "Yes, please." He waits until he's gone. "Don't you think you should talk this out with Isabel? See what she says about it? You might be surprised, Sophie."

I shake my head. "Dad, this whole time I've been trying to figure out what made it so hard for me to tell her. And I finally know. I figured it out yesterday when we went to the cupcake shop after school. She cares about her family so much. Things with her mom haven't always been easy, but she loves her! And I'm her best friend, so of course she cares about me too. How can I tell her that I want to do the commercial, but only if she says it's okay? I'd be asking her to make an impossible choice."

"But I don't think—"

I interrupt Mom. "Isabel is one of the nicest people I know. People at school gave her a bad time about winning the contest, and she never got mad. They thought she was buying stuff, being selfish, and what is she doing with the money? Taking *me* on a trip to Seattle. See? Nice! This is my chance to do

• 361 •

something nice for Isabel. Don't you understand? I need to make the choice for her."

Dad looks at Mom. "I think it should be Sophie's decision. If she doesn't want to do it, we need to respect that."

I stand up. "Good. I'm not doing the commercial."

Mom comes over and gives me a hug. "Okay. If that's what you want. I'll call Candace first thing in the morning, when the office is open. It's too late now."

"Okay. Can I go back to my room, please?"

Mom nods. "I'll call you when dinner is ready. Should be about twenty minutes."

I look at her. "Please don't. I'm not hungry."

Dream #10—
I dream of more chances.
Please let there be
more chances.

After I write in my dream journal, a gift from the nicest friend in the universe, I think about calling Isabel to apologize for what Lily said.

But I can't. Because I'm too busy crying.

Chapter 21

chocolate-flavored lip gloss

IT CAN HELP YOU THROUGH THE DAY

I think I got thirty minutes of sleep. Maybe forty. But I am ready to tell Isabel about the audition and now, with me turning down the commercial, I can honestly tell her I did it just for the practice.

I put on my favorite jeans and my favorite black blouse, and while I put on my favorite chocolate cherry lip gloss, I give myself a pep talk in the bathroom.

"You are going to get this thing over with, Sophie Wright. Walk up to her at the locker, tell her you have something to say, and tell her. Get it all out, let her know how sorry you are for lying, but you really didn't want to upset her. Then it's over with. Along with your friendship. And your acting career." I shake my head. "Stop it. It'll be fine."

It'll be fine.

I keep telling myself those three words over and over as I walk to the kitchen. Mom is there, and I swear she looks like the dog has just died. In fact, it makes me wonder. "Where's Daisy?" I call for her. "Daisy? Daisy, come here!"

She comes running from the family room, carrying a rawhide bone in her mouth. I reach down and scoop her up into my arms, leaving the slimy bone on the floor.

"I have some bad news, Sophie," Mom says.

I knew it. "What? Tell me!"

She throws the *Willow Gazette* onto the table. I look down and see a picture of me along with the headline "Local Willow Girl to Star in National Ad Campaign for Beatrice's Brownies."

"What?" I yell so loudly it scares Daisy and she jumps out of my arms. I look at Mom. "How did this happen?"

Mom speaks slowly, like her words are tiptoeing out of her mouth. "I think Candace must have sent out a press release yesterday."

I shake my head. "No. No, no, no, no, no! Mom, wouldn't she talk to me about it first? Make sure I wanted to do the commercial?"

"You went on the audition. I think to her that meant you wanted to do the commercial."

I start pacing, back and forth, back and forth, my mind racing with questions and worries. I check the clock, and then realize I have to talk to Isabel before she sees it. I run to the phone and dial her number, but no one answers.

"Mom, will you drive me to school? Now?"

"Do you want to eat anything first?"

"No. I need to go!"

"Okay, but we have to take Hayden too, and he needs to eat breakfast."

I throw my hands in the air. "Never mind. I can get there faster on my bike."

I run to my room, grab my coat and backpack, and head to the garage. When I open the door, I see it's raining. Perfect. I put my hood up and off I go.

All I can think about the whole way to school, rain pelting my face, is that this is what I get for lying to Isabel. My mother couldn't have put together a better punishment than this if she'd tried.

When I pull up to the bike rack, Isabel is there too, putting her bike into one of the spaces.

I jump off my bike and run over to her. "Isabel, I have to talk to you."

Even with her wet, rain-covered face, I can tell in an instant that she knows. I imagine her and her parents seeing the picture and the headline and looking at one another, stunned. Disgusted. All because of me, the person who is supposed to be Isabel's best friend in the world.

"I don't have anything to say to you," she says, bending down to secure her lock.

"Please, Chickarita, I can explain."

She stands up, her bottom lip quivering, because she's trying so hard not to cry. "You lied to me. You stabbed my family in the back. That pretty much explains it all, doesn't it?" She turns and runs into the school before I can say anything else.

I turn my face to the sky and let the rain pound my face. I don't know what to do now. How can I go in there? If my best friend is mad at me, everyone else will be too. No one will want to hear my side of the story.

I start to head back home, because I feel like there's no where else to go, when Dennis comes running up, the black hood on his hoodie covering his head.

"Sophie, I saw the paper," he says. "Congratulations. You never told me you were doing that. Wait. Why is your bike headed away from school? Where are you going?"

"Home." And as soon as the word is out, I start crying. The warm tears blend in with the cold raindrops, and it feels funny. "I can't believe what a mess I've made." He takes my bike and parks it. Then he walks back to me, takes my hand, and pulls me toward the front steps, which are covered. He sits down and pulls me down next to him. He lets me cry for a few minutes. Then he asks, "Isabel didn't know about the commercial?"

I shake my head. "She knew I was auditioning, but she thought it was for something else." I look at him. I can barely see his eyes behind his wet glasses. It's like he can read my mind, because he takes them off and starts wiping them on his jeans. I never noticed Dennis's eyes before. They're green with little yellow specks around the middle. Different. Nice.

"You lied to her?" he asks.

"I know, I'm horrible." I bite my lip to keep from crying some more. Then I take a deep breath. "I was going to tell her everything today. I swear. And I didn't want to do the commercial. I went to the audition just to see what it was like. But yesterday my mom told my agent I'd do it, even though she hadn't talked to me about it yet."

He puts his glasses back on. "Yep. That's a mess."

He stands and pulls me up with him.

"Where are we going?"

"You're going to lock your bike, and then we're going to science class. You can't run away, Sophie. Everything will still be here tomorrow. And the next day. And the day after that."

"But—"

"Nope. You have to go in. Trust me. You may not have had friend troubles before, but I have."

"Dennis—"

He turns and faces me. "I will be with you whenever I can. Between classes. At lunch. After school. People will leave you alone if you're with me. And we'll figure out a plan to get Isabel to forgive you. I'm going to help you. I promise. Okay?"

I feel like I'm putting my life in Dennis Holt's hands. And for some strange reason, I'm okay with that.

Chapter 22

brownies

A WONDERFUL DESSERT TO SHARE
WITH A FRIEND

Dream #11—
I dream of forgiveness.
Lots and lots of forgiveness.

Somehow with Dennis's help I make it through the morning. I hear kids whispering about me, but I keep my head down and tell myself *It doesn't matter, it doesn't matter, it doesn't matter.* Even though it really does. I remember how I told Isabel I could do something terrible to take the attention off of her and the baking contest. Well, looks like I succeeded.

A couple of teachers congratulate me on the commercial, and one actually hangs the newspaper article in the hallway, outside her door. Dennis asks her to take it down. She does.

Isabel doesn't even look at me in Math or English. I try passing her a note. She rips it up without even reading it.

At lunch, Dennis and Austen walk me through the lunch line. I tell Dennis I don't want anything to eat, but he doesn't listen to me. For lunch I'm having a grilled-cheese sandwich, French fries, apple slices, and a brownie. Guess he wasn't thinking when he picked the brownie for me. I'm pretty sure I'll never want to eat another brownie as long as I live.

When we sit down, I pass it to Austen. He stuffs the whole thing in his mouth and just like that, it's gone. If only I could have him do that with all of my brownie problems.

While I tear my sandwich into pieces, Dennis gives

Austen a quick rundown of what's going on between Isabel and me.

"Can we just talk about movies or something?" I ask. I look at Dennis. "Did you ask him what his favorite movie is, like you're supposed to?"

"Didn't even have to," Dennis says. "If I said something stupid, he just laughed and said something stupid back."

If I wasn't so upset, this would make me very happy.

"You need a plan," Austen says, reaching for my fries because he's already eaten all of his.

"Right," Dennis says. "Something big. Really big."

They start talking about what their favorite superheroes would do while I scan the cafeteria, looking for Isabel. I don't see her anywhere. I start to get up, but Dennis grabs my arm.

"Where are you going?"

"To find Isabel, so I can talk to her. She needs to hear the whole story. She only knows part of it right now."

"Sit down," he says. "You need to give her a couple of days to cool off."

"And don't do it here at school," Austen says.

"One person will hear you and in five minutes, the whole school will know what you said."

"Plus, they'll throw in things that aren't true," Dennis says. "A five-minute conversation will morph into a thirty-minute fight out on the football field."

I sit back down. They're right. I can't do it here. Maybe I can get her to meet me at the Blue Moon Diner after school. Ha, who am I kidding?

Dennis and Austen are still talking, and now they've turned the fight on the football field into one that includes ninjas and pirates. While they battle it out over who would win, I rack my brain trying to think of what I can do to get Isabel to realize how sorry I am.

Something big.

Something eye-catching.

Something really, really awesome.

I wish I could hire a television crew and pay for advertising. I'd put the best commercial ever on television. But that costs thousands of dollars and after spending all of my money on Christmas gifts, I don't even have five dollars in my wallet.

But I keep rolling that idea around in my head,

and it gets bigger and bigger, like a snowball rolling down a hill. Pretty soon my head is so full of this idea, I can hardly see straight.

"No, see," Dennis is saying, "the pirates would bring their cannons and—"

"I know what to do. I'm going to dress up like a cupcake."

They both turn and look at me like I just said there are no such things as pirates and ninjas.

"What do you mean?" Austen asks. "Frosting is really messy. I think it'd be hard to wash out of your hair."

"No, not a real cupcake. A pretend cupcake. Can you guys help me? I think we'll need to make a trip to the craft store."

"What's a craft store?" Dennis asks as he straightens his glasses.

I put my head in my hands while Austen and Dennis laugh over the idea that there are actual stores that sell craft-making supplies.

Boys.

My mom said one time, "Can't live with them, can't live without them." I'm pretty sure now I know what she meant.

Chapter 23

ice-cream sandwiches

THEY'RE EASY TO MAKE AND YUMMY

Saturday morning, I wake up to rain pounding the roof. In my nightmare, it was Isabel pounding on my window, yelling, "You're the worst friend ever! Worst. Friend. Ever!"

I make myself open my eyes, and I go to my window. The sky is a dark, dark gray and the trees are blowing left, then right, then left again, the wind whipping them around like puppets.

I plop back on my bed, pull the covers over my head, and decide I will just stay there forever. But eventually, my bladder overrules my decision. As much as I love my bed, I don't love it *that* much.

I run into Mom in the hallway. "Any big plans for today?" she asks.

"I was thinking about staying in bed forever. But since I'm up, could you take me to the craft store later? And give me an advance on my allowance? I have some things I need to pick up. My friends Dennis and Austen are going to help me. Is it okay if they come over here this afternoon?"

"Sure. That's fine."

I slip past her and use the bathroom, then go back to my room. Mom comes in a little while later with a plate of toast and a cup of orange juice. She takes a seat on the chair that sits by my desk. She's been really great, leaving me alone like I've asked the past few days. I haven't wanted to talk about it. But I guess the time has come.

"I'm assuming you haven't talked to Isabel yet," she says. "When are you planning on doing that?"

I set the juice on my nightstand. "Mom, she is so mad. She avoided me at school all week like she'd break out with some terrible disease if she even looked at me. I tried writing her notes. I tried talking to her at our locker. She didn't want anything to do with any of it."

Mom sighs. "You girls are so dramatic, you know that?"

"I'm an actress," I tell her. "Drama is my specialty."

"And apparently Isabel's too. Honey, I have faith that you girls will work this out. I think you just have to keep trying. She can't ignore you forever."

I nod. I hope this plan I have works.

"Mom, do you think Isabel is mad that the commercial is with Beatrice's Brownies? Or is she mad about me not telling her the truth?"

"Have you finished watching that movie your friend loaned you?" she asks.

"Not yet."

"Well, I don't want to give anything away, but you should finish watching it. And think about what makes Jess and Leslie's friendship so strong. They want to help each other find their true selves. To celebrate that which is special about each of them. Don't you think Isabel wants that for you, Sophie, just like you want it for her?"

"I don't know," I tell her.

Mom pats my leg and then gets up to leave. "I think you do."

Dream #12—
I dream
my plan will work.

I call Dennis and tell him to be at the craft store at one o'clock. He says he'll call Austen and let him know to meet us there too.

When I get there, Dennis and Austen are waiting for me by a big display of papier-mâché reindeer. They each have two reindeer in their hands.

"So here's our plan," Austen says in a deep voice with a funny accent. "We wait until Santa isn't looking. Then we grab all of the video games."

"And comic books," Dennis says, trying to copy Austen's weird reindeer voice. "Don't forget the comic books."

"Like you can do that with four hooves," I say as I take the reindeer away from Dennis and put them back on the display. "Come on. We have some shopping to do."

I grab a cart and we begin strolling the aisles of the store. Shopping in a craft store is pretty entertaining with two boys. Every aisle, they have something new to say about what they see.

"So this is where cemeteries get all those fake flowers."

"Was my grandma just here? This place smells like her house."

"Everything better be half-off, since everything's only half put-together."

"What's a hot-melt glue gun? Sounds like a torture device for aliens."

"Boys," I say. "Focus. Giant cupcake. Remember?"

"Right," Dennis says. "Hey, I sketched out an idea last night. We need a big, round laundry basket, though. Do you have one at your house?"

"Yeah," I say, "we do. Why?"

"Think your mom will mind if we cut the bottom out of it?"

Dennis pulls a piece of paper out of his pocket and shows me the design. It is perfect. Genius! It's so good, I almost want to kiss him. Almost.

The laundry basket will be the bottom half of the cupcake. We'll wrap it in something to make it look like a cupcake wrapper, then we'll put a whole bunch of fabric on the top, and sort of puff it out somehow, to make it look like lots of frosting. To wear the costume, I'll have to attach straps to the laundry basket. Then I'll step into the basket with my feet, pull it up to my hips, put the straps over my shoulders, and suddenly I'm a walking, talking cupcake.

We go to work filling the shopping cart with the supplies we need. When we go to the cash register, our cart holds three rolls of aluminum foil, a pink fleece blanket, cardboard, some purple and red felt, a roll of pink ribbon, a Styrofoam ball, red spray paint, glue, thick masking tape, and a big poster board.

After I pay for the stuff, Mom is in the parking lot waiting for us, and she helps me put the bags in the trunk of the car. The boys get in the back and I sit up front with my mom.

"You want to tell me what you kids are up to?" Mom asks.

"Sorry, ma'am," Dennis says. "Top-secret operation."

"Yes, and our top-secret operation requires a round laundry basket," Austen says. "We understand you have one. Could we use it, please? We won't be able to give it back, since we have interesting things planned. But don't worry. Nothing illegal."

I watch as Mom looks in the rearview mirror, smiling. "You want my laundry basket? It's full of laundry, you know."

"If we do the laundry, can we have the basket?" Dennis asks.

Mom looks at me. "Sophie, I like these boys."

When we get home, we go into the garage and get to work on what is now called "Operation Cupcake." Never has making a cupcake been so important.

We have so much fun, and I can't stop laughing. They don't settle for good or okay. If I say, "That looks okay," they start over and try again. Everything has to be over-the-top, out of this world, amazing. And when the whole thing is done, that's exactly what it is.

The laundry basket is covered in silver foil. The fleece blanket is rolled and puffed out on top of the laundry basket, with a little bit of help from some cardboard. Hearts made out of red and purple felt are glued all over the pink fleece, like pink and red sprinkles. The Styrofoam ball is bright red, and has a stick poking out the top, which Dennis got from our yard. The red ball is glued to a pink ski hat I found in my closet. Yes, the walking, talking cupcake will even have a cherry on top. I decide that tomorrow, when I put Operation Cupcake into play, I'll wear some pink tights and old ballet slippers to complete the look.

After a couple of hours, Mom brings us a plate of homemade ice-cream sandwiches—a scoop of chocolate ice cream between two oatmeal cookies. When she sees me in the costume, she almost drops the plate.

"What do you think?" I ask, twirling around for her.

"I think you are the cutest cupcake I've ever seen!"

I hold up the poster board and show her the sign I've made that I'll carry tomorrow.

BUY A CUPCAKE
AT IT'S RAINING CUPCAKES
AND TELL THEM SOPHIE
SENT YOU!

"Operation Cupcake is complete," Dennis says.

"Good," Austen says. "Because my stomach is telling me it's time for Operation Ice-Cream Sandwich."

I go over to my mom and tell her thanks for the snack. "Operation Cupcake is a great idea," she tells me.

"I just hope it works, Mom."

She reaches for my hand and gives it a little squeeze. "It looks like a winning recipe to me."

Chapter 24

cherry cupcakes

DRIZZLE THEM WITH WHITE CHOCOLATE

TO SHOW YOUR LOVE

It's Sunday afternoon. Time to put Operation Cupcake into action.

Dennis called earlier and gave me a pep talk. It went something like this:

"You have to be the best cupcake that's ever walked the face of the earth."

"And how exactly do I do that?" I asked him.

"I don't know," he said. "But something will come to you."

"Hey, Dennis?"

"Yeah?"

"Remember how you said you were going to get me for bringing up the Power Rangers? Operation Cupcake isn't going to show up in the school newspaper tomorrow, is it?"

"You know, that's not a bad idea." He paused. "Just kidding. You have nothing to worry about, I promise. I just want things to be better with Isabel."

"Yeah. Me too."

He might not have been as motivational as Uncle Pete would have been, but he was all right. And I'm ready to do what I have to do. Mom drops me off around the corner from It's Raining Cupcakes. Before I get out of the car, she says, "Good luck, honey. Remember to speak from your heart."

If she gives me the chance to speak at all. "Okay. Thanks, Mom."

"What time should I pick you up?" she asks.

"I can walk home."

She hands me her phone. "Take this, just in case. And don't lose it!"

I slip it into the pocket of the shorts I'm wearing over my tights. I get out of the car, pull the costume and sign out of the backseat, and slip the costume on. Mom waves good-bye and pulls away. I suddenly wish I had asked Dennis to come with me. No, that wouldn't have been right. I have to do this by myself. This is about me and Isabel, and I have to show her I'll do whatever it takes to make things right between us.

With my cherry-topped hat in place and the sign in front of me, I begin walking up and down the sidewalk. I do this for probably thirty minutes, back and forth, from one end of the sidewalk to the other. But then I realize I'll have more visibility if I increase the size of the area I'm covering.

So I broaden my path. I go across the street and make a big loop. Around the bookstore, past the post office, past the big park where some kids are playing, and back around to the cupcake shop.

After an hour of doing this, my legs are starting to get tired of walking and my shoulders are sore from the straps holding up my costume. Still, I'm not ready to give up. I create an even bigger loop. With every route, I make sure that I pass by the cupcake shop at some point.

Cars drive by and honk, and I wave, and soon I notice that traffic has increased a lot in front of the shop, and I see person after person going into the store and coming out with their boxes of cupcakes.

It's working.

People are buying cupcakes!

And so it goes, hour after hour, until every muscle in my body aches and I've waved at so many cars, my arm feels like it's going to fall off.

And yet, not one sign of Isabel.

A raindrop falls, and then another one, and soon it's not just sprinkling, it's outright pouring. My stomach, as well as the darkened sky, tells me it's time to go home. Four hours of total humiliation must not have been enough to show Isabel how sorry I am.

I thought she'd realize how bad I feel.

I thought she'd come see me, tell me it's okay, and that I'm forgiven.

It wasn't enough.

Obviously, there's still more I have to do.

Maybe it's what Dad said to me that one night I couldn't sleep. Sometimes you know how someone feels, but it's nice to hear it too.

I walk to the side of a building and stand underneath the awning, to stay dry. I take the phone out of my pocket and dial Isabel's number.

"Hello?"

"Isabel, it's me, Sophie. Please don't hang up. Look, maybe it's not going to make much difference, but I want you to know how sorry I am that I lied to you about the audition. I didn't want to make you choose between me and your family. I never planned on actually doing the commercial. I went to the audition for practice. But then my agent called, and my mom was so excited, and neither of them asked me if I wanted to do the commercial. And I don't! If it means losing you as a friend, I don't want to do it. I'm not doing it. Isabel, you have to believe me. I'm so sorry."

She doesn't say anything for a long time. And then finally, she lets out a sigh and says, "Okay. Thanks for calling." And she hangs up.

I stand there, watching the rain fall. It's definitely not raining cupcakes.

As if the day hasn't been bad enough, now I get to walk home in the rain. Perfect. Just perfect.

I've about reached the corner when I hear a voice.

"Hey! Sophie Bird!"

I turn around and there's Isabel. She gives me a little wave.

I try to run, but laundry baskets aren't really made to run in. So I walk, really, really fast. When I reach her, she pulls me under the awning of Stan's barber shop.

"How is it possible that you look so amazing and so ridiculous all at the same time?" she asks.

"Takes a special talent," I say.

"You got that right. What kind of cupcake are you, anyway?"

"Cherry and white chocolate. It's a special creation, just for you. I hope you like it."

She pauses, and then says, "You shouldn't have lied to me."

"I know." I start to cry. "I'm so sorry. I handled it all really badly, and I want to talk to you about it some more. Can we go upstairs, to your place?"

She looks at me. "Under one condition."

"Anything."

"That you do the commercial."

"But—"

She shakes her head. "It's a chance of a lifetime, Soph! You have to do it. Whatever happens to the cupcake shop is going to happen whether you do the commercial or not."

"Let's talk about it. I want you to be sure, okay? And your parents too."

"Okay," she says. "But you have to take that ridiculous cherry off your head. Fruit should be eaten, not worn as decorative headwear. Don't you know that?"

"What about the cupcake costume? Can I take that off?"

"No," she says. "Keep it on. I like it. It sold a lot of cupcakes today."

I smile through my tears. And then I reach out and hug her.

"Careful," she says. "I don't want to get frosting on my new shirt."

"I love you, Chickarita," I tell her.

"I love you too, Sophie Bird."

Dream #13—
I have the best friend
a girl could ever dream of.

Chapter 25

marshmallow
chocolate-chip pie

OOEY, GOOEY PERFECTION

Christmas is wonderful. Dad loves his new robe, although he says he's keeping the old one as a memento of the good old days. Spit-up equals good old days? Okay, whatever. Mom is totally surprised by her box of tea, and proceeds to make herself a cup of it right away.

As for Hayden, I used my December allowance and got him three *Star Wars* figures, one of which is Yoda, his favorite character.

"Happy Jedi, I am," he says after he opens it. "Thank you."

Yes, we are now sharing a house with Yoda, which is about as much fun as wearing a cupcake costume in the pouring rain.

My haul includes new clothes, a bunch of new books, including *Bridge to Terabithia*, a gift certificate for an acting class, and my very own cell phone!

"Don't lose it" is the first thing my parents say to me after I open it.

Mom also got me a new purse, which has a special pocket inside specifically for the cell phone. And surprisingly enough, she did a good job picking out the purse. Although she went the easy route—she picked one that is almost identical to my old one. She's a smart one, my mother.

The day after Christmas, Mom drops me off at Isabel's house with my suitcase in hand. It's time to make the trek to Seattle, and I'm so excited!

Isabel takes me to her room and shows me all the cool stuff she got for Christmas—lots of cute clothes, an art set, a cute apron that says, "Top Chef," and a new suitcase.

"Wow, a suitcase, huh?" I ask her. "Does that mean there's a lot more traveling in your future?"

"I hope so," she says.

I help her finish packing, and then we head downstairs and wait for her parents in the cupcake shop. Her grandma is there, helping a couple of customers.

When she's finished, she says, "Hi, Sophie! So nice to see you! Ready to visit the Space Needle in the sky?"

"I'm ready!" I say. "It's going to be so much fun!"

"But don't forget," Isabel says. "First we have to stop and have pie at Penny's Pie Place."

I nudge Isabel and suddenly notice her hair looks really nice today. Like she spent a long time on it this morning. "Are you excited to see Jack?" I ask.

She smiles. "Maybe."

"Okay, girls," Isabel's mom says, peeking her head through the door. "We're ready to go. Thank you,

Mother, for holding down the fort while we're gone."

"You know I'm happy to do it. You guys have a wonderful time, all right?"

"We will," Isabel says. "Bye, Grandma!"

"Bye!"

Isabel and I pass the time in the car by playing cards with a deck she brought along and munching on Goldfish crackers and apples.

When we get to Seattle, it's blue skies and sunny, but cold. Perfect weather for going up in the Space Needle. The plan is to have some pie, and then we'll head over and spend the rest of the afternoon there.

The outside of the restaurant is bright yellow and red, and the words PENNY'S PIE PLACE are printed right on the building, above the awning. And next to the words is a big piece of apple pie on a yellow plate.

We go inside and a woman greets us. She's wearing a yellow dress with an apron. Her name tag says "Karen."

"Hello, can I help you?" she asks.

"I'm friends with Jack," Isabel tells her. "I told him we'd be coming this way today. Is he here?"

Just then, a cute boy with straight dark hair and

big brown eyes comes from around the corner. He smiles and shows his two dimples.

"Hey, Isabel," he says. He gives her a really quick hug, and then she introduces all of us to him.

"We're going to go sit down," Isabel's mom says. She looks at Isabel. "We know you want to catch up with your friend, so go ahead and get a table and order, okay?"

"Okay. Thanks, Mom."

Jack leads us over to a booth in the corner. I slide in one side of the booth, while Isabel slides in next to Jack.

"So, girls, welcome to Seattle," he says. "Otherwise known as the Emerald City. Unfortunately, we've given all of our emeralds away today, so all I have to give you is pie."

"Pie is good," Isabel says. "How many flavors do you have, anyway?"

"Twelve. But you have to trust me on this one, okay? Marshmallow chocolate-chip pie is the specialty pie this week, and I really think you should try it'"

"Marshmallow chocolate-chip pie?" I ask. "It sounds a little bit like a s'more."

"You're right!" he says. "It's actually the recipe I entered for the contest."

Both of our mouths drop open. "Really?" Isabel says. "I entered a s'more cupcake recipe. Well, until Mom sent in the recipe I really wanted to enter, which was for chocolate jam tarts."

Jack looks confused.

"Never mind," Isabel says. "Long story. The important thing is that it sounds delicious, and of course I want to try it!"

"Me too," I chime in.

Jack turns and looks at me. "Isabel told me in her last letter you're going to be in a commercial. You trying to put the rest of us out of business?"

I know he's joking, but it isn't very funny to me. It's still a sensitive topic, I guess.

Isabel smiles and says, "Sophie, maybe you could make a pie costume next. I bet people would love that. You'd sell hundreds of pies for them, I just know it."

I shout "No!" while Jack shouts "Yes!"

We laugh and then Jack's face gets all serious. "Actually," he says, leaning in and whispering, "just between us, Mom and Dad are thinking of closing the place down. Business hasn't been very good lately."

"Oh no," Isabel says as I feel my heart breaking in half.

"Is there anything we can do?" I ask.

"Nah, I don't think there's anything anyone can do. I mean, cupcakes are all the rage. They're cute, they're fun, and kids love them. Pies are sort of boring, you know?"

"I don't think so," I say. "I love pie."

"Do you love it more than cupcakes?" he asks.

I look at him. I look at Isabel. Then I throw my hands in the air. "Don't put me in another impossible situation! I've had my share, thank you very much."

They laugh at me, and then Karen comes to take our order and brings our slices of pie back a few minutes later.

"Oh my gosh, Jack," I say, "this is seriously the best pie I've *ever* had. Can I get the recipe?"

"Didn't Isabel tell you?" he whispers. "It's top-secret. If I told you, I'd have to kill you. But get me those secret brownie recipes and you might have a deal."

"That's it, Sophie!" Isabel squeals. "You can be

a spy for us. Find the secret to Beatrice's Brownie's success, and we can bring them down!"

"But I don't want to be a spy," I tell them. "I just want to be an actress. Is that too much to ask?" And with that, I throw my head down on the table and pretend to weep.

"She's good," I hear Jack say.

"You're telling me," Isabel says.

After we finish eating, I excuse myself to use the bathroom so Isabel can have a few minutes alone with Jack. I scrub my hands for a good five minutes, trying to drag out the inevitable. She's going to have to leave him, and I know she's not going to want to.

Finally, I walk out to find them standing by the front door with Isabel's parents, waiting on me.

"Bye, Jack," I say. "The pie was fabulous. Tell your parents I hope they can hang in there."

"Bye, Sophie. I will."

I head toward the car with Isabel's parents. Isabel stays behind a minute, saying good-bye to Jack in private.

When she finally gets in the car, she's beaming.

"To the Space Needle?" Isabel's dad asks.

"To the Space Needle!" we all shout back.

And as we drive away, Isabel opens her hand and shows me the silver necklace with the pink cupcake charm she's holding.

Awww. What a *sweet* guy.

Chapter 26

chocolate-dipped fortune cookie

IT SAYS YOUR FUTURE IS BRIGHT

For three days we have fun exploring Seattle. The Space Needle is really high. Like, amazingly high. I can't even go out on the viewing deck because it freaks me out.

We spend a whole afternoon shopping at Pike Place Market. We watch the men throw the fish over customers' heads and we eat all kinds of good food. We go to two museums, the Museum of Flight as well as the Science Fiction Museum. The whole time I'm there, I think of Hayden. He'd love it. He should *live* here!

And before I know it, we're driving back, heading toward Willow where school will be starting back up in just a few days.

Isabel is sad to be leaving, I can tell. She stayed happy through most of the trip, wearing the necklace he gave her the whole time, and reaching up to touch it every once in a while, like it made her feel close to him. But now we're heading home, and home is a long, long way from Seattle.

"Maybe he'll come visit you," I whisper.

"I hope so."

Isabel is writing stuff down in her little notebook, so I pull out my dream notebook and write:

Dream #14—
I dream of a happily ever after
for everyone.

When I get home, Mom and Dad are glad to see me. Hayden says, "Good trip, was it?"

"Yes, a most excellent trip, Yoda wannabe. Mom, Dad, we have to take Hayden to the Science Fiction Museum someday. He would love it!"

"Maybe this summer," Dad says. "I haven't been to Seattle in a long time. It'd be fun to spend some time up there."

"Oh, and there's this great pie restaurant we have to go to." *If it stays open that long.* "Maybe I could bring Isabel with us, since she was nice enough to invite me to come with her."

"I don't see why not," Mom says.

Oh, wait until I tell Isabel! She'll be over-the-moon happy about the possibility of seeing Jack again.

At school I take Dennis Holt's movie back to him. I feel bad I had it for so long, but I kept forgetting to watch the ending. I finally found time last night. It was good, but sad, like everyone said. I definitely want to read the book now.

I find Dennis at his locker before school starts.

When he turns around, I can't believe what I see. Is this really him?

"Dennis, what . . . what happened?"

"I got contacts. And I finally listened to my mom and got my hair cut. I'm not sure about it. What do you think?"

"I think it looks fantastic." As soon as I say it, I feel my cheeks getting warm.

"Well, thanks," he says. "If you like it, then it must be all right."

We chat for a while, about Christmas and stuff, and then the warning bell rings, telling us it's time to head to class.

"Oh, wait, I almost forgot. I brought your movie back. Thanks for letting me borrow it. It was really good."

"You're welcome," he says as he throws the movie into his locker and shuts the door. "Someday I bet I'll be watching you in a movie like that."

I shrug. "Maybe. We'll see what people have to say about the commercial first."

"Yeah, when do we get to watch it?" he asks.

"We shot the commercial last week, when I got back from Seattle. They're saying it will air for the first time in a couple of weeks. I'm so nervous!"

"It'll be great," he says. "That reminds me, I have something for you, too. I'm not sure what you're going to think, but uh, well, I want to give it to you."

He stops and rummages around in that messy binder of his, and pulls out something in a plastic wrapper. He hands it to me and says, "I hope it's not broken."

I look at it closely and see it's a chocolate-dipped fortune cookie with sprinkles on the outside. And it isn't broken. It's really pretty. Almost too pretty to eat.

"A fortune cookie?" I ask.

"Yeah," he says. "My way of saying congratulations on the commercial. Open it!"

I take off the plastic wrap, and break the cookie open to read the fortune.

It says: "In the shadowy light of the stronghold everything seemed possible."—From *Bridge to Terabithia* (Remember—everything is possible!)

Aw. What a *sweet* guy!

"Thanks, Dennis. I love it." I hand him a piece of the cookie, and we eat as we walk to class. When we get there, he stops just outside the doorway.

"I almost forgot to tell you," he says. "I got the best camera for Christmas. My mom said a little elf helped her pick it out. Do you know anything about that?"

I try to look shocked. "No! Why would you think that?"

He smiles. "I don't know. Just a guess. Hey, Austen and I are going to enter a photography contest. Grand prize is five hundred bucks! What do you think? You in?"

I laugh. "No, thanks. No more contests for me for a while."

"Okay, well, maybe you can help me with mine."

"As long as it doesn't involve dead birds or gutted fish, I'll help you."

And then, he leans in a little bit. "Sophie, do you know how I said one time I wished you were a boy?"

"Yes."

"I just want you to know, I think I've changed my mind on that."

As I walk to my desk I feel my heart beating really

hard. Almost as hard as the moment I found out Mom was taking me to see *Wicked*.

Does this mean I like Dennis Holt almost as much as I like musicals?

Oh. My. Gosh.

I think it does!

Chocolate Jam Tarts

2 ⅔ cups flour

1 cup butter, chilled

⅓ cup unsweetened cocoa

4 tablespoons sugar

½ teaspoon baking powder

1 egg yolk

⅓ cup ice-cold water

½ cup strawberry jam

Preheat oven to 400°. Blend flour and butter together using butter knives and/or a pastry blender until butter is marble size. Stir in cocoa. Make a well and add the sugar, baking powder, egg yolk, and water. Quickly combine all ingredients. Use hands to knead the dough into a ball, then place on a floured surface and roll to ¼-inch thickness.

Using a butter knife, cut into 3-inch squares. Put a tablespoonful of jam in the center of each square, fold into a triangle, and crimp the edges together.

Place on a greased baking sheet and bake for 10 minutes. Cool for 30 minutes and sift powdered sugar over the top of the tarts.

Monster Cookies

1 cup brown sugar

1 cup granulated sugar

½ cup butter or margarine

1 ½ cups creamy peanut butter

3 eggs

1 teaspoon vanilla

1 tablespoon Karo syrup

4 ½ cups rolled oats

½ cup flour

2 teaspoons baking soda

1 cup M&M's

1 cup chocolate chips

With a mixer, beat together sugars, butter, and peanut butter. Add the eggs, vanilla, and Karo syrup, and mix well. Gradually add in the rolled oats, flour, and baking soda, and mix until well blended. Stir in the M&M's and chocolate chips. Refrigerate dough for at least 3 hours (can even be overnight) to help cookies mound up better. When ready to bake, preheat oven to 350°, and use a teaspoon to drop onto ungreased baking sheets. Bake about 12 minutes, until a light golden brown.

acknowledgments

First and foremost I have to thank all of the kids who wrote to me, letting me know how much they enjoyed the book *It's Raining Cupcakes*. It's because of *you* that I decided to write another book about Isabel and Sophie. I hope you find this book just as sweet!

Deena Lipomi, you helped me come up with the premise, so I'm not sure this book would exist without you! Thanks also to Kate, Emily, and Tina for helping to brainstorm ideas.

Lindsey and Lisa, you thought long and hard on titles, so I have to say thanks for that. Triple Ls, always and forever.

I want to send a big thank-you out to Allie Costa and Amanda Morgan, who answered my questions about commercial auditions and provided valuable feedback on an important part of the book.

Thank you to my editor, Alyson, and all of the fine people at Aladdin who helped bake this book into something that's not only pretty to look at but also delicious to read.

Thanks, as always, to my agent, Sara.

Thank you, Katherine Paterson, for writing *Bridge to Terabithia*, one of the greatest books of all time.

When I needed to brainstorm funny things boys would say, I turned to my husband, Scott, who is an expert at being funny. I like funny boys, and I'm glad I'm married to one.

My kids have to put up with many dinner conversations that start out, "I need some help with . . ." Thanks, boys, for not only putting up with me but also for being the best kids a mom could ask for. I want to say something really mushy, but I'll refrain. You're welcome.

Frosting and Friendship

For my friend Lindsey Leavitt,
who pointed me in the right direction
by sharing her baking disaster stories.
You are the best.

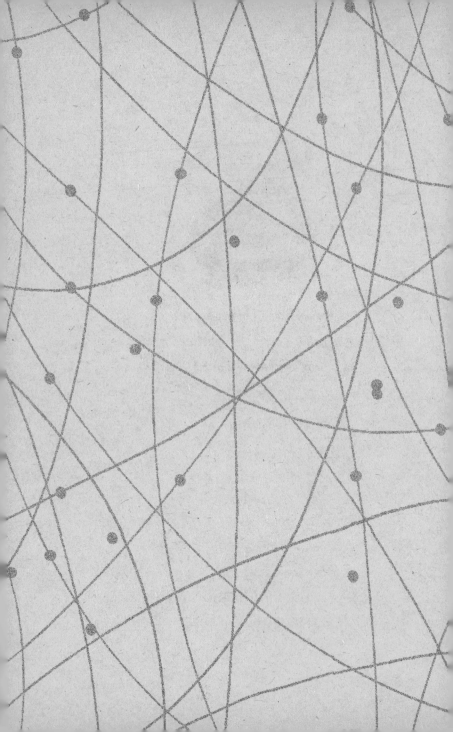

Chapter 1

apple-blackberry pie

BECAUSE BOOK CLUBS DESERVE

THE BERRY BEST

On a scale of one to ten, I am a zero when it comes to baking. I've tried, but it seems like every single time, something goes wrong. Here are just a few examples of some of my kitchen disasters.

In fifth grade, I misread the recipe and added a tablespoon of salt to a batch of sugar-cookie dough instead of a teaspoon. I'd planned on giving a plate of pretty, decorated cookies to my teacher for a holiday gift. It was a good thing we sampled them first. I gave her a coffee mug instead.

In sixth grade, my school had a bake sale to raise money for new computers in the library. I tried to make a decadent layered chocolate cake, but when I put the layers together, the cake was so uneven, it looked like the Leaning Tower of Pisa in Italy.

And then there was the time I helped Mom make a lemon cake for a meeting at our house. It looked really dark on top, but we figured some powdered sugar would fix that problem. We later discovered the bottom of the cake was even darker than the top. As in, black. The next time Mom had a meeting, we bought cupcakes.

My mom says she doesn't have the baking gene either, so I shouldn't feel bad. But I do. It seems like every girl I know loves to bake and is an expert at whipping up delicious treats.

My sad skills in the kitchen are the reason I'm secretly freaking out about the discussion going on right now in Sophie's living room. There are five girls and their moms here for the first meeting of the mother/daughter book club that Sophie decided to start. I was so flattered when she asked if my mom and I would like to be a part of it. Sophie and I have been good friends for a few years, ever since we met in theater camp, but we don't go to the same middle school, so it would have been easy for her to leave me out.

Sophie has been explaining to us how the club will work. We'll meet the first Sunday of every month and take turns hosting the club. In addition to the meeting place, the hostesses will provide a list of discussion questions and delicious snacks.

Wait. That's not exactly right. I believe Sophie's exact words were "amazing, delicious, out-of-this-world homemade snacks."

I raise my hand.

"Lily?" Sophie says.

"So, we can't buy snacks?" I ask. "Like at a bakery or grocery store?"

Sophie's best friend, Isabel, replies. "Sophie and I have talked about the snacks a lot. I know we're all busy, but we'll be taking turns, so each of us will only have to bake for the club two or three times a year. We really think homemade treats will make the meetings extra special. We can even exchange recipes, if everyone's interested."

I glance sideways at my mother to see if she's freaking out as much as I am, but my mother is the Queen of Calm. If she's bothered by their homemade requirement, her face doesn't show it.

I take a deep breath and try to copy my mom. She's keeping her eyes focused on the speaker. Her lips are upturned in a slight smile. And her hands are folded in her lap.

Then I give myself a pep talk. My dad taught me this trick because he says there are times in life you need one and the only person available is yourself. I believe this is one of those times.

Lily, stop freaking out about the snacks! Geez, it's not like someone's in the hospital or something. So many people have bigger things to worry about. Get over it. You'll make something and it will be fine. It might taste horrible. Or be black around the edges. Or require a steak knife to cut into it. But it'll be fine.

Sophie continues. "I told my mom that next to seeing friends once a month and reading good books, sharing yummy snacks was at the top of the list as to why I wanted to start a mother/daughter book club. The book club gives us girls a reason to play around in the kitchen and try new recipes. It'll be fun, right?"

I watch as the three other girls nod their heads in agreement with Sophie. I remain calm, all the while thinking how awesome it would be to have a book club with pizza delivered at every meeting.

Sophie looks at a piece of paper in front of her before she says, "Okay, I think I've covered everything. After we discuss *A Wrinkle in Time* this afternoon, we'll choose books for the rest of the year while we eat our snack."

One of the girls I just met today, Dharsanaa, points to the pie on the coffee table. "What kind of pie did you make? It looks really good."

"It's apple-blackberry, and I hope it's good," Sophie replies. "It's the first time I've ever made a pie. Mom helped me with the crust."

"And Jack gave you a few pie-baking tips, right?" Isabel asks. Sophie nods while Isabel explains. "Jack is a friend of mine who lives in Seattle. His mom owns Penny's Pie Place, so he knows a lot about pies."

"Yeah," Sophie says. "He told me to wrap the edge of the pie crust up with aluminum foil the last twenty minutes, to keep it from getting too dark."

Isabel rubs her hands together. "I can't wait to try it, Soph. It looks like something out of a magazine."

"But first we have to eat the jam sandwiches," Katie says. "Like Meg and Charles did in the book, the night of the storm."

"We're going to have hot cocoa too," Sophie says.

"Are we ready to start the discussion?" Dharsanaa asks.

"What about a name for our club?" Isabel asks. "Remember, Sophie? We were going to see if anyone had any suggestions."

The fifth girl, Katie, raises her hand. "I have an idea. How about the Baking Bookworms?"

Sophie and Isabel squeal at the exact same time. "I love it!" Sophie says. "It's perfect! Is that okay with everyone?"

I look at my mom again. She looks at me. The Queens of Calm have vanished from the room. We are the Princesses of Panic, because now there's no denying that this club is going to be as much about baking as it is about reading. But everyone is talking and agreeing that it's the best name ever, so neither of us says a word. I try to think of something else, a different name they'd love just as much, but my mind is completely blank.

Sophie's dog, Daisy, barks, asking to be let in from the backyard. Sophie's mom is in the kitchen getting the hot cocoa ready. "Is it okay if I let her in?" I ask.

"Oh, sure. Thanks, Lily."

I go to the back door and open it, and Daisy is so happy to see me. It's started to rain outside. That's probably why she wanted inside. She follows me back to the living room, where I rejoin everyone. Daisy sits near the coffee table and licks her chops as she eyes the pie.

"Oh, no you don't," Sophie says. She picks up the pie and walks toward the kitchen.

"Let's go around the room and assign a month for hosting," Isabel says. "I'll take April. Lily, you get May, Dharsanaa hosts in June, and in July, it'll be Katie. Is that okay with everyone?"

We all nod our heads. I tell myself two months is plenty of time to find a delicious recipe and practice making it a hundred times. Oh my gosh. Does that mean I have to eat it a hundred times? Maybe my sister will help me. She's athletic and always hungry.

Or maybe we can read a historical book when it's my turn to host. Something from back in the days when sugar was expensive and most people couldn't afford to bake anything really fancy. My great-grandma told me that when she was a little girl she'd get an orange and a few nuts in her stocking at Christmastime and she'd be thrilled. I need a book like that. Then I could serve oranges and nuts and call it good.

Except Sophie wasn't satisfied with just serving hot cocoa and jam sandwiches. She had to go above and beyond what was in the book and bake a beautiful, complicated pie.

I am so doomed.

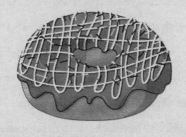

Chapter 2

chocolate-chip-cookie-dough cupcakes

DEFINITELY IMPRESSIVE

"The girls seem really nice," Mom says to me on the drive home. "And their moms too. I think it's a good group. They seem to enjoy baking more than we do, but that's all right. We'll do something simple when it's our turn. I'll go to the bookstore this week and buy the next two books."

We stop at a light near the cupcake shop, It's

Raining Cupcakes. The shop is dark since it's closed on Sundays, but I remember how adorable the shop is inside, with the mural on the wall and the large glass cases filled with pretty cupcakes. I wonder if Isabel and her mom know how lucky they are to be able to bake treats that everyone loves. Next month, when it's Isabel's turn to host the club, she'll probably serve the most spectacular cupcakes, like chocolate-chip cookie dough or caramel Oreo. Everyone will *ooh* and *aah* over them. A month later, it'll be my turn. The girls and their moms will go from being dazzled to being disappointed.

"Lily, are you all right?" Mom asks.

"I guess so. I was just thinking how I wish I could be a good baker like Isabel. Did you know she won the baking contest in New York City a few months back?"

"Yes, I did," she says as the light turns green. "And while it's impressive, you have to remember, you have other talents. It's impossible to be good at everything. That reminds me. When are your bandmates coming over to practice again? Have you worked out a regular schedule?"

"They're coming over tomorrow night. We don't

have a schedule, but I'll ask them about it at practice. We really want to try and find a party or event where we could perform, so then we have something to work toward, you know?"

Mom pats my leg. "Honey, I think it's great that you girls have taken the initiative and formed this band. I'm proud of you, and I know your father is too. But if I were you, I wouldn't worry about performances right now. Focus on playing together. Write more songs. Have fun. Make it about the music."

I sigh. "You sound like Dad."

"Well, he should know. He's been a musician for a long time, right?"

"But, Mom, our dream is to perform for other people. What's the point of practicing if there's no performance to look forward to?"

"Lily, I'm not saying it won't ever happen. But you've only been a band for a couple of months. You have a lot of years ahead of you. For now, focus on the music. Practice because it will make you better musicians. Isn't that what is most important? Becoming the best band you can be?"

"Yeah. I guess so."

I still don't think there's anything wrong with looking for a chance to perform for other people. There's this other band, the New Pirates, made up of a few kids from school, and they're already performing. Zeke Bernstein's parents hired them to play at his Bar Mitzvah party. Belinda McGuire is the lead singer of the New Pirates. Every time our choir director, Mr. Weisenheimer, has us compete for a solo performance in choral practice, it comes down to Belinda and me. She's a really good singer.

To be honest, I don't like Belinda McGuire very much. It seems like she thinks she's better than everyone else. Maybe she is, as far as her talent goes, but it makes her come across as stuck-up.

Someone else who has a lot of talent is my sister, who jumps out from behind the bushes holding a basketball just as we pull into the driveway. She's talented in all things athletic—and now, at almost giving us a heart attack. Fortunately, Mom is a slow driver.

"Good grief, Madison," Mom mutters under her breath.

"Sorry," my sister says as we get out of the car. "The basketball got away from me and I didn't hear you pull up."

"Look before you leap next time," Mom says, walking toward the front door. "Dinner will be ready in an hour, girls."

Mom goes inside while my sister, Miss Show-off, twirls the ball on her pointer finger. Her short brown hair is matted to her face and her cheeks are all red. She's probably been out here shooting hoops most of the afternoon. "How was the book club?"

"It was all right."

"Do you guys have a name?" she asks me, now doing some fancy dribbling move between her legs.

"Do you ever get tired of showing off?" I ask.

She grins. "Not really."

Yeah. That's what I thought.

"Come on," she says. "You must have come up with a name, right?"

I don't want to tell her. She'll make fun of it the second I say it. But she'll find out sooner or later. "The Baking Bookworms."

She stops dribbling and laughs. "When they taste

something you make, you'll have to change your name to the Burnt Bookworms."

I knock the ball out of her hands before I turn to go inside. She scrambles after the ball rolling toward the bushes again. As I approach the front door, I hear her running on the pavement and, a couple of seconds later, the ball swooshing through the net. No doubt a perfect shot.

After I hang up my coat, I head to the family room. The television is on and Dad is just getting up out of his chair, holding his guitar with a broken string hanging from it.

"Hey, Lily Dilly," he says. "Your mom said the book club was fun."

"Yeah. I guess so."

He squints his dark brown eyes at me. "That doesn't sound very convincing."

"Did she tell you that baking seems to be just as important as reading in this club?"

"No, she didn't."

"I really like the girls in the club," I tell Dad. "And I want them to like me. Sophie and I have been friends for a quite a while, but sometimes it feels like I'm second best to her other friends, especially Isabel. This book club is my chance to show Sophie I fit in, you know?"

He pats me on the shoulder before I take a seat on the sofa. "It'll be okay. The most important thing is to have fun. And the more you practice, the better your baking will be. You know, because practice makes . . ."

He wants me to say "perfect." I think it's his favorite saying. I'm sick of the saying myself. "Makes delicious brownies?"

He laughs. "You betcha." He walks past me. "I need to fix this thing since I have a gig tonight. See you at dinner." He flashes me the peace sign, which is his way of saying "see you later." My dad is cool like that.

"Okay, Mr. Peace. See ya."

I pick up the remote and flip through the channels, trying to find something good to watch. I stop when I see a round man with bright red hair and lots of freckles on his face holding a fork. There's a piece of cake on a plate in front of him, and after he takes a bite, he exclaims, "Sweet Uncle Pete, that's good!"

He sets the plate down and smiles at the camera. "I hope you enjoyed the lesson today on how to make a decadent coconut cake. Please tune in to *Secrets of a Pastry Chef* next week, when I'll show you how to bake a white-chocolate-raspberry cheesecake. This is Chef Smiley signing off. Remember: With the right tools and the right attitude, baking is a piece of cake!"

I immediately program the DVR to record the series.

Mr. Smiley, where have you been all my life?

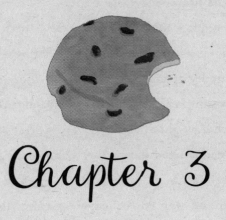

Chapter 3

salted-caramel-mocha cupcakes

SWEET YET SOPHISTICATED

The next day at school, my friend and bandmate Abigail is waiting for me at my locker, her wavy red hair pulled back into a ponytail with a green ribbon around it. Green is her favorite color. She's wearing a cute T-shirt with a picture of an owl. It says I'M A HOOT.

"Your hair sure is getting long," I tell her as I go

to work on my locker combination. "I'm surprised your mom hasn't cut it off yet."

"She really wants to, actually. Said she has a new style she wants to try out on me." She reaches over and pats my straight brown hair. "Hey, maybe I should volunteer you to be her guinea pig. You'd *love* a new style, wouldn't you?"

I shake my head hard. Abigail's mom is going to beauty school. She decided she was tired of working in retail and wanted to become a hairstylist. "You know I haven't changed my hair in, like, four years. Why should I start now?"

"Maybe it's time for a new look. A new Lily! Something that screams rock star."

I laugh as I pull out my algebra textbook and notebook. "We're not really a rock band, are we? More like a pop band."

We walk toward math class, which we have together. "We need to come up with a name," Abigail says. "How can we be a real band without a name?"

"I know. We should work on that tonight."

"Tonight?" she asks, looking at me. "Are we practicing tonight?"

"Abigail, did you forget? Seven o'clock. My dad's playing every night this week at the Wallflower, so we can use the studio as much as we want."

We stop outside the classroom, waiting for the bell to ring.

"Hey, girls," we hear behind us. "How's it going?"

We turn and find Belinda flanked by the other Pirates, Bryan and Sydney. Belinda always dresses like she's about to go on stage. Today she's wearing a purple miniskirt with a black blouse and black boots. My mom would never let me come to school dressed like that. I look down at my jeans and pink Converse sneakers and realize I wouldn't *want* to come to school dressed like that.

"Have you heard the news?" Belinda asks, twirling one of her blond corkscrew curls around her finger. She's got more curls than a toy poodle.

"What news?" Abigail asks.

"Mr. Weisenheimer convinced Ms. Presley to let some local talent perform at the Spring Fling."

Every April, our middle school has a Spring Fling on a Friday night for the seventh and eighth graders. They set up games in the gym, like badminton and

Ping-Pong, and some of the classrooms have activities like a cakewalk, bean-bag toss, and bingo. There's music in the gym, too, usually with a DJ, and kids can dance if they want to, although most of us just stand around with a soda in our hand and talk while we listen to the music. A few kids who are amazing dancers might go on the dance floor to show off what they can do, but that's about it.

"What do you mean by 'local talent'?" I ask.

"From our school," Sydney says. "They're going to have tryouts and let someone, a singer or a band or whatever, perform a few songs on stage."

"Pretty awesome, right?" Bryan says as he swings his head back to get the bangs out of his eyes. I have to say, I am a little bit envious that Belinda is in a band with Bryan. He is so cute. He keeps talking. "We already know what song we're going to do for the audition."

I swallow hard. "Audition? When's the audition?"

"We don't know yet," Belinda says. "They're supposed to let us know sometime this week." She smiles a big, fake smile. The kind of smile that says, *I look forward to beating the pants off you in that audition.* "Think you guys will try out?"

Abigail starts to reply. "I don't—"

"Of course we will," I say. "Yeah, we're all over that. We have some great songs. One of them is *really* awesome. It's the kind you can't help but dance to, no matter how shy you might be."

Abigail looks at me like I've lost my mind. "Which song is that?" she asks.

I nudge her with my elbow. "Remember? That one song? Um, what's it called?" My eyes dart around, looking for something to say, and land on Sydney's T-shirt, which is pink and glittery and has a big cupcake on it. "The cupcake song. Remember?"

Abigail pinches her lips together, like she's trying not to laugh. My eyes beg her to keep her ridiculous thoughts to herself. She nods. "Oh. Right! The cupcake song. Yeah, it's really fun." She tells the New Pirates, "If you guys come to the dance, we'll teach you how to do the cupcake dance too. How's that?"

Belinda laughs. "Oh, you've made up a cupcake dance to go with the song? Wow, that's impressive, since cupcakes don't really do anything but sit there and look cute."

As if a cupcake song wasn't bad enough, now we've

promised them we have a dance to go with the song? Oh boy. This is worse than a bunch of my mom's friends eating burnt lemon cake that I made for them.

The warning bell rings, thank goodness. The three turn to head to class, but not before Sydney says, "I doubt you'll get to show us your dance. Because we're gonna own that audition. I promise you, the New Pirates will be the ones performing on that stage at the Spring Fling."

"Whatever," I mumble as Abigail pulls me into class.

We take our seats in the back row.

"Really, Lily?" Abigail asks me. "The cupcake song? What are we, six?"

"Hey, cupcakes can be sophisticated," I say, trying to convince myself just as much as Abigail. "What about coffee-flavored cupcakes? I had this salted-caramel-mocha cupcake one time, and it was so good. I wonder if they use real coffee when they make them."

She waves her hand in front of my face. "Earth to Lily, Earth to Lily. That's enough about cupcakes. What about our band? Do you think we can beat the New Pirates?"

"I think it depends on when the auditions are and how long we have to practice," I say.

Immediately after the second bell rings, our principal, Ms. Presley, comes over the intercom with Monday-morning announcements. She talks about a disaster drill we'll be doing in the next few days and an assembly we have coming up on Friday. I doodle in my notebook as she rambles on.

"Finally, plans are under way for our Spring Fling, coming up on Friday, April twelfth." I sit up straight and listen. "Our choir director, Mr. Weisenheimer, and our band director, Ms. Adams, have decided it would be fun to allow a student or group of students to perform at the Spring Fling this year. Auditions will be held after school in just a few weeks, right before spring break, on Thursday, March twenty-first. A group of teachers will choose the act they believe to be the best fit. Good luck, everyone!"

I look at Abigail and give her a thumbs-up. Three weeks is plenty of time to get a song or two ready.

Isn't it?

Chapter 4

peanut-butter cookies
IT'S EASY TO SING THEIR PRAISES

The doorbell rings right at seven. Mom is in her office on the phone, lining up houses to show to a client tomorrow. She's a real estate agent, so she works a lot. She loves her job, though—helping people find their dream homes.

I hurry to the door and find Zola there, holding her drumsticks. Dad has a drum set in his studio that he lets us use, but Zola likes to use her own sticks.

She says using someone else's drumsticks is like using someone else's toothbrush. Ew! Her parents bought her a drum set for Christmas last year, when she was one of the students selected to play drums for the school band. She's really good. When kids try out for the drums, the band teacher looks for kids who can pick up a rhythm really quickly, and Zola blew everyone away with her performance the first time she played.

"Hey, Lily," she says.

"Hi, Zola. Come in. Abigail isn't here yet."

Zola is one of the most popular girls at school. She is cute and fun and it seems like everything she does, she does well. Kind of like my sister. When Abigail and I asked her if she'd like to join our band, I was so nervous, but I shouldn't have been. She was really excited that we'd asked her, and happily said yes.

"I love your shoes," I tell her. "I didn't know they made polka-dot ones."

"Yeah," she says, looking down at her purple sneakers. "I think they're kind of a new thing." She looks over at my pink ones. "Dude, you should get yourself some."

Zola says "dude" a lot. Maybe because she has three older brothers. I don't know, but I don't mind. I kind of like it.

I lean up against the staircase. "Do you think it's important to be really stylish when you're in a band? Like, are we supposed to dress up or something?"

She shrugs. "I don't want to dress up. I like being comfortable, don't you? Maybe we'll be known as that cool band with girls who wear awesome sneakers. Nothing wrong with that."

I nod, because she's right. There's a knock at the door, which means Abigail's here. We say hello and head down to the basement. When Mom and Dad bought this house ten years ago, it was the soundproof studio Dad loved the most. And I have to say, it's pretty great knowing that when we shut the door, our noise—I mean, our music—won't bother anyone. Abigail goes to work hooking up her pretty red guitar to the amplifier. My dad's been really nice about letting us use his studio equipment. He has top-of-the-line equipment that he uses for his performances, but the stuff in his studio wasn't cheap either.

He spent an hour or so going over rules with us. Everything basically came down to this one: Do not break anything or you will be grounded for the rest of your life.

"Before we start playing, I really think we should come up with a name," Abigail says, fishing a guitar pick out of her jeans pocket. She's been taking guitar lessons for about six months, and she's getting pretty good.

"I hate coming up with names," I say, thinking about the Baking Bookworms and how my mind went blank and I couldn't even offer any other suggestions. "It's so hard. How do people do it? Where do you think the New Pirates got their name?"

"I don't know," Zola says as she takes a seat behind the drum set. "It's an awesome name, if you ask me."

"What about the Cherry Pickers?" Abigail asks. "I'd love something fun like that."

"Um, I don't like cherries," Zola says. "No offense."

"Maybe we can stay away from food-related names?" I suggest. "They kind of make me nervous. Long story."

"We could go with something like the Zombies or the Ninjas," Zola says. "I'd rather be a ninja than a pirate any day."

Abigail slips the guitar strap around her neck and strums. It's really loud, so she turns the volume down on the amp. "Nah. Too much like the Pirates. I want to be different from them."

I look around the room, trying to think of something that's fun and unique. Something that feels like us. I keep looking at Zola's shoes, wondering if we could do something related to them. The Polka Dots is a cute name, but people would probably expect us to play polka music, and polka is about the last thing I want to play.

The Sneakers?

The Sneaker Dots?

The Dots?

"You guys," I say, "what about something really simple? Like the Dots?"

"Hey, I like it," Zola says. "Do you think it's too simple, though?"

Abigail smiles. "The Dots. No. It's easy to remember, and that's good."

"Yeah, I like it too," I say. "Here, let me try it out. Ladies and gentlemen, for this year's Spring Fling, I'm pleased to introduce to you a band that's as fun as their name—the Dots!"

Abigail and Zola clap and cheer. It makes me laugh.

After we calm down, I say, "So now that our name is settled, do you guys want to compete in the auditions coming up in a few weeks?"

"Yes," they say at the exact same time.

"But shouldn't we perform an original song?" I ask.

Abigail pulls a crumpled piece of paper out of her back pocket. "Well, I've been working on something. We can try it out, if you want to."

"Is it a cupcake song?" I ask.

She shakes her head. "No, it isn't. Lily, you are the one who got us into that mess, so I think you're the one who gets to work on a cupcake song."

Zola looks at us like we are crazy. "Dudes, what are you talking about?"

"Lily promised the New Pirates that if we're chosen to play at the Spring Fling," Abigail explains, "we'll play a cupcake song they'll love."

"Don't forget the dance," I say, cringing. "That was your idea, Abigail."

"Sorry, Lily. If you write the song, I think it makes sense you come up with the dance too," Abigail says.

"So what's the song called you've been working on?" Zola asks.

"'Wishing.' Here, I'll play a little bit for you."

Abigail puts the piece of paper on the music stand in front of her and then strums her guitar and starts to sing.

> *I blew on the dandelion, and watched the wishes fly.*
> *Some fell to the ground while others floated high.*
> *Maybe life is hard sometimes, but that's just how it goes.*
> *If we hope and if we wish, life might change, who knows."*

She stops playing. "That's all I've got. Sorry. I need to work on the chorus. Maybe you guys can help me?"

"Abigail, that's really good," I say. "If we can finish it and then practice like crazy the next couple of weeks, we might have a chance at winning that audition."

"Can you play it from the top?" Zola asks, which sounds so professional and like we're really a band.

That's when it hits me, and I want to squeal and jump around because I'm in a *real* band and we have a name and we might even have a song!

I'm so excited, but I tell myself to calm down because there is still a lot of work to do. Before we're able to get too far into the song, someone knocks on the studio door. I open the door just enough to peek out and see my mom standing there.

"Sorry to bother you," she says. She's holding a piece of paper with a phone number written on it. "Isabel just called and I thought you might want to call her back before it gets too late. She said it was important, and she didn't have your cell number, so she called the house."

"We're right in the middle of something," I tell her as I take the piece of paper. "I'll have to wait and call her in a little while."

Mom nods. "Well, if you girls want to take a break pretty soon, I bought some peanut-butter cookies at the store. They're really good."

"Okay. Thanks."

I shut the door and go back to the band. Not just any band. My band—the Dots!

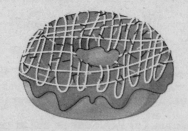

Chapter 5

applesauce cake
GOOD FOR CALMING NERVES

We manage to get some more lyrics written to our song, though it's still not finished. I sing while the girls play the instruments, and we don't sound half-bad. We don't sound great yet either, but that's to be expected with a brand-new song.

I ask the girls if we can take a break, so we go upstairs and Abigail and Zola munch on cookies at the kitchen table while I excuse myself for a minute and take the phone into the living room.

"Isabel?" I say when she answers. "This is Lily."

"Oh, thanks for calling me back. Your mom said your band is practicing tonight. That's so amazing you're in a band. What do you play?"

I take a seat on the sofa. "I don't play an instrument. I'm the lead singer. I should probably learn guitar at some point, but my parents have been paying for voice lessons, and lessons are pretty expensive."

"Yeah. I bet. Hey, the reason I called is because Sophie's thirteenth birthday is coming up in a couple of weeks. I want to have a surprise party for her."

"Oh, wow, I love that idea," I say. "Is there anything I can do to help?"

"Actually, there is. Our apartment isn't very big, so I was hoping you might be willing to have the party at your house. Do you think your mom would mind?"

"Oh, um, I don't think so." I get up and walk toward Mom's office. "Let me ask her right now. When's her birthday?"

"It's March sixteenth, which is a Saturday, lucky for

us. You could have it in the afternoon or evening, whatever you think is best."

"Okay. Can you hold on a second, Isabel?"

"Sure."

I knock lightly on Mom's office door.

"Come in," Mom calls out.

I cover the phone with the palm of my hand and go in. "Mom, Isabel wants to have a surprise party for Sophie. She's turning thirteen in a couple of weeks. Do you think we could have the party here?"

Mom smiles. "Oh, sweetie, I'd love to do that! Sophie has been such a good friend to you. What's the date? I'll check my calendar to make sure we're free."

"March sixteenth."

She clicks on her laptop, studies it for a second, and then says, "Yep. That'll be fine. Oh, how fun! I love surprise parties!"

I step out of her office and shut the door as I put the phone back to my ear. "Isabel? My mom said we could have the party here."

"Perfect! We have a lot we need to talk about and so much to do, but I know you need to get back to your band. We'll need to meet up at least once this week and get invitations made and buy some decorations and figure out food. Do you have time tomorrow?"

I'm thinking fast, trying to figure out how I can make this work. I have an essay for social studies I have to work on after school. "After dinner would probably be best. Where do you want to meet?"

"If your mom can bring you here, we can sit in the cupcake shop and eat cupcakes while we talk about the party."

"Sounds good. I'll be there around seven."

"Great. Thanks, Lily. See you then."

I head back to the kitchen, where Abigail and Zola have finished off the cookies and are entertaining themselves by playing table hockey with a guitar pick.

"Sorry about that," I tell them. "We can head back to the studio now and work on those song lyrics some more."

Zola looks at her phone. "Actually, my dad is on his way to pick me up. He's going to be here any minute. I need to get my sticks from downstairs."

"Should we set up another time to practice?" Abigail asks as she and Zola stand up. "What about tomorrow night?"

"Sorry. I can't," I say. "I have something else I have to do." Now I feel guilty about making plans with Isabel before checking with Abigail and Zola. "What about Wednesday?"

"Wednesday I have guitar lessons," Abigail says.

"And Thursday night I have drum lessons," Zola says.

"Friday?" I ask.

They both nod. "Yeah, that should work," Zola says.

I breathe a sigh of relief. "Okay, good. Friday it is."

"Work on that cupcake song between now and then, okay?" Abigail says with a wink.

"How about if I eat a cupcake instead?" I say, thinking of the cupcake shop where I'll be meeting Isabel tomorrow night.

We hustle down to the studio and collect their things. Both of their parents arrive a few minutes later.

After they leave, I rustle around in the kitchen, looking for something to eat, when Madison comes in.

"How'd band practice go?" she asks.

I turn around as she sets a plastic bag on the counter. "It was fun. What's that?"

"Leftover applesauce cake from the potluck tonight. You can have some if you want. It's pretty good. Mom picked it up at the bakery."

I take the cake out of the bag. "Was the potluck a basketball thing?"

She leans against the counter, and I can't help but notice how strong she looks. Her arms have so much definition to them, and I wonder if she lifts weights on top of everything else she does to stay fit.

"Yeah. End-of-the-season party. I was kind of down about the season ending, but I'm feeling better now."

I cut a piece of cake and put it on a plate. "How come?"

"Some of my friends talked me into going out for softball. Tryouts are this week."

I get a fork out of the silverware drawer. "Softball? But you've never played. Volleyball and basketball have always been your sports."

She shrugs. "I figure it doesn't hurt to try. My friends tell me softball is a blast. And if I make the team, it'll be a good way to keep myself in shape."

"Well, good luck with that," I say as I sit at the table with my piece of cake.

Mom comes out of her office and joins us. "Lily, here's the book for our next book club meeting. I bought two copies for us, so you don't have to worry about rushing through it."

She sets a copy of *The View from Saturday* down in front of me. I feel a tiny knot in the pit of my stomach, because there's one more thing on my growing list of things I have to do in the next few weeks. I take a bite of cake to distract myself from the nervous-making thoughts.

"Mom," I say, "I told Isabel I'd meet up with her at the cupcake shop tomorrow night, to start planning for Sophie's party. Can you drive me there after dinner?"

"Yes," she says as she gets herself a piece of cake. "I'm happy to do that." She looks at Madison. "We're having a surprise party for a friend of Lily's here in a couple of weeks."

Madison nods. "Please remind me a couple of days before the party so I can make sure I have something else to do far, far away that day. I don't want to get sucked into cleaning house or decorating or baking or any of the other hundred things you guys will be doing."

I gulp.

"It probably will be a lot of work," Mom says, "but it'll be worth it. Right, Lily?"

I take another bite of cake, hoping to distract myself again.

What have I gotten myself into?

Chapter 6

cookies-'n'-cream cupcakes

FLAVOR OVERLOAD

When I get to It's Raining Cupcakes on Tuesday evening, it's almost dark, but I can see Isabel waiting in front of the brightly lit shop.

"I'm going grocery shopping while you two chat," Mom says. "I'll be back in about an hour."

"Okay," I tell her as I get out of the car. "Thanks, Mom."

She waves and drives off.

"Hi, Isabel," I say.

"Hey, Lily. Thanks for coming." She opens the door to the shop and we step inside. It smells like freshly baked cake. Delicious! Isabel locks the door and says, "We're not actually open right now, but my mom said we could sit at a table and have a cupcake while we talk about the party."

"Where are all the cupcakes?" I ask as I scan the empty cases.

"Oh, we take them out of the cases before we close every afternoon," Isabel explains. "Whatever is left over, we sell the following day at a discount. They're called day-old cupcakes. They still taste good, but we want people to know that the cupcakes in the cases are always really fresh, baked the same day. Follow me. I'll show you."

We go around the cash register and back into the kitchen. She walks over to a big plastic tub on the counter.

"Let's see," she says as she pops the lid off. "You get to choose from cookies 'n' cream, coconut bliss, banana-cream pie, or red velvet. What looks good?"

"They all look fantastic." I try to imagine what each one might taste like. Red velvet is my favorite, but I kind of want to try something different tonight. "I think I'll go with the cookies 'n' cream."

Isabel smiles. "Excellent choice." She grabs a pair of plastic tongs, picks up a cookies-'n'-cream cupcake for me, and places it on a pretty yellow plate. She chooses banana-cream pie for herself.

"You must feel like the luckiest girl in the world," I tell her. "You get to eat cupcakes anytime you want."

"I kind of get sick of them sometimes, to be honest. But my mom loves her cupcake shop, and while business was slow for a while, things have picked up, so that's good. We have Sophie to thank for that. I feel lucky to have Sophie as a best friend, that's for sure."

The way she says it, I feel like I'm watching two friends whisper back and forth, sharing a secret. "What did she do?"

"Once a month or so, she comes and walks around the neighborhood, wearing a cupcake costume she made, to help bring us business. She looks amazing and, at the same time, a little bit ridiculous, but she doesn't care. She's helping us, and that's all that matters to her."

"Wow," I say. In that moment, I'm so jealous of Isabel and the close friendship she has with Sophie, but I try to not let it show. Softly, I say, "You are lucky. What a good friend. She's never said anything about that to me."

Isabel hands me the plates. "That's Sophie for you. She's not the type to brag about herself, right?" She points toward the dining area. "Find the table with the pad of paper and pen, and take a seat. I'll get us some milk."

"Okay, thanks." I go back to the dining area and see the paper she was talking about. I sit down in one of the two chairs, still thinking about what Isabel said. This surprise party is my chance to show Sophie she's one of my best friends. I have to do everything I can to make it a really great party.

I turn the pad of paper toward me and read what Isabel has written.

Things to do for Sophie's party:

1. Make a list of people to invite
2. Make or buy invitations
3. Pass out invitations
4. Buy decorations
5. Plan menu
6. Games or something else fun to do?
7. Come up with a plan to get Sophie to Lily's house
8. Buy gift

"My dad loves lists," Isabel says as she sits down with the glasses of milk. "I guess I take after him."

"Yeah, it's a good way to really see everything that needs to be done," I tell her, secretly panicking inside at all the things that need to be done.

I peel the liner off of my cupcake.

"I've been working on a list of people to invite," Isabel says, flipping the pad to another piece of paper. "I hope thirty isn't too many?"

I almost drop my cupcake. "Thirty?"

"It's really hard to narrow it down any more than that because I don't want anyone to feel left out. And

I think I should invite both boys and girls, because we have some boys who we're good friends with at school. Think your mom will be okay with thirty kids, both boys and girls?"

"Uh, sure."

She smiles. "Oh, good. I was hoping you'd say that. My dad said he'd help me make some invitations on the computer, so I'm going to do that tonight, when we're done here. I should be able to hand them out to everyone tomorrow."

I am giving myself a little pep talk right now. This is what it sounds like in my brain.

It'll be okay, Lily. Think of your algebra class—that's about thirty kids. It's not so many, right? It'll be fun. What does Dad always say? The more the merrier? The important thing is to make Sophie happy. Isabel is going to help you with everything, so it's not like you're going to have that much to do. Look. She's handling all of the invitations, and that's a big job. Remain calm. Eat your cupcake. It will be fine.

I bite into my cupcake and the creamy taste of vanilla frosting mixed with Oreo cookie hits my tongue, and it's really, really good. I take a deep breath and close my eyes for a second, savoring the flavor.

"What time do you want to have the party?" Isabel asks.

And just like that, I'm back from the sweetness of cupcakes to the business of party planning. "Mom and I talked about it on the ride over," I tell her. "Is seven o'clock okay? That way we don't have to worry about serving a meal."

"Perfect," Isabel says, writing down seven o'clock on her pad of paper. "Can you give me your address?"

She hands me the pen and paper, and I write down all of my information, including my cell phone number. While I'm doing that, she says, "I figure I'll get purple and silver decorations. Purple and silver look pretty together, don't you think?"

"Ooooh, that sounds nice."

"I can come to your house early that day and help you decorate. I don't want you to have to do it all alone."

Isabel looks at the list and points to number five. "So, what do you think we should do for food?"

"I wonder if your mom might want to donate some cupcakes," I say. It seems like a good solution to me. And who doesn't like cupcakes?

She taps the pen on the table, thinking about my question. "The thing is, Sophie has cupcakes here all the time. I want something special for her birthday. This is the big thirteen, right? She should have an amazing dessert for becoming a teenager."

I feel my cheeks getting warm. Isabel must think I'm an idiot. I have to show her that I want something amazing for Sophie too. "Right. Of course she should have something really special. I bet I can find a dessert that's out of this world."

"Really?"

I try to sound excited, even though I'm actually terrified as to whether or not I can pull it off. "Sure."

"Awesome," she says, writing my name next to number five on her list. "I know you'll make something fantastic."

When she says the word "make," my stomach lurches. It feels like I'm on a giant roller coaster, heading down, down, down. "Well," I quickly say, "we have this great bakery nearby that my mom goes to . . ." I stop because Isabel looks like I've just told her I want to serve asparagus and mud pies at the party. It's like the mother/daughter book club meeting all over again. She really wants me to make something. I try to save myself from complete embarrassment. "Maybe I can get some ideas there."

"Maybe. I bet your mom would love to help you make something. And what about your older sister? Does she like to bake?"

"Not really. She's into sports."

She nods, like it makes complete sense. "Well, you're one of the Baking Bookworms," she says, taking a bite of her cupcake. When she's done chewing, she smiles. "Which means there isn't a single baking challenge you can't handle, right?"

I should have suggested a different name.

The Bashful Bookworms.

The Babbling Bookworms.

The Brilliant Bookworms.

Why didn't I suggest a different name? And why did I agree to cohost Sophie's birthday party?

Chapter 7

cinnamon rolls

A COMFORTING SNACK

From the time I was three years old, I loved to sing. Mom says I could sing better than I could talk. I get that from my dad. If my dad isn't playing music, he's usually listening to it, and apparently I loved to sing along to whatever song was on the radio, whether I knew all the words or not.

I wish other things came as easily to me. When I was six, Mom signed me up for soccer. It seems like there's always one kid who can't do anything right and runs the wrong way down the field and scores a goal for the other team. I was that kid. I was horrible. My dad tried to tell me it didn't matter, that the most important thing was to have fun. Easy for him to say. I'm pretty sure he'd never scored a point for the opposite team.

When I get home from school on Wednesday, I take out every cookbook we own. All three of them. They look brand-new. Mom probably got them at her bridal shower years ago, stuck them in the cupboard, and hasn't looked at them since. She's a pretty basic cook. Tacos are about as complicated as she gets in the kitchen.

I flip through the cookbook by Betty Crocker and find the dessert section. I don't know what I'm looking for, exactly, other than something that says Sophie and birthday party. I figure I'll know it when I see it.

"Hey, Lily Dilly." Dad strolls over to the fridge and pulls out a bottle of water.

"Hey, Dad."

After he takes a drink, he rummages around

for a minute, until he eventually pulls out a tube of something. "Think I'll make cinnamon rolls. Sounds like a good afternoon snack, right?"

My stomach grumbles at the mention of those two pretty words. It's been a few hours since I ate my peanut-butter-and-honey sandwich for lunch.

"Right."

He hits a couple of buttons on the oven and it starts preheating. Then he pulls a baking pan out of the cupboard, pops the tube open, and places the unbaked cinnamon rolls in a circle on the pan.

Maybe I could do that for Sophie's party. Buy a bunch of tubes of cinnamon rolls from the grocery store, bake them up ahead of time, frost them, and pass them off as homemade. Would anyone even know the difference?

Dad sits down across from me and takes another swig from his water bottle. His cheeks are really pink and his short brown hair is sticking every which way. Either he's been working on a new song for hours and hours or he just got off his treadmill.

He must know I'm trying to figure out why he

looks the way he does because he says, "I went for a four-mile run on the treadmill."

I nod. "I didn't think you got that sweaty playing music."

He smiles. "Not in the studio, no. Playing on a stage with hot lights for two hours, yes."

"Are your shows at the Wallflower going all right?" I ask.

"Oh, yeah. They're great. We've had a good crowd every night." The oven beeps, letting us know it's preheated, so he jumps up and sticks the rolls in. "What about you? How's your band coming along?"

I sigh. "We have half a song written. We're getting together again Friday night. I hope we can finish it. We want to audition for the Spring Fling at school."

He sits down again and raises his eyebrows. "You guys are trying out for a gig? That's awesome, kiddo! You're going big-time." He raises his hand and we high-five. "Just remember what I told you. Make the music your priority. All the rest will work out if you focus on making great music."

I nod. "I'm supposed to write a cupcake song. A

sophisticated cupcake song. Think you can help me with that?"

He points to the cookbooks in front of me. "Is that what you're doing? Looking for a little inspiration in those books?"

"No. The cookbooks are because I'm supposed to make a fabulous dessert for thirty people at a surprise birthday party in a week and a half."

He laughs and leans back in his chair. "Hold on a second. What are you doing to yourself, Lily? That's an awful lot you've got on your plate."

I shake my head. "Believe me. I know."

"Can't you just buy a dessert for the party?" he asks. "That's what I'd do. I'm happy to give you some money to shop at Mom's favorite bakery. Or what if we get a whole bunch of brownies from Beatrice's Brownies?"

I laugh. "Dad, the party is for Sophie. She's the girl who's done television commercials for Beatrice's Brownies. She's probably sick of those things by now."

"Well, what's wrong with a huge bakery cake, then? I know. We can have it decorated like that musical you saw with Sophie a few months back. What was it called?"

"*Wicked*," I tell him. "And I'm not really sure a cake with the Wicked Witch of the West's face in green frosting would be very appetizing."

"Hmm," he says. "You may be right. Well, think it over. I'm happy to help however I can. Though if you're going to try and make something yourself, I'm probably not your guy. Wait. That reminds me. There's a chef on TV I was watching last Sunday when I was fiddling around on my guitar. Have you ever seen the show *Secrets of a Pastry Chef*?"

I close the cookbook because all it's doing is making me even more hungry. The cinnamon rolls are starting to smell really good. "I scheduled the DVR to record it. I think it only shows on Sundays."

"You should double-check," he says. "They might be playing reruns on other days of the week. Chef Smiley takes you through all of the steps of a recipe, and he makes it look so easy. I'm telling you, Lily, he might be the answer to your baking problems."

"Okay. I'll see what I can find."

He stands up and walks over to the oven. "As far

as the cupcake song, I'll let you know if any lyrics or a fun melody come to mind."

The timer goes off. The cinnamon rolls are done. I wish I could just pop a few notes in the oven and have a complete song come out. Someone needs to invent that—a song-writing oven.

But knowing me, I'd probably mess that up too.

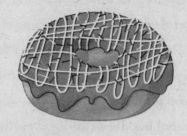

Chapter 8

strawberry cake

PRETTY ENOUGH TO WEAR

Dad was right. They do play reruns of Chef Smiley's show on the Food Channel. After dinner, I settle in on the sofa with a notebook and our kitty, Oscar, to watch an episode. The funny chef takes us start to finish through a strawberry cake made from scratch. The secret ingredient is strawberry-flavored gelatin.

"I know it sounds strange," Chef Smiley says as he

pours the red powdery stuff into the bowl, "but it gives the cake a delicious strawberry flavor. Remember, it isn't always about being fancy and using expensive or exotic ingredients. It's about finding what works. In fact, that's one of my mottos in the kitchen—whatever works!"

I write everything down while Chef Smiley shows us, step by step, how to make the cake. It really doesn't look too hard, and I'm getting more and more excited as the show winds down. When he takes a bite of the cake, he says, "Sweet Uncle Pete, that's good," just like he did last time. I wonder if he has an uncle Pete who's really sweet.

When I'm finished watching, I give the cat one last pet and then go looking for my mom. I find her in the kitchen, unloading the dishwasher. "Good," she says. "I could use an extra set of hands. Can you help me, please?"

I set my notebook down and grab a couple of glasses from the top rack. "Mom, I need a few things from the store so I can make a strawberry cake. Can you take me?"

"Oh, honey, I can't. I need to get a house listed

on the computer tonight. Maybe your sister can take you. Unless it can wait until tomorrow?"

I sigh. "No. I don't want to wait. I have to find something amazing to make for Sophie's party. This strawberry cake may be the answer. It looks so good. And pretty."

She goes to work putting the silverware away. "When we're done here, we'll go find your sister and I'll ask her to drive you."

Madison won't like it, but I know she'll do it. When Madison got the used Ford Escort that Mom and Dad helped pay for, they told her she had a responsibility to help out with errands when necessary.

After we've finished, we head upstairs to Madison's room. Mom knocks. Music is playing. Loudly. She knocks again.

"Come in," Madison calls out. The music gets quieter.

Mom opens the door and we peer inside. Madison is sitting at her desk. Dirty clothes are scattered across the floor and all over her bed. On her nightstand are a whole bunch of dirty dishes.

"Madison, I need you to take your sister to the store, please."

"But, Mom, I'm—"

"Please don't argue. I need you to get up and take her right now. It'll only take a few minutes and then you can get back to whatever it is you're working on. And when you're done with that, you get to clean your room. For goodness' sake, Madison. It smells like a cat died in here."

Madison scrunches up her nose. "Gross. No, it doesn't."

I nod my head. "Yes, it does. I'd start digging around for Oscar if I hadn't just seen him in the family room. It really does stink."

Madison stands up. "Okay, okay, so I've been super busy and haven't had time to clean." She looks at me. "Give me a minute to change out of these shorts. I'll meet you downstairs."

"Thank you, honey," Mom says.

Five minutes later, we're in the car, on our way to the store. "What are you up to?" Madison asks me.

"Isabel expects me to make the dessert for

Sophie's party," I tell her. "So I want to try and make this strawberry cake I just saw on TV. It doesn't look *too* hard."

She shakes her head. "Lily, maybe you should tell your book club friends you're not a baker. I bet they'd understand."

"But maybe I am a baker," I say. "Maybe I just haven't practiced enough. You know what Dad says. Practice makes—"

"Perfect? Look, you know I'm a big believer in practicing myself. But here's the thing—sometimes there are things we just aren't good at doing. I mean, what if I told you I wanted to be a ballerina? Would you tell me if I practice enough, I'll be good enough to perform the *Nutcracker* come Christmastime?"

I look out my window and watch raindrops skip across the glass. "Maybe," I say quietly. "I mean, who knows? Anything is possible, isn't it? Mom and Dad have told us that our whole lives. Are you saying you don't believe it?"

Madison pulls into the Safeway parking lot and parks the car. After she turns the motor off, she looks at me. "Lily, that's what parents are supposed to say. It's okay if you're good at some things and not so good at others. I mean, look around. Who's good at everything?"

I think for a few seconds, and only one person pops into my head, though I'm sure there must be plenty of people. "You?" I say to my sister.

She laughs. "Oh, that is funny. Do you really think I'm good at everything? Come on. Don't you remember how I sing? What'd you say I sounded like last time I tried to sing with you?"

"A seal with the flu."

"Right. And what about my decorating skills? Or my cleaning skills? You saw my room—nothing to brag about there."

I grab my purse and start to get out. "Okay, okay, maybe you're right. But I want to feel like I fit in with the Baking Bookworms. I like those girls, and I want them to like me. I want to be good at baking, Madison. So I'm going to see if Chef Smiley can teach me. It doesn't hurt to try."

"All right. Hurry up and buy what you need," she says as I get out. "I have a paper to write and a room to clean, thanks to you, Miss Baker-Wannabe."

I grab a grocery cart and make my way through the store, crossing things off my list. The recipe calls for sifted flour, and I remember what Chef Smiley said. *With the right tools and the right attitude, baking is a piece of cake.* I throw a flour sifter in my cart, because I'm pretty sure we don't have one at home.

I buy the stuff with the money Mom gave me and hurry back to the car. Madison gives me a hard time about taking forever, but geez, I had to make sure I got everything on my list.

When we get home, Madison retreats to her room and I go to work making the cake. I cream the butter, sugar, and gelatin together with the mixer, just like Chef Smiley said to do. Then I separate the eggs and add the yolks, followed by the whipped egg whites. I mix the flour and baking powder together, and stir that in with the milk. I add the vanilla, and the only thing left to do is puree the frozen strawberries.

I get the blender out, put a bunch of strawberries in along with some water, and hit blend.

"Lily!" Mom yells behind me. "You don't have the . . ."

But it's too late. Bright red strawberries go

everywhere—on the counter, the cupboards, the floor, the ceiling, and yes, some get on me too.

I push the off button and turn around to face my mother.

"Oh, honey," she says, trying not to laugh, which I guess is better than yelling at me. "Always make sure to put the lid on the blender."

I am so embarrassed. And everything was going so well. "Yeah, I think I know that now."

I look down at my white shirt, dots of strawberry juice all over it. It's probably ruined.

"Why don't you go change your clothes?" Mom says. "I'll start cleaning up in here."

"But what about the cake? I'm almost done with the batter. I just need to add the pureed strawberries and bake it."

"Do you have any berries left?"

Thankfully, I'd dumped only half of the big bag into the blender. "Yes. They're in the freezer. Can I finish really quickly and then go shower?"

"All right," she says, wetting a rag in the sink. "I'll work around you."

I blend more strawberries, this time keeping

everything inside the blender. I pour them into the batter and mix it well. Then I put the parchment paper in the bottom of the pans, just like Chef Smiley instructed. He said it keeps the cakes from sticking. He also said the batter makes enough for three pans, but we have only two, so I split the batter between the two pans. After I pop them in the oven, I set the timer and thank Mom for helping to clean up.

"You're welcome," she says. "Come and help me when you're finished, okay?"

"I think I might take a shower. If I'm not down in twenty-five minutes, can you check the cakes? Check them with a toothpick. It should come out clean."

"Okay," she says, grabbing a stool so she can get to the ceiling.

"I'm really sorry, Mom," I tell her again. "Hopefully, the cake will taste delicious and you can have a big piece."

She holds up her hand with her fingers crossed. "That's what I'm hoping for!"

Chapter 9

glazed doughnuts

A TRUE JOY

I'm heading to choir, and I'm so tired, I could probably lie down in the hallway and take a nap. Okay, maybe not. After all, the hallway is where hundreds of kids walk and it wouldn't be very nice to take a nap where I'd be trampled. Not to mention the fact that I'd be sleeping in dirt.

But I am *so* tired.

Last night, after I took a shower and dried my

hair, I went downstairs and smelled something bad. Mom was nowhere in sight. The timer was beeping and the cakes were done. They weren't burnt, but the oven was filled with smoke because I guess I filled the cake pans too full. The bottom of the oven was covered with burnt batter that had dripped from the pans as the cake rose.

My mother had stepped away to take a call. When my mom gets on the phone, the sky could be falling and she wouldn't notice.

After I opened the windows to clear out the smoke, I considered my options. I could call the whole thing a disaster and throw out the cakes. Or I could frost the cakes even though they weren't perfect and see how they tasted, and then decide if I wanted to attempt it all over again for Sophie's party.

I decided I wanted to see my recipe through to the end. I'd already put in a lot of work, plus I was curious how the cake would taste. Mom came back a while later and felt really bad. While she frosted the cake, I finished wiping down the kitchen.

The cake was not pretty, due to the layers being uneven. When I took a bite, I thought for sure it would taste as bad as it looked. What a surprise when it turned out to be delicious! Mom and I were still up when Dad got home, and he thought it tasted good too.

Now I'm trying to decide if I want to try again on Sophie's big day, or look for a different recipe. Maybe something a little easier. I figure I'd have to make two cakes in order to feed thirty people, which means I'd have twice the chances of messing up.

"Hey, Lily," Belinda says as I enter the choir room. She never really talks to me. Weird.

"Hey," I say. "How's it going?"

"Fine." She smiles. "How's the audition practicing going?"

I try to sound happy. Confident. "Oh, it's going really well."

She narrows her eyes. "Really? That's great. Are you guys going to audition with your cupcake song?"

I cross my arms. "Oh no. We want to save that song for the Spring Fling. Because it's . . . special, you know?"

She smirks. "Right. I'm sure it is."

"What about you guys? Have you decided what

song you're going to play in the audition?"

She casually picks at one of her fingernails. "No, not yet. We have over thirty songs to choose from, so it's not easy. We want to perform one that shows our experience and our depth as musicians." She looks at me. "We *really* want to win."

I gulp. Thirty songs? Depth as musicians? What does that even mean? I'm not sure how to reply and lucky for me, the bell rings, so I don't have to.

We start to move toward the risers, where we'll take our places, but Mr. Weisenheimer calls out, "Kids, I brought doughnuts for you today. Come over and get one and take a seat in the chairs. I want to talk to you for a few minutes before we start singing."

I make my way toward the table with the boxes of doughnuts. Everyone is smiling and laughing and thanking Mr. Weisenheimer for bringing us an unexpected treat.

After we're all seated and munching away, he stands in front of us and smiles. "Wow. What a bunch of happy kids. Wish I could bring doughnuts for you every day."

"You should!" someone from the back calls out.

Everyone laughs.

"You all know that I think you did an amazing job at the winter concert. And I've talked about how I want the spring concert in May to be even better. And while we've worked hard on the technical aspects, like breathing, pitch, and tone, I haven't spent any time talking about what I believe to be most important when it comes to singing. Does anyone want to take a guess as to what I think is most important?"

No one answers.

He walks over to the dry-erase board on the wall and writes the word "Joy."

"I want to talk to you about singing with feeling and pulling on the heart strings of the people listening to you. Just like you're eating those doughnuts with joy, I want you to sing with joy. To feel the music with your entire body and to let your audience in on what you're feeling." He pauses and looks at us. "Yes, you have to have a certain amount of talent to go far as a singer. But I truly believe that talent will only get you so far. The people who go to the top are the people who sing because they love it more than anything else. And it shows."

Belinda raises her hand. "I disagree."

Our teacher nods and smiles. "Okay. How come?"

"Without talent," Belinda says, "and I'm talking true talent, you're nothing. You'll get nowhere."

"You may be right," Mr. Weisenheimer says. "But my point is, be excited about what you're doing. Don't just go through the motions. When you're singing, feel the song and let the audience see and hear and feel those emotions as well. Understand?"

I think I understand, so I nod my head, along with most everyone else.

"All right," he says. "Then let's do what we love to do, shall we? Let's sing!"

After school, Isabel calls me. I'm sitting at the kitchen table, looking through the cookbooks again, eating an apple.

"I just wanted to check in with you," she says, "and let you know the invitations are all passed out. I'm already starting to get replies from people about whether or not they can come. I'll try to have a final count to you by Monday or Tuesday. Is that okay?"

"Sure," I say. "That'll be fine."

"Have you decided what you're going to bake for the big day?"

I laugh nervously. "Not yet. I'm trying out some recipes, hoping to find something really wonderful."

"You know," Isabel says, "I was thinking that it should be something chocolate. Sophie loves chocolate. She even loves chocolate chips in her pancakes."

When I slept over at Sophie's house one time, we had chocolate-chip pancakes for breakfast. Isabel's right. The dessert needs to be chocolate. That means the strawberry cake is definitely out. I think of the white-chocolate raspberry cheesecake recipe Chef Smiley is supposed to talk about on Sunday. "Do you think white chocolate is okay?" I ask.

"Yeah. I think so. I mean, chocolate is chocolate, right?" In my mind it is. Isabel continues. "I'm going to buy the decorations this weekend. We still need to come up with a plan to get Sophie to your house. So let's think about that. Maybe you can call her and invite her over there to do something. I don't know. But we need to come up with an idea soon, so Sophie doesn't make other plans for that night."

I tell her I'll brainstorm ideas and we agree to talk again on Monday.

After we hang up, I give myself a pep talk because I want to believe everything is going to turn out fine. Maybe even better than fine. I'll find a delicious chocolate dessert and Sophie is going to come to my house and be totally surprised. She'll be so impressed with everything I did for her, our friendship will be just as strong as the one she has with Isabel.

Here's the thing about pep talks given by yourself and to yourself. It's too easy to roll your eyes and say, "What do you know, anyway?"

Chapter 10

cocoa fudge cake

MUSIC TO A CHOCOHOLIC'S EAR

After dinner Friday night, while Mom goes to watch Dad's last night at the Wallflower, I decide to bake a chocolate cake from a recipe I found in one of our three cookbooks. Mom said it would be okay, since Madison is home, but she made me promise not to burn the house down.

Obviously, my mom has a lot of confidence in my baking skills.

I have about thirty minutes before Zola and Abigail will arrive for practice. I figure it's enough time to get the cake batter mixed up, and then it can bake while we're practicing.

The recipe is called cocoa fudge cake, probably because cocoa is one of the ingredients. I love hot cocoa as a drink, so I figure I'll love the cake too. After I put on an apron, I pull out the flour, sugar, the can of hot cocoa powder, baking soda, salt, and shortening from the pantry. I get the eggs and milk from the refrigerator and the vanilla from the cupboard where we keep the spices.

I measure the ingredients out one by one and put everything in a large mixing bowl. I've just added the last ingredient, the teaspoon of vanilla, when the doorbell rings.

Both Zola and Abigail are standing on the porch when I open the door.

"Hey. Cute apron," Abigail says as the girls step inside.

"Thanks." I look down at the apron I'm wearing. It's yellow and pink with little daisies all over it. I'm pretty sure this is the first time it's been worn. After all, my mom doesn't need to wear an apron to drive to the bakery.

"What are you baking?" Zola asks as I lead them into the kitchen.

"A cocoa fudge cake," I say as I stick the beaters into the mixer. "I'm having a birthday party for a friend from theater camp here next Saturday, and I'm trying to figure out what dessert to serve. As soon as I get the cake in the oven, we can go downstairs."

Zola looks behind me. "Dude, it doesn't look like your oven is preheating. My grandma, the best cake maker on the planet, says you always have to preheat the oven."

I set the mixer down and turn around. "Thanks. You're right. I forgot." Once the oven is turned on, I go back to the ingredients. The recipe says to beat on low speed for thirty seconds and then on high speed for three minutes after that. I don't have a watch, so I eye the clock on the microwave as I mix.

When I'm done, I start to walk toward the sink, holding the dirty beaters, when Abigail asks, "Hold on, Lily. Aren't you going to lick the beaters? That's the best part of making a cake."

I run my finger up the side of one of them and taste the batter before I hand both of them off to my friends.

"Wow," I say. "It's really sweet. Do you think it's supposed to be that sweet?"

Zola and Abigail both taste the batter and eye me suspiciously. "How much sugar did you add?" Zola asks.

"One and a half cups, just like it says. I was really careful with every single ingredient. I want this cake to turn out, you guys. Actually, I *need* this cake to turn out."

Abigail shrugs. "It's probably fine. I mean, it's not horrible. When it bakes up, I bet it'll taste good. I haven't ever tried a chocolate cake made from scratch. It's probably supposed to be really sweet. Right?"

Zola doesn't say anything as she takes the beater from Abigail and tosses both of them in the sink. She has her drumsticks stuck in the back pocket of her jeans. She looks so awesome, with her hair in adorable cornrows. And she's wearing her polka-dot shoes again. It's like you can tell she's in a band just by looking at her. I look down at myself, with the cute apron, and realize I look nothing like a person in a band.

"All right. Get that cake in the oven so we can go make some music," Zola says when she turns around. I pour the batter into the cake pans and slide them into the oven just as the oven beeps that it's done preheating.

I set the timer for thirty minutes before we head downstairs.

"Belinda told me the New Pirates have thirty songs written," I tell the girls when we get to Dad's studio. "Can you believe that? We barely have one."

"A half a song," Abigail says as she passes out music for each of us. "That's what we have."

"Just remember," Zola says with a smile, "all we need is one. One amazing song, one amazing performance, and we're in. So let's focus on that. You ready, Dots? From the top!"

I sing while they play, and when we get to the end of what we have written, we brainstorm some more lyrics. Actually, Zola and Abigail brainstorm some more lyrics. I'm too busy watching the clock on the wall to make sure I don't let the cake burn.

"Earth to Lily, Earth to Lily," Abigail says as she brushes the bangs out of her eyes. "Can you help us out here? Please? This is really important. If we don't finish writing the song, we can't practice the song."

"And if we can't practice the song," Zola says, "we can't win the audition. Guaranteed."

Fifteen minutes. That's how long I have before I need to check on the cake. I grab a pencil from Dad's small desk in the corner. "Okay, sorry. I'll focus. How about this? Let's all think quietly on our own for, like, five minutes, and then we'll share and decide which sounds the best. Okay?"

I get two more pencils and pass them to Abigail and Zola. I read over the chorus again and hum the tune in my head.

> *Wishes swirl and*
> *wishes twirl,*
> *around and around they spin.*
> *Wishes here and*
> *wishes there,*
> *when one comes true, I win.*
> *Wish on stars or*

wish with coins,

who cares, all right, just wish!

When you wish, my wish for you

is that your wish comes true.

I wish for my cake to turn out. I wish for it to taste delicious. I wish for the birthday party to be so much fun that Sophie will never forget it. I wish to be remembered forever as the nicest friend in Willow, Oregon, and the best cake baker too.

And so it goes, wish after wish, until Zola says, "Okay. Time's up. Let's share what we have."

I look down at my blank piece of paper. Did I really just spend practically the entire time wishing? Oh brother.

Abigail shares her lyrics, which sound great, and then Zola shares hers, which are good, but not quite as good as Abigail's. When it's my turn, I say, "I really love Abigail's lyrics. I mean, I like yours too, Zola, but can we just go with Abigail's? Mine are pretty terrible, honestly."

"I didn't see you writing anything down," Zola says, her arms crossed as she sits on the stool behind the drums.

I bite my lip, trying to think of how to respond. "Oh, right, well, they're in my head. But I knew they were bad, so I didn't even bother writing them down."

Abigail shrugs. "Okay, let's add my lyrics to the song and we can try them out. See how it sounds." She looks at Zola. "Is that all right with you?"

"I guess so. Seems like this song is going to be Abigail's song, not the Dots' song, but if that's the way you guys want to roll, whatever."

Abigail looks hurt. "Zola, please don't be upset," she says. "Please? You want to write the last verse all by yourself? If you want to do that, it's fine with me. I don't care. Really."

"Maybe we should make Lily write it," Zola says. "Make sure she's committed to this band."

I look at the clock for the fiftieth time tonight and then jump out of my chair. "You guys, I'm sorry, but I have to check on the cake. I'll be right back. I promise. And of course I'm committed to the band. Not everyone can be good at songwriting, okay? I think there are lots of bands where one person mostly writes the songs. It's a special talent, and obviously, Abigail has that talent."

Neither of them says a word, and Zola still looks kind of mad, but I don't have time to try and smooth things over right now. I run out the door and up the stairs. I find Madison at the oven, peeking in on the cake.

"I could smell the chocolate all the way in my room," Madison says. She shuts the oven door and turns around. Her eyebrows are scrunched up and I can tell something's wrong before she even says it. "Something doesn't look right, Lily. They're about done baking, but the cakes didn't rise very much. I don't know what happened, but I think you did something wrong."

The story of my baking life.

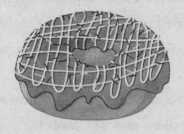

Chapter 11

chocolate
marshmallow cookies

PERFECT TO SHARE WITH A FRIEND

After we pulled the pans out of the oven, with the very flat cakes inside of them, I wanted to cry. Madison tried to make me feel better by telling me the cake still might taste good, but it was no use. I felt like a failure.

Abigail and Zola came upstairs a little while later to see why I hadn't come back, their faces telling me they weren't too happy with me. I tried to apologize and offered to go back downstairs with them to practice a while longer, but they just wanted to go home. Madison offered to give them a ride home, so they took off and left me alone with the pathetic cakes. I almost threw them out, but I was curious how they tasted, so I sat there and stared at them, waiting for them to cool off.

Later that night, when my mom got home, she went over the recipe with me. I learned regular milk shouldn't be substituted for buttermilk. Apparently, the buttermilk has an ingredient in it that works with the baking soda to make the cake rise.

That's not the only thing I did wrong, though. When we tried the cake, it tasted terrible. My mom asked what kind of cocoa I used and when I told her about the hot cocoa mix, she explained that when a recipe calls for cocoa, it means unsweetened baking cocoa.

No wonder cake mixes are so popular. Baking a cake from scratch is hard! Like, harder than singing the national anthem at the Super Bowl. Not that I've ever sung the national anthem at the Super Bowl, but still, I can imagine.

Now it's Saturday morning, and I'm trying to figure out what to do next. Mom said she would take me to the store to get the ingredients to try making the cake again, but I don't know if I even want to have the party now.

Actually, I want to have the party and give Sophie a thirteenth birthday she'll never forget, but I don't think I'm good enough to pull it off. What will she think of me if the party turns out to be a disaster just like every recipe I try to make? I want to be someone Sophie admires, not someone she's ashamed of.

I'm trying to get up the nerve to call Isabel, to tell her I can't do it. I stare at the phone, trying to find the right words, when it rings.

"Hello?"

"Hey, Lily. It's Sophie! How are you?"

"Oh, hi, Sophie. I'm all right. What's up?"

"My mom needs to do some shopping for Hayden. He's had a growth spurt and all of his pants are way too short. Every time I see him with his high-water pants and his white socks showing, I can't help but laugh. I guess my mom finally got the hint and figured out she needs to buy him some new ones.

"Anyway, we're going to the mall this afternoon. Thought I'd see if you might want to go with us. We don't have to hang out with them, of course. I want to shop for some new shoes. You know how I love shoes!"

I smile. She does love shoes. I do too. But I should call Isabel. I should practice the audition song. I should write a cupcake song. I should start reading the book for the next book club meeting. I should do a lot of things. But going to the mall for the afternoon sounds like fun and I'm tired of worrying about everything in my life right now.

"Sure. I'd love to go with you."

"Okay," Sophie says. "We'll pick you up around one o'clock. See you then."

"Bye."

Mom tells me she thinks it's a good idea for me to get out of the house and take a break from worrying about the party and everything else. So I eat lunch and get myself ready, and with each passing minute, I'm feeling happier and happier. Sophie and I haven't hung out together in a while and I'm so excited to see her and to do something that doesn't involve flour, sugar, and eggs.

When we get to the mall, Sophie's mom and little brother head in one direction, while Sophie and I take off in another. I have thirty dollars from my allowance that I've saved up, and my mom gave me twenty more, in case I find something special to buy.

We walk toward the big department store, and before we know it, we are laughing our heads off.

First, there's the kiosk in the middle of the mall with the special hand cream called Marvel a salesperson wants us to try. When we say, "No thanks," and keep walking, she walks along with us, begging us to stop and try it.

Then there's the remote-control flying helicopter toy I almost run into, and Sophie can't stop giving me a hard time about it. I was busy making sure the hand cream lady had stopped chasing us down, so I didn't notice the small helicopter flying in the air.

When we finally make it to the shoe department, we collapse into two chairs, trying to keep the laughing tears back.

"I can see it now," Sophie says between her laughs. "The headline reads, 'Girl at mall is seriously injured when she collides with a toy helicopter because she was too busy running from the crazy hand cream lady.'"

"Can I help you?" a man asks us. He's about my dad's age and dressed in a nice, silvery gray suit, with a white shirt and a purple tie.

We stop laughing, because I think that's his way of telling us to behave, in the nicest way possible.

"Look, Sophie," I say, trying to catch my breath, pointing at his tie. "Purple. Your favorite color."

"Or purplicious, as Isabel and I like to say." As I learn of yet another special thing Isabel and Sophie have between them, it feels like someone pokes my heart with a needle. I tell myself it's just a silly word and to forget about it. "I've never seen a purple tie before," Sophie continues. "It goes really well with your silver suit."

"Hey, silver and purple, just like the colors for the . . ." I stop, my hand flying up to my mouth. I can't believe I almost gave it away. I almost told her about the surprise party we've been planning for her. The man must see that I could use some help about now.

"Thank you," he says as he runs his fingers down the side of the tie. "I'm glad you like it. It's one of my favorites. My wife and two sons gave it to me for Father's Day last year. She wasn't sure I'd wear it, but I think it's awesome."

Sophie looks at me. "What were you going to say?"

I'm thankful the guy gave me a minute to think of a good cover. "Oh, um, just that my mom told me when she and my dad got married, their wedding colors were silver and purple."

"That must have been so pretty," she says. "Maybe I'll have those colors at my wedding."

The salesman is still standing there. "We're going to look around," I tell him. "If that's okay."

He nods and smiles. "Absolutely. Just let me know if there's a shoe you'd like to try."

"We will," Sophie says.

Between the two of us, we must try on twenty pairs of shoes. I'm pretty sure the man with the purple tie regrets ever approaching us in the first place.

Sophie ends up with a cute pair of wedge sandals, and I buy a pair of polka-dot sneakers, like Zola's, except black with off-white dots. I love them. As I pay for the shoes at the register, I realize I need to call both Abigail and Zola and apologize again for getting distracted last night. Our song isn't finished and it's all my fault. I hope they'll forgive me.

We have some time before we're supposed to meet up with Sophie's mom and brother, so Sophie and I get two giant cookies and two cartons of milk from the Cookie Shack and sit down at a table.

"Yum," Sophie says as she takes a bite of the chocolate marshmallow cookie. "This cookie reminds me of the piece of pie Isabel and I had at Penny's Pie Place. It was the pie Jack made for the baking contest. That's where Isabel met him." We both take a bite at the same time. "Good, huh?"

I nod as I wonder if there's anything that doesn't remind Sophie of Isabel. I start to say something about it and stop myself. That won't do any good. If I want to be as good of a friend to Sophie as Isabel, I have to show her how much she means to me. I realize that one of the best things I can do to make our friendship stronger is to be the person who gives her an amazing birthday party.

She takes another bite of her cookie and I decide to pick her brain while I have the chance. "So if you had to pick one dessert, and that's the only dessert you could eat for the rest of your life, what would it be?"

She sets her cookie down on the plate and wipes her mouth with her napkin. "Well, definitely not brownies. I like them, but after doing the commercials for Beatrice's Brownies, I'm a little tired of them."

"Are you done with those commercials for a while?" I ask as I pick up my carton of milk.

"Yep. All done. My agent is looking for new opportunities for me now."

"Okay," I say, "so no brownies. What would it be, then?"

She leans back in her chair and stares at her plate. "One dessert. And only one. Hm. I guess I'd have to go with the classic chocolate-chip cookie. I mean, no one ever gets tired of chocolate-chip cookies, right?"

"Really? You wouldn't want something more special? More . . . complicated?"

She gives me a funny look. "Complicated? I don't think something has to be complicated to taste good. Sometimes the best things in life are the simplest things, you know?" She smiles. "Like shoe shopping with a friend. Or reading a good book. Which reminds me, have you started the next book yet?"

"No," I say. "I've been so busy with school and my band. Hopefully soon."

"I love the name we came up with for the book club, don't you? The Baking Bookworms. I think it's great we all love to bake."

Just hearing her say that makes my stomach hurt. After all of my recent disasters in the kitchen, I would be thrilled if I never had to turn the oven on again.

I wonder what she'd say if I told her. What would she say if I told her that I wish I could bake as well as she and Isabel do, but baking and I don't seem to get along? Would they kick me out of the book club? I'd hate that. I want to be in the club. More than that, I want to be Sophie's other best friend.

"What about you?" she asks.

I gulp. "What do you mean?"

"If you could only eat one dessert for the rest of your life, what would it be?"

"Oh." I think for a few seconds. "Probably doughnuts. I love doughnuts."

She smiles. "See? You like simple too."

As we eat our cookies, I think about that. Would Isabel be disappointed if I decided to serve something simple, like cookies or doughnuts, at the party? What was it that she said? *She should have an amazing dessert for becoming a teenager.*

Suddenly, making both Isabel and Sophie happy seems about as impossible as beating the New Pirates at the Spring Fling audition.

Chapter 12

white-chocolate raspberry cheesecake

A TRUE BAKER'S DELIGHT

It's Sunday night and I'm watching Chef Smiley make cheesecake. And so far I've learned one thing. Sweet Uncle Pete, that's complicated! Yeah, nothing simple about cheesecake, that's for sure.

When I'm done watching, I go find Mom in her office. Her door is open, so I walk in and sit on one of the chairs she has in front of her desk.

"Hi, Lily," she says, not even looking up from her computer. "How's it going?"

"Not so good."

Now she looks up. "How come?"

"Tomorrow Isabel wants me to tell her what I've decided to do as far as food goes for Sophie's birthday party, and I have absolutely no idea."

Now she stops what she's doing and looks at me. "Honey, if it were up to you, and it didn't matter what anyone else thought, what would you serve at the party?"

"I don't know. I've been trying to think of something fun and different. Something . . . special. But not too hard. That's the problem. Everything I might like to make just seems too complicated."

Mom types something into her computer. "You know what I think we could make fairly easily? And would be really fun and unique? I saw some at the coffee shop earlier today."

"What?"

"Cake pops. Have you heard of those? They're little pieces of frosted cake on a stick. Here, I found a how-to video. Come watch."

I hop up and go stand behind her. The lady in the video walks us through how to make them. You bake a cake using a mix in a rectangle pan, let it cool, and then you break up the cake into pieces in a big mixing bowl. You add some canned frosting to the bowl (that helps the cake stick together), mix again, and roll the mixture into small balls. They go in the freezer for a few hours before they're dipped in icing made by melting chocolate coating pieces, either white or regular chocolate. You put lollipop sticks into the balls, dip them in the icing, and finally, roll them in decorations.

"Mom, those are so cute!" I say. "And because you crumble the cake up after it's baked, it doesn't matter if it comes out of the oven crooked or lumpy or a hundred other things."

Mom smiles. "Exactly. And we could use a cake mix from the store. I think together you and I could make these cake pops."

"You really think so?" I ask her.

She stands up and pulls me into a hug. "Yes. I do. I'm pretty sure it'll be a piece of cake."

I smile at her joke, even though I've heard it

before from Chef Smiley, as I pull away. "Should we practice first?"

"Lily, I have a really busy week. And I know you have other things you should be doing too. Let's wait and deal with them on Saturday. We'll make them work. I promise. Is there anything else you'd like to serve?"

"Maybe some chocolate-chip cookies? They're Sophie's favorite."

She nods. "How about if we get some cookie dough at the store? That way all you have to do is bake up the cookies Friday night or Saturday morning."

"Mom, I think Isabel wants everything to be homemade."

"You don't think that's going to be too much work? Making cookies and cake pops?"

"I want to show Sophie and Isabel I'm a Baking Bookworm too."

"All right. But try not to worry, okay?" She strokes my hair. "Everything will be fine. Now, why don't you go relax for a change? Read some of that book for our club, and try to forget about baked goods, okay?"

I take a deep breath. "Okay. Thanks, Mom."

❀ ❀ ❀

The next day at school, Abigail gives me the cold shoulder. I'd tried to call her Saturday night and apologize for how our practice turned out, but she didn't answer her phone.

I'm standing at her locker, trying to get her to turn around and talk to me.

"Abigail, please. I'm sorry. I really am. I know I shouldn't have let the cake take over the evening. I want to make the party coming up on Saturday really special, you know? But Friday night was for practicing, and I'm sorry I let other things get in the way."

She slams the door and turns around. "Can I ask you something, Lily?"

"Yeah. Of course."

"Do you want to be a baker or a singer?"

"You already know the answer to that question. Why are you even asking me that? Music and singing, they mean everything to me."

She gives me a look I don't like. A look that says she's disappointed in me. "Well, you're sure not acting like it."

And then she heads off to class without me.

Chapter 13

butterscotch pudding

COMFORT IN A BOWL

When school is over, I chase after Zola as she walks toward the front door. I pull her to the side of the hallway as kids rush past us.

"Hey, do you want to come over and practice tonight?" I ask. "I promise there'll be no interruptions this time. I'm really sorry about Friday night."

She sighs. "Lily, maybe this band thing isn't such a great idea. It takes work, you know? And you seem to have lots of other stuff going on."

I can't believe what I'm hearing.

"Please don't say that. I love our band." I point down at my new shoes. "See? I even bought new shoes."

When she sees my shoes, it makes her smile. Then she looks at me and says, "Dude, you gotta understand something, though. It takes more than cute shoes to make a band."

"I know," I tell her as I lightly squeeze her arm. "I'm really sorry. So will you help me talk Abigail into coming over tonight? We'll get that song finished and we will rock it. I know we will." I glance around the hallway before I say, "Don't you want to show the New Pirates they're not the only band in town?"

I can tell by the look on her face she does. "Yeah. Of course. But we all have to work at it. We each have to do our share. It's not fair otherwise."

I nod. "You're totally right. Please forgive me and let's start over, okay? We'll have an awesome practice. Just wait."

Abigail walks by just then. "Hey," Zola calls out to her. "Come here for a second."

She stops but doesn't seem too happy about it. "I need to go. My mom's waiting for me."

"Can you practice tonight?" Zola asks. "Lily feels really bad, and I think we need to give it another chance."

"I don't know," she says, fiddling with the zipper on her hoodie. "I mean, what's the point? The New Pirates are going to win. There's no way we can beat them."

I remember what my parents have been telling me all along. "So let's not worry about them. Let's just play for ourselves. I want to finish that song. I want to hear what it sounds like from start to finish, with you guys playing it. How many people can say they actually wrote a song and played it? I bet not very many, but I want to be able to do that."

Abigail looks at me and I can tell she's thinking about what I said. "Okay," she finally says. "But no phone calls or cake baking. Please?"

"Don't worry," I tell her. "No more distractions."

"What about the cupcake song?" Abigail asks, half smiling.

"I'm on it," I tell her. "Soon. I mean, probably after I get this party out of the way."

"Wait a minute," Zola says, her brown eyes big and round. "I have an idea. How about we play at the party? It'd be good practice for the audition."

Abigail's face lights up. "I love that idea. We can play 'Happy Birthday' for the birthday girl and then play our song. See what people think."

I shrug. "Okay. Yeah, we can do that. My dad will need to move the instruments upstairs for us, but I can help him. It shouldn't be a problem."

"I gotta run," Abigail says. "Later, alligators."

We wave good-bye, and as Zola and I walk outside, into the gray and cloudy March day, I'm feeling better about things than I've felt in a long time.

We head our separate ways and I feel good as I walk home.

Even when Isabel calls, I don't panic. After all, Mom and I have a plan. We know what we're doing with the food, and it's going to be amazing. I just know it. I can picture the table of sweet treats in my head. I can hear the compliments everyone gives me about the cake pops.

"Hello?" I say with a smile when I answer my phone.

"Lily, it's Isabel. I have good news! Guess what I just did!"

"What?"

"I got a band to agree to play at Sophie's birthday party. The best part is, they'll do it for free. Can you believe that?"

I stand inside the refrigerator door, letting the cold air wash over me. I feel faint. Sick. I don't want to ask the question, but I have to. Even though I'm pretty sure I know the answer.

"What's the name of the band?" I ask.

"The New Pirates. Have you heard of them? There's this kid Bryan in the band, and my dad and his dad are good friends. Bryan goes to your school. Maybe you know him? Anyway, we ran into them yesterday at the grocery store, and when his dad told us Bryan was in a band, I had the brilliant idea to ask if they might like to play at the party. He said he had to check with his bandmates. I just got off the phone with him, and they said they'd do it! They want to practice for some big audition coming up."

I grab one of the leftover bowls of instant butterscotch pudding Mom made last night for dessert and then I shut the refrigerator door. After I get a spoon, I sink into a chair at the kitchen table.

I sigh. "Isabel, I—"

"Oh no," she interrupts. "I should have checked with you first. I'll be so sad if they can't play. I know Sophie will love having live music. I thought about asking you and your band to play, but you're hosting the party and that's enough for you to worry about. Besides, who won't love a band called the New Pirates, right? I hope it's okay. Can you check with your parents and get back to me? Please?"

My heart feels like it's a rope in a tug-of-war game. Isabel and Sophie are on one end while Abigail and Zola are pulling on the other.

Part of me wants to tell her no. The New Pirates can't play because my band should perform if we're going to have a band. The other part of me wants to tell her yes, of course the New Pirates can play, because she loves the idea, which means Sophie will love the idea, and I *really* want Sophie to be happy.

I don't know what to do. All I know is my heart

hurts from all that pulling. I can tell she is in love with this idea. Offering up my band as a replacement won't be the same. After all, her dad and Bryan's dad are friends. And Bryan's cute. I know I should say something—stand up for the Dots. But just the thought exhausts me. "Sure. I'll ask them tonight and see what they say."

"Thank you so much, Lily. You're the best. How's the food planning coming along?"

I take a bite of the pudding. It is delicious. "Mom and I are going to make cake pops. Little cake balls on sticks? Have you seen them?"

"Oh, fun! That's a great idea."

"Sophie loves chocolate-chip cookies, so we'll probably have some of those too. Don't worry. My mom and I have it under control. It's all good."

"Yay!" she squeals. "It's going to be fabulous! Oh, and I wanted to tell you, I've had seven people say they can't make it. So counting you and me, we'll have about twenty-five people there. Now all we need is a way to get Sophie to your house."

I set the spoon down and lean back in the chair. "Maybe we should talk to Sophie's mom. You know, tell her about our surprise. They might be planning a special dinner or something for her that night."

"You're probably right," Isabel says. "Should one of us call her? Or go over there? What do you think?" I start to answer, but Isabel keeps talking. "You know what? I'll just call her mom right now. I'll use my mom's cell phone. That way Sophie won't recognize the number, and if she answers, I'll just hang up."

"Good idea."

"Let's talk again tomorrow, okay? I'll tell you what her mom and I come up with and you can tell me what your parents say about the band."

"Okay. Bye, Isabel."

"Bye."

I take another bite of pudding as I think about the New Pirates playing at the party. The more I think about it, the angrier I get. Isabel should have asked me about our band. It's not right to assume I wouldn't want to do it.

Now she's pushed me into a corner, and I have to figure out how to get myself out.

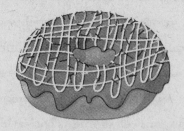

Chapter 14

strawberry-lime cupcakes

A SPECIAL AND EXCITING DESSERT

I'm in my room at my desk doing homework when my mother bursts through the door, a smile as big as the sun on her face.

"Guess what," she says.

"What?"

She doesn't answer right away. It's like she's trying to figure out if she should drag the surprise out any longer. "Who is your favorite chef on TV?"

I give her a curious look. "Chef Smiley?"

She rushes over, takes my hands, and pulls me out of my chair. She's dressed up in a suit and her long brown hair is pulled back in a bun. She must have had meetings today at work. "Yes! We're going to see him. Tonight! He's in Portland this week. The radio station is hosting a class for radio listeners, and I just won two tickets!"

My mouth drops open. "Mom, are you kidding?"

"No," she says, holding up her hand like she's being sworn into court. "I swear it's true. We need to get ready right now so we can leave in thirty minutes. It'll be rush hour soon, and we'll have to stop for dinner on the way too. So get ready and I'll see you downstairs."

She starts to leave, but I call out, "Mom. Wait! My bandmates are coming over tonight. I can't go. I promised them we'd finish our song tonight."

"Lily, this is the chance of a lifetime. Call them and explain. They'll understand. Now, please hurry. I don't want to be late."

She doesn't give me time to protest any further. Her mind is made up. We're going. And I admit, it sounds fun, but how can I let Abigail and Zola down again? I wish she'd won four tickets. I'd invite the two of them to go with us.

I get my phone and call Abigail, hoping I can figure out how to break the news to her gently. When she answers, she doesn't even say hello.

"If you're going to cancel practice tonight," she says, "I might have to take you to the zoo and feed you to the bears."

I close my eyes and wish for forgiveness. "Abigail, I'm sorry. It's just, my mom won two tickets and it's a once-in-a-lifetime chance."

"Bears, Lily. Big, hungry bears." She sighs. "Tickets? Like, concert tickets?"

I feel my chest tighten. "No."

"What kind of tickets, then?"

I open my eyes and pace the floor. "My mom won them on the radio. Isn't that cool? They were giving tickets away for a special class, and she won. She just left my room to get ready. You know, she really didn't give me a choice. I have to go."

"What kind of class?"

Obviously, she is not going to let me off the hook.

"Have you ever watched Chef Smiley on TV?"

It's silent for a few seconds. Finally, she says, "You're kidding, right?"

"He's in Portland this week, and the radio show is sponsoring a class for some of its listeners. Doesn't that sound amazing?"

I cross my fingers and hope she agrees with me. "Wow," she says. "I guess you really do want to be a baker, don't you?"

I shake my head and plop down on my bed. She doesn't get it. "I don't want to be a baker. But I do want to be a *better* baker than I am now, which is a terrible one. What's wrong with wanting to learn how to bake?"

"Nothing, Lily, if you have all the time in the world. But you don't! Those auditions are coming up fast, and it seems like you don't even care."

"I do care. Honest."

"Then tell your mom you want to stay home and practice. Maybe she can find a friend to go with her."

I take a deep breath and try not to get upset that she's making this so difficult. "We can practice tomorrow night. You guys don't have lessons, so that should work, right? Look, I have to go. Can you call Zola and ask if we can change practice to tomorrow?"

"Lily."

"Abigail, please? If it were you, I'd understand. I'd want you to go and have a good time. It's one night. That's all. Okay?"

She pauses before she replies in a softer voice. "Okay. I'll call her. Will you be at school tomorrow?"

"Yes. We'll probably get home late, but my mom won't let me stay home. I'll see you then, okay?"

"Bye."

I hang up and rush to my closet, trying to figure out what a person should wear to meet a well-known pastry chef. I decide on a simple black jersey knit dress. I wear my new polka-dot sneakers, too, for luck. I really hope a little bit of Chef Smiley's baking skills can rub off on me.

A few hours later, we're seated in a classroom at the Western Culinary Institute. On the way over, Mom explained it's a school where people learn how to become chefs. The classroom has a counter covered with kitchen tools and ingredients. Behind the counter, along the wall, are a stove, a sink, and a refrigerator. It looks like a small kitchen in a home, but is set up so people can sit and watch what's happening in the kitchen.

I was hoping it'd be more of a hands-on class, where we'd all get to bake something, but that would probably be really hard to do.

When Chef Smiley comes out, wearing his white chef shirt, he says, "Good evening, friends. I'm so glad you're here to bake with me!" Everyone applauds.

"Tonight you're in for a real treat. Literally." He rubs his belly and laughs. "We are going to make strawberry-lime cupcakes. But as you'll see, these aren't your normal cupcakes. They have a tasty surprise in each one."

Mom and I look at each other and smile, and I admit, I'm excited. Maybe I can learn how to make fabulous cupcakes like Isabel.

Chef Smiley continues. "Before I get started, I want you to reach under your chairs. Taped to one of them is a bright orange piece of paper with a few words written on it. Everyone check, please, and if you find the piece of paper, raise it high in the air, so I can see it."

I lean to the side of my seat and then reach up and search the bottom of the chair with my hand. When I feel something on my fingertips, I have to cover my mouth with my other hand to keep from squealing.

I pull the piece of paper away from the chair and read what it says.

CHEF SMILEY'S

PERSONAL ASSISTANT

FOR THE EVENING

Mom and I look at each other again. She puts her arm around me and gives me a squeeze. "Looks like you get the best seat in the house."

"Mom, what if I mess up?" I whisper to her. "In front of all of these people? Maybe you should do it."

"It'll be fine," she says. "Don't worry. He'll help you."

I guess I don't have a choice. Everyone is looking

around, wondering who found the note. My heart races as I hold the sheet high in the air, just like Chef Smiley said to do.

"Oh, good," the chef says. "Come on up here, please. Let's meet the person who will be my helper this evening."

I force my shaky legs to stand up and somehow I make it to the front of the room without falling down. Chef Smiley directs me to go around the counter until I'm standing right next to him.

"Well, hello there," he says. He looks just as nice and friendly up close. "Can you tell us your name, good and loud, so everyone can hear you?"

"Lily."

"It's wonderful to meet you, Lily. I assume you like to bake, if you're here tonight?"

I hold on to the counter for support. "Well, I'm here because I want to be a better baker. I'm pretty much a disaster in the kitchen."

He gives me a look of concern. "Disaster? What do you mean?"

"Nothing ever seems to go right when I'm baking. I overfill the cake pans or use the wrong ingredients or I forget to do something important, like put the lid on the blender."

He puts his arm around me and talks to the audience. "I already like this girl. Don't you love her honesty?"

Everyone claps, and I feel my cheeks getting warm.

"Here's what I want you to remember, Lily. More than anything, baking should be fun. Do your best and have fun! If something doesn't turn out, well, you've learned something for the next time, right? It took a lot of years and a lot of practice for me to get to where I am now. So let's see if I can teach you a few things tonight. How do you like the sound of that?"

I nod as I feel myself relax a little bit. Chef Smiley is so nice and maybe I will learn something.

He claps his hands together. "All right, then. Let's get started. Lily, I'll have you wash your hands behind me while I go over the ingredients with our guests."

I turn toward the sink and pinch my hand to make sure I'm not dreaming. Nope. Wide awake. This is really happening. I'm baking with a famous pastry chef. Unbelievable.

Chef Smiley talks while I turn the faucet on and

pick up the bar of soap. "Lily mentioned using the wrong ingredients, and that's our first lesson tonight. It's so important to follow the recipe closely and make sure you use the correct ingredients. For example, this recipe calls for all-purpose flour, so you want to make sure that's what you're using."

I dry my hands and go back to standing next to him. He points to each ingredient, which seem to be all measured out in various-sized bowls along the counter, while he talks about each one.

"Lily," he says as he puts the beaters into the mixer, "I'm going to ask you to go through the fresh strawberries in that bowl and pick out the best ones for our recipe. While she does that, I'm going to cream the butter, sugar, and eggs until fluffy. That's another mistake people make—when mixing ingredients, don't undermix or overmix. If the recipe says this mixture should be fluffy, then I'm going to keep beating until it's fluffy. Okay?"

He passes me the bowl of strawberries before he starts mixing the ingredients. A wave of panic washes over me. What does he mean by best? Biggest? Reddest? Juiciest?

I wait until he's done. When the mixer stops, I ask, "Um, what are you going to use the strawberries for?"

He's scraping the bowl with a spatula. "Lily, that's an excellent question. Do you know why, audience? I wasn't specific enough in my directions. If we're going to chop them up and use them in the recipe, she might choose different strawberries than if we were going to use them as a topping on the cupcake."

Chef Smiley reaches under the counter and pulls out a small plate with a pretty, frosted cupcake on it. The cupcake is cut in half, and when he spreads the halves apart, it makes me smile, because right there, in the middle of the cupcake, is a fresh strawberry, cut in half as well. When he shows the cupcake to the audience, everyone says, "Ooooh." It's pretty funny.

"After we bake the cupcakes," he explains, "we're going to cut a cone-shaped hole in each one and insert a small strawberry into that hole. We'll put our special lime buttercream frosting on the top, and you won't even know there's a strawberry inside until you bite into it." He looks at me, his green eyes sparkling. "Isn't that a fun surprise?"

"Yes, but it sounds kind of hard. How do you keep the cupcake from crumbling apart when you put the strawberry down the middle of the cupcake?"

Now he starts mixing the dry ingredients together. "It is a bit tricky. You'll want to choose strawberries that aren't too large. And you don't want to cut the hole for the berry too big. This is definitely a recipe that's easier with a friend, and one that requires you to really take your time and not rush through it."

Now that I know what kind of berries to look for, I go through the bowl and pick out the ones that are on the small side but look red and juicy.

When I'm finished, he's almost done getting the batter all mixed up. "Excellent work, Lily. Would you like to drop the batter into our cupcake pan that I've already filled with liners?"

I shake my head. "Not really. I'll just make a mess and get more batter on the countertop than in the liners."

He frowns. "Oh no. Have a bit more confidence in yourself, my dear. We'll use a gravy ladle to scoop up the batter and then carefully pour the batter into the liners. See?" He demonstrates for us. "Easy as pie."

"Easy as pie?" I say without thinking. "Pie is totally complicated, isn't it?"

Everyone laughs.

Chef Smiley winks at me. "You're right. Baking a pie isn't exactly easy. I think the saying is referring to eating them. Now, that's easy!" He hands me the gravy ladle. "But you keep practicing in the kitchen, and I bet you'll be baking a pie in no time." He looks into my eyes and with more confidence than I've ever heard in anyone's voice, he says, "I believe in you, Lily."

Chapter 15

fruit smoothie

EASY TO MAKE, EASY TO DRINK

At the end of the class, after Chef Smiley tastes one of the cupcakes and yells, "Sweet Uncle Pete, that's good," everyone gets a cupcake to try. Mom and I agree that the strawberry-lime cupcakes are amazing. The fresh strawberry inside each one is like nothing I've ever seen, or tasted, before.

Chef Smiley shakes hands with everyone on their way out. He asks my mom and me to step aside so he can speak to us after everyone else is gone, so that's what we do.

When he comes over to us, he says, "Lily, thank you for being a delightful assistant tonight. You did a wonderful job."

"This is my mom, Connie." Chef Smiley shakes her hand. "Thank you for everything I learned tonight. It was fun."

"I hope you'll keep practicing," he says. "I know baking can be frustrating sometimes, but it can also be very rewarding, working hard at something and then being able to share the results with people you care about."

"She tries really hard," my mom tells him as she strokes my hair. "I'm proud of how hard she tries."

"I want to give you something," he says as he steps over to the counter. He comes back carrying a book and a pen. "This is my first cookbook, coming out next month. You get one of the first copies, Lily."

He opens the cover, writes something, and then hands the book to me.

"Wow," I say. "Thank you! This will be a huge help."

He smiles. "I hope it is!"

We say good-bye and as we walk to the car, I read what he wrote. It says:

For Lily ~
It's true. One cannot live on dessert alone. But a treat now and then makes life extra sweet. Happy baking! Remember one of my favorite sayings—whatever works!
Your friend,
Chef Smiley

The next morning, Dad is up bright and early to help get me off to school, so Mom can sleep in a little bit. I wish I could have slept in too. We didn't get home until eleven, since Portland is about a two-hour drive from Willow. I feel like a stale, dried-out cupcake.

I slide into a chair at the kitchen table.

"Good morning," Dad says as he sets a glass of something purple in front of me. "I made you a smoothie. It's yogurt, a little orange juice, and frozen berries all blended together. It's kind of like a breakfast shake."

I take a sip through the straw. "Yum, Dad. And I

see you remembered to put the lid on the blender, which is always a good thing."

He chuckles before he turns back to the stove. "I'm glad you like it. I'll have your cheesy eggs ready in a minute. Did you have fun last night?"

I set the smoothie down. "Yeah. It was a lot of fun. We made cupcakes, and I got to be Chef Smiley's personal assistant."

"Cool. I bet you learned a lot, huh?"

"I guess," I say. "I'm not sure I could make those cupcakes without the chef to help me. He makes it look so easy, but it's really not easy at all."

He brings me my plate of scrambled eggs with shredded cheese melting on top of them. Curls of steam rise up from the plate. It looks delicious. I take a bite while Dad sits down across from me. "It's a lot like making music," he says. "Taylor Swift makes it look simple, but your band has probably discovered by now, it's a combination of hard work, talent, and more hard work."

"Oh, Dad, that reminds me. The Dots are going to practice tonight. Can we use your studio? We're really close to finishing a song."

He smiles. "The Dots. Nice. I like it. And yes, you can use the studio tonight for a couple of hours."

"And if we decide to play at Sophie's birthday party Saturday night, could we move the equipment upstairs? I can help you."

He raises his eyebrows at me. "You want to play at the party? You think you're ready for that?"

"After tonight, we will be. I hope. We think it's a good way for us to practice for the audition coming up soon."

"How many songs do you have ready?"

I slink down into my seat and shovel more eggs into my mouth, trying to decide how to answer that question. I finally decide I can't lie to my dad, no matter how embarrassed I am about the answer. "Um, almost one."

He looks surprised. "Almost one? As in, not even one?"

"We have a song that's almost finished. It sounds really good. Tonight we're going to finish it and then maybe we can play it on Saturday."

He leans in and looks at me with his warm brown eyes. "Lily, don't rush things, okay? Do you remember what I told you? Play because you love it, not to try and impress other people. I'd hate to see you do too much and then have regrets. I've seen far too many musicians turn away from music because they hurried things along and weren't happy with the results."

"But, Dad—"

"Honey, I know what it feels like to want to share your music with other people. To want to give and get back something in return. But I'm telling you, if you aren't ready, wait. Keep practicing. Have fun. There will be more opportunities in the future."

"You don't know that, Dad," I say as I stand up and take my dishes to the sink. "What if our band doesn't stay together? What if this is the only chance I'll ever have to be in a band?"

Dad comes over and gives me a hug. "You are so talented, Lily. You have a lifetime of singing ahead of you."

I know he's trying to be helpful, but that is so not helpful! We want to play on Saturday and I have to figure out how to make it happen. I just have to.

Chapter 16

caramel apple

ONE STICKY SITUATION

It's so hard to be a good student when you're exhausted. How do kids who are allowed to stay up late all the time do it? They must have some superpower that helps them get by on a tiny bit of sleep. I know for a fact I was not born with that superpower. I have to keep pinching myself the next day at school to stay awake. I'm happy to get to choir, because I'm pretty sure it's impossible to sing and fall asleep at the same time.

Belinda is waiting for me again before class. "So, I hear our band will be playing at your house on Saturday night."

It catches me by surprise. But then I realize Isabel had to tell Bryan where they'd be playing, and she probably asked him if he knew me.

"Maybe," I tell her. "I'm not sure yet. I still need to talk to my parents about it and see what they think."

"But they'll say yes, right? Isabel made it sound like it's practically a done deal. You must have a huge house."

"Not really. Just average, I guess. Why?"

"Isabel said she wanted us to play for at least an hour. Because once people start dancing, they'll want to keep it going for a while."

I wait for her to smile and say, "Just kidding." Except she looks totally serious. Oh my gosh. She is totally serious. Dancing? In my house? Is there enough room for that? Even if there is, that's not the kind of party I had in mind.

I feel a little sick to my stomach. "She said that?"

Belinda crosses her arms over her chest. "Why do you look so surprised? Of course people are going to want to dance when they hear us play. That's what people do at a party with a band, Lily. You didn't know that?"

I scramble to save myself from looking stupid. "No, I did. I guess I'm surprised you could perform for a full hour, that's all. Are you sure you guys can pull it off?"

The bell rings. "Don't worry about us," she says. "We know what we're doing." Before she walks away, she whispers, "Do you?"

As we take our places on the risers, I try to imagine a group of kids dancing in my living room. If we can fit everyone, how will people dance, exactly? Like at a concert, where everyone kind of bounces to the music? Or will boys and girls pair up and dance as, like, couples? And if that happens, what if they get . . . carried away? I put my hand on my stomach, because I really don't feel well.

This is the pep talk I give myself. Except it turns into more of an argument inside my head:

Calm down, Lily. Nothing is decided. You'll talk to Isabel, and you'll work everything out. Maybe you can suggest some really fun games.

Right. Because games sound so much fun compared to dancing to a live band. Lily, get real. Face the truth!

What's the truth?

If you want to give Sophie the best birthday party ever, you have to let the New Pirates play. It's what Isabel wants, and you know it'll be a party Sophie will never forget. Abigail and Zola will understand. You can get the song ready for the audition. That's the important thing anyway.

I'm relieved when Mr. Weisenheimer asks us to start singing, because it makes the noise in my brain stop. Temporarily, anyway.

After school, when I've finished eating a sliced apple with caramel dip along with some crackers, I give Isabel a call.

"Lily," she says, "please tell me your parents said the band is okay. Please? I really want to hear them play. I think Sophie will love them."

I take a deep breath. "Hi, Isabel. So, I talked to Belinda today, one of the band members of the

New Pirates. And she said you want everyone to dance. I'm not sure we have enough room for that."

She laughs nervously. "Oh, I didn't mean dance, like at the prom or something. More like at a concert. You get what I mean, right?"

"Yeah. That makes sense, I guess." I swallow hard. "Still, it seems like this party is turning into something really different from what I thought it would be. And a lot more complicated. I'm just not sure—"

She doesn't let me finish. "You know, maybe we should have the party somewhere else. I can check with some other people today and see if I can find a different place."

"But the invitations are already out," I say. "Wouldn't that be weird, to make a change now?"

"I'd have to give everyone a corrected invitation. It would mean some extra work, but I'll do it if I have to. The important thing is to give Sophie a great birthday party."

I can see it now: everyone talking about me, about how I almost ruined the surprise party for Sophie. When it's all over, what would Isabel say about me to

Sophie? Instead of growing closer to Sophie and the other girls in the book club, I'd be pushing myself farther away.

The words come rushing out, because as difficult as everything is, I think changing things now would be a lot worse. "No, it's fine," I tell her, trying not to be mad that Isabel keeps getting her way while I have to push what I want aside. "My dad said a band at the party is okay." Which is true. He just thought it would be my band.

She squeals with excitement. "Thank you so much! This party is going to be amazing. Like, the best birthday party in the history of the universe. Oh, and Sophie's mom is going to tell Sophie she's taking her out for a nice dinner, just the two of them, for some special mother-daughter time. Then she'll pretend they have to stop at your house because you have a gift you want to give the birthday girl. They'll walk into the house, we'll yell surprise, and the party begins!"

"That sounds good," I tell her. "What time should I have the New Pirates arrive?"

"I'd say seven, like everyone else. Sophie's mom is

going to get her there around seven thirty."

"Okay," I say. "So, is there anything else? If not, I'll just see you Saturday, I guess."

"Yeah, I think we're good," she says. "I'll be there around five, with the decorations."

We say good-bye, and after we hang up, I start to think about how I'm going to break the news to Zola and Abigail. I don't want to be upset with Isabel, but I can't deny that I am. She basically demanded the New Pirates play at the party. If I had said no, then I would have looked like the bad guy—or girl in this case.

I really wish she hadn't put me in this position. But here I am, and now I have to figure out what to do about it.

Do I wait for the perfect moment during practice tonight and try to break it to Abigail and Zola gently, or is it better to get it over quickly, right when they get here, kind of like ripping off a Band-Aid?

My mom is a rip-off-the-Band-Aid kind of person. I've never liked that method. I think it hurts a lot more that way.

So I decide I'll wait for the right time tonight and explain, as nicely as I can, what happened. Hopefully they'll understand. Because something tells me if they don't, the Dots may be finished before we ever had a chance to really begin.

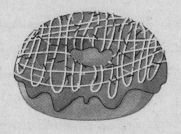

Chapter 17

hot-fudge sundaes

NO BAKING REQUIRED

After dinner, Mom brings four bowls, a half gallon of vanilla ice cream, hot fudge, and whipped cream to the table.

"Sundaes?" I ask.

"Yep," Mom says. "We have something to celebrate tonight."

I look at Dad, but he doesn't say a word. He just smiles and stands up to help scoop ice cream.

I turn to Madison. "Do you know why we're celebrating?"

She beams. "I made the varsity softball team."

"You did?" I ask. "But . . . how?"

She shrugs. "The coach said I've got what it takes."

"Madison has what you and I don't have, Lily Dilly," Dad says, drizzling hot fudge over the scoops of ice cream. "Innate athletic ability."

Mom takes a bowl from Dad and puts a dollop of whipped cream on top before she passes it to Madison. I feel anger boiling up inside of me. She wanted to play softball, she tried out for the team, and without having to practice at all, she made the team. Easy as pie.

Why is everything *so* easy for her, and why does it have to be *so* hard for me?

Mom passes me my sundae, and now I feel too upset to eat. It's not fair. Everything goes Madison's way.

Everything.

"Aren't you going to congratulate me?" Madison asks me before she takes a big bite of her sundae.

Pep talk time.

Your sister can't help it if she's naturally good at almost everything.

It's not her fault. It's not going to do any good to be mad at her. Remember how she was really nice to you when the chocolate cake didn't turn out? You owe it to her. Be nice. You know what Mom always says—life isn't always fair. So you have to work harder at things. Maybe that's a good thing somehow. Okay, maybe not, but still . . . do the right thing.

"Congratulations," I say as I look her right in the eyes. "I hope you make it to the championships."

"Wouldn't that be wonderful?" Mom says, sitting back down to eat her hot-fudge sundae.

I don't answer that question. But I do take a bite of my sundae, and it tastes fantastic. I think ice cream may be my new favorite dessert. After all, you don't even have to turn on the oven.

When Abigail and Zola arrive, I stay focused on finishing the song. All three of us know that's the number one priority.

It takes us a good hour to figure out the right notes and the perfect words to go with those notes, but we keep at it.

Until finally "Wishing" by the Dots is complete!

We play it three times, from start to finish, and each time, it sounds better and better.

After the third time through, Zola gives me and Abigail high fives. "Dudes, we are on our way. I can't wait for Saturday night."

Abigail grins. "Me either. Did you check with your dad? Is he cool with moving the equipment upstairs?"

"Yeah," I tell them. "But—"

I don't get a chance to finish. Zola interrupts me. "Hey, we should practice 'Happy Birthday.' We need to spice the original version up a bit. Put our own spin on it, you know?"

Abigail plays a chord on her guitar and Zola starts beating out a rhythm. It sounds so fun, I can't help but start to sing when it's time for the vocals to come in. We mess around with it for a while, and we're laughing and having such a good time, I look at my friends and think, *This is how it's supposed to be.* This is what I dreamed of when I thought about being in a band, and it's come true. It's really come true!

The moment is gone quickly, though, when Abigail looks at the clock and starts scurrying around, gathering her things. "Oh shoot. Zola, come on, we have to go. My dad is probably waiting out front for us."

The voice in my head starts screaming, *Tell them, tell them!* I need to tell them we're not playing at the party, but I can't do it. Everything has been so perfect, I don't want to ruin it.

"Bye, Lily," Abigail says as they head out the door of the studio. "Thanks for a great practice."

"See you tomorrow," Zola says.

And just like that, they're gone, and I'm left holding a song about wishing, while I'm doing a little of my own wishing.

I wish Isabel hadn't run into Bryan and his dad.

I wish the New Pirates weren't our musical enemies.

I wish we had thirty songs ready, so I could cancel the New Pirates' appearance at Sophie's party and we could easily take their place.

The more I wish, the more I realize wishing is kind of silly, because no matter how hard I wish, none of it's going to come true.

Suddenly, I'm not so sure I like the song we wrote. When you wish, you hope something good is going to happen. And when it doesn't, which is a lot of the time, then you feel bad. Like, so bad, you just want to crawl in bed and stay there.

The party is on Saturday. No matter how hard I might wish that it all goes perfectly and everyone gets along and no one is upset with me, that's probably not going to happen.

Maybe our next song should be titled "Life Isn't Fair, Deal with It."

Chapter 18

candy orange slice

TASTES LIKE A SLICE OF SUNSHINE

On Tuesday, I promised myself I'd tell Abigail and Zola on Wednesday about the New Pirates playing at the party.

On Wednesday, I promised myself I'd tell Abigail and Zola on Thursday about the New Pirates playing at the party.

On Thursday, as I'm trying really, really hard to think of an excuse not to tell Abigail and Zola about the New Pirates playing at the party, I get a brilliant idea.

Both of us can play at the party! I can't believe I didn't think of it before. It makes so much sense. Isabel gets what she wants and I don't have to make any band members angry.

It's perfect!

I'm so happy and relieved, when Mom asks me if I'll go see my great-grandpa with her after school on Thursday, I don't whine or complain like I sometimes do. I just say, "Sure."

My great-grandpa Frank lives in a retirement home called New Beginnings. That means he has his own little apartment in a big building where a whole bunch of other old people also have their own apartments. The people who live there go to a big dining room three times a day for their meals. There's an activity coordinator who comes up with things for them to do. Some of the activities I've heard about are yoga, aerobics, bingo, sing-alongs, and poker night. Grandpa Frank says poker night is his favorite. He plays cards and bets with chips. The chips are like pretend money, so if he loses all of his chips, it doesn't matter. Although, he hates to lose, so I guess it does matter a little bit.

When we get to Grandpa Frank's room, Mom knocks, but the television is turned up so loud, he doesn't hear it. My great-grandma passed away a few years ago. He's lived here ever since, and I think the television may be his best friend since she died. It's kind of sad, but I guess it's good that he has something to keep him company during the day, when he's not doing some kind of activity. I told him once that he should try yoga. This is what he said: "Yoga is for young chickens. In case you haven't noticed, I am not a young chicken." I didn't argue with him, even though no one doing yoga at New Beginnings is a young chicken.

Finally Grandpa Frank opens the door and invites us in. His room smells like pine trees, like always. He buys little green trees at the store that are actually car fresheners and hangs one from the latch on one of the windows. He says the smell reminds him of the days he was a park ranger, walking around the forests of Oregon.

After he says hello and turns the television off,

he picks up the candy dish off the coffee table and offers me a candy orange slice. They are little sugary candies in the shape of an orange wedge. They're soft and chewy, sweet and delicious. And orange-flavored, of course. Every time we come to visit, I wonder if this will be the time when he doesn't have any candy in the bowl. I'd be so disappointed. But he hasn't let me down yet.

"How's the cat?" he asks.

"Good," I say. "Soft and fluffy, just the way you like him."

It makes him smile. He asks about Oscar every time we see him. He's a big fan of cats. Of all animals, really. He keeps asking the administration to make an exception and let him have his own cat, but they keep turning him down.

"You're here just in time," he tells us. He puts on a navy blue sweater-vest over his white button-down shirt and slips on his brown loafers. I guess we're going somewhere.

"In time for what?" I ask.

"They're having a sing-along downstairs."

"But you hate to sing," my mother says.

"Not since I met Betty," says Grandpa.

"Betty?" both my mom and I say at the same time.

"She sings like an angel," he says. "Just like you, Lily." He takes my hand in his and leads me to the door. "She wants to meet you."

I look at my mother, and she shrugs. What else can we do but follow Grandpa Frank to the sing-along and meet this angel named Betty?

When we get downstairs, we go to the music room. A lady is sitting at the piano flipping through sheet music, and in the center of the room are chairs in a circle. About half of them are filled with people. As soon as we walk in the room, a tall, thin woman with gray hair and a big smile outlined in red lipstick gets out of her chair and walks over to greet us.

"You must be Lily," she says to me, her hand extended. I shake it as I say, "Yes. Hi." She looks at my mom and says, "And, Connie. So nice to meet you. I'm Betty."

My mother shakes her hand and says hello.

"She's new here," Grandpa says. "Do you know what she used to do? She used to be a psychologist.

She specialized in helping people overcome their fears and achieve their dreams."

"How interesting," my mom says. "What a wonderful way to help people."

Before she can reply, Mr. Green, a longtime resident of New Beginnings, walks up to us and says, "Why did the chicken cross the road?"

"I don't know," I say like I always do when I see Mr. Green and he asks me this question. I guess it's his favorite joke, though he never gives the same answer twice.

"Well, you see, he was a rubber chicken and he wanted to stretch his legs."

It makes me smile. Mr. Green turns around and takes a seat in the circle.

"In your opinion," Mom asks Betty, "what's the biggest mistake people make when it comes to their lives and their dreams?"

"Oh, that's easy," Betty says. "They let other things get in the way. They put it off and put it off, doing other things, telling themselves it's okay because there will be time later. Really, deep down, the truth is, most of them are afraid."

"Afraid of what?" I ask.

"Oh, any number of things, I suppose. They're afraid of making mistakes. Of not getting it right the first time. Of having people make fun of them. But see, what you have to remember is that the people who made their dreams come true felt afraid too, but they didn't let it stop them. That's the difference."

The lady at the piano runs her hands across the ivory keys, and it gets everyone's attention. The four of us take a seat in the circle.

A woman wearing a purple and red dress with matching red shoes and dainty white gloves on her hands gives each of us a songbook.

"Thanks for coming today, everyone," the piano lady says. "We're going to start with 'You Are My Sunshine' on page six."

After she plays the introduction, we're all singing along. Betty is sitting beside me. When I glance over at her, I notice how her pretty green eyes sparkle like emeralds and she sings with a slight grin. Her voice is smooth and nice, but it's the happiness I notice the most. Anyone could look at her and tell that she loves to sing.

And when I look at Grandpa Frank, he is a picture of happiness too. He doesn't care if he can't sing a single note on key. He's here and there's music and Betty's smiling. There's a lot for him to be happy about.

I close my eyes for a moment, and as I start to sing, I know that for now, I don't have to try to chase away a bunch of worries about a hundred different things. It's just me and the cheerful, sweet song. Every cell in my body remembers how much I love this—music and singing.

And I never want to forget how it feels.

Chapter 19

chocolate-chip brownies

CHOCOLATE CURES ALMOST EVERYTHING

An hour of singing with a bunch of people who are not young chickens but are nice to be around anyway seems to be just what I needed. On Friday, I float through the day, hardly a care in the world. I tell Belinda to be at my house at seven o'clock Saturday night, with all of their equipment. She says, "I'm so glad you changed your mind." Like I had a choice?

Friday evening, right after dinner, Madison takes me grocery shopping because Mom is busy closing a deal. Whatever that means. I think it means she's sold a house. Or almost sold a house and is trying to get the paperwork signed to make it official.

Madison is a huge help and suggests items I hadn't even thought of getting, like some cartons of lemonade so we have something to drink besides water. We also buy paper plates, cups, and napkins, and all of the stuff I need to make the cake pops and cookies.

"Are you feeling pretty good?" Madison asks on the drive home. "About the party?"

"I think so."

"Mom's going to help you make the cake pops?"

"Yes. We're going to do that tomorrow. Tonight I'm baking the chocolate-chip cookies."

Madison turns on her blinker before turning onto our street. "I saw Mom had a cleaning lady come today. That was a smart thing to do. I was worried we'd be up until midnight tonight, dusting and vacuuming."

"Wow, talk about a fun Friday night," I tease.

"Are you guys gonna play games at the party or what?" she asks.

"I don't know. Isabel had that on her to-do list, but we never talked about it. Do you know any good ones?"

She pulls into the driveway. "Let's see. How about pass the orange? You use either your feet or your neck to pass the orange from person to person. No hands allowed."

"That sounds hard," I say, trying to imagine playing that game with Sophie's friends. "And awkward."

A sudden wave of panic washes over me. I'm not going to know most of the kids at the party. They'll all be from Sophie's school. I'll know Sophie and Isabel, of course. And the other two girls from the book club, Katie and Dharsanaa, will probably be there. But that's it. I'm going to have a bunch of strangers in my house. Everyone will know everyone, except me. That seems so . . . weird. At least Abigail and Zola will be there. It makes me more thankful than ever that I kept quiet about the whole band thing.

Madison turns the car off. "You guys could go

on a scavenger hunt. You know, come up with lists of random items like dice and rubber bands and a stuffed rabbit or whatever. Then break up into groups and go around the neighborhood to find the stuff. First group back wins."

"I don't know," I say. "We might not have that much time. I mean, the New Pirates are going to be playing for an hour."

She gives me a funny look. "The New Pirates? Who are they?"

"A band."

"And Mom and Dad said that's okay?"

"Well, Dad said my band could play, but then Isabel wanted this other band, so I'm sure it's fine."

Now Madison looks really confused. "Why isn't your band playing?"

I open the car door. "We're going to play too." I sigh. "It's a long story. And it's not really important now. Come on. Help me carry this stuff inside."

When we get to the kitchen, something smells really good. Dad is there, pulling a pan out of the oven.

"What is that?" Madison asks.

"Your mother is really stressed out," he says. "I found a box of chocolate-chip brownie mix in the cupboard, so I decided to whip up a batch." He smiles. "You know, because chocolate makes everything better. Or so I've heard, anyway."

"Wow, Dad," I say as I peer in the pan. "They look really good. Maybe you should help me with the cake pops tomorrow instead of Mom."

"Sorry, kiddo. I won't be here. Another band had to back out of a wedding reception due to illness, so we're filling in. It's a couple of hours away, which means I'm going to have to leave here in the morning, and I won't be back until tomorrow night." He rubs my head as he walks by. "I'm sure you and your mom are going to do a fantastic job. Those brownies need to cool for thirty minutes, so don't have any yet, okay?"

Both Madison and I nod. "Man, they smell amazing," she says after he's gone.

"I know," I say, my stomach begging for one. "I'm so impressed Dad made them."

"Well, I'm going to go change and then I'm out of here," Madison says. "I'm meeting up with some friends at the movies."

"Okay," I say. "Hey, are you going to be around here tomorrow? In case Mom and I need some help?"

She shakes her head. "No way. I told you, I'm staying far, far away from here. You and Mom are on your own."

"Madison, come on," I say, giving her a little shove. "That's mean."

She laughs. "Well, even if I wanted to help, I can't. I have a preseason doubleheader tomorrow afternoon that the coach set up. She wants to move us around to different positions and figure out where we play best.

"It'll be okay," she says as she reaches for the silverware drawer and pulls out a knife. "I'm sure everything will be fine."

She goes to the pan and cuts into the brownies. "Hey, it hasn't been thirty minutes yet," I say.

She takes a bite of the ooey, gooey brownie that's falling apart in her hands. She catches a big chunk that falls off as it drops toward the floor and pops it in her mouth.

"Mmmm. Good," she mumbles. "See? It's gonna be a piece of cake. Nothing to worry about, Lily Dilly."

I nod as she heads out of the kitchen, leaving me alone with the big pan of brownies. I'm going to be good and wait the right amount of time before I have one, like Dad said.

If there's one thing I've learned, it's that things turn out best when you follow the instructions. Now, if only I had instructions for how to make a surprise party turn out perfectly from start to finish, I'd be set.

I guess I'll just have to cross my fingers and hope for the best.

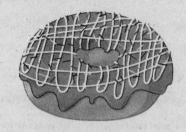

Chapter 20

chocolate-chip cookies

SWEET PERFECTION

When I wake up Saturday morning and see my alarm clock says 10:15, I jump out of bed. I didn't mean to sleep so late. It must have been because I had trouble falling asleep the night before, thinking about the party.

I make my way downstairs, but no one is around. It seems strange. I go back upstairs and find the door to my parents' bedroom shut. I knock softly. "Mom? Are you in there?"

I hear a soft moan and then, "Yes. Lily, come in."

I open the door and see her curled up, under the covers. This is not like my mother. She's always the first one up on Saturdays, with a to-do list a mile long and lots of energy to get it all done.

"Mom, are you okay?"

She doesn't move. "Don't come any closer, sweetie. I have the stomach flu, and I don't want you to get sick."

I can feel my heart racing. This is not good. In fact, it's terrible. "Are you sure? I mean, maybe you just ate too many brownies."

She chuckles. "I wish, but I don't think so. I have a fever. And I'm achy."

"Where's Dad?"

"He left a little while ago. He told you about the wedding reception, right? I'm sorry, Lil. You're going to have to make the cake pops by yourself."

"Mom, I don't think—"

"You can do it. I saw the cookies you made last night, and they turned out great. Did you try one?"

"Yeah. They're really good."

"See?" she says. "You're halfway there. Now close the door and go downstairs. If I rest, maybe I'll feel better and can help you this afternoon."

If she has a fever, that seems like wishful thinking. But I don't say anything. I don't want to make her feel any worse than she already does.

"Can I get you anything?" I ask, feeling slightly sick myself that this is happening on the worst possible day.

"No, I'm fine. Don't worry about me. I know you have enough on your plate today."

After I close the door, I try to give myself a pep talk, but I'm freaking out so much, it's impossible. No amount of pep talking is going to keep me calm right now.

I run into my room, shut the door, and yell into my pillow. It helps. A little. When I sit up, I ask myself what it is that I need more than anything. And an answer pops into my brain right away.

I need a friend. Someone who will help me get the cake pops ready, but more than that, someone who will help me get through the day without falling apart like a really dry cupcake. I need someone to help me keep it together.

I go to the phone and call Abigail.

"Hello?"

"Oh good, you're home."

"Hey. What's going on? You excited about tonight?"

"I have a huge favor to ask you," I say as I sit on my bed. "Can you come over and help me bake some cake pops?"

She laughs. "You just will not let this baking thing go, will you?"

"My mom was going to help me," I explain, "but she's sick. And I already promised Isabel we'd have cake pops at the party. She was really excited about them when I told her. Please, Abigail? It'd mean a lot to have you here."

"Okay," she says. "I'll have one of my parents bring me over after lunch. Is that enough time?"

"I think so. We need to have everything done by five, when Isabel is scheduled to get here with the decorations."

"Oh yeah, we can do it," she says. "Piece of cake."

I'm starting to get a little bit annoyed by that saying.

"Thanks, Abigail. See you in a while."

"Okay, bye."

I quickly take a shower and get myself ready. I throw on old clothes, since I'll be baking all afternoon. I can change later, after Isabel and I finish decorating the house.

When I go back downstairs, I find Madison, dressed in her softball uniform, rummaging around in the refrigerator.

"Mom's sick," I tell her.

She turns around, holding a small bottle of orange juice, and shuts the fridge door.

"Yeah. I know. I'm sorry, Lil. You gonna be okay? I hope you have a backup plan in case your cake pops don't turn out."

I cross my arms over my chest. "Backup plan? You think I'm going to need a backup plan? Thanks a lot, Madison."

"Hey," she says as she twists the lid off of the bottle, "it's good to be prepared. That's all I'm saying."

"Well, I don't have a backup plan, so be quiet. Abigail's coming over in a little while to help me make the cake pops. Together, we'll be fine."

She takes a long drink of her juice before she asks, "Where's the band going to set up? They're bringing their own equipment, right?"

"Yeah. I've been thinking about where to put them, and I think maybe the garage is the best place. I mean, you know how Dad is. It's spotless out there, and it's bigger than any room in the house. We can put some balloons and streamers out there too, right?"

She shrugs. "Whatever you want to do. It's your party." She starts to leave and then she turns around and says, "So did the other band say they were fine with your band using their instruments? Because some people are really uptight about that kind of thing, you know."

I gulp. "No. I just assumed they would let us use their equipment. I thought it would be easier that way."

"You didn't ask them?" I shake my head. "Are they good friends of yours?"

I'm pretty sure my sister can tell by the look on my face the answer to that question is a big, fat no.

Chapter 21

lollipops

HAPPINESS ON A STICK

I remember that I'd talked to Dad about moving his studio equipment upstairs for the party before I found out the New Pirates were going to play. My heart skips a beat at the thought that maybe he remembered to move the equipment before he left this morning. It's not anywhere in the house, so I cross my fingers as I check the garage. But it's empty. He forgot. And I didn't think to ask him.

Just as I'm shutting the door to the garage, my phone vibrates in my pocket.

"Hi, Dad," I say. "I was just thinking about you."

"Lily, I'm so sorry. I forgot to ask you if your band had decided to play tonight. Was I supposed to move the equipment and instruments upstairs for you?"

I sink down into the sofa in the family room and lean my head back. Then I tell him about the New Pirates and the plan to have them play and how I was hoping our band could play too.

"What do you think?" I ask. "Will they let us use their stuff?"

"I doubt it. Most people are really protective of their instruments. It's kind of like letting someone else drive your really fancy sports car when you don't know if her driving skills are any good."

"But we won't break anything," I say, trying to keep the tears back.

"You can't promise that, sweetie," he says softly. "I know you'd be really careful, but what if something did happen? It'd be pretty horrible, right?"

"Zola and Abigail really wanted to play tonight. I don't know how I can tell them the whole deal is off. Abigail's going to be here soon to help me, since Mom is sick."

"You're just going to have to tell them. And please apologize for me. It's partly my fault."

"Okay," I mutter.

"And, Lily, I know I probably don't have to tell you this, but you kids can't move that equipment. It needs to stay in the studio. Understand?"

"Yes."

"Look, I have to go. We stopped to get gas, and the guys are ready to roll. I'm really sorry. But don't let this ruin the party, okay? You'll have other opportunities to perform."

"Bye, Dad."

"Bye."

I make myself eat some cheese and crackers and a banana because I know hunger doesn't help my mood. When I'm finished, I check on my mom. She's sleeping, so I tiptoe out of the room and quietly shut the door.

Abigail arrives a little while later. She knows right away that something is wrong.

"Uh-oh. Are you feeling sick too?" Abigail asks.

"Not that kind of sick."

She grabs my hands. "Come on. It's not that bad. We are going to make the best cake pops you've ever seen. It'll be okay. I know you're probably worried they're not going to turn out, but you really shouldn't be. I've come prepared."

She reaches into the bag she's carrying and pulls out a pink and white apron, a bag of lollipops, and something else. It's white and shaped like an egg.

"What is that?" I ask.

"My mom's lucky timer."

"Why's it lucky?"

"Because nothing has ever burned when she's used this timer. It's like . . . magic."

"What are the lollipops for?"

"My backup plan. If the cake pops are a disaster, you just serve lollipops instead. They're cute and delicious too, right?"

It makes me smile. She is trying so hard to help me and to cheer me up. She loops her arm through mine and says, "Come on. Let's get baking!"

Abigail is being really sweet and I'm already feeling better. I know it's time to tell her the news and get it over with. Then we can focus on the cake pops.

"I need to tell you something," I say when we reach the kitchen. "I have some bad news."

She sets her bag on the kitchen table and then walks over and places the timer on the counter. "What?"

"My dad left this morning to play at a wedding reception this afternoon, and he forgot to move the instruments and equipment upstairs."

"What do you mean?"

"I mean we can't play. We can't play our songs at the party tonight."

Abigail's face droops like a wilted daisy. "We can't move the stuff ourselves?"

I shake my head. "He specifically told me not to. I'm really sorry, Abigail. He feels bad, and so do I."

She takes a deep breath. "Oh well. Guess there's nothing we can do then."

There's one more thing I have to do. A part of me is still hoping I can convince Belinda and the rest of the band to let us use their instruments when they're done. It's going to be tricky, trying to get my friends to come to the party when they don't even know Sophie.

But I want to try. I don't know what they'll say when they find out the New Pirates are playing and we aren't, but I figure I'll deal with that later. One thing at a time, like my mom always says.

"I still want you and Zola to be here tonight," I tell Abigail. "I don't know most of the kids coming and I'd love it if you'd stay and hang out. Keep me company."

She slips the apron over her head and ties the straps behind her back. "You don't think your friend would mind, when she doesn't even know us?"

"Oh no. She's really nice. I can tell her you're my helpers. Or something."

She shrugs. "I don't have anything better to do. My dad is going to pick me up at four. I'll go home, eat dinner, and come back. You should call Zola and tell her we're not playing. She might be upset if she shows up here and finds out."

"Okay. I'll give her a call while the cake is in the oven."

Abigail claps her hands together. "All right. Get your apron, Lily. You think Chef Smiley's a genius in the kitchen? Well, he'll be shaking in his boots when the entire state of Oregon is talking about our magnificent cake pops."

I giggle. "Shaking in his boots? He's a pastry chef, not a cowboy, silly."

"Fine. He'll be shaking in his chef's hat. Or apron. Whatever. He's gonna be scared—that's what I'm trying to say."

Abigail's confidence makes me feel like I can do anything. Like I'm putting on a cape instead of an apron. Now let's just hope her superfriend powers combined with the magical egg timer work!

Chapter 22

cake pops

ALL THE RAGE, LITERALLY

While the cake bakes in the oven, I call Zola and tell her the bad news. She's disappointed we won't be playing, but I beg her to come anyway, and she finally gives in.

I also get my mom's laptop and look up the video on how to make cake pops and show it to Abigail. We watch it three times.

"Piece of cake," she says once again, like it's the funniest thing ever.

That joke is really getting old.

I also show her the cookbook Chef Smiley gave me.

"Whatever works?" she asks when she reads the page that he signed. "What does that mean?"

"If there's an easier way to do something, even if it's not fancy or the most popular way, it's okay. You shouldn't feel bad about doing something that works for you."

The egg timer lets out a really loud, annoying screech, making us both jump.

She runs over and turns it off while I check the oven. "So that's why it's magic," I say. "That thing's loud enough to let the people across the street know the cake's done."

"Exactly," she says.

The chocolate cake looks good. It's a little lopsided, but it doesn't bother me at all because I know it doesn't matter.

While the cake cools, I find a tablecloth and throw it on the dining room table. Abigail helps me arrange the plates, napkins, cups, and silverware.

Then we go to work making the cake balls, following the instructions in the video. When we have four dozen and the bowl is empty, I stick them in the freezer to harden for an hour.

"Man, baking is exhausting," Abigail says as she plops down at the kitchen table. She reaches back and tightens up her ponytail.

"Thanks for helping me," I say as I sit down across from her. "It means a lot."

"We're halfway there, right?" she says. "We'll get the chocolate candies melted, do some dipping, and we're done. You can finally call yourself a baker, Lily! Just like you've wanted, right?"

I smile. "Yeah. I guess I can."

The doorbell rings.

"Who's that?" Abigail asks me as I stand up.

"I have no idea."

Abigail comes with me. When I peek out the peephole, I see Bryan standing there, his hands in his jeans pockets, looking as cute as ever.

"Hey," Bryan says after I open the door. "I know I'm way early, but my dad said it'd be a good idea to come and get everything set up now. I hope it's okay. I figured you'd be here, getting ready for the party."

Abigail looks at me. And then back at Bryan. "What's he talking about?"

"I'll tell you in a minute," I say quickly before I step outside. It's nice today. Sunny and warm, a rare thing in March in Oregon. "Let me punch in the code and open the garage door for you." I shut the front door and hustle over to the garage. Fortunately, Mom's car is parked in the driveway, and since both Dad and Madison are gone, the garage will be empty.

"You sure the garage is the best place for us?" Bryan asks as I punch in the code that opens the door.

"I'm sure," I say, hoping he approves of the space.

After the door is up, he stares at the neatly organized shelves along the walls. "Ah. I see. Your dad's a neat freak. It's perfect."

He motions to his dad, who's in a white van parked in front of our house, to pull into the driveway.

"Well, let me know if you need anything," I tell him. "I'll be inside, making cake pops."

He gives me a curious look. "Cake pops? What's that, cake mixed with soda pop or something?"

Oh brother. "Never mind. Just shut the door when you're done, okay?"

I head back toward the house, when he calls out, "Hey, Lily?"

I turn around and face Bryan. "Yeah?"

"I think it's really great you're letting us play when you're probably bummed and wishing your band could play. What's your band's name again?"

"The Dots."

"Nice. Anyway, I want you to know, we'll make it a fun party. I promise."

It's a kind thing to say, and I'm glad he's not rubbing it in my face. But right now, with Abigail inside probably fuming about this whole thing, I wish more than anything that we were playing instead. I wave to Bryan and run back inside the house.

"Lily," Abigail says with her arms crossed over her chest, "please tell me the New Pirates are not playing at this party tonight."

"I wish I could," I say softly, "but they are playing."

She starts to say something else, but I keep going. "Isabel's dad knows Bryan's dad. She asked Bryan about playing at the party before she said anything to me. She was so excited about them playing, I couldn't say no. I mean, you should have heard her, Abigail. She wouldn't stop talking about the New Pirates and how good-looking Bryan is and how much Sophie will love having them play for her thirteenth birthday."

"So how long have you known about this?"

"For a while," I say. "The thing is, I thought we could play too. That way everyone would be happy. Until I found out that bands don't really like other bands to use their instruments."

Abigail walks past me without another word and into the kitchen. I follow her like a puppy with its tail between its legs. She takes her apron off and stuffs it into her bag, and then she gets the magical egg timer and the lollipops and puts those in the bag too.

"Where are you going?" I ask.

"Home."

"Abigail, wait, please."

She turns and looks at me. "You should have told us about the New Pirates."

"You're right. I'm sorry."

"I feel like I don't know you anymore, Lily. What's

happened? Ever since you decided to have this party, it's like you're a different person. I hope you have fun tonight, with your other friends, since them and baking seem to be more important than anything to you."

And then she's gone. I think about chasing after her, but I can tell it wouldn't do any good. She's too mad right now.

I blink back tears as I slink into the living room and collapse on the couch, thinking about what Abigail said. Have I become a different person? Did I go too far with this party, wanting so badly for it to be the very best it could be for Sophie?

Maybe I did, but that's because I care about her. I care about Abigail and Zola too, though. Don't they know that?

An image of Abigail's face, covered in sadness, pops into my head. Obviously, she didn't know, because I did a terrible job of showing them.

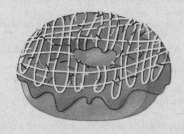

Chapter 23

chocolate

DELICIOUS HOT OR COLD

After I let myself pout for a little while, I go upstairs to check on Mom. She's fast asleep, and as much as I want to wake her and tell her what's happened, I know she needs her rest.

I'm on my own.

As I'm heading back to the kitchen to finish making the cake pops, there's a knock at the door.

Hoping it's Abigail, I rush to the door and fling

it open. But it's not Abigail. It's Bryan.

"Oh. Hi," I say.

He gives me a concerned look. "Hi. Are you okay?"

I try to smile. "Yeah. Fine. Are you all set up?"

"Almost. I forgot an extension cord and wondered if you might have one we could borrow."

I could be mean and say no and slam the door in his face, after everything that's happened. But I'm not going to do that. It's not his fault that I've messed up so badly with my bandmates. "Sure. Come in. I think my dad has some extras in his studio."

He steps into the entryway and I point him to the kitchen and tell him he can get a glass of water if he's thirsty, while I go down to the studio.

"I smell chocolate," he says when I come back. I watch as he surveys the kitchen, which is a mess right now. "Is it those cake pops you were talking about?"

I hand him the cord. "Yeah. They're in the freezer right now. I need to finish them. Abigail was supposed to help me but . . . she left."

He leans up against the counter. "I saw her leave. She didn't look very happy. Was she mad about something?"

"You could say that."

"Let me guess," he says, sweeping the bangs out of his eyes. "She's mad you guys aren't playing tonight?"

I look down at my shoes and nod. It's so embarrassing, talking to him about this.

"I'm sorry," he says. And the way he says it, I know he means it. "Is there anything I can do? Want me to stay and help you?"

I jerk my head up, surprised by his offer. "Really? You'd do that?"

He shrugs. "Sure. Let me finish in the garage and then I'll tell my dad I'll walk home when we're done."

After he leaves, I go to work cleaning off the counters and making room for the next part of the process: icing and decorating the pops. The whole time I'm thinking how nice Bryan is to offer to stay and help me. I'm kind of nervous about him seeing me fumble around in the kitchen, but I know the extra set of hands will be worth it.

I get out the double boiler, fill the bottom of the pan with water, and put it on the stove. While I wait for the water to boil, I take the cake pops out of the freezer and put the sticks in them. When Bryan knocks on the door again, I run to let him in and then lead him to the kitchen and show him what we'll be doing.

After the water boils, I put the white-chocolate candy pieces in the pan that sits on top of the pan of hot water. The heat from the hot water below is what will melt the chocolate.

"Can you stir while I add in the food coloring?" I ask.

He takes the wooden spoon from me and I pick up the little bottle with a red cap. I squirt in a few drops while he stirs. It becomes a pretty pink color.

"So now what?" he asks.

"Now we roll each ball of cake in the melted chocolate and then in some sprinkles. Oh, wait, I need to put the decorations in bowls."

"Where do we set the cake pops to dry?" he asks, still stirring. "If we lay them down on the counter, one side will be smooshed, you know? I'm guessing smooshed isn't the look you're going for."

He's right. I remember the lady in the video stuck the cake pops in a piece of Styrofoam so they could stand straight up as they dried. I'm looking around the kitchen as I'm pouring sprinkles into bowls, trying to think of something that would work as well as a piece of Styrofoam. But I can't think of anything.

"This chocolate is getting pretty hot," he says. "Should I turn off the heat?"

"Um, I don't think so," I say, opening a cupboard door full of bowls. "We don't want the chocolate to harden. Maybe turn it down a little bit?"

I'm staring into the cupboard when he says, "What about that thing?"

"What thing?" I ask.

He points at the top shelf. "I don't know what it's called. You put spaghetti noodles in it so the water drains? Here, let me get it."

He reaches up and takes out the silver colander. By turning it upside down, he's created a dome of holes and I realize it's perfect. "You are a genius, Bryan."

A smile spreads across his face. "Well, thanks. Pretty sure that's the first time I've heard my name and the word 'genius' in the same sentence."

"Come on," I say. "Help me roll the balls in the chocolate."

"I'll watch you do it first," he says. "To make sure I do it right."

"I've never made them before, so I'm not really

an expert," I tell him as I pick up a cake pop. "Cross your fingers it works!"

I roll the ball through the melted chocolate and then roll it around in some green sprinkles. When I turn the cake pop upright so I can put it in the colander to cool, the whole ball slides down the stick.

"Oh no," I say. "What'd I do wrong?"

"Maybe you need to work faster," he says. He does one and goes through the motions much faster, but this time the cake ball falls apart before he even rolls it in the sprinkles.

I can't believe this is happening. My chest tightens and it takes every ounce of strength I have not to burst into tears in front of him.

"I think the chocolate may be too hot," he says as he turns the burner off. "Let's keep trying."

Again and again, the cake balls either fall apart or slide down the stick. I wash my hands before I sink into the kitchen chair, checking the clock on the microwave. It's just after four o'clock. We have less than an hour to pull some amazing dessert out of thin air.

Bryan pops one of the cake balls into his mouth. "They taste pretty good," he says. I can tell he's trying to make me feel better, but it's not working.

"I'm such an idiot," I say, putting my face into my hands. "Why did I think I could pull this off?"

Bryan comes over and sits across from me. "Lily? Are you okay?"

I shake my head.

"Do you have any other food?"

I look up at him. "I made chocolate-chip cookies last night. But this is a birthday party. A surprise birthday party! I should have an amazing dessert for Sophie, and I have . . . nothing."

With a crooked smile he says, "At least you have an amazing band, right?"

Before I can tell him it's so funny I forgot to laugh, the doorbell rings. I get up and Bryan follows me.

When I open the door, the situation goes from bad to worse.

Isabel, Katie, and Dharsanaa are on my porch. The silver balloons they brought float above them.

"Hi, Lily," Isabel says, holding a giant shopping bag in one hand and a big bowl of caramel corn in the other. "Are you ready to make Sophie over-the-moon happy with the best surprise party ever?"

Chapter 24

caramel corn

A PERFECT ADDITION TO ANY PARTY

I stand there with my mouth open, unable to speak.

"I know we're early," Isabel says, "but I wanted to make sure we had plenty of time to get things ready. Oh, and I hope it's okay that I brought a couple of helpers along. And some homemade caramel corn."

I think I might be sick. And not because of the

caramel corn, which I love. Somehow I manage to say, "Yeah, it's fine."

We stand there a few seconds, looking at each other, and it feels like my heart is going to pop right out of my chest, it's beating so hard. All I can think is, *What am I going to do? What am I going to do?*

"So, can we come in?" Katie asks with a nervous giggle.

"Oh, sorry. Yes, please."

Once they're inside, I take the bowl from Isabel and introduce them to Bryan. I explain that he came over early to set up the band equipment and then stayed to help me with the cake pops.

"Can we see them?" Isabel asks. She looks at Bryan as she says, "I bet they're perfect!"

He doesn't say anything, just raises his eyebrows and looks at me to answer.

My brain is scrambling, trying to figure out how I can get out of this awful situation. But there's no way out. The Baking Bookworms are here and the kitchen looks like a tornado has hit, and I know I have to tell them the truth.

"Follow me," I say.

When we get into the kitchen, I set the bowl down on the counter and watch the three girls as they take in the sight of abandoned cake balls and empty sticks all over the countertops.

Isabel's mouth drops to the floor. "What happened?"

"Something went wrong," I tell them. "I'm not sure what I did. All I know is the cake pops didn't turn out. I should have practiced making them first. I'm so sorry, you guys. I wasn't honest with you. I'm a terrible baker. I try and I try, and every time, something like this happens."

They look horrified. It's like I've told them there are zombies trying to break down the front door. "So, we have no food?" Isabel asks.

"There's still time," Bryan says. "We can run to the bakery." He looks at me. "Can't we? Is your mom or dad here?"

"My dad's out of town and my mom's upstairs, sick with the flu."

Now Isabel is the one who looks sick. "Lily, you have to do something. I've worked so hard to get people here, get a band, and all you had to do was make a dessert. Sophie's party is ruined unless you think of something fast."

The way she says it, like I had the easy part, makes me upset. "You asked me to cohost this party. To have it here, at my house. You've barely let me have a say in *anything*. I would have bought a nice cake and some other treats at the bakery, but you didn't think that was special enough. And then there's the band. Did you ever think about what it would be like for me to have to listen to another band play at my house? My friends are mad at me because you just had to have the New Pirates play at this party." I take a deep breath. "I've worked so hard to make this party the best it could be. And you're saying it's going to be a failure because one thing didn't go right? Well, it's not going to be a failure. Sophie is going to have a great birthday party. Just wait and see."

It's quiet for a few awkward seconds before Bryan claps his hands together and says, "Okay, you know what I want to do? I want to hang some streamers. It's, like, my favorite thing in the world. Come on, Isabel. You must have brought some streamers, right?

Let's go. Everything's going to be fine. Streamers will help. You'll see."

I turn around and go to work cleaning the kitchen. Bryan's chatting up a storm with the other girls, trying to lighten the mood, as they go through the decorations Isabel brought along. We become robots, doing what we need to do to get the place ready. As I clean, I try to think if there's anything I can make quickly with the ingredients on hand. I check the flour and sugar containers and remember I used the last of our supply when I baked the cookies last night. And we don't have any cake mixes in the pantry, so whipping up a cake isn't a possibility.

As I pull out the containers of chocolate-chip cookies, I spy the pan of brownies Dad made last night. I have four dozen cookies and probably a dozen brownies. There's got to be something I can do with them to turn them into some kind of fun dessert. I think and I think, and then an idea comes to me. The question is, can I make it work?

I run upstairs to Mom's office and get a huge cardboard box she folded up and put in the closet. Before I go downstairs, I peek in and check on her. She's awake and so I take a minute to tell her what happened, along with my latest and greatest idea.

"I'm proud of you, Lily," she says. "I think it sounds fabulous."

I run downstairs and cut one of the sides off of the box. Then I cover the large piece of cardboard with aluminum foil and set it in the middle of the dining room table. I line up the brownies from top to bottom to make a gigantic number one. Next to it, I put the cookies in the shape of a number three.

"Wow," Isabel says behind me. "A sweet thirteen. It looks amazing, Lily."

"Yeah. I made the chocolate-chip cookies last night, since they're Sophie's favorite dessert. It's kind of a fun creation, right?"

She softly says, "They're Sophie's favorite? Really? I don't think I knew that."

I shrug. "One of them, yeah." I continue. "We have lots of vanilla ice cream and hot fudge sauce. After Sophie blows out her candles, everyone can make a brownie or cookie sundae. Does that sound okay?"

She nods, and I see tears forming in her eyes.

"I'm really sorry. About everything. I wanted to show Sophie how much she means to me, you know?" She looks down and picks at her thumbnail. "I was afraid I was losing her to you. That's why I got the New Pirates to play and not your band."

I stand there, my mouth gaping open. I can't believe she was worried about losing her best friend to me. I'm the one who's the outsider. The one who wants so badly to fit in with the Baking Bookworms.

"And I'm sorry I didn't say anything about my horrible baking skills," I say. "I didn't want you guys to kick me out of the book club. I really want to be a part of it."

"So, can we start over?" Isabel asks. "Put the stupid jealousy behind us and just be friends?"

I point to the number thirteen made out of brownies and cookies. "That's one thing I'm really good at," I say, smiling. "Starting over."

Chapter 25

brownie sundaes

A GREAT WAY TO SAY "SURPRISE!"

Purple streamers twist and turn through the air, to the center of the dining room, where they gather at the sparkly chandelier. A dozen silver balloons, filled with helium, bob across the ceiling, with long, curly ribbons in a variety of colors streaming down from each one. We also hung strips of streamers in the doorways and other spaces throughout the bottom floor of the house, like curtains. It looks really cool.

The garage is decorated with streamers and balloons as well. And we moved an area rug from the basement to the garage, to make it feel more comfortable—less like a garage and more like a bonus room.

Mom came downstairs in her pink bathrobe to refill her water cup just as I was getting ready to go and change out of my grubby clothes and into my purple and black striped dress. The look on her face as she scanned the decorations and treats told me we had done a fantastic job.

Now Isabel and I are greeting kids as they arrive, taking their gifts and putting them on the coffee table in the family room. I totally forgot to get Sophie a gift. When I ran upstairs to ask Mom, who'd gone back to bed, if we had anything fun tucked away for emergencies like this, she told me the party is the best gift I could give her.

Bryan ran home to get ready and then returned with the rest of his band a little before seven. They're hanging out in the garage until we're ready to move the party out there. Zola hasn't shown up, so I figure Abigail must have called her and now I'm in double trouble. There's no time to worry about it, though.

I'll have to wait until tomorrow to figure out how to fix that mess.

As Sophie's friends arrive, Isabel is great about introducing me as she greets each person. One of her friends, Dennis, comes in carrying the biggest gift bag I think I've ever seen.

After she introduces us, Isabel asks him, "What'd you get her? A new television?"

He laughs. "No." He looks around, then leans in and whispers, "It's this really awesome picture I took of her dog, Daisy. I blew it up and made it into a poster. Wait until you see it. It's the best gift ever, if I do say so myself."

"Can I see it now?" she asks him.

"No, you cannot. The birthday girl has to be the first one to see it. She's particular about those kinds of things, you know."

"She is?" Isabel asks.

"No," Dennis says. "I just like saying that word. Particular. Don't I sound really mature when I say it?"

She points Dennis to the family room so he can put his gift with the others, and after he's gone, she whispers, "That's Sophie's almost-boyfriend."

"Almost-boyfriend? As in, she likes him but he doesn't like her?"

"No, they both like each other, and they hang out all the time and talk on the phone and stuff."

"So . . . they're basically friends?"

"Yeah. But the way she talks, sometimes I think she wants to be more, you know? So, he's her almost-boyfriend in my mind."

I nod like I understand, but I'm not sure I really do.

Five minutes before seven thirty, I go through the house and shut off the lights. Then we all gather in the entryway.

"After Sophie rings the bell, Lily will go to the door," Isabel explains to everyone. "She's going to open the door really wide, and when she does, I'm going to flip on the light. As soon as the light goes on, you all yell, 'Surprise!' Until then, we have to be super quiet, so she doesn't suspect anything."

"I don't think most of the girls here know what super quiet means," I hear Dennis say.

A few people hush him.

We stand there quietly, waiting. My heart is pounding. Will she be surprised? Happy? Excited to see all of her friends in one place? Thrilled to see all the colorful packages and the delicious food?

I hope so, I hope so, I hope so.

When the doorbell finally rings, I'm shaking so bad, I can hardly make myself move. It's even worse than when I got called up to be Chef Smiley's assistant. I don't know why I'm so nervous. As I reach for the doorknob, I take a deep breath. And then I swing the door open quickly, and as I do, the lights come on and everyone yells, "Surprise!"

Sophie squeals. Isabel and I jump out and we both say, "Happy birthday," like we'd planned it, even though we hadn't. It makes us laugh and then Sophie is inside, hugging us and bouncing up and down because she's so excited.

I peek outside and see her mom wave. I wave back before I shut the door.

"I can't believe you guys did this," Sophie says, her eyes taking in the curtains of streamers and all the smiling faces.

"So, you're surprised?" Isabel asks.

Sophie laughs. "More like shocked!"

We take her into the dining room and show her

my special brownie and cookie creation. "That's so clever," she says. "How did you come up with that?"

I smile. "It's kind of a long story. I think I'll wait and tell you about it another time."

"Well, I love it."

Next we take her into the family room to show her all the gifts. Isabel says, "Lily and I have been working on this party for weeks. I was so worried you'd find out."

Sophie is beaming. She hugs us again. "Thank you guys so much. You're the best friends a girl could have." Isabel and I look at each other and smile.

"We're going to have brownie and cookie sundaes in a little while," I say. "But first, we have another surprise. A really big one that Isabel arranged. Think you can handle one more?"

She claps her hands together. "I can't wait!"

I wish I could borrow a little bit of her excitement. I'm afraid seeing the New Pirates perform might make me even sadder than seeing all of the cake pops fall apart.

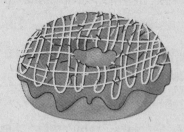

Chapter 26

dots

WHETHER A TYPE OF CANDY OR A BAND, THEY'RE PRETTY SWEET

*E*veryone follows Isabel and me out to the garage. When we go in, the band stops their warm-up. Sophie squeals, "Oh my gosh! You got me a *band*?"

Belinda takes the microphone and holds it like a pro. "I guess we should start by saying happy birthday, Sophie!"

The party guests clap and cheer as they gather

in the middle of the garage, all eyes on the stage. Belinda puts the microphone back in the stand and picks up a black electric guitar. As she puts the strap around her neck, she says, "We're the New Pirates and we're here to give Sophie a night she won't ever forget. So let's get this party started, what do you say? Our first song is called 'This Life.'"

Sydney and Belinda start jamming on their guitars while Bryan drums out the beat. The crowd is cheering and jumping up and down.

They play and sing like they've been doing this their whole lives. It's incredible. I had no idea they were so talented. I remember what Belinda said in choir class that one day. *Without talent . . . you're nothing. You'll get nowhere.*

They definitely have talent. And they seem to be enjoying themselves too. The crowd loves them.

When they're finished, everyone raises their hands in the air and screams. Who knew twenty-five kids could make so much noise? Belinda says "Thank you" six or seven times, waiting until it's quieted down before they go into their next song.

They play one amazing song after another. Their

songs are upbeat and fun and full of lyrics that are easy to remember, so by the time the chorus comes around for the third time, everyone's singing along. Like this one:

> *"I like you,*
> *you like me,*
> *that's the way*
> *it's supposed to be."*

For a whole hour, we are entertained. Dazzled. Inspired. They must practice constantly. There's no way they could be this good otherwise. I remember what Betty said to my mom when we visited Grandpa Frank, about people's dreams and how it's too easy to let things get in the way. Obviously, the New Pirates haven't let anything get in their way.

But I have.

I was trying so hard to be something I'm not—a good baker—that I didn't let myself follow my real dream. All of that time and energy should have been spent on what really matters to me. Music is what matters to me. It's what's always mattered to me.

As the show winds down, all I can think about is how badly I've messed up. I want to hug Abigail and Zola a million times over. I can only hope they'll give me another chance.

When I think the New Pirates are going to wrap up and say good night, Bryan picks up his microphone and says, "You know, I think we might have time for another song or two."

Everyone cheers.

"But I think you've heard enough from us," he says. "So I'm going to invite the Dots up here to play."

I'm looking at him, shaking my head, trying to get him to understand this won't work. I know he's trying to be nice, but I'm the only Dot who's here.

At least, I thought I was. In a matter of seconds, Abigail and Zola are on either side of me. They've been here watching? How did I not see them?

"What?" I say. "How—"

"Bryan called us," Abigail says in my ear. "He convinced us to come and play."

I give each of them a quick hug. "I'm so sorry," I tell them.

They both nod, as if to say, "We forgive you." Zola

pulls her sticks from her back pocket and holds them in the air. "Let's do this thing!"

I watch as Belinda turns around and whispers something angrily to Bryan, but he pulls her off the stage. Sydney follows them.

I suddenly feel dizzy and I can hardly breathe. Is this really happening? We're actually going to play? Zola starts walking toward the stage. Abigail grabs my hand and pulls me along, the crowd parting for us as we go. I take my place at the front of the small stage, while Zola moves to the drums and Abigail picks up one of the guitars.

"First," I say, "we have a little song for the birthday girl. Happy birthday, sweet Sophie."

We break out into our fun and up-tempo version of "Happy Birthday," and the crowd claps along to the beat. It sounds really good. I look down at Sophie, standing in the front row, and I can tell she loves it.

When we finish, it feels like there are a million butterflies swarming inside my stomach. I don't think I've ever felt this nervous before. What if we can't pull off the song we wrote? What if no one likes it? The New Pirates were so good, and they've obviously practiced a lot more than we have.

I turn and look at my bandmates, and their eyes are questioning me. I bite my lip, wondering if I should just end it now. Maybe I should say, "That's all, folks," and quit while we're ahead.

But Betty's voice echoes in my brain.

The people who made their dreams come true felt afraid too, but they didn't let it stop them.

I wanted a chance to prove to Zola and Abigail that I'm committed to this band. I can show them here and now that my heart is in it a hundred percent. I messed up. I forgot what mattered most to me. This is my chance to show them who I really am.

It's my chance to show everyone. I want to be a singer.

No.

I am a singer.

I take the microphone and say, "This next song we wrote over the past few weeks. I want to play this song for you guys because I'm proud of it and I'm proud of my band. I want to say thanks to my bandmates, Zola and Abigail, for sticking with me when I let other things get in the way. I was trying to be someone I'm not.

"See, I thought I wanted to be a good baker like my friends Sophie and Isabel. The truth is, I'm a horrible baker. And maybe I'm better now than I was a month ago, but I don't even really like baking. So I'll leave the baking to the people who do like it, while I work hard on what really matters to me.

"This next song is called 'Wishing.' And tonight, my greatest wish, beyond Sophie having a great birthday, is that Abigail and Zola will forgive me. And that we have the chance to write many more songs together in the future."

I put the microphone back in the stand. I listen to my band play the introduction. And then I sing like I've never sung before.

I'm pretty sure it's the best three minutes of my entire life.

Chapter 27

music lovers cupcakes

A PERFECT HARMONY OF
CHOCOLATE AND VANILLA

There's a whole bunch of kids standing outside the choir room, waiting for Mr. Weisenheimer to announce who will be playing at the Spring Fling. Abigail and Zola are passing the time by listening to a song on Zola's iPod. They each have an earbud in one of their ears.

My gaze meets Bryan's across the sea of people. He

gives me a thumbs-up. I smile. Ever since Sophie's party, we talk almost every day. Abigail and Zola like to tease me about it, even though he's just a friend. They probably can't understand how we bonded over failed cake pops and how much it means that he helped get my band back together.

Bryan told me that when he called Abigail the day of Sophie's party, he explained how bad I felt about everything. He told her he knows what it's like to be torn in two different directions. Bryan's parents own rental property along the Oregon coast and lots of times, on the weekends, they want to drag him along with them so he can learn about home maintenance and repairs. On the one hand, he wants to help his parents, but on the other hand, his band likes to practice on the weekends, when there's not as much school stuff to worry about.

Abigail told me later that as he talked, she realized I wasn't trying to hurt anyone. I was just trying to make everyone happy. And how could she stay mad at me for something like that?

Of course, now that everyone knows the truth about my baking skills, life has been much easier. Since the party, Abigail, Zola, and I have become a music-making machine. We wrote two more songs, and when we played them for my parents, my dad said he was honestly impressed with how far we'd come in such a short amount of time.

Our audition for the Spring Fling went well, although I was really nervous, so my voice shook a little bit. That's one thing I need to work on. Dad says it just takes practice, and some musicians get a little case of stage fright every time they have to perform. He says either I'll get over it or I'll learn to live with it. I hope he's right, because I don't ever want to stop singing.

The doors to the choir room open. Mr. Weisenheimer steps out and everyone backs up a little bit to give him some room. Zola and Abigail tear the earbuds out of their ears so they can hear what he has to say.

"Thanks for your patience, everyone," Mr. Weisenheimer says. "I want you to know, this was a really difficult decision. I said we'd have an announcement for you today by four o'clock, and here we are, a half hour late, and I apologize for that. It makes me extremely proud to work at a school with such talented musicians and singers. If I could, I'd let you all play at the Spring Fling. I truly hope all of you will decide to perform at the talent show at the end of the year. I'd love for the community to see and hear you perform."

I look at Zola and Abigail, and we all nod, as if to say, "We're in for the talent show."

Abigail squeezes my hand as we wait in agony for him to tell us who they've chosen. I'm glad he's proud of all of us, but come on, the waiting is torture!

He must read my mind because he says, "All right, enough of that. I know you're all dying to learn who will be playing at your Spring Fling. This band has some of the most talented young people I've ever seen. I can't believe they are eighth graders. I won't be surprised at all if they're touring the country someday, playing their music to millions of adoring fans.

"So, it's my pleasure to say congratulations to the New Pirates! You'll be playing at our Spring Fling this year! Let's give them a round of applause."

Everyone claps. I look over at Bryan, and now I give him a thumbs-up. I'm truly happy for them. They totally deserve it.

"To show my appreciation to all of you for your efforts," Mr. Weisenheimer says, "come in and grab a special treat I picked up on my way to work this morning. When I called It's Raining Cupcakes a few days ago and asked if they could make something special for this occasion, they came up with some fabulous music lovers cupcakes, just for you."

We make our way into the choir room and then over to a long table, where the cupcakes are spread out along with plates and napkins. Each cupcake has vanilla frosting with a black musical note piped on top. They are gorgeous.

I grab one and slowly peel off the wrapper. The cake appears to be chocolate. I take a bite, and the way the chocolate and vanilla blend together in my mouth, it's almost magical. The chocolate flavor is different from anything I've ever tasted. It has a little bit of a spicy taste to it. Cinnamon, maybe? I don't know, but it tastes really, really good.

I turn and see Belinda standing next to me. "Congratulations," I tell her. "I can't wait to hear you guys play again."

"Thanks. We're excited. Except I'm bummed we

won't get to hear your cupcake song. Do you want to sing it for me now?" she teases.

I smile. "You know, I've learned I don't like baking cupcakes. And singing about them really isn't all that fun either. I think I'll stick to what I do best, as far as cupcakes are concerned."

And with that, I take another bite and leave to find my bandmates.

"Dudes, when do we start practicing for the talent show?" Zola asks.

Abigail and I answer at the exact same time. "Tonight!"

Chapter 28

chocolate no-bake cookies

WHATEVER WORKS,

AND THESE WORK VERY WELL

What are you making?" Madison asks me as she saunters into the kitchen, holding her water bottle. She's wearing her uniform, off to play a game, I'm guessing.

"Chocolate no-bake cookies," I say. "The ones with the oatmeal and peanut butter. You've had them before, right?"

"I love those cookies," she says, peering into the saucepan. "Save me some, okay?"

"There's only ten of us, so there'll be some left over."

"I gotta run," she says. "Have a fun meeting."

"We will. Bye."

Today is the day I host the Baking Bookworms. Last month, when Isabel hosted, she made us little fruit tarts and lemon bars. Everyone couldn't stop talking about how good everything tasted.

But it didn't bother me.

That's who Isabel is. A wonderful baker. And today I will show the girls who I am. A girl who will make easy snacks, because they're good too, and it's okay. Whatever works, just like Chef Smiley told me.

When the dough is done, I lick the wooden spoon before I throw it in the sink.

"Sweet Uncle Pete, that's good!" I say.

"I recognize that saying," Mom says as she and Dad walk into the kitchen. "Are your no-bake cookies almost done?"

"I just need to put them on wax paper and let them set up."

"Want me to help you?" Dad asks.

"Okay. Thanks."

"How's that new song coming along?" he asks as he gets two spoons out of the drawer for us.

"We finished it and started working on another," I tell him as I scoop up a big chunk of dough.

"Wow. I'm so proud of how hard you guys have been working. How many songs are you up to?"

"Six," I tell him. "Six good ones. We wrote a couple that we ended up throwing out. They just weren't good enough."

Dad stops and looks at me. He's got a funny look in his eyes. A look that says, *I think you're going to like what I'm about to say.*

"You know, I was thinking . . ."

He waits.

I poke him in the stomach. "What? Tell me."

"Five songs is a good little set. My band's been asked to play at a company picnic coming up in June. It'll be a great venue—outside, at the park, while people mingle and eat their hamburgers and hot dogs. I'm thinking it'd be nice to have a little opening act. There'll be quite a few kids there who don't really want to hear a bunch of old fogies singing."

I drop my spoon on the counter. "Really? Dad, are you serious? You don't think they'd mind?"

"Actually, I already asked the guy who hired me," he says with a smile. "He loved the idea."

I stand on my tiptoes, throw my arms around my dad's neck, and give him a big hug. "Thank you! Abigail and Zola are going to be so excited."

The doorbell rings, interrupting our special father-daughter moment.

I pull away from Dad and check the clock. Then I look at Mom. "Uh-oh. Somebody's early."

"Go see who it is," Mom says. "Dad and I'll finish these."

I quickly wipe my hands on a towel and then head to the door. It's Sophie and Isabel and their moms.

"Hi, Lily," Sophie's mom says. "Hope it's okay we're a little early."

"Sure. Come in."

My mom comes out of the kitchen and greets the moms and asks them if they'd like some tea. They do, so they follow her back to the kitchen.

"Did you like the book *Ella Enchanted*?" Isabel asks us.

Sophie nods while I say, "I loved it. My mom did too."

"So what kinds of snacks are we having?"

I'm about to tell them about the easy things I made when the doorbell rings again. The other girls, Katie and Dharsanaa, have arrived with their moms.

"Everyone's early," Katie says. "I guess we're excited about this book!"

I lead the girls into our family room, where we'll have our discussion, while the moms visit in the kitchen.

"So, did you bake a beautiful six-layer cake, like Ella had on her fifth birthday?" Dharsanaa asks me. I can tell she's teasing me. They know that I'm not a baker, and I'm no longer afraid to admit it.

I laugh. "Um, no, there will be no homemade six-layer cake today. But I did make a cream trifle, which was mentioned in the book. We bought a pound cake, some jam and berries, and whipped cream. It was super easy to make and it looks so pretty. Wait until you see it. We layered pieces of cake, the berries, and the cream in a pretty glass bowl."

"Yum," Katie says. "That sounds good."

"And because Sophie loves chocolate," I say, "I made really easy chocolate no-bake cookies too."

"Yay!" Sophie says.

Chef Smiley was right. "Whatever works" is the best saying ever. I still have great homemade snacks and I didn't have to bake a thing.

"Are you okay with our name staying the Baking Bookworms, Lily?" Isabel asks me. "Or do you want to change it? We don't want you to feel left out."

"No, it's fine. We're all used to the name by now. You guys can do the baking. And I'll do the eating."

Everyone laughs.

Sweet Uncle Pete, I like my friends!

Chocolate No-Bake Cookies

1¾ cups sugar

4 tablespoons baking cocoa

½ cup milk

½ cup (1 stick) butter

a pinch of salt

1 tablespoon vanilla

1 cup peanut butter

3 cups quick 1-minute oats

Carefully measure out the sugar and baking cocoa into a saucepan and mix well. Slowly stir in the milk and blend well with the sugar mixture. Next, add the butter by cutting it with a knife into tablespoon-sized pats. Add a pinch of salt. Turn the burner on medium heat and stir frequently until mixture boils. Let mixture boil for two full minutes while stirring and then remove from heat. Add the vanilla and stir. Finally, add the peanut butter and oats and mix until well blended. Drop by rounded teaspoons onto a sheet of wax paper and cool. Makes about two dozen.

Strawberry Cake

Cake

1 cup (2 sticks) butter, softened

1½ cups white sugar

1 (3 oz.) package strawberry-flavored gelatin

4 eggs, room temperature

2½ cups sifted all-purpose flour

2½ teaspoons baking powder

1 cup whole milk, room temperature

½ cup strawberry puree made from frozen
   unsweetened strawberries

1 tablespoon vanilla

Take eggs, milk, and butter out of the refrigerator a few hours before making the batter.

Preheat oven to 350 degrees. Grease and flour two 9-inch round pans or one 9 x 13 pan.

In a large bowl, combine the butter, sugar, and strawberry gelatin. Mix on medium speed until light and fluffy. Separate the eggs; add the yolks to the batter and mix well. Whip the egg whites vigorously until soft peaks form before mixing them into the batter.

Sift flour, then measure and put into a separate bowl. Combine the baking powder with the sifted flour. Alternate adding the flour mixture and milk to the batter, mixing with each addition.

Use the blender to make a strawberry puree from a ...g of frozen unsweetened strawberries. Add a little bit of water and blend until smooth. Add ½ cup puree to the batter along with the vanilla and mix well. Pour batter into prepared pans. For round pans, bake 25 to 30 minutes, for a 9 x 13, bake for 35 to 40 minutes, until a toothpick comes out clean. If you're making a layered cake, allow the cakes to cool on a wire rack for 10 minutes before removing them from the pans to cool completely.

Frosting
1 cup (2 sticks) unsalted butter, softened
8 oz. cream cheese, softened
2 teaspoons vanilla
4 cups powdered sugar

Mix butter on low until fluffy. Add cream cheese and vanilla and mix for one minute. Add powdered sugar one cup at a time, mixing thoroughly. When all powdered sugar has been added, whip the frosting on high for 30 seconds to make it nice and smooth. Spread onto cooled cake. Top with sliced strawberries, if desired.

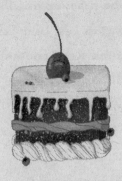

acknowledgments

A huge thank-you to Nathalie Dion for creating such fantastic art for this book as well as for *It's Raining Cupcakes* and *Sprinkles and Secrets*. You've done an amazing job, and every time I look at the covers, I feel like I've won the cover lottery.

Thanks to Mary Hays, a fan of the first two books, who wrote to me and helped me come up with the title of this book. It's perfect!

Thanks to the amazing team at Aladdin for all your hard work and support: Bethany Buck,

Mara Anastas, Fiona Simpson, Lydia Finn, Karin Paprocki, Karina Granda, Julie Doebler, Katherine Devendorf, Andrea Kempfer, and Alyson Heller. Cupcakes for all!

A special shout-out to Jen and Katie Manullang for your support from the very beginning of this cupcake-filled journey.

Thank you to Sara Gundell for so many things, but especially for featuring my books on your blog and working your magic to get me on TV.

To the librarians and booksellers, thanks for all you do to get books into the hands of readers.

Finally, thank you to *all* you young readers who have enjoyed my books and told your friends about them. Your enthusiasm makes me over-the-moon happy, and I want you to know I appreciate you more than words can say. Keep reading!